ALL-TIME FAVORITE
COWBOY
STORIES

Edited and with an Introduction by
ROCHELLE KRONZEK

D0639508

DOVER PUBLICATIONS, INC.
Mineola, New York

Bibliographical Note

All-Time Favorite Cowboy Stories, first published by Dover Publications, Inc.,
in 2009, is a new compilation of unabridged stories from standard sources.

Library of Congress Cataloging-in-Publication Data

All-time favorite cowboy stories / edited and with an introduction by Rochelle
 Kronzek.
  p. cm.
 ISBN-13: 978-0-486-46906-5
 ISBN-10: 0-486-46906-9
  1. Cowboys—Fiction. 2. Western stories. I. Kronzek, Rochelle.

PS648.W4A5 2009
813'.087408—dc22

2008044795

Manufactured in the United States of America
Dover Publications, Inc., 31 East 2nd Street, Mineola, N.Y. 11501

Dedication

SOME WRITERS bring their readers to faraway galaxies that no one has seen before with science fiction. Other readers walk through a closet into a fantastic world where lions talk and good triumphs over evil. All of us had favorite movies, television programs, and books during our youth that have pulled us into another time, another place, dangerous adventures, detective stories, cartoons and yes . . . even drawn us into "shoot 'em up" Westerns. I've spoken to many friends and colleagues in my adult life who seem to share a common memory with me—their fathers or grandfathers loved to read and watch Westerns. My dad Joe read the dime store novels of Zane Grey and Max Brand when he was a boy, and loved watching Western movies and television programs as an adult. His interest and enthusiasm for the Old West never waned. He'd eat his dinner in front of the television set where he'd watch *Gunsmoke, Bonanza, Rawhide, The Wild Wild West, The Virginian,* and *The Rifleman.* I often joined him and over time became a fan myself.

My dad worked twelve to fourteen hours a day, six days a week as a kosher butcher. Dad's day off was Saturday. He loved watching old Western movies on television on Saturday afternoons, as if the ones we had watched during the week weren't enough. He seemed to relax and forget his financial concerns and ongoing family squabbles. John Wayne, Henry Fonda, Kirk Douglas, James Stewart, Gary Cooper, Lee Marvin, James Coburn, and Clint Eastwood loomed larger than life. *High Noon, Shane, The Magnificent Seven, Cat Ballou, How the West Was Won, The Good, the Bad and the Ugly,* and *A Fistful of Dollars* are all classic American Westerns. We saw them and countless others again and again.

Gone are the days of old TV Westerns and their stars: *Wild Wild West's* Jim West and Artemus Gordon; Little Joe and Ben Cartwright on *Bonanza*; Marshall Dillon and Festus with *Gunsmoke*; Lucas on

The Rifleman and Rowdy on *Rawhide*. Only the occasional Western movie or TV show comes along anymore, such as *Walker, Texas Ranger, Lonesome Dove,* and the *Deadwood* TV series, as well as *Unforgiven, Blazing Saddles,* and *City Slickers.*

None of the heroic ranch hands, cowpokes, lawmen, or moralist land owners of the vintage 1960s or 1970s could ever stand as tall, as wise, as brave, and as important as my dad. But he loved them and I loved him and we shared our Westerns together.

I dedicate this volume to JOE KRONZEK
(April 18, 1923–August 25, 2004)

Say hello to John Wayne for me.

Contents

v

Introduction

TWENTIETH- AND twenty-first-century Americana is epitomized by baseball and football, hotdogs, apple pie, country fairs and outdoor music, beauty contests, rodeos, fireworks on the Fourth of July, barbeques, and action heroes. All these things are tasty, nostalgic, and typify the old-fashioned American Way but, there's nothing more American than a good cowboy story depicting life on the Western frontier.

The cowboy is one of the greatest personas in United States history and fiction. He is the figure of a man riding his horse across the dusty plains, through streams, and into the mountains. He is not of one time period alone, but has come to epitomize strength, strong character, and the Old West. The golden days of the Old West date from the close of the Civil War through the turn of the century. In actuality, most cowboys came from the lower social classes and the pay was poor. Many cowboys were men of color recently freed from the bondage of slavery. The average cowboy earned approximately a dollar a day, plus food, and when near the home ranch, had a bed in the bunkhouse: a single open room shared with other hired hands like him. Settlers in the West had to brave the elements, which were harsh, but at least they had one another. The cowboy was often alone, a wanderer, seeking work, food, and shelter, and perhaps some money for a drink. His horse was his closest companion and confidant, while other cowboys came and went, often competing for jobs.

This collection comprises a choice variety of cowboy stories, including one written by a woman, Bertha Muzzy Bower, and another by and about a black cowboy, Nat Love. An illustrious president, Theodore Roosevelt, has a tale to tell about his experiences in the Dakota Territory, where he lived and worked as a rancher, deputy sheriff, and naturalist. Mark Twain recounts in vivid detail one of his own mighty struggles in the untamed West. No collection of cowboy lore would be complete without a piece by Frederic Remington, American painter, sculptor, and illustrator, famous for his treasured depictions of cowboys and the Old West. And while not well known for his Western stories, O. Henry's portrait of an outlaw killer is a grim reminder of the lawlessness that often reigned supreme on the open range.

When we think of the Old West, we think of Jesse James and Wild Bill Hickok, Calamity Jane, great train robberies, and tumbleweeds. The Old West is not typified by the ghost town nor the outlaw, but by the cowboys and the Indians, whose stories have been romanticized and demonized, but whose realities were often harsh—ones of survival and protection of heritage and family. Let's take a step back in time, a hundred years and more, when survival meant taming the wilderness, braving the elements, and providing food for the table.

Cowboy stories, fact or fiction? Many of the stories presented here are based on the authors' own experiences. Many are true, with only the names changed in some cases. They are sure to linger in your memory, drawing you away to a remote and untamed wilderness that looms larger than life. The words paint pictures of hardships and loss, as well as the tenacity and pluck necessary to conquer nature and the elements. To wander along the open dusty trail . . . the stuff that dreams are made of.

Owen Wister (1860–1938)

OWEN WISTER was born in Germantown, Pennsylvania (near Philadelphia). His father was a wealthy physician and his mother, the daughter of famous actress Fanny Kemble. Owen Jr. attended schools in Great Britain and Switzerland and later studied in New Hampshire and at Harvard University, where he was a classmate of Theodore Roosevelt. After graduating from Harvard, Wister studied music in Paris, but returned to America in 1883. Although he graduated from Harvard Law School in 1888 and practiced in Philadelphia for a time, he had little interest in pursuing a career as a lawyer. Due to ill health, Wister had spent several summers in the West and had become fascinated with the region. On an 1893 visit to Yellowstone Park, Wister met the Western painter Frederic Remington and they became lifelong friends. When Wister began writing, he naturally gravitated toward writing about the Old West. His most famous work to this day is his 1902 novel *The Virginian: A Horseman of the Plains,* which he dedicated to his good friend and former classmate, Theodore Roosevelt.

The Virginian, published in 1902, is considered the first Western. It is widely credited with molding the future of cowboy novels to come. In this book, Wister fashioned a style, theme, and characterization that still influence Western writers more than a century later.

"Enter the Man," the first chapter of *The Virginian,* follows.

Enter the Man

FROM *The Virginian: A Horseman of the Plains,* 1902

Some notable sight was drawing the passengers, both men and women, to the window; and therefore I rose and crossed the car to see what it was. I saw near the track an enclosure, and round it some laughing men, and inside it some whirling dust, and amid the dust some horses, plunging, huddling, and dodging. They were cow ponies in a corral, and one of them would not be caught, no matter who threw the rope. We had plenty of time to watch this sport, for our train had stopped that the engine might take water at the tank before it pulled us up beside the station platform of Medicine Bow. We were also six hours late, and starving for entertainment. The pony in the corral was wise, and rapid of limb. Have you seen a skilful boxer watch his antagonist with a quiet, incessant eye? Such an eye as this did the pony keep upon whatever man took the rope. The man might pretend to look at the weather, which was fine; or he might affect earnest conversation with a bystander: it was bootless. The pony saw through it. No feint hoodwinked him. This animal was thoroughly a man of the world. His undistracted eye stayed fixed upon the dissembling foe, and the gravity of his horse-expression made the matter one of high comedy. Then the rope would sail out at him, but he was already elsewhere; and if horses laugh, gayety must have abounded in that corral. Sometimes the pony took a turn alone; next he had slid in a flash among his brothers, and the whole of them like a school of playful fish whipped round the corral, kicking up the fine dust, and (I take it) roaring with laughter. Through the window-glass of our Pullman the thud of their mischievous hoofs reached us, and the strong, humorous curses of the cow-boys. Then for the first time I noticed a man who sat on the high gate of the corral, looking on. For he now climbed down with the undulations of a tiger, smooth and easy, as if his muscles flowed beneath his skin. The others had all visibly whirled the rope, some of them even shoulder high.

I did not see his arm lift or move. He appeared to hold the rope down low, by his leg. But like a sudden snake I saw the noose go out its length and fall true; and the thing was done. As the captured pony walked in with a sweet, church-door expression, our train moved slowly on to the station, and a passenger remarked "That man knows his business."

But the passenger's dissertation upon roping I was obliged to lose, for Medicine Bow was my station. I bade my fellow-travellers good-by, and descended, a stranger, into the great cattle land. And here in less than ten minutes I learned news which made me feel a stranger indeed.

My baggage was lost; it had not come on my train; it was adrift somewhere back in the two thousand miles that lay behind me. And by way of comfort, the baggage-man remarked that passengers often got astray from their trunks, but the trunks mostly found them after a while. Having offered me this encouragement, he turned whistling to his affairs and left me planted in the baggage-room at Medicine Bow. I stood deserted among crates and boxes, blankly holding my check, hungry and forlorn. I stared out through the door at the sky and the plains; but I did not see the antelope shining among the sage-brush, nor the great sunset light of Wyoming. Annoyance blinded my eyes to all things save my grievance: I saw only a lost trunk. And I was muttering half-aloud, "What a forsaken hole this is!" when suddenly from outside on the platform came a slow voice:—

"Off to get married *again?* Oh, don't!"

The voice was Southern and gentle and drawling; and a second voice came in immediate answer, cracked and querulous:—

"It ain't again. Who says it's again? Who told you, anyway?"

And the first voice responded caressingly:—

"Why, your Sunday clothes told me, Uncle Hughey. They are speakin' mighty loud o' nuptials."

"You don't worry me!" snapped Uncle Hughey, with shrill heat.

And the other gently continued, "Ain't them gloves the same yu' wore to your last weddin'?"

"You don't worry me! You don't worry me!" now screamed Uncle Hughey.

Already I had forgotten my trunk; care had left me; I was aware of the sunset, and had no desire but for more of this conversation. For it resembled none that I had heard in my life so far. I stepped to the door and looked out upon the station platform.

Lounging there at ease against the wall was a slim young giant, more beautiful than pictures. His broad, soft hat was pushed back; a loose-knotted, dull-scarlet handkerchief sagged from his throat; and one casual thumb was hooked in the cartridge-belt that slanted across his hips. He had plainly come many miles from somewhere across the vast horizon, as the dust upon him showed. His boots were white with it. His overalls were gray with it. The weather-beaten bloom of his face shone through it duskily, as the ripe peaches look upon their trees in a dry season. But no dinginess of travel or shabbiness of attire could tarnish the splendor that radiated from his youth and strength. The old man upon whose temper his remarks were doing such deadly work was combed and curried to a finish, a bridegroom swept and garnished; but alas for age! Had I been the bride, I should have taken the giant, dust and all.

He had by no means done with the old man.

"Why, yu've hung weddin' gyarments on every limb!" he now drawled, with admiration. "Who is the lucky lady this trip?"

The old man seemed to vibrate. "Tell you there ain't been no other! Call me a Mormon, would you?"

"Why, that—"

"Call me a Mormon? Then name some of my wives. Name two. Name one. Dare you!"

"—that Laramie wido' promised you—"

"Shucks!"

"—only her docter suddenly ordered Southern climate and—"

"Shucks! You're a false alarm."

"—so nothing but her lungs came between you. And next you'd most got united with Cattle Kate, only—"

"Tell you you're a false alarm!"

"—only she got hung."

"Where's the wives in all this? Show the wives! Come now!"

"That corn-fed biscuit-shooter at Rawlins yu' gave the canary—"

"Never married her. Never did marry—"

"But yu' come so near, uncle! She was the one left yu' that letter explaining how she'd got married to a young cyard-player the very day before her ceremony with you was due, and—"

"Oh, you're nothing; you're a kid; you don't amount to—"

"—and how she'd never, never forgot to feed the canary."

"This country's getting full of kids," stated the old man, wither-

ingly. "It's doomed." This crushing assertion plainly satisfied him.
And he blinked his eyes with renewed anticipation. His tall tormen-
tor continued with a face of unchanging gravity, and a voice of
gentle solicitude:—

"How is the health of that unfortunate—"

"That's right! Pour your insults! Pour 'em on a sick, afflicted
woman!" The eyes blinked with combative relish.

"Insults? Oh, no, Uncle Hughey!"

"That's all right! Insults goes!"

"Why, I was mighty relieved when she began to recover her
mem'ry. Las' time I heard, they told me she'd got it pretty near all
back. Remembered her father, and her mother, and her sisters and
brothers, and her friends, and her happy childhood, and all her doin's
except only your face. The boys was bettin' she'd get that far too,
give her time. But I reckon afteh such a turrable sickness as she had,
that would be expectin' most too much."

At this Uncle Hughey jerked out a small parcel. "Shows how
much you know!" he cackled. "There! See that! That's my ring she
sent me back, being too unstrung for marriage. So she don't remember me, don't she? Ha-ha! Always said you were a false alarm."

The Southerner put more anxiety into his tone. "And so you're
a-takin' the ring right on to the next one!" he exclaimed. "Oh, don't
go to get married again, Uncle Hughey! What's the use o' being married?"

"What's the use?" echoed the bridegroom, with scorn. "Hm!
When you grow up you'll think different."

"Course I expect to think different when my age is different. I'm
havin' the thoughts proper to twenty-four, and you're havin' the
thoughts proper to sixty."

"Fifty!" shrieked Uncle Hughey, jumping in the air.

The Southerner took a tone of self-reproach. "Now, how could I
forget you was fifty," he murmured, "when you have been telling it
to the boys so careful for the last ten years!"

Have you ever seen a cockatoo—the white kind with the top-
knot—enraged by insult? The bird erects every available feather upon
its person. So did Uncle Hughey seem to swell, clothes, mustache,
and woolly white beard; and without further speech he took himself
on board the East-bound train, which now arrived from its siding in
time to deliver him.

Yet this was not why he had not gone away before. At any time he could have escaped into the baggage-room or withdrawn to a dignified distance until his train should come up. But the old man had evidently got a sort of joy from this teasing. He had reached that inevitable age when we are tickled to be linked with affairs of gallantry, no matter how.

With him now the East-bound departed slowly into that distance whence I had come. I stared after it as it went its way to the far shores of civilization. It grew small in the unending gulf of space, until all sign of its presence was gone save a faint skein of smoke against the evening sky. And now my lost trunk came back into my thoughts, and Medicine Bow seemed a lonely spot. A sort of ship had left me marooned in a foreign ocean; the Pullman was comfortably steaming home to port, while I—how was I to find Judge Henry's ranch? Where in this unfeatured wilderness was Sunk Creek? No creek or any water at all flowed here that I could perceive. My host had written he should meet me at the station and drive me to his ranch. This was all that I knew. He was not here. The baggage-man had not seen him lately. The ranch was almost certain to be too far to walk to, to-night. My trunk—I discovered myself still staring dolefully after the vanished East-bound; and at the same instant I became aware that the tall man was looking gravely at me,—as gravely as he had looked at Uncle Hughey throughout their remarkable conversation.

To see his eye thus fixing me and his thumb still hooked in his cartridge-belt, certain tales of travellers from these parts forced themselves disquietingly into my recollection. Now that Uncle Hughey was gone, was I to take his place and be, for instance, invited to dance on the platform to the music of shots nicely aimed?

"I reckon I am looking for you, seh," the tall man now observed.

Theodore Roosevelt (1858–1919)

THEODORE ROOSEVELT, historian, naturalist, explorer, author, hunter, soldier, conservationist, governor of New York, and twenty-sixth President of the United States, was born to a prominent New York family of Dutch provenance. His boyhood was spent in New York City and Oyster Bay, Long Island. Roosevelt graduated from Harvard University in 1880, and entered a career in public service shortly thereafter. In 1881, he was elected to the New York State Legislature.

In 1884, after his wife died two days after childbirth and his mother died on the same day, Roosevelt put his career on hold. Leaving his baby daughter in his sister's care, he bought two cattle ranges on the Little Missouri River in North Dakota and spent the next two years there. He learned to ride, rope, and hunt, and even served a short time as a deputy sheriff. He began writing about frontier life for magazines. After the harsh winter of 1886–87 wiped out his cattle, he returned to the home he had built for his wife and child, Sagamore Hill, in Oyster Bay.

"In Cowboy Land" is from his autobiography (1913).

In Cowboy Land

FROM *Theodore Roosevelt: An Autobiography*, 1913

Though I had previously made a trip into the then Territory of Dakota, beyond the Red River, it was not until 1883 that I went to the Little Missouri, and there took hold of two cattle ranches, the Chimney Butte and the Elkhorn.

It was still the Wild West in those days, the Far West, the West of Owen Wister's stories and Frederic Remington's drawings, the West of the Indian and the buffalo-hunter, the soldier and the cowpuncher. That land of the West has gone now, "gone, gone with lost Atlantis," gone to the isle of ghosts and of strange dead memories. It was a land of vast silent spaces, of lonely rivers, and of plains where the wild game stared at the passing horseman. It was a land of scattered ranches, of herds of long-horned cattle, and of reckless riders who unmoved looked in the eyes of life or of death. In that land we led a free and hardy life, with horse and with rifle. We worked under the scorching midsummer sun, when the wide plains shimmered and wavered in the heat; and we knew the freezing misery of riding night guard round the cattle in the late fall round-up. In the soft springtime the stars were glorious in our eyes each night before we fell asleep; and in the winter we rode through blinding blizzards, when the driven snow-dust burnt our faces. There were monotonous days, as we guided the trail cattle or the beef herds, hour after hour, at the slowest of walks; and minutes or hours teeming with excitement as we stopped stampedes or swam the herds across rivers treacherous with quicksands or brimmed with running ice. We knew toil and hardship and hunger and thirst; and we saw men die violent deaths as they worked among the horses and cattle, or fought in evil feuds with one another; but we felt the beat of hardy life in our veins, and ours was the glory of work and the joy of living.

It was right and necessary that this life should pass, for the safety of our country lies in its being made the country of the small homemaker. The great unfenced ranches, in the days of "free grass," necessarily represented a temporary stage in our history. The large migratory flocks of sheep, each guarded by the hired shepherds of absentee owners, were the first enemies of the cattlemen; and owing to the way they ate out the grass and destroyed all other vegetation, these roving sheep bands represented little of permanent good to the country. But the homesteaders, the permanent settlers, the men who took up each his own farm on which he lived and brought up his family, these represented from the National standpoint the most desirable of all possible users of, and dwellers on, the soil. Their advent meant the breaking up of the big ranches; and the change was a National gain, although to some of us an individual loss.

I first reached the Little Missouri on a Northern Pacific train about three in the morning of a cool September day in 1883. Aside from the station, the only building was a ramshackle structure called the Pyramid Park Hotel. I dragged my duffle-bag thither, and hammered at the door until the frowsy proprietor appeared, muttering oaths. He ushered me upstairs, where I was given one of the fourteen beds in the room which by itself constituted the entire upper floor. Next day I walked over to the abandoned army post, and, after some hours among the gray log shacks, a ranchman who had driven into the station agreed to take me out to his ranch, the Chimney Butte ranch, where he was living with his brother and their partner.

The ranch was a log structure with a dirt roof, a corral for the horses near by, and a chicken-house jabbed against the rear of the ranch house. Inside there was only one room, with a table, three or four chairs, a cooking-stove, and three bunks. The owners were Sylvane and Joe Ferris and William J. Merrifield. Later all three of them held my commissions while I was President. Merrifield was Marshal of Montana, and as Presidential elector cast the vote of that State for me in 1904; Sylvane Ferris was Land Officer in North Dakota, and Joe Ferris Postmaster at Medora. There was a fourth man, George Meyer, who also worked for me later. That evening we all played old sledge round the table, and at one period the game was interrupted by a frightful squawking outside which told us that a bobcat had made a raid on the chicken-house.

After a buffalo hunt with my original friend, Joe Ferris, I entered into partnership with Merrifield and Sylvane Ferris, and we started a cow ranch, with the maltese cross brand—always known as "maltee cross," by the way, as the general impression along the Little Missouri was that "maltese" must be a plural. Twenty-nine years later my four friends of that night were delegates to the First Progressive National Convention at Chicago. They were among my most constant companions for the few years next succeeding the evening when the bobcat interrupted the game of old sledge. I lived and worked with them on the ranch, and with them and many others like them on the round-up; and I brought out from Maine, in order to start the Elkhorn ranch lower down the river, my two backwoods friends Sewall and Dow. My brands for the lower ranch were the elkhorn and triangle.

I do not believe there ever was any life more attractive to a vigorous young fellow than life on a cattle ranch in those days. It was a fine, healthy life, too; it taught a man self-reliance, hardihood, and the value of instant decision—in short, the virtues that ought to come from life in the open country. I enjoyed the life to the full. After the first year I built on the Elkhorn ranch a long, low ranch house of hewn logs, with a veranda, and with, in addition to the other rooms, a bedroom for myself, and a sitting-room with a big fire-place. I got out a rocking-chair—I am very fond of rocking-chairs—and enough books to fill two or three shelves, and a rubber bathtub so that I could get a bath. And then I do not see how any one could have lived more comfortably. We had buffalo robes and bearskins of our own killing. We always kept the house clean—using the word in a rather large sense. There were at least two rooms that were always warm, even in the bitterest weather; and we had plenty to eat. Commonly the mainstay of every meal was game of our own killing, usually antelope or deer, sometimes grouse or ducks, and occasionally, in the earlier days, buffalo or elk. We also had flour and bacon, sugar, salt, and canned tomatoes. And later, when some of the men married and brought out their wives, we had all kinds of good things, such as jams and jellies made from the wild plums and the buffalo berries, and potatoes from the forlorn little garden patch. Moreover, we had milk. Most ranchmen at that time never had milk. I knew more than one ranch with ten thousand head of cattle where there was not a cow that could be milked. We made up our minds that we would be more enterprising. Accordingly, we started to domesticate some of the cows. Our first effort was not successful, chiefly because we did not devote the needed time and patience to the matter. And we found that to race a cow two miles at full speed on horseback, then rope her, throw her, and turn her upside down to milk her, while exhilarating as a pastime, was not productive of results. Gradually we accumulated tame cows, and, after we had thinned out the bobcats and coyotes, more chickens.

The ranch house stood on the brink of a low bluff overlooking the broad, shallow bed of the Little Missouri, through which at most seasons there ran only a trickle of water, while in times of freshet it was filled brimful with the boiling, foaming, muddy torrent. There was no neighbor for ten or fifteen miles on either side of me. The river twisted down in long curves between narrow bottoms bordered by sheer cliff walls, for the Bad Lands, a chaos of peaks, plateaus, and ridges, rose abruptly from the edges of the level, tree-clad, or grassy, alluvial meadows. In front of the ranch-house veranda was a row of cottonwood trees with gray-green leaves which quivered all day long if there was a breath of air. From these trees came the far-away, melancholy cooing of mourning doves, and little owls perched in them and called tremulously at night. In the long summer afternoons we would sometimes sit on the piazza, when there was no work to be done, for an hour or two at a time, watching the cattle on the sandbars, and the sharply channeled and strangely carved amphitheater of cliffs across the bottom opposite; while the vultures wheeled overhead, their black shadows gliding across the glaring white of the dry river-bed. Sometimes from the ranch we saw deer, and once when we needed meat I shot one across the river as I stood on the piazza. In the winter, in the days of iron cold, when everything was white under the snow, the river lay in its bed fixed and immovable as a bar of bent steel, and then at night wolves and lynxes traveled up and down it as if it had been a highway passing in front of the ranch house. Often in the late fall or early winter, after a hard day's hunting, or when returning from one of the winter line camps, we did not reach the ranch until hours after sunset; and after the weary tramping in the cold it was keen pleasure to catch the first red gleam of the fire-lit windows across the snowy wastes.

The Elkhorn ranch house was built mainly by Sewall and Dow, who, like most men from the Maine woods, were mighty with the ax. I could chop fairly well for an amateur, but I could not do one-third the work they could. One day when we were cutting down the cottonwood trees, to begin our building operations, I heard some one ask Dow what the total cut had been, and Dow, not realizing that I was within hearing, answered: "Well, Bill cut down fifty-three, I cut forty-nine, and the boss he beavered down seventeen." Those who have seen the stump of a tree which has been gnawed down by a beaver will understand the exact force of the comparison.

In those days on a cow ranch the men were apt to be away on the various round-ups at least half the time. It was interesting and exciting work, and except for the lack of sleep on the spring and summer round-ups it was not exhausting work; compared to lumbering or mining or blacksmithing, to sit in the saddle is an easy form of labor. The ponies were of course grass-fed and unshod. Each man had his own string of nine or ten. One pony would be used for the morning work, one for the afternoon, and neither would again be used for the next three days. A separate pony was kept for night riding.

The spring and early summer round-ups were especially for the branding of calves. There was much hard work and some risk on a round-up, but also much fun. The meeting-place was appointed weeks beforehand, and all the ranchmen of the territory to be covered by the round-up sent their representatives. There were no fences in the West that I knew, and their place was taken by the cowboy and the branding-iron. The cattle wandered free. Each calf was branded with the brand of the cow it was following. Sometimes in winter there was what we called line riding; that is, camps were established and the line riders traveled a definite beat across the desolate wastes of snow, to and fro from one camp to another, to prevent the cattle from drifting. But as a rule nothing was done to keep the cattle in any one place. In the spring there was a general round-up in each locality. Each outfit took part in its own round-up, and all the outfits of a given region combined to send representatives to the two or three round-ups that covered the neighborhoods near by into which their cattle might drift. For example, our Little Missouri round-up generally worked down the river from a distance of some fifty or sixty miles above my ranch toward the Kildeer Mountains, about the same distance below. In addition we would usually send representatives to the Yellowstone round-up, and to the round-up along the upper Little Missouri; and, moreover, if we heard that cattle had drifted, perhaps toward the Indian reservation southeast of us, we would send a wagon and rider after them.

At the meeting-point, which might be in the valley of a half-dry stream, or in some broad bottom of the river itself, or perchance by a couple of ponds under some queerly shaped butte that was a landmark for the region round about, we would all gather on the appointed day. The chuck-wagons, containing the bedding and food, each drawn by four horses and driven by the teamster cook, would come jolting and rattling over the uneven sward. Accompanying each wagon were eight or ten riders, the cow-punchers, while their horses, a band of a hundred or so, were driven by the two herders, one of whom was known as the day wrangler and one as the night wrangler. The men were lean, sinewy fellows, accustomed to riding half-broken horses at any speed over any country by day or by night. They wore flannel shirts, with loose handkerchiefs knotted round their necks, broad hats, high-heeled boots with jingling spurs, and sometimes leather shaps, although often they merely had their trousers tucked into the tops of their high boots. There was a good deal of rough horse-play, and, as with any other gathering of men or boys of high animal spirits, the horse-play sometimes became very rough indeed; and as the men usually carried revolvers, and as there were occasionally one or two noted gun-fighters among them, there was now and then a shooting affray. A man who was a coward or who shirked his work had a bad time, of course; a man could not afford to let himself be bullied or treated as a butt; and, on the other hand, if he was "looking for a fight," he was certain to find it. But my own experience was that if a man did not talk until his associates knew him well and liked him, and if he did his work, he never had any difficulty in getting on. In my own round-up district I speedily grew to be friends with most of the men. When I went among strangers I always had to spend twenty-four hours in living down the fact that I wore spectacles, remaining as long as I could judiciously deaf to any side remarks about "four eyes," unless it became evident that my being quiet was misconstrued and that it was better to bring matters to a head at once.

If, for instance, I was sent off to represent the Little Missouri brands on some neighboring round-up, such as the Yellowstone, I usually showed that kind of diplomacy which consists in not uttering one word that can be avoided. I would probably have a couple of days' solitary ride, mounted on one horse and driving eight or ten others before me, one of them carrying my bedding. Loose horses drive best at a trot, or canter, and if a man is traveling alone in this fashion it is a good thing to have them reach the camp ground suf-ficiently late to make them desire to feed and sleep where they are until morning. In consequence I never spent more than two days on the journey from whatever the point was at which I left the Little

Missouri, sleeping the one night for as limited a number of hours as possible.

As soon as I reached the meeting-place I would find out the wagon to which I was assigned. Riding to it, I turned my horses into the saddle-band and reported to the wagon boss, or, in his absence, to the cook—always a privileged character, who was allowed and expected to order men around. He would usually grumble savagely and pro- fanely about my having been put with his wagon, but this was merely conventional on his part; and if I sat down and said nothing he would probably soon ask me if I wanted anything to eat, to which the cor- rect answer was that I was not hungry and would wait until meal- time. The bedding rolls of the riders would be strewn round the grass, and I would put mine down a little outside the ring, where I would not be in any one's way, with my six or eight branding-irons beside it. The men would ride in, laughing and talking with one another, and perhaps nodding to me. One of their number, usually the wagon foreman, might put some question to me as to what brands I represented, but no other word would be addressed to me, nor would I be expected to volunteer any conversation. Supper would consist of bacon, Dutch oven bread, and possibly beef; once I won the good graces of my companions at the outset by appearing with two antelope which I had shot. After supper I would roll up in my bedding as soon as possible, and the others would follow suit at their pleasure.

At three in the morning or thereabouts, at a yell from the cook, all hands would turn hurriedly out. Dressing was a simple affair. Then each man rolled and corded his bedding—if he did not, the cook would leave it behind and he would go without any for the rest of the trip—and came to the fire, where he picked out a tin cup, tin plate, and knife and fork, helped himself to coffee and to whatever food there was, and ate it standing or squatting as best suited him. Dawn was probably breaking by this time, and the trampling of unshod hoofs showed that the night wrangler was bringing in the pony herd. Two of the men would then run ropes from the wagon at right angles to one another, and into this as a corral the horses would be driven. Each man might rope one of his own horses, or more often point it out to the most skillful roper of the outfit, who would rope it for him—for if the man was an unskillful roper and roped the wrong horse or roped the horse in the wrong place there was a chance of the whole herd stampeding. Each man then saddled and bridled his horse. This was usually followed by some resolute bucking on the part of two or three of the horses, especially in the early days of each round-up. The bucking was always a source of amusement to all the men whose horses did not buck, and these fortunate ones would gather round giving ironical advice, and especially adjuring the rider not to "go to leather"—that is, not to steady himself in the saddle by catching hold of the saddle-horn.

As soon as the men had mounted, the whole outfit started on the long circle, the morning circle. Usually the ranch foreman who bossed a given wagon was put in charge of the men of one group by the round-up foreman; he might keep his men together until they had gone some ten or fifteen miles from camp, and then drop them in couples at different points. Each couple made its way toward the wagon, gathering all the cattle it could find. The morning's ride might last six or eight hours, and it was still longer before some of the men got in. Singly and in twos and threes they appeared from every quarter of the horizon, the dust rising from the hoofs of the steers and bulls, the cows and calves, they had collected. Two or three of the men were left to take care of the herd while the others changed horses, ate a hasty dinner, and then came out to the afternoon work. This consisted of each man in succession being sent into the herd, usually with a companion, to cut out the cows of his brand or brands which were followed by unbranded calves, and also to cut out any mavericks or unbranded yearlings. We worked each animal gently out to the edge of the herd, and then with a sudden dash took it off at a run. It was always desperately anxious to break back and rejoin the herd. There was much breakneck galloping and twisting and turning before its desire was thwarted and it was driven to join the rest of the cut—that is, the other animals which had been cut out, and which were being held by one or two other men. Cattle hate being alone, and it was no easy matter to hold the first one or two that were cut out; but soon they got a little herd of their own, and then they were contented. When the cutting out had all been done, the calves were branded, and all misadventures of the "calf wrestlers," the men who seized, threw, and held each calf when roped by the mounted roper, were hailed with yelling laughter. Then the animals which for one reason or another it was desired to drive along with the round-up were put into one herd and left in charge of a couple of night guards, and the rest of us would loaf back to the wagon for supper and bed.

By this time I would have been accepted as one of the rest of the outfit, and all strangeness would have passed off, the attitude of my fellow cow-punchers being one of friendly forgiveness even toward my spectacles. Night guards for the cattle herd were then assigned by the captain of the wagon, or perhaps by the round-up foreman, according to the needs of the case, the guards standing for two hours at a time from eight in the evening till four in the morning. The first and last watches were preferable, because sleep was not broken as in both of the other two. If things went well, the cattle would soon bed down and nothing further would occur until morning, when there was a repetition of the work, the wagon moving each day eight or ten miles to some appointed camping-place.

Each man would picket his night horse near the wagon, usually choosing the quietest animal in his string for that purpose, because to saddle and mount a "mean" horse at night is not pleasant. When utterly tired, it was hard to have to get up for one's trick at night herd. Nevertheless, on ordinary nights the two hours round the cattle in the still darkness were pleasant. The loneliness, under the vast empty sky, and the silence, in which the breathing of the cattle sounded loud, and the alert readiness to meet any emergency which might suddenly arise out of the formless night, all combined to give one a sense of subdued interest. Then, one soon got to know the cattle of marked individuality, the ones that led the others into mischief; and one also grew to recognize the traits they all possessed in common, and the impulses which, for instance, made a whole herd get up towards midnight, each beast turning round and then lying down again. But by the end of the watch each rider had studied the cattle until it grew monotonous, and heartily welcomed his relief guard. A newcomer, of course, had any amount to learn, and sometimes the simplest things were those which brought him to grief.

One night early in my career I failed satisfactorily to identify the direction in which I was to go in order to reach the night herd. It was a pitch-dark night. I managed to get started wrong, and I never found either the herd or the wagon again until sunrise, when I was greeted with withering scorn by the injured cow-puncher, who had been obliged to stand double guard because I failed to relieve him.

There were other misadventures that I met with where the excuse was greater. The punchers on night guard usually rode round the cattle in reverse directions; calling and singing to them if the beasts seemed restless, to keep them quiet. On rare occasions something happened that made the cattle stampede, and then the duty of the riders was to keep with them as long as possible and try gradually to get control of them.

One night there was a heavy storm, and all of us who were at the wagons were obliged to turn out hastily to help the night herders. After a while there was a terrific peal of thunder, the lightning struck right by the herd, and away all the beasts went, heads and horns and tails in the air. For a minute or two I could make out nothing except the dark forms of the beasts running on every side of me, and I should have been very sorry if my horse had stumbled, for those behind would have trodden me down. Then the herd split, part going to one side, while the other part seemingly kept straight ahead, and I galloped as hard as ever beside them. I was trying to reach the point— the leading animals—in order to turn them, when suddenly there was a tremendous splashing in front. I could dimly make out that the cattle immediately ahead and to one side of me were disappearing, and the next moment the horse and I went off a cut bank into the Little Missouri. I bent away back in the saddle, and though the horse almost went down he just recovered himself, and, plunging and struggling through water and quicksand, we made the other side. Here I discovered that there was another cowboy with the same part of the herd that I was with; but almost immediately we separated. I galloped hard through a bottom covered with big cottonwood trees, and stopped the part of the herd that I was with, but very soon they broke on me again, and repeated this twice. Finally toward morning the few I had left came to a halt.

It had been raining hard for some time. I got off my horse and leaned against a tree, but before long the infernal cattle started on again, and I had to ride after them. Dawn came soon after this, and I was able to make out where I was and head the cattle back, collecting other little bunches as I went. After a while I came on a cowboy on foot carrying his saddle on his head. He was my companion of the previous night. His horse had gone full speed into a tree and killed itself, the man, however, not being hurt. I could not help him, as I had all I could do to handle the cattle. When I got them to the wagon, most of the other men had already come in and the riders were just starting on the long circle. One of the men changed my horse for me while I ate a hasty breakfast, and then we were off for the day's work.

As only about half of the night herd had been brought back, the circle riding was particularly heavy, and it was ten hours before we were back at the wagon. We then changed horses again and worked the whole herd until after sunset, finishing just as it grew too dark to do anything more. By this time I had been nearly forty hours in the saddle, changing horses five times, and my clothes had thoroughly dried on me, and I fell asleep as soon as I touched the bedding. Fortunately some men who had gotten in late in the morning had had their sleep during the daytime, so that the rest of us escaped night guard and were not called until four next morning. Nobody ever gets enough sleep on a round-up.

The above was the longest number of consecutive hours I ever had to be in the saddle. But, as I have said, I changed horses five times, and it is a great lightening of labor for a rider to have a fresh horse. Once when with Sylvane Ferris I spent about sixteen hours on one horse, riding seventy or eighty miles. The round-up had reached a place called the ox-bow of the Little Missouri, and we had to ride there, do some work around the cattle, and ride back.

Another time I was twenty-four hours on horseback in company with Merrifield without changing horses. On this occasion we did not travel fast. We had been coming back with the wagon from a hunting trip in the Big Horn Mountains. The team was fagged out, and we were tired of walking at a snail's pace beside it. When we reached country that the driver thoroughly knew, we thought it safe to leave him, and we loped in one night across a distance which it took the wagon the three following days to cover. It was a beautiful moonlight night, and the ride was delightful. All day long we had plodded at a walk, weary and hot. At supper time we had rested two or three hours, and the tough little riding horses seemed as fresh as ever. It was in September. As we rode out of the circle of the fire-light, the air was cool in our faces. Under the bright moonlight, and then under the starlight, we loped and cantered mile after mile over the high prairie. We passed bands of antelope and herds of long-horn Texas cattle, and at last, just as the first red beams of the sun flamed over the bluffs in front of us, we rode down into the valley of the Little Missouri, where our ranch house stood.

I never became a good roper, nor more than an average rider, according to ranch standards. Of course a man on a ranch has to ride a good many bad horses, and is bound to encounter a certain number of accidents, and of these I had my share, at one time cracking a rib, and on another occasion the point of my shoulder. We were hundreds of miles from a doctor, and each time, as I was on the round-up, I had to get through my work for the next few weeks as best I could, until the injury healed of itself. When I had the opportunity I broke my own horses, doing it gently and gradually and spending much time over it, and choosing the horses that seemed gentle to begin with. With these horses I never had any difficulty. But frequently there was neither time nor opportunity to handle our mounts so elaborately. We might get a band of horses, each having been bridled and saddled two or three times, but none of them having been broken beyond the extent implied in this bridling and saddling. Then each of us in succession would choose a horse (for his string), I as owner of the ranch being given the first choice on each round, so to speak. The first time I was ever on a round-up Sylvane Ferris, Merrifield, Meyer, and I each chose his string in this fashion. Three or four of the animals I got were not easy to ride. The effort both to ride them and to look as if I enjoyed doing so, on some cool morning when my grinning cowboy friends had gathered round "to see whether the high-headed bay could buck the boss off," doubtless was of benefit to me, but lacked much of being enjoyable. The time I smashed my rib I was bucked off on a stone. The time I hurt the point of my shoulder I was riding a big, sulky horse named Ben Butler, which went over backwards with me. When we got up it still refused to go anywhere; so, while I sat it, Sylvane Ferris and George Meyer got their ropes on its neck and dragged it a few hundred yards, choking but stubborn, all four feet firmly planted and plowing the ground. When they released the ropes it lay down and wouldn't get up. The round-up had started; so Sylvane gave me his horse, Baldy, which sometimes bucked but never went over backwards, and he got on the now rearisen Ben Butler. To my discomfiture Ben started quietly beside us, while Sylvane remarked, "Why, there's nothing the matter with this horse; he's a plumb gentle horse." Then Ben fell slightly behind and I heard Sylvane again, "That's all right! Come along! Here, you! Go on, you! Hi, hi, fellows, help me out! he's lying on me!" Sure enough, he was; and when we dragged Sylvane from under him the first thing the rescued Sylvane did was to execute a war-dance, spurs and all, on the iniquitous Ben. We could do nothing with him that day; subsequently we got him so that we could ride him; but he never became a nice saddle-horse.

As with all other forms of work, so on the round-up, a man of ordinary power, who nevertheless does not shirk things merely because they are disagreeable or irksome, soon earns his place. There were crack riders and ropers who, just because they felt such over-weening pride in their own prowess, were not really very valuable men. Continually on the circles a cow or a calf would get into some thick patch of bulberry bush and refuse to come out; or when it was getting late we would pass some bad lands that would probably not contain cattle, but might; or a steer would turn fighting mad, or a calf grow tired and want to lie down. If in such a case the man steadily persists in doing the unattractive thing, and after two hours of exas-peration and harassment does finally get the cow out, and keep her out, of the bulberry bushes, and drives her to the wagon, or finds some animals that have been passed by in the fourth or fifth patch of bad lands he hunts through, or gets the calf up on his saddle and takes it in anyhow, the foreman soon grows to treat him as having his uses and as being an asset of worth in the round-up, even though neither a fancy roper nor a fancy rider.

When at the Progressive Convention last August, I met George Meyer for the first time in many years, and he recalled to me an incident on one round-up where we happened to be thrown together while driving some cows and calves to camp. When the camp was only just across the river, two of the calves positively refused to go any further. He took one of them in his arms, and after some hazard-ous maneuvering managed to get on his horse, in spite of the objec-tions of the latter, and rode into the river. My calf was too big for such treatment, so in despair I roped it, intending to drag it over. However, as soon as I roped it, the calf started bouncing and bleating, and, owing to some lack of dexterity on my part, suddenly swung round the rear of the horse, bringing the rope under his tail. Down went the tail tight, and the horse "went into figures," as the cow-puncher phrase of that day was. There was a cut bank about four feet high on the hither side of the river, and over this the horse bucked. We went into the water with a splash. With a "pluck" the calf fol-lowed, described a parabola in the air, and landed beside us. Fortunately, this took the rope out from under the horse's tail, but left him thoroughly frightened. He could not do much bucking in the stream, for there were one or two places where we had to swim, and the shallows were either sandy or muddy; but across we went, at speed, and the calf made a wake like Pharaoh's army in the Red Sea.

On several occasions we had to fight fire. In the geography books of my youth prairie fires were always portrayed as taking place in long grass, and all living things ran before them. On the Northern cattle plains the grass was never long enough to be a source of danger to man or beast. The fires were nothing like the forest fires in the Northern woods. But they destroyed large quantities of feed, and we had to stop them where possible. The process we usually followed was to kill a steer, split it in two lengthwise, and then have two riders drag each half-steer, the rope of one running from his saddle-horn to the front leg, and that of the other to the hind leg. One of the men would spur his horse over or through the line of fire, and the two would then ride forward, dragging the steer bloody side downward along the line of flame, men following on foot with slickers or wet horse-blankets to beat out any flickering blaze that was still left. It was exciting work, for the fire and the twitching and plucking of the ox carcass over the uneven ground maddened the fierce little horses so that it was necessary to do some riding in order to keep them to their work. After a while it also became very exhausting, the thirst and fatigue being great, as, with parched lips and blackened from head to foot, we toiled at our task.

In those years the Stockman's Association of Montana was a powerful body. I was the delegate to it from the Little Missouri. The meetings that I attended were held in Miles City, at that time a typical cow town. Stockmen of all kinds attended, including the biggest men in the stock business, men like old Conrad Kohrs, who was and is the finest type of pioneer in all the Rocky Mountain country; and Granville Stewart, who was afterwards appointed Minister by Cleveland, I think to the Argentine; and "Hashknife" Simpson, a Texan who had brought his cattle, the Hashknife brand, up the trail into our country. He and I grew to be great friends. I can see him now the first time we met, grinning at me as, none too comfortable, I sat a half-broken horse at the edge of a cattle herd we were working. His son Sloan Simpson went to Harvard, was one of the first-class men in my regiment, and afterwards held my commission as Postmaster at Dallas.

At the stockmen's meeting in Miles City, in addition to the big stockmen, there were always hundreds of cowboys galloping up and down the wide dusty streets at every hour of the day and night. It was a picturesque sight during the three days the meetings lasted. There was always at least one big dance at the hotel. There were few dress suits, but there was perfect decorum at the dance, and in the square dances most of the men knew the figures far better than I did. With such a crowd in town, sleeping accommodations of any sort were at a premium, and in the hotel there were two men in every bed. On one occasion I had a roommate whom I never saw, because he always went to bed much later than I did and I always got up much earlier than he did. On the last day, however, he rose at the same time and I saw that he was a man I knew named Carter, and nicknamed "Modesty" Carter. He was a stalwart, good-looking fellow, and I was sorry when later I heard that he had been killed in a shooting row.

When I went West, the last great Indian wars had just come to an end, but there were still sporadic outbreaks here and there, and occasionally bands of marauding young braves were a menace to outlying and lonely settlements. Many of the white men were themselves lawless and brutal, and prone to commit outrages on the Indians. Unfortunately, each race tended to hold all the members of the other race responsible for the misdeeds of a few, so that the crime of the miscreant, red or white, who committed the original outrage too often invited retaliation upon entirely innocent people, and this action would in its turn arouse bitter feeling which found vent in still more indiscriminate retaliation. The first year I was on the Little Missouri some Sioux bucks ran off all the horses of a buffalo-hunter's outfit. One of the buffalo-hunters tried to get even by stealing the horses of a Cheyenne hunting party, and when pursued made for a cow camp, with, as a result, a long-range skirmish between the cowboys and the Cheyennes. One of the latter was wounded; but this particular wounded man seemed to have more sense than the other participants in the chain of wrong-doing, and discriminated among the whites. He came into our camp and had his wound dressed.

A year later I was at a desolate little mud road ranch on the Deadwood trail. It was kept by a very capable and very forceful woman, with sound ideas of justice and abundantly well able to hold her own. Her husband was a worthless devil, who finally got drunk on some whisky he obtained from an outfit of Missouri bullwhackers—that is, freighters, driving ox wagons. Under the stimulus of the whisky he picked a quarrel with his wife and attempted to beat her. She knocked him down with a stove-lid lifter, and the admiring bull-whackers bore him off, leaving the lady in full possession of the ranch. When I visited her she had a man named Crow Joe working for her, a slab-sided, shifty-eyed person who later, as I heard my foreman explain, "skipped the country with a bunch of horses." The mistress of the ranch made first-class buckskin shirts of great durability. The one she made for me, and which I used for years, was used by one of my sons in Arizona a couple of winters ago. I had ridden down into the country after some lost horses, and visited the ranch to get her to make me the buckskin shirt in question. There were, at the moment, three Indians there, Sioux, well behaved and self-respecting, and she explained to me that they had been resting there waiting for dinner, and that a white man had come along and tried to run off their horses. The Indians were on the lookout, however, and, running out, they caught the man; but, after retaking their horses and depriving him of his gun, they let him go. "I don't see why they let him go," exclaimed my hostess. "I don't believe in stealing Indians' horses any more than white folks'; so I told 'em they could go along and hang him—I'd never cheep. Anyhow, I won't charge them anything for their dinner," concluded my hostess. She was in advance of the usual morality of the time and place, which drew a sharp line between stealing citizens' horses and stealing horses from the Government or the Indians.

A fairly decent citizen, Jap Hunt, who long ago met a violent death, exemplified this attitude towards Indians in some remarks I once heard him make. He had started a horse ranch, and had quite honestly purchased a number of broken-down horses of different brands, with the view of doctoring them and selling them again. About this time there had been much horse-stealing and cattle-killing in our Territory and in Montana, and under the direction of some of the big cattle-growers a committee of vigilantes had been organized to take action against the rustlers, as the horse thieves and cattle thieves were called. The vigilantes, or stranglers, as they were locally known, did their work thoroughly; but, as always happens with bodies of the kind, toward the end they grew reckless in their actions, paid off private grudges, and hung men on slight provocation. Riding into Jap Hunt's ranch, they nearly hung him because he had so many horses of different brands. He was finally let off. He was much upset by the incident, and explained again and again, "The idea of saying that I was a horse thief! Why, I never stole a horse in my life— leastways from a white man. I don't count Indians nor the Government, of course." Jap had been reared among men still in the stage of tribal morality, and while they recognized their obligations to one another, both the Government and the Indians seemed alien bodies, in regard to which the laws of morality did not apply.

On the other hand, parties of savage young bucks would treat lonely settlers just as badly, and in addition sometimes murder them. Such a party was generally composed of young fellows burning to distinguish themselves. Some one of their number would have obtained a pass from the Indian Agent allowing him to travel off the reservation, which pass would be flourished whenever their action was questioned by bodies of whites of equal strength. I once had a trifling encounter with such a band. I was making my way along the edge of the bad lands, northward from my lower ranch, and was just crossing a plateau when five Indians rode up over the further rim. The instant they saw me they whipped out their guns and raced full speed at me, yelling and flogging their horses. I was on a favorite horse, Manitou, who was a wise old fellow, with nerves not to be shaken by anything. I at once leaped off him and stood with my rifle ready.

It was possible that the Indians were merely making a bluff and intended no mischief. But I did not like their actions, and I thought it likely that if I allowed them to get hold of me they would at least take my horse and rifle, and possibly kill me. So I waited until they were a hundred yards off and then drew a bead on the first. Indians— and, for the matter of that, white men—do not like to ride in on a man who is cool and means shooting, and in a twinkling every man was lying over the side of his horse, and all five had turned and were galloping backwards, having altered their course as quickly as so many teal ducks.

After this one of them made the peace sign, with his blanket first, and then, as he rode toward me, with his open hand. I halted him at a fair distance and asked him what he wanted. He exclaimed, "How! Me good Injun, me good Injun," and tried to show me the dirty piece of paper on which his agency pass was written. I told him with sincerity that I was glad that he was a good Indian, but that he must not come any closer. He then asked for sugar and tobacco. I told him I had none. Another Indian began slowly drifting toward me in spite of my calling out to keep back, so I once more aimed with my rifle, whereupon both Indians slipped to the other side of their horses and galloped off, with oaths that did credit to at least one side of their acquaintance with English. I now mounted and pushed over the plateau on to the open prairie. In those days an Indian, although not as good a shot as a white man, was infinitely better at crawling under and taking advantage of cover; and the worst thing a white man could do was to get into cover, whereas out in the open if he kept his head he had a good chance of standing off even half a dozen assailants. The Indians accompanied me for a couple of miles. Then I reached the open prairie, and resumed my northward ride, not being further molested.

In the old days in the ranch country we depended upon game for fresh meat. Nobody liked to kill a beef, and although now and then a maverick yearling might be killed on the round-up, most of us looked askance at the deed, because if the practice of beef-killing was ever allowed to start, the rustlers—the horse thieves and cattle thieves—would be sure to seize on it as an excuse for general slaughter. Getting meat for the ranch usually devolved upon me. I almost always carried a rifle when I rode, either in a scabbard under my thigh, or across the pommel. Often I would pick up a deer or antelope while about my regular work, when visiting a line camp or riding after the cattle. At other times I would make a day's trip after them. In the fall we sometimes took a wagon and made a week's hunt, returning with eight or ten deer carcasses, and perhaps an elk or a mountain sheep as well. I never became more than a fair hunter, and at times I had most exasperating experiences, either failing to see game which I ought to have seen, or committing some blunder in the stalk, or failing to kill when I fired. Looking back, I am inclined to say that if I had any good quality as a hunter it was that of perseverance. "It is dogged that does it" in hunting as in many other things. Unless in wholly exceptional cases, when we were very hungry, I never killed anything but bucks.

Occasionally I made long trips away from the ranch and among the Rocky Mountains with my ranch foreman Merrifield; or in later years with Tazewell Woody, John Willis, or John Goff. We hunted bears, both the black and the grizzly, cougars and wolves, and moose, wapiti, and white goat. On one of these trips I killed a bison bull, and I also killed a bison bull on the Little Missouri some fifty miles south of my ranch on a trip which Joe Ferris and I took together. It was rather a rough trip. Each of us carried only his slicker behind him on the saddle, with some flour and bacon done up in it. We met with all kinds of misadventures. Finally one night, when we were sleeping by a slimy little prairie pool where there was not a stick of wood, we had to tie the horses to the horns of our saddles; and then we went to sleep with our heads on the saddles. In the middle of the night something stampeded the horses, and away they went, with the saddles after them. As we jumped to our feet Joe eyed me with an evident suspicion that I was the Jonah of the party, and said: "O Lord! *I've* never done anything to deserve this. Did *you* ever do anything to deserve this?"

In addition to my private duties, I sometimes served as deputy sheriff for the northern end of our county. The sheriff and I crisscrossed in our public and private relations. He often worked for me as a hired hand at the same time that I was his deputy. His name, or at least the name he went by, was Bill Jones, and as there were in the neighborhood several Bill Joneses—Three Seven Bill Jones, Texas Bill Jones, and the like—the sheriff was known as Hell Roaring Bill Jones. He was a thorough frontiersman, excellent in all kinds of emergencies, and a very game man. I became much attached to him. He was a thoroughly good citizen when sober, but he was a little wild when drunk. Unfortunately, toward the end of his life he got to drinking very heavily. When, in 1905, John Burroughs and I visited the Yellowstone Park, poor Bill Jones, very much down in the world, was driving a team in Gardiner outside the park. I had looked forward to seeing him, and he was equally anxious to see me. He kept telling his cronies of our intimacy and of what we were going to do together, and then got drinking; and the result was that by the time I reached Gardiner he had to be carried out and left in the sagebrush. When I came out of the park, I sent on in advance to tell them to be sure to keep him sober, and they did so. But it was a rather sad interview. The old fellow had gone to pieces, and soon after I left he got lost in a blizzard and was dead when they found him.

Bill Jones was a gun-fighter and also a good man with his fists. On one occasion there was an election in town. There had been many threats that the party of disorder would import section hands from the neighboring railway stations to down our side. I did not reach Medora, the forlorn little cattle town which was our county seat, until the election was well under way. I then asked one of my friends if there had been any disorder. Bill Jones was standing by. "Disorder hell!" said my friend. "Bill Jones just stood there with one hand on his gun and the other pointing over toward the new jail whenever any man who didn't have a right to vote came near the polls. There was only one of them tried to vote, and Bill knocked him down. Lord!" added my friend, meditatively, "the way that man fell!"

"Well," struck in Bill Jones, "if he hadn't fell I'd have walked round behind him to see what was propping him up!"

In the days when I lived on the ranch I usually spent most of the winter in the East, and when I returned in the early spring I was always interested in finding out what had happened since my departure. On one occasion I was met by Bill Jones and Sylvane Ferris, and in the course of our conversation they mentioned "the lunatic." This led to a question on my part, and Sylvane Ferris began the story: "Well, you see, he was on a train and he shot the newsboy. At first they weren't going to do anything to him, for they thought he just had it in for the newsboy. But then somebody said, 'Why, he's plumb crazy, and he's liable to shoot any of *us!*' and then they threw him off the train. It was here at Medora, and they asked if anybody would take care of him, and Bill Jones said he would, because he was the sheriff and the jail had two rooms, and he was living in one and would put the lunatic in the other." Here Bill Jones interrupted: "Yes, and more fool me! I wouldn't take charge of another lunatic if the whole county asked me. Why" (with the air of a man announcing an astounding discovery), "that lunatic didn't have his right senses! He wouldn't eat, till me and Snyder got him down on the shavings and *made* him eat." Snyder was a huge, happy-go-lucky, kind-hearted Pennsylvania Dutchman, and was Bill Jones's chief deputy. Bill continued: "You know, Snyder's soft-hearted, he is. Well, he'd think that lunatic looked peaked, and he'd take him out for an airing. Then the boys would get joshing him as to how much start he could give him over the prairie and catch him again." Apparently the amount of the start given the lunatic depended upon the amount of the bet to which the joshing led up. I asked Bill what he would have done if Snyder hadn't caught the lunatic. This was evidently a new idea, and he responded that Snyder always did catch him. "Well, but suppose he hadn't caught him?" "Well," said Bill Jones, "if Snyder hadn't caught the lunatic, I'd have whaled hell out of Snyder!"

Under these circumstances Snyder ran his best and always did catch the patient. It must not be gathered from this that the lunatic was badly treated. He was well treated. He became greatly attached to both Bill Jones and Snyder, and he objected strongly when, after the frontier theory of treatment of the insane had received a full trial, he was finally sent off to the territorial capital. It was merely that all the relations of life in that place and day were so managed as to give ample opportunity for the expression of individuality, whether in sheriff or ranchman. The local practical joker once attempted to have some fun at the expense of the lunatic, and Bill Jones described the result. "You know Bixby, don't you? Well," with deep disapproval, "Bixby thinks he is funny, he does. He'd come and he'd wake that lunatic up at night, and I'd have to get up and soothe him. I fixed Bixby all right, though. I fastened a rope on the latch, and next time Bixby came I let the lunatic out on him. He 'most bit Bixby's nose off. I learned Bixby!"

Bill Jones had been unconventional in other relations besides that of sheriff. He once casually mentioned to me that he had served on the police force of Bismarck, but he had left because he "beat the Mayor over the head with his gun one day." He added: "The Mayor, he didn't mind it, but the Superintendent of Police said he guessed I'd better resign." His feeling, obviously, was that the Superintendent of Police was a martinet, unfit to take large views of life.

It was while with Bill Jones that I first made acquaintance with Seth Bullock. Seth was at that time sheriff in the Black Hills district, and a man he had wanted—a horse thief—I finally got, I being at the time deputy sheriff two or three hundred miles to the north. The man went by a nickname which I will call "Crazy Steve"; a year or two afterwards I received a letter asking about him from his uncle, a thoroughly respectable man in a Western State; and later this uncle and I met at Washington when I was President and he a United States Senator. It was some time after "Steve's" capture that I went down to Deadwood on business, Sylvane Ferris and I on horseback, while Bill Jones drove the wagon. At a little town, Spearfish, I think, after crossing the last eighty or ninety miles of gumbo prairies, we met Seth Bullock. We had had rather a rough trip, and had lain out for a fortnight, so I suppose we looked somewhat unkempt. Seth received us with rather distant courtesy at first, but unbent when he found out who we were, remarking, "You see, by your looks I thought you were some kind of a tin-horn gambling outfit, and that I might have to keep an eye on you!" He then inquired after the capture of "Steve"—with a little of the air of one sportsman when another has shot a quail that either might have claimed—"My bird, I believe?" Later Seth Bullock became, and has ever since remained, one of my stanchest and most valued friends. He served as Marshal for South Dakota under me as President. When, after the close of my term, I went to Africa, on getting back to Europe I cabled Seth Bullock to bring over Mrs. Bullock and meet me in London, which he did; by that time I felt that I just had to meet my own people, who spoke my neighborhood dialect.

When serving as deputy sheriff I was impressed with the advantage the officer of the law has over ordinary wrong-doers, provided he thoroughly knows his own mind. There are exceptional outlaws, men with a price on their heads and of remarkable prowess, who are utterly indifferent to taking life, and whose warfare against society is as open as that of a savage on the war-path. The law officer has no advantage whatever over these men save what his own prowess may—or may not—give him. Such a man was Billy the Kid, the notorious man-killer and desperado of New Mexico, who was himself finally slain by a friend of mine, Pat Garrett, whom, when I was President, I made collector of customs at El Paso. But the ordinary criminal, even when murderously inclined, feels just a moment's hesitation as to whether he cares to kill an officer of the law engaged in his duty. I took in more than one man who was probably a better man than I was with both rifle and revolver; but in each case I knew just what I wanted to do, and, like David Harum, I "did it first," whereas the fraction of a second that the other man hesitated put him in a position where it was useless for him to resist.

I owe more than I can ever express to the West, which of course means to the men and women I met in the West. There were a few people of bad type in my neighborhood—that would be true of every group of men, even in a theological seminary—but I could not speak with too great affection and respect of the great majority of my friends, the hard-working men and women who dwelt for a space of perhaps a hundred and fifty miles along the Little Missouri. I was always as welcome at their houses as they were at mine. Everybody worked, everybody was willing to help everybody else, and yet nobody asked any favors. The same thing was true of the people whom I got to know fifty miles east and fifty miles west of my own range, and of the men I met on the round-ups. They soon accepted me as a friend and fellow-worker who stood on an equal footing with them, and I believe the most of them have kept their feeling for me ever since. No guests were ever more welcome at the White House than these old friends of the cattle ranches and the cow camps—the men with whom I had ridden the long circle and eaten at the tail-board of a chuck-wagon—whenever they turned up at Washington during my Presidency. I remember one of them who appeared at

Washington one day just before lunch, a huge, powerful man who, when I knew him, had been distinctly a fighting character. It happened that on that day another old friend, the British Ambassador, Mr. Bryce, was among those coming to lunch. Just before we went in I turned to my cow-puncher friend and said to him with great solemnity, "Remember, Jim, that if you shot at the feet of the British Ambassador to make him dance, it would be likely to cause international complications"; to which Jim responded with unaffected horror, "Why, Colonel, I shouldn't think of it, I shouldn't think of it!"

Not only did the men and women whom I met in the cow country quite unconsciously help me, by the insight which working and living with them enabled me to get into the mind and soul of the average American of the right type, but they helped me in another way. I made up my mind that the men were of just the kind whom it would be well to have with me if ever it became necessary to go to war. When the Spanish War came, I gave this thought practical realization.

Fortunately, Wister and Remington, with pen and pencil, have made these men live as long as our literature lives. I have sometimes been asked if Wister's "Virginian" is not overdrawn; why, one of the men I have mentioned in this chapter was in all essentials the Virginian in real life, not only in his force but in his charm. Half of the men I worked with or played with and half of the men who soldiered with me afterwards in my regiment might have walked out of Wister's stories or Remington's pictures.

There were bad characters in the Western country at that time, of course, and under the conditions of life they were probably more dangerous than they would have been elsewhere. I hardly ever had any difficulty, however. I never went into a saloon, and in the little hotels I kept out of the bar-room unless, as sometimes happened, the bar-room was the only room on the lower floor except the dining-room. I always endeavored to keep out of a quarrel until self-respect forbade my making any further effort to avoid it, and I very rarely had even the semblance of trouble.

Of course amusing incidents occurred now and then. Usually these took place when I was hunting lost horses, for in hunting lost horses I was ordinarily alone, and occasionally had to travel a hundred or a hundred and fifty miles away from my own country. On one such occasion I reached a little cow town long after dark, stabled my horse in an empty outbuilding, and when I reached the hotel was informed in response to my request for a bed that I could have the last one left, as there was only one other man in it. The room to which I was shown contained two double beds; one contained two men fast asleep, and the other only one man, also asleep. This man proved to be a friend, one of the Bill Joneses whom I have previously mentioned. I undressed according to the fashion of the day and place, that is, I put my trousers, boots, shaps, and gun down beside the bed, and turned in. A couple of hours later I was awakened by the door being thrown open and a lantern flashed in my face, the light gleaming on the muzzle of a cocked .45. Another man said to the lantern-bearer, "It ain't him"; the next moment my bedfellow was covered with two guns, and addressed, "Now, Bill, don't make a fuss, but come along quiet." "I'm not thinking of making a fuss," said Bill. "That's right," was the answer; "we're your friends; we don't want to hurt you; we just want you to come along, you know why." And Bill pulled on his trousers and boots and walked out with them. Up to this time there had not been a sound from the other bed. Now a match was scratched, a candle lit, and one of the men in the other bed looked round the room. At this point I committed the breach of etiquette of asking questions. "I wonder why they took Bill," I said. There was no answer, and I repeated, "I wonder why they took Bill." "Well," said the man with the candle, dryly, "I reckon they wanted him," and with that he blew out the candle and conversation ceased. Later I discovered that Bill in a fit of playfulness had held up the Northern Pacific train at a near-by station by shooting at the feet of the conductor to make him dance. This was purely a joke on Bill's part, but the Northern Pacific people possessed a less robust sense of humor, and on their complaint the United States Marshal was sent after Bill, on the ground that by delaying the train he had interfered with the mails.

The only time I ever had serious trouble was at an even more primitive little hotel than the one in question. It was also on an occasion when I was out after lost horses. Below the hotel had merely a bar-room, a dining-room, and a lean-to kitchen; above was a loft with fifteen or twenty beds in it. It was late in the evening when I reached the place. I heard one or two shots in the bar-room as I came up, and I disliked going in. But there was nowhere else to go, and it was a cold night. Inside the room were several men, who, including the bartender, were wearing the kind of smile worn by men who are making believe to like what they don't like. A shabby individual in a broad hat with a cocked gun in each hand was walking up and down the floor talking with strident profanity. He had evidently been shooting at the clock, which had two or three holes in its face.

He was not a "bad man" of the really dangerous type, the true man-killer type, but he was an objectionable creature, a would-be bad man, a bully who for the moment was having things all his own way. As soon as he saw me he hailed me as "Four eyes," in reference to my spectacles, and said, "Four eyes is going to treat." I joined in the laugh and got behind the stove and sat down, thinking to escape notice. He followed me, however, and though I tried to pass it off as a jest this merely made him more offensive, and he stood leaning over me, a gun in each hand, using very foul language. He was foolish to stand so near, and, moreover, his heels were close together, so that his position was unstable. Accordingly, in response to his reiterated command that I should set up the drinks, I said, "Well, if I've got to, I've got to," and rose, looking past him.

As I rose, I struck quick and hard with my right just to one side of the point of his jaw, hitting with my left as I straightened out, and then again with my right. He fired the guns, but I do not know whether this was merely a convulsive action of his hands or whether he was trying to shoot at me. When he went down he struck the corner of the bar with his head. It was not a case in which one could afford to take chances, and if he had moved I was about to drop on his ribs with my knees; but he was senseless. I took away his guns, and the other people in the room, who were now loud in their denunciation of him, hustled him out and put him in a shed. I got dinner as soon as possible, sitting in a corner of the dining-room away from the windows, and then went upstairs to bed where it was dark so that there would be no chance of any one shooting at me from the outside. However, nothing happened. When my assailant came to, he went down to the station and left on a freight.

As I have said, most of the men of my regiment were just such men as those I knew in the ranch country; indeed, some of my ranch friends were in the regiment—Fred Herrig, the forest ranger, for instance, in whose company I shot my biggest mountain ram. After the regiment was disbanded the careers of certain of the men were diversified by odd incidents. Our relations were of the friendliest, and, as they explained, they felt "as if I was a father" to them. The manifestations of this feeling were sometimes less attractive than the phrase sounded, as it was chiefly used by the few who were behaving like very bad children indeed. The great majority of the men when the regiment disbanded took up the business of their lives where they had dropped it a few months previously, and these men merely tried to help me or help one another as the occasion arose; no man ever had more cause to be proud of his regiment than I had of mine, both in war and in peace. But there was a minority among them who in certain ways were unsuited for a life of peaceful regularity, although often enough they had been first-class soldiers.

It was from these men that letters came with a stereotyped opening which always caused my heart to sink—"Dear Colonel: I write you because I am in trouble." The trouble might take almost any form. One correspondent continued: "I did not take the horse, but they say I did." Another complained that his mother-in-law had put him in jail for bigamy. In the case of another the incident was more markworthy. I will call him Gritto. He wrote me a letter beginning: "Dear Colonel: I write you because I am in trouble. I have shot a lady in the eye. But, Colonel, I was not shooting at the lady. I was shooting at my wife," which he apparently regarded as a sufficient excuse as between men of the world. I answered that I drew the line at shooting at ladies, and did not hear any more of the incident for several years.

Then, while I was President, a member of the regiment, Major Llewellyn, who was Federal District Attorney under me in New Mexico, wrote me a letter filled, as his letters usually were, with bits of interesting gossip about the comrades. It ran in part as follows: "Since I last wrote you Comrade Ritchie has killed a man in Colorado. I understand that the comrade was playing a poker game, and the man sat into the game and used such language that Comrade Ritchie had to shoot. Comrade Webb has killed two men in Beaver, Arizona. Comrade Webb is in the Forest Service, and the killing was in the line of professional duty. I was out at the penitentiary the other day and saw Comrade Gritto, who, you may remember, was put there for shooting his sister-in-law [this was the first information I had had as to the identity of the lady who was shot in the eye]. Since he was in there Comrade Boyne has run off to old Mexico with his (Gritto's) wife, and the people of Grant County think he ought to be let out." Evidently the sporting instincts of the people of Grant County had been roused, and they felt that, as Comrade Boyne had had a fair start, the other comrade should be let out in order to see what would happen.

The men of the regiment always enthusiastically helped me when I was running for office. On one occasion Buck Taylor, of Texas, accompanied me on a trip and made a speech for me. The crowd took to his speech from the beginning and so did I, until the peroration, which ran as follows: "My fellow-citizens, vote for my Colonel! vote for my Colonel! *and he will lead you, as he led us, like sheep to the slaughter!*" This hardly seemed a tribute to my military skill; but it delighted the crowd, and as far as I could tell did me nothing but good.

On another tour, when I was running for Vice-President, a member of the regiment who was along on the train got into a discussion with a Populist editor who had expressed an unfavorable estimate of my character, and in the course of the discussion shot the editor—not fatally. We had to leave him to be tried, and as he had no money I left him $150 to hire counsel—having borrowed the money from Senator Wolcott, of Colorado, who was also with me. After election I received from my friend a letter running: "Dear Colonel: I find I will not have to use that $150 you lent me, as we have elected our candidate for District Attorney. So I have used it to settle a horse transaction in which I unfortunately became involved." A few weeks later, however, I received a heartbroken letter setting forth the fact that the District Attorney—whom he evidently felt to be a cold-blooded formalist—had put him in jail. Then the affair dropped out of sight until two or three years later, when as President I visited a town in another State, and the leaders of the delegation which received me included both my correspondent and the editor, now fast friends, and both of them ardent supporters of mine.

At one of the regimental reunions a man, who had been an excellent soldier, in greeting me mentioned how glad he was that the judge had let him out in time to get to the reunion. I asked what was the matter, and he replied with some surprise: "Why, Colonel, don't you know I had a difficulty with a gentleman, and . . . er . . . well, I killed the gentleman. But you can see that the judge thought it was all right or he wouldn't have let me go." Waiving the latter point, I said: "How did it happen? How did you do it?" Misinterpreting my question as showing an interest only in the technique of the performance, the ex-puncher replied: "With a .38 on a .45 frame, Colonel." I chuckled over the answer, and it became proverbial with my family and some of my friends, including Seth Bullock. When I was shot at Milwaukee, Seth Bullock wired an inquiry to which I responded that it was all right, that the weapon was merely "a .38 on a .45 frame." The telegram in some way became public, and puzzled outsiders. By the way, both the men of my regiment and the friends I had made in the old days in the West were themselves a little puzzled at the interest shown in my making my speech after being shot. This was what they expected, what they accepted as the right thing for a man to do under the circumstances, a thing the non-performance of which would have been discreditable rather than the performance being creditable. They would not have expected a man to leave a battle, for instance, because of being wounded in such fashion; and they saw no reason why he should abandon a less important and less risky duty.

One of the best soldiers of my regiment was a huge man whom I made marshal of a Rocky Mountain State. He had spent his hot and lusty youth on the frontier during its viking age, and at that time had naturally taken part in incidents which seemed queer to men "accustomed to die decently of zymotic diseases." I told him that an effort would doubtless be made to prevent his confirmation by the Senate, and therefore that I wanted to know all the facts in his case. Had he played faro? He had; but it was when everybody played faro, and he had never played a brace game. Had he killed anybody? Yes, but it was in Dodge City on occasions when he was deputy marshal or town marshal, at a time when Dodge City, now the most peaceful of communities, was the toughest town on the continent, and crowded with man-killing outlaws and road agents; and he produced telegrams from judges of high character testifying to the need of the actions he had taken. Finally I said: "Now, Ben, how did you lose that half of your ear?" To which, looking rather shy, he responded: "Well, Colonel, it was bit off." "How did it happen, Ben?" "Well, you see, I was sent to arrest a gentleman, and him and me mixed it up, and he bit off my ear." "What did you do to the gentleman, Ben?" And Ben, looking more coy than ever, responded: "Well, Colonel, we broke about even!" I forebore to inquire what variety of mayhem he had committed on the "gentleman." After considerable struggle I got him confirmed by the Senate, and he made one of the best marshals in the entire service, exactly as he had already made one of the best soldiers in the regiment; and I never wish to see a better citizen, nor a man in whom I would more implicitly trust in every way.

When, in 1900, I was nominated for Vice-President, I was sent by the National Committee on a trip into the States of the high plains and the Rocky Mountains. These had all gone overwhelmingly for

Mr. Bryan on the free-silver issue four years previously, and it was thought that I, because of my knowledge of and acquaintanceship with the people, might accomplish something towards bringing them back into line. It was an interesting trip, and the monotony usually attendant upon such a campaign of political speaking was diversified in vivid fashion by occasional hostile audiences. One or two of the meetings ended in riots. One meeting was finally broken up by a mob; everybody fought so that the speaking had to stop. Soon after this we reached another town where we were told there might be trouble. Here the local committee included an old and valued friend, a "two-gun" man of repute, who was not in the least quarrelsome, but who always kept his word. We marched round to the local opera-house, which was packed with a mass of men, many of them rather rough-looking. My friend the two-gun man sat immediately behind me, a gun on each hip, his arms folded, looking at the audience; fixing his gaze with instant intentness on any section of the house from which there came so much as a whisper. The audience listened to me with rapt attention. At the end, with a pride in my rhetorical powers which proceeded from a misunderstanding of the situation, I remarked to the chairman: "I held that audience well; there wasn't an interruption." To which the chairman replied: "Interruption? Well, I guess not! Seth had sent round word that if any son of a gun peeped he'd kill him!"

There was one bit of frontier philosophy which I should like to see imitated in more advanced communities. Certain crimes of revolting baseness and cruelty were never forgiven. But in the case of ordinary offenses, the man who had served his term and who then tried to make good was given a fair chance; and of course this was equally true of the women. Every one who has studied the subject at all is only too well aware that the world offsets the readiness with which it condones a crime for which a man escapes punishment, by its unforgiving relentlessness to the often far less guilty man who *is* punished, and who therefore has made his atonement. On the frontier, if the man honestly tried to behave himself there was generally a disposition to give him fair play and a decent show. Several of the men I knew and whom I particularly liked came in this class. There was one such man in my regiment, a man who had served a term for robbery under arms, and who had atoned for it by many years of fine performance of duty. I put him in a high official position, and no man under me rendered better service to the State, nor was there any man whom, as soldier, as civil officer, as citizen, and as friend, I valued and respected—and now value and respect—more. Now I suppose some good people will gather from this that I favor men who commit crimes. I certainly do not favor them. I have not a particle of sympathy with the sentimentality—as I deem it, the mawkishness—which overflows with foolish pity for the criminal and cares not at all for the victim of the criminal. I am glad to see wrong-doers punished. The punishment is an absolute necessity from the standpoint of society; and I put the reformation of the criminal second to the welfare of society. But I do desire to see the man or woman who has paid the penalty and who wishes to reform given a helping hand—surely every one of us who knows his own heart must know that he too may stumble, and should be anxious to help his brother or sister who has stumbled. When the criminal has been punished, if he then shows a sincere desire to lead a decent and upright life, he should be given the chance, he should be helped and not hindered; and if he makes good, he should receive that respect from others which so often aids in creating self-respect—the most invaluable of all possessions.

O. Henry (1862–1910)

WILLIAM SYDNEY PORTER, better known as "O. Henry," is remembered as the father of the short story, but his connection with the cowboy story is less well known. O. Henry was the creator of the "Cisco Kid," a character nothing like the good-natured, Robin Hood-like personality portrayed on television in the early 1950s. O. Henry's Cisco Kid was a cold-hearted, cold-blooded killer.

Porter was born in Greensboro, North Carolina. His mother died when Porter was three so he was raised by his grandmother and aunt. He was an avid reader and good student but left school at fifteen to find a job. He trained to be a pharmacist but moved to a sheep farm in Texas in 1882 hoping to recover from ill health and persistent coughs. Much improved, he left the farm for city life in Austin two years later. He took a variety of jobs and began writing on the side. He married and began working as a bank teller, but lost his first banking job due to suspicion of embezzlement. He then worked full-time on a satirical weekly, which published some of Porter's own short stories and artwork. After that effort eventually failed, he moved his family to Houston in 1895, and began writing for *The Post*. His wife died of tuberculosis in 1897 and Porter was convicted of his earlier bank embezzlement a year later. He served five years for his bookkeeping inconsistencies. While in prison, he worked as a licensed pharmacist and continued to write, since he needed to make money for his daughter's support. He had fourteen stories published during his prison term. Once released from prison, he continued to write under the name "O. Henry." His short stories are widely read, and remain popular one hundred years later. Unfortunately, O. Henry's latter days were clouded by alcoholism, ill health, and continued financial problems.

"The Caballero's Way" is from the *Heart of the West* (1907) story collection.

The Caballero's Way

FROM *Heart of the West*, 1907

The Cisco Kid had killed six men in more or less fair scrimmages, had murdered twice as many (mostly Mexicans), and had winged a larger number whom he modestly forbore to count. Therefore a woman loved him.

The Kid was twenty-five, looked twenty; and a careful insurance company would have estimated the probable time of his demise at, say, twenty-six. His habitat was anywhere between the Frio and the Rio Grande. He killed for the love of it—because he was quick-tempered—to avoid arrest—for his own amusement—any reason that came to his mind would suffice. He had escaped capture because he could shoot five-sixths of a second sooner than any sheriff or ranger in the service, and because he rode a speckled roan horse that knew every cow-path in the mesquite and pear thickets from San Antonio to Matamoras.

Tonia Perez, the girl who loved the Cisco Kid, was half Carmen, half Madonna, and the rest—oh, yes, a woman who is half Carmen and half Madonna can always be something more—the rest, let us say, was humming-bird. She lived in a grass-roofed *jacal* near a little Mexican settlement at the Lone Wolf Crossing of the Frio. With her lived a father or grandfather, a lineal Aztec, somewhat less than a thousand years old, who herded a hundred goats and lived in a continuous drunken dream from drinking *mescal*. Back of the *jacal* a tremendous forest of bristling pear, twenty feet high at its worst, crowded almost to its door. It was along the bewildering maze of this spinous thicket that the speckled roan would bring the Kid to see his girl. And once, clinging like a lizard to the ridge-pole, high up under the peaked grass roof, he had heard Tonia, with her Madonna face and Carmen beauty and humming-bird soul, parley with the sheriff's posse, denying knowledge of her man in her soft *mélange* of Spanish and English.

One day the adjutant-general of the State, who is, *ex offico,* commander of the ranger forces, wrote some sarcastic lines to Captain Duval of Company X, stationed at Laredo, relative to the serene and undisturbed existence led by murderers and desperadoes in the said captain's territory.

The captain turned the colour of brick dust under his tan, and forwarded the letter, after adding a few comments, per ranger Private Bill Adamson, to ranger Lieutenant Sandridge, camped at a water hole on the Nueces with a squad of five men in preservation of law and order.

Lieutenant Sandridge turned a beautiful *couleur de rose* through his ordinary strawberry complexion, tucked the letter in his hip pocket, and chewed off the ends of his gamboge moustache.

The next morning he saddled his horse and rode alone to the Mexican settlement at the Lone Wolf Crossing of the Frio, twenty miles away.

Six feet two, blond as a Viking, quiet as a deacon, dangerous as a machine gun, Sandridge moved among the *jacales,* patiently seeking news of the Cisco Kid.

Far more than the law, the Mexicans dreaded the cold and certain vengeance of the lone rider that the ranger sought. It had been one of the Kid's pastimes to shoot Mexicans "to see them kick": if he demanded from them moribund Terpsichorean feats, simply that he might be entertained, what terrible and extreme penalties would be certain to follow should they anger him! One and all they lounged with upturned palms and shrugging shoulders, filling the air with "*quien sabes*" and denials of the Kid's acquaintance.

But there was a man named Fink who kept a store at the Crossing—a man of many nationalities, tongues, interests, and ways of thinking.

"No use to ask them Mexicans," he said to Sandridge. "They're afraid to tell. This *hombre* they call the Kid—Goodall is his name, ain't it?—he's been in my store once or twice. I have an idea you might run across him at—but I guess I don't keer to say, myself. I'm two seconds later in pulling a gun than I used to be, and the difference is worth thinking about. But this Kid's got a half-Mexican girl at the Crossing that he comes to see. She lives in that *jacal* a hundred yards down the arroyo at the edge of the pear. Maybe she—no, I don't suppose she would, but that *jacal* would be a good place to watch, anyway."

Sandridge rode down to the *jacal* of Perez. The sun was low, and the broad shade of the great pear thicket already covered the grass-thatched hut. The goats were enclosed for the night in a brush corral near by. A few kids walked the top of it, nibbling the chaparral leaves. The old Mexican lay upon a blanket on the grass, already in a stupor from his mescal, and dreaming, perhaps, of the nights when he and Pizarro touched glasses to their New World fortunes—so old his wrinkled face seemed to proclaim him to be. And in the door of the *jacal* stood Tonia. And Lieutenant Sandridge sat in his saddle staring at her like a gannet agape at a sailorman.

The Cisco Kid was a vain person, as all eminent and successful assassins are, and his bosom would have been ruffled had he known that at a simple exchange of glances two persons, in whose minds he had been looming large, suddenly abandoned (at least for the time) all thought of him.

Never before had Tonia seen such a man as this. He seemed to be made of sunshine and blood-red tissue and clear weather. He seemed to illuminate the shadow of the pear when he smiled, as though the sun were rising again. The men she had known had been small and dark. Even the Kid, in spite of his achievements, was a stripling no larger than herself, with black, straight hair and a cold, marble face that chilled the noonday.

As for Tonia, though she sends description to the poorhouse, let her make a millionaire of your fancy. Her blue-black hair, smoothly divided in the middle and bound close to her head, and her large eyes full of the Latin melancholy, gave her the Madonna touch. Her motions and air spoke of the concealed fire and the desire to charm that she had inherited from the *gitanas* of the Basque province. As for the humming-bird part of her, that dwelt in her heart; you could not perceive it unless her bright red skirt and dark blue blouse gave you a symbolic hint of the vagarious bird.

The newly lighted sun-god asked for a drink of water. Tonia brought it from the red jar hanging under the brush shelter. Sandridge considered it necessary to dismount so as to lessen the trouble of her ministrations.

I play no spy; nor do I assume to master the thoughts of any human heart; but I assert, by the chronicler's right, that before a quarter of an hour had sped, Sandridge was teaching her how to plait a six-strand rawhide stake-rope, and Tonia had explained to him that were it not for her little English book that the peripatetic *padre* had given her and the little crippled *chivo*, that she fed from a bottle, she would be very, very lonely indeed.

Which leads to a suspicion that the Kid's fences needed repairing, and that the adjutant-general's sarcasm had fallen upon unproductive soil.

In his camp by the water hole Lieutenant Sandridge announced and reiterated his intention of either causing the Cisco Kid to nibble the black loam of the Frio country prairies or of haling him before a judge and jury. That sounded business-like. Twice a week he rode over to the Lone Wolf Crossing of the Frio, and directed Tonia's slim, slightly lemon-tinted fingers among the intricacies of the slowly growing lariata. A six-strand plait is hard to learn and easy to teach.

The ranger knew that he might find the Kid there at any visit. He kept his armament ready, and had a frequent eye for the pear thicket at the rear of the *jacal*. Thus he might bring down the kite and the humming-bird with one stone.

While the sunny-haired ornithologist was pursuing his studies the Cisco Kid was also attending to his professional duties. He moodily shot up a saloon in a small cow village on Quintana Creek, killed the town marshal (plugging him neatly in the centre of his tin badge), and then rode away, morose and unsatisfied. No true artist is uplifted by shooting an aged man carrying an old-style .38 bulldog.

On his way the Kid suddenly experienced the yearning that all men feel when wrong-doing loses its keen edge of delight. He yearned for the woman he loved to reassure him that she was his in spite of it. He wanted her to call his bloodthirstiness bravery and his cruelty devotion. He wanted Tonia to bring him water from the red jar under the brush shelter, and tell him how the *chivo* was thriving on the bottle.

The Kid turned the speckled roan's head up the ten-mile pear flat that stretches along the Arroyo Hondo until it ends at the Lone Wolf Crossing of the Frio. The roan whickered; for he had a sense of locality and direction equal to that of a belt-line street-car horse; and he knew he would soon be nibbling the rich mesquite grass at the end of a forty-foot stake-rope while Ulysses rested his head in Circe's straw-roofed hut.

More weird and lonesome than the journey of an Amazonian explorer is the ride of one through a Texas pear flat. With dismal monotony and startling variety the uncanny and multiform shapes of the cacti lift their twisted trunks, and fat, bristly hands to encumber the way. The demon plant, appearing to live without soil or rain, seems to taunt the parched traveller with its lush grey greenness. It warps itself a thousand times about what look to be open and inviting paths, only to lure the rider into blind and impassable spine-defended "bottoms of the bag," leaving him to retreat, if he can, with the points of the compass whirling in his head.

To be lost in the pear is to die almost the death of the thief on the cross, pierced by nails and with grotesque shapes of all the fiends hovering about.

But it was not so with the Kid and his mount. Winding, twisting, circling, tracing the most fantastic and bewildering trail ever picked out, the good roan lessened the distance to the Lone Wolf Crossing with every coil and turn that he made.

While they fared the Kid sang. He knew but one tune and he sang it, as he knew but one code and lived it, and but one girl and loved her. He was a single-minded man of conventional ideas. He had a voice like a coyote with bronchitis, but whenever he chose to sing his song he sang it. It was a conventional song of the camps and trail, running at its beginning as near as may be to these words:

> Don't you monkey with my Lulu girl
> Or I'll tell you what I'll do—

and so on. The roan was inured to it, and did not mind.

But even the poorest singer will, after a certain time, gain his own consent to refrain from contributing to the world's noises. So the Kid, by the time he was within a mile or two of Tonia's *jacal,* had reluctantly allowed his song to die away—not because his vocal performance had become less charming to his own ears, but because his laryngeal muscles were aweary.

As though he were in a circus ring the speckled roan wheeled and danced through the labyrinth of pear until at length his rider knew by certain landmarks that the Lone Wolf Crossing was close at hand. Then, where the pear was thinner, he caught sight of the grass roof of the *jacal* and the hackberry tree on the edge of the arroyo. A few yards farther the Kid stopped the roan and gazed intently through the prickly openings. Then he dismounted, dropped the roan's reins, and proceeded on foot, stooping and silent, like an Indian. The roan, knowing his part, stood still, making no sound.

The Kid crept noiselessly to the very edge of the pear thicket and reconnoitered between the leaves of a clump of cactus.

Ten yards from his hiding-place, in the shade of the *jacal,* sat his Tonia calmly plaiting a rawhide lariat. So far she might surely escape condemnation; women have been known, from time to time, to engage in more mischievous occupations. But if all must be told, there is to be added that her head reposed against the broad and comfortable chest of a tall red-and-yellow man, and that his arm was about her, guiding her nimble small fingers that required so many lessons at the intricate six-strand plait.

Sandridge glanced quickly at the dark mass of pear when he heard a slight squeaking sound that was not altogether unfamiliar. A gun-scabbard will make that sound when one grasps the handle of a six-shooter suddenly. But the sound was not repeated; and Tonia's fingers needed close attention.

And then, in the shadow of death, they began to talk of their love; and in the still July afternoon every word they uttered reached the ears of the Kid.

"Remember, then," said Tonia, "you must not come again until I send for you. Soon he will be here. A *vaquero* at the *tienda* said to-day he saw him on the Guadalupe three days ago. When he is that near he always comes. If he comes and finds you here he will kill you. So, for my sake, you must come no more until I send you the word."

"All right," said the stranger. "And then what?"

"And then," said the girl, "you must bring your men here and kill him. If not, he will kill you."

"He ain't a man to surrender, that's sure," said Sandridge. "It's kill or be killed for the officer that goes up against Mr. Cisco Kid."

"He must die," said the girl. "Otherwise there will not be any peace in the world for thee and me. He has killed many. Let him so die. Bring your men, and give him no chance to escape."

"You used to think right much of him," said Sandridge.

Tonia dropped the lariat, twisted herself around, and curved a lemon-tinted arm over the ranger's shoulder.

"But then," she murmured in liquid Spanish, "I had not beheld thee, thou great, red mountain of a man! And thou art kind and good, as well as strong. Could one choose him, knowing thee? Let him die; for then I will not be filled with fear by day and night lest he hurt thee or me."

"How can I know when he comes?" asked Sandridge.

"When he comes," said Tonia, "he remains two days, sometimes three. Gregorio, the small son of old Luisa, the *lavendera,* has a swift pony. I will write a letter to thee and send it by him, saying how it will be best to come upon him. By Gregorio will the letter come. And bring many men with thee, and have much care, oh, dear red one, for the rattlesnake is not quicker to strike than is '*El Chivato,*' as they call him, to send a ball from his *pistola.*"

"The Kid's handy with his gun, sure enough," admitted Sandridge, "but when I come for him I shall come alone. I'll get him by myself or not at all. The Cap wrote one or two things to me that make me want to do the trick without any help. You let me know when Mr. Kid arrives, and I'll do the rest."

"I will send you the message by the boy Gregorio," said the girl. "I knew you were braver than that small slayer of men who never smiles. How could I ever have thought I cared for him?"

It was time for the ranger to ride back to his camp on the water hole. Before he mounted his horse he raised the slight form of Tonia with one arm high from the earth for a parting salute. The drowsy stillness of the torpid summer air still lay thick upon the dreaming afternoon. The smoke from the fire in the *jacal,* where the *frijoles* blubbered in the iron pot, rose straight as a plumb-line above the clay-daubed chimney. No sound or movement disturbed the serenity of the dense pear thicket ten yards away.

When the form of Sandridge had disappeared, loping his big dun down the steep banks of the Frio crossing, the Kid crept back to his own horse, mounted him, and rode back along the tortuous trail he had come.

But not far. He stopped and waited in the silent depths of the pear until half an hour had passed. And then Tonia heard the high, untrue notes of his un-musical singing coming nearer and nearer; and she ran to the edge of the pear to meet him.

The Kid seldom smiled; but he smiled and waved his hat when he saw her. He dismounted, and his girl sprang into his arms. The Kid looked at her fondly. His thick, black hair clung to his head like a wrinkled mat. The meeting brought a slight ripple of some undercurrent of feeling to his smooth, dark face that was usually as motionless as a clay mask.

"How's my girl?" he asked, holding her close.

"Sick of waiting so long for you, dear one," she answered. "My eyes are dim with always gazing into that devil's pincushion through which you come. And I can see into it such a little way, too. But you are here, beloved one, and I will not scold. *Qué mal muchacho!* not to come to see your *alma* more often. Go in and rest, and let me water your horse and stake him with the long rope. There is cool water in the jar for you."

The Kid kissed her affectionately.

"Not if the court knows itself do I let a lady stake my horse for me," said he. "But if you'll run in, *chica,* and throw a pot of coffee together while I attend to the *caballo,* I'll be a good deal obliged."

Besides his marksmanship the Kid had another attribute for which he admired himself greatly. He was *muy caballero,* as the Mexicans express it, where the ladies were concerned. For them he had always gentle words and consideration. He could not have spoken a harsh word to a woman. He might ruthlessly slay their husbands and brothers, but he could not have laid the weight of a finger in anger upon a woman. Wherefore many of that interesting division of humanity who had come under the spell of his politeness declared their disbelief in the stories circulated about Mr. Kid. One shouldn't believe everything one heard, they said. When confronted by their indignant men folk with proof of the *caballero's* deeds of infamy, they said maybe he had been driven to it, and that he knew how to treat a lady, anyhow.

Considering this extremely courteous idiosyncrasy of the Kid and the pride he took in it, one can perceive that the solution of the problem that was presented to him by what he saw and heard from his hiding-place in the pear that afternoon (at least as to one of the actors) must have been obscured by difficulties. And yet one could not think of the Kid overlooking little matters of that kind.

At the end of the short twilight they gathered around a supper of *frijoles,* goat steaks, canned peaches, and coffee, by the light of a lantern in the *jacal.* Afterward, the ancestor, his flock corralled, smoked a cigarette and became a mummy in a gray blanket. Tonia washed the few dishes while the Kid dried them with the flour-sacking towel. Her eyes shone; she chatted volubly of the inconsequent happenings of her small world since the Kid's last visit; it was as all his other home-comings had been.

Then outside Tonia swung in a grass hammock with her guitar and sang sad *canciones de amor.*

"Do you love me just the same, old girl?" asked the Kid, hunting for his cigarette papers.

"Always the same, little one," said Tonia, her dark eyes lingering upon him.

"I must go over to Fink's," said the Kid, rising, "for some tobacco. I thought I had another sack in my coat. I'll be back in a quarter of an hour."

"Hasten," said Tonia, "and tell me—how long shall I call you my own this time? Will you be gone again to-morrow, leaving me to grieve, or will you be longer with your Tonia?"

"Oh, I might stay two or three days this trip," said the Kid, yawning. "I've been on the dodge for a month, and I'd like to rest up."

He was gone half an hour for his tobacco. When he returned Tonia was still lying in the hammock.

"It's funny," said the Kid, "how I feel. I feel like there was somebody lying behind every bush and tree waiting to shoot me. I never had mullygrubs like them before. Maybe it's one of them presumptions. I've got half a notion to light out in the morning before day. The Guadalupe country is burning up about that old Dutchman I plugged down there."

"You are not afraid—no one could make my brave little one fear."

"Well, I haven't been usually regarded as a jack-rabbit when it comes to scrapping; but I don't want a posse smoking me out when I'm in your *jacal*. Somebody might get hurt that oughtn't to."

"Remain with your Tonia; no one will find you here."

The Kid looked keenly into the shadows up and down the arroyo and toward the dim lights of the Mexican village.

"I'll see how it looks later on," was his decision.

At midnight a horseman rode into the rangers' camp, blazing his way by noisy "halloes" to indicate a pacific mission. Sandridge and one or two others turned out to investigate the row. The rider announced himself to be Domingo Sales, from the Lone Wolf Crossing. He bore a letter for Señor Sandridge. Old Luisa, the *lavendera,* had persuaded him to bring it, he said, her son Gregorio being too ill of a fever to ride.

Sandridge lighted the camp lantern and read the letter. These were its words:

Dear One: He has come. Hardly had you ridden away when he came out of the pear. When he first talked he said he would stay three days or more. Then as it grew later he was like a wolf or a fox, and walked about without rest, looking and listening. Soon he said he must leave before daylight when it is dark and stillest. And then he seemed to suspect that I be not true to him. He looked at me so strange that I am frightened. I swear to him that I love him, his own Tonia. Last of all he said I must prove to him I am true. He thinks that even now men are waiting to kill him as he rides from my house. To escape he says he will dress in my clothes, my red skirt and the blue waist I wear and the brown mantilla over the head, and thus ride away. But before that he says that I must put on his clothes, his *pantalones* and *camisa* and hat, and ride away on his horse from the *jacal* as far as the big road beyond the crossing and back again. This before he goes, so he can tell if I am true and if men are hidden to shoot him. It is a terrible thing. An hour before daybreak this is to be. Come, my dear one, and kill this man and take me for your Tonia. Do not try to take hold of him alive, but kill him quickly. Knowing all, you should do that. You must come long before the time and hide yourself in the little shed near the *jacal* where the wagon and saddles are kept. It is dark in there. He will wear my red skirt and blue waist and brown mantilla. I send you a hundred kisses. Come surely and shoot quickly and straight.

THINE OWN TONIA.

Sandridge quickly explained to his men the official part of the missive. The rangers protested against his going alone.

"I'll get him easy enough," said the lieutenant. "The girl's got him trapped. And don't even think he'll get the drop on me."

Sandridge saddled his horse and rode to the Lone Wolf Crossing. He tied his big dun in a clump of brush on the arroyo, took his Winchester from its scabbard, and carefully approached the Perez *jacal*. There was only the half of a high moon drifted over by ragged, milk-white gulf clouds.

The wagon-shed was an excellent place for ambush; and the ranger got inside it safely. In the black shadow of the brush shelter in front of the *jacal* he could see a horse tied and hear him impatiently pawing the hard-trodden earth.

He waited almost an hour before two figures came out of the *jacal*. One, in man's clothes, quickly mounted the horse and galloped past the wagon-shed toward the crossing and village. And then the other figure, in skirt, waist, and mantilla over its head, stepped out into the faint moonlight, gazing after the rider. Sandridge thought he would take his chance then before Tonia rode back. He fancied she might not care to see it.

"Throw up your hands," he ordered loudly, stepping out of the wagon-shed with his Winchester at his shoulder.

There was a quick turn of the figure, but no movement to obey, so the ranger pumped in the bullets—one—two—three—and then twice more; for you never could be too sure of bringing down the Cisco Kid. There was no danger of missing at ten paces, even in that half moonlight. The old ancestor, asleep on his blanket, was awakened by the shots. Listening further, he heard a great cry from some man in mortal distress or anguish, and rose up grumbling at the disturbing ways of moderns.

The tall, red ghost of a man burst into the *jacal,* reaching one hand, shaking like a *tule* reed, for the lantern hanging on its nail. The other spread a letter on the table.

"Look at this letter, Perez," cried the man. "Who wrote it?"

"*Ah, Dios!* it is Señor Sandridge," mumbled the old man, approaching. "*Pues, señor,* that letter was written by '*El Chivato,*' as he is called—by the man of Tonia. They say he is a bad man; I do not know. While Tonia slept he wrote the letter and sent it by this old hand of mine to Domingo Sales to be brought to you. Is there anything wrong in the letter? I am very old; and I did not know. *Valgame Dios!* it is a very foolish world; and there is nothing in the house to drink—nothing to drink."

Just then all that Sandridge could think of to do was to go outside and throw himself face downward in the dust by the side of his humming-bird, of whom not a feather fluttered. He was not a *caballero* by instinct, and he could not understand the niceties of revenge.

A mile away the rider who had ridden past the wagon-shed struck up a harsh, untuneful song, the words of which began:

> Don't you monkey with my Lulu girl
> Or I'll tell you what I'll do—

Emerson Hough (1857–1923)

EMERSON HOUGH was born in Newton, Iowa, and graduated from the University of Iowa in 1880. He moved to White Oaks, New Mexico, where he practiced law and worked as a reporter for the local newspaper. He married in 1897 and made Chicago his home thereafter. Hough was hired by *Field and Stream* magazine in 1899 to manage their Chicago office. He also traveled widely and wrote the "Out of Doors" column for *The Saturday Evening Post* for many years. Hough was a conservationist, and was instrumental in getting a law passed to protect the buffalo in Yellowstone National Park. He served as a captain in the Army Intelligence Division during World War I.

Hough is best remembered for his Western stories and is considered one of the authors who helped to create and define the Western genre. Two of his novels, *The Covered Wagon* (1922) and *North of Thirty-Six* (1923), were turned into screenplays and became enormously popular silent films, making him one of the first Western authors to enter into the motion picture industry.

"The Cowboy" is chapter 4 from *The Passing of the Frontier, A Chronicle of the Old West* (1918).

The Cowboy

FROM *The Passing of the Frontier, A Chronicle of the Old West,* 1918

The Great West, vast and rude, brought forth men also vast and rude. We pass today over parts of that matchless region, and we see the red hills and ragged mountain-fronts cut and crushed into huge indefinite shapes, to which even a small imagination may give a human or more than human form. It would almost seem that the same great hand which chiseled out these monumental forms had also laid its fingers upon the people of this region and fashioned them rude and ironlike, in harmony with the stern faces set about them. Of all the babes of that primeval mother, the West, the cowboy was perhaps her dearest because he was her last. Some of her children lived for centuries; this one for not a triple decade before he began to be old. What was really the life of this child of the wild region of America, and what were the conditions of the experience that bore him, can never be fully known by those who have not seen the West with wide eyes—for the cowboy was simply a part of the West. He who does not understand the one can never understand the other.

If we care truly to see the cowboy as he was and seek to give our wish the dignity of a real purpose, we should study him in connection with his surroundings and in relation to his work. Then we shall see him not as a curiosity but as a product—not as an eccentric driver of horned cattle but as a man suited to his times.

Large tracts of that domain where once the cowboy reigned supreme have been turned into farms by the irrigator's ditch or by the dry-farmer's plan. The farmer in overalls is in many instances his own stockman today. On the ranges of Arizona, Wyoming, and Texas and parts of Nevada we may find the cowboy, it is true, even today: but he is no longer the Homeric figure that once dominated the plains. In what we say as to his trade, therefore, or his fashion in the practice of it, we speak in terms of thirty or forty years ago, when wire was unknown, when the round-up still was necessary, and the cowboy's life was indeed that of the open.

By the costume we may often know the man. The cowboy's costume was harmonious with its surroundings. It was planned upon lines of such stern utility as to leave no possible thing which we may call dispensable. The typical cowboy costume could hardly be said to contain a coat and waistcoat. The heavy woolen shirt, loose and open at the neck, was the common wear at all seasons of the year excepting winter, and one has often seen cowboys in the winter-time engaged in work about the yard or corral of the ranch wearing no other cover for the upper part of the body but one or more of these heavy shirts. If the cowboy wore a coat he would wear it open and loose as much as possible. If he wore a "vest" he would wear it slouchily, hanging open or partly unbuttoned most of the time. There was a reason for this slouchy habit. The cowboy would say that the vest closely buttoned about the body would cause perspiration, so that the wearer would quickly chill upon ceasing exercise. If the wind were blowing keenly when the cowboy dismounted to sit upon the ground for dinner, he would button up his waistcoat and be warm. If it were very cold he would button up his coat also.

The cowboy's boots were of fine leather and fitted tightly, with light narrow soles, extremely small and high heels. Surely a more irrational foot-covering never was invented; yet these tight, peaked cowboy boots had a great significance and may indeed be called the insignia of a calling. There was no prouder soul on earth than the cowboy. He was proud of being a horseman and had a contempt for all human beings who walked. On foot in his tight-toed boots he was lost; but he wished it to be understood that he never was on foot. If we rode beside him and watched his seat in the big cow saddle we found that his high and narrow heels prevented the slipping forward of the foot in the stirrup, into which he jammed his feet nearly full length. If there was a fall, the cowboy's foot never hung in the stir-rup. In the corral roping, afoot, his heels anchored him. So he found his little boots not so unserviceable and retained them as a matter of pride. Boots made for the cowboy trade sometimes had fancy tops of bright-colored leather. The Lone Star of Texas was not infrequent in their ornamentation.

The curious pride of the horseman extended also to his gloves. The cowboy was very careful in the selection of his gloves. They were made of the finest buckskin, which could not be injured by wetting. Generally they were tanned white and cut with a deep cuff or gauntlet from which hung a little fringe to flutter in the wind when he rode at full speed on horseback.

The cowboy's hat was one of the typical and striking features of his costumes. It was a heavy, wide, white felt hat with a heavy leather band buckled about it. There has been no other head covering devised so suitable as the Stetson for the uses of the Plains, although high and heavy black hats have in part supplanted it today among stockmen. The boardlike felt was practically indestructible. The brim flapped a little and, in time, was turned up and perhaps held fast to the crown by a thong. The wearer might sometimes stiffen the brim by passing a thong through a series of holes pierced through the outer edge. He could depend upon his hat in all weathers. In the rain it was an umbrella; in the sun a shield; in the winter he could tie it down about his ears with his handkerchief.

Loosely thrown about the cowboy's shirt collar was a silk kerchief. It was tied in a hard knot in front, and though it could scarcely be said to be devoted to the uses of a neck scarf, yet it was a great comfort to the back of the neck when one was riding in a hot wind. It was sure to be of some bright color, usually red. Modern would-be cowpunchers do not willingly let this old kerchief die, and right often they over-play it. For the cowboy of the "movies," however, let us register an unqualified contempt. The real range would never have been safe for him.

A peculiar and distinctive feature of the cowboy's costume was his "chaps" (chaparejos). The chaps were two very wide and full-length trouser-legs made of heavy calfskin and connected by a narrow belt or strap. They were cut away entirely at front and back so that they covered only the thigh and lower legs and did not heat the body as a complete leather garment would. They were intended solely as a protection against branches, thorns, briers, and the like, but they were prized in cold or wet weather. Sometimes there was seen, more often on the southern range, a cowboy wearing chaps made of skins tanned with the hair on; for the cowboy of the Southwest early learned that goatskin left with the hair on would turn the cactus thorns better than any other material. Later, the chaps became a sort of affectation on the part of new men on the range; but the old-time cowboy wore them for use, not as a uniform. In hot weather he laid them off.

In the times when some men needed guns and all men carried them, no pistol of less than 44-caliber was tolerated on the range, the solid framed 45-caliber being the one almost universally used. The barrel was eight inches long, and it shot a rifle cartridge of forty grains of powder and a blunt-ended bullet that made a terrible missile. This weapon depended from a belt worn loose resting upon the left hip and hanging low down on the right hip so that none of the weight came upon the abdomen. This was typical, for the cowboy was neither fancy gunman nor army officer. The latter carries the revolver on the left, the butt pointing forward.

An essential part of the cow-puncher's outfit was his "rope." This was carried in a close coil at the side of the saddle-horn, fastened by one of the many thongs scattered over the saddle. In the Spanish country it was called reata and even today is sometimes seen in the Southwest made of rawhide. In the South it was called a lariat. The modern rope is a well-made three-quarter-inch hemp rope about thirty feet in length, with a leather or rawhide eye. The cowboy's quirt was a short heavy whip, the stock being of wood or iron covered with braided leather and carrying a lash made of two or three heavy loose thongs. The spur in the old days had a very large rowel with blunt teeth an inch long. It was often ornamented with little bells or oblongs of metal, the tinkling of which appealed to the childlike nature of the Plains rider. Their use was to lock the rowel.

His bridle—for, since the cowboy and his mount are inseparable, we may as well speak of his horse's dress also—was noticeable for its tremendously heavy and cruel curbed bit, known as the "Spanish bit." But in the ordinary riding and even in the exciting work of the old round-up and in "cutting out," the cowboy used the bit very little, nor exerted any pressure on the reins. He laid the reins against the neck of the pony opposite to the direction in which he wished it to go, merely turning his hand in the direction and inclining his body in the same way. He rode with the pressure of the knee and the inclination of the body and the light side-shifting of both reins. The saddle was the most important part of the outfit. It was a curious thing, this saddle developed by the cattle trade, and the world has no other like it. Its great weight—from thirty to forty pounds—was readily excusable when one remembers that it was not only seat but workbench for the cowman. A light saddle would be torn to pieces at the first rush of a maddened steer, but the sturdy frame of a cow-saddle would throw the heaviest bull on the range. The high cantle would give a firmness to the cowboy's seat when he snubbed a steer with a sternness sufficient to send it rolling heels over head. The high pommel, or "horn," steel-forged and covered with cross braids of leather, served as anchor post for this same steer, a turn of the rope about it accomplishing that purpose at once. The saddle-tree forked low down over the pony's back so that the saddle sat firmly and could not readily be pulled off. The great broad cinches bound the saddle fast till horse and saddle were practically one fabric. The strong wooden house of the old heavy stirrup protected the foot from being crushed by the impact of the herd. The form of the cow-saddle has changed but little, although today one sees a shorter seat and smaller horn, a "swell front" or roll, and a stirrup of open "ox-bow" pattern.

The round-up was the harvest of the range. The time of the calf round-up was in the spring after the grass had become good and after the calves had grown large enough for the branding. The State Cattle Association divided the entire State range into a number of round-up districts. Under an elected round-up captain were all the bosses in charge of the different ranch outfits sent by men having cattle in the round-up. Let us briefly draw a picture of this scene as it was.

Each cowboy would have eight or ten horses for his own use, for he had now before him the hardest riding of the year. When the cow-puncher went into the herd to cut out calves he mounted a fresh horse, and every few hours he again changed horses, for there was no horse which could long endure the fatigue of the rapid and intense work of cutting. Before the rider stretched a sea of interwoven horns, waving and whirling as the densely packed ranks of cattle closed in or swayed apart. It was no prospect for a weakling, but into it went the cow-puncher on his determined little horse, heeding not the plunging, crushing, and thrusting of the excited cattle. Down under the bulks of the herd, half hid in the whirl of dust, he would spy a little curly calf running, dodging, and twisting, always at the heels of its mother; and he would dart in after, following the two through the thick of surging and plunging beasts. The sharp-eyed pony would see almost as soon as his rider which cow was wanted and he needed small guidance from that time on. He would follow hard at her heels, edging her constantly toward the flank of the herd, at times nipping her hide as a reminder of his own superiority. In spite of herself the cow would gradually turn out toward the edge, and at last would be swept clear of the crush, the calf following close behind her. There was a whirl of the rope and the calf was laid by the heels and dragged to the fire where the branding irons were heated and ready.

Meanwhile other cow-punchers are rushing calves to the brand-ing. The hubbub and turmoil increase. Taut ropes cross the ground in many directions. The cutting ponies pant and sweat, rear and plunge. The garb of the cowboy is now one of white alkali which hangs gray in his eyebrows and moustache. Steers bellow as they surge to and fro. Cows charge on their persecutors. Fleet yearlings break and run for the open, pursued by men who care not how or where they ride.

We have spoken in terms of the past. There is no calf round-up of the open range today. The last of the roundups was held in Routt County, Colorado, several years ago, so far as the writer knows, and it had only to do with shifting cattle from the summer to the winter range.

After the calf round-up came the beef round-up, the cowman's final harvest. This began in July or August. Only the mature or fatted animals were cut out from the herd. This "beef cut" was held apart and driven on ahead from place to place as the round-up progressed. It was then driven in by easy stages to the shipping point on the rail-road, whence the long trainloads of cattle went to the great mar-kets.

In the heyday of the cowboy it was natural that his chief amuse-ments should be those of the outdoor air and those more or less in line with his employment. He was accustomed to the sight of big game, and so had the edge of his appetite for its pursuit worn off. Yet he was a hunter, just as every Western man was a hunter in the times of the Western game. His weapons were the rifle, revolver, and rope; the latter two were always with him. With the rope at times he cap-tured the coyote, and under special conditions he has taken deer and even antelope in this way, though this was of course most unusual and only possible under chance conditions of ground and cover. Elk have been roped by cowboys many times, and it is known that even the mountain sheep has been so taken, almost incredible as that may seem. The young buffalo were easy prey for the cowboy and these he often roped and made captive. In fact the beginnings of all the herds of buffalo now in captivity in this country were the calves roped and secured by cowboys; and these few scattered individuals of a grand race of animals remain as melancholy reminders alike of a national shiftlessness and an individual skill and daring.

The grizzly was at times seen by the cowboys on the range, and if it chanced that several cowboys were together it was not unusual to give him chase. They did not always rope him, for it was rarely that the nature of the country made this possible. Sometimes they roped him and wished they could let him go, for a grizzly bear is uncommonly active and straightforward in his habits at close quarters. The extreme difficulty of such a combat, however, gave it its chief fascination for the cowboy. Of course, no one horse could hold the bear after it was roped, but, as one after another came up, the bear was caught by neck and foot and body, until at last he was tangled and tripped and hauled about till he was helpless, strangled, and nearly dead. It is said that cowboys have so brought into camp a grizzly bear, forcing him to half walk and half slide at the end of the ropes. No feat better than this could show the courage of the plainsman and of the horse which he so perfectly controlled.

Of such wild and dangerous exploits were the cowboy's amusements on the range. It may be imagined what were his amusements when he visited the "settlements." The cow-punchers, reared in the free life of the open air, under circumstances of the utmost freedom of individual action, perhaps came off the drive or round-up after weeks or months of unusual restraint or hardship, and felt that the time had arrived for them to "celebrate." Merely great rude children, as wild and untamed and untaught as the herds they led, they regarded their first look at the "settlements" of the railroads as a glimpse of a wider world. They pursued to the uttermost such avenues of new experience as lay before them, almost without exception avenues of vice. It is strange that the records of those days should be chosen by the public to be held as the measure of the American cowboy. Those days were brief, and they are long since gone. The American cowboy atoned for them by a quarter of a century of faithful labor.

The amusements of the cowboy were like the features of his daily surroundings and occupation—they were intense, large, Homeric. Yet, judged at his work, no higher type of employee ever existed, nor one more dependable. He was the soul of honor in all the ways of his calling. The very blue of the sky, bending evenly over all men alike, seemed to symbolize his instinct for justice. Faithfulness and manliness were his chief traits; his standard—to be a "square man."

Not all the open range will ever be farmed, but very much that was long thought to be irreclaimable has gone under irrigation or is being more or less successfully "dryfarmed." The man who brought water upon the arid lands of the West changed the entire complexion of a vast country and with it the industries of that country. Acres redeemed from the desert and added to the realm of the American farmer were taken from the realm of the American cowboy. The West has changed. The curtain has dropped between us and its wild and stirring scenes. The old days are gone. The house dog sits on the hill where yesterday the coyote sang. There are fenced fields and in them stand sleek round beasts, deep in crops such as their ancestors never saw. In a little town nearby is the hurry and bustle of modern life. This town is far out upon what was called the frontier, long after the frontier has really gone. Guarding its ghost here stood a little army post, once one of the pillars, now one of the monuments of the West.

Out from the tiny settlement in the dusk of evening, always facing toward where the sun is sinking, might be seen riding, not so long ago, a figure we should know. He would thread the little lane among the fences, following the guidance of hands other than his own, a thing he would once have scorned to do. He would ride as lightly and as easily as ever, sitting erect and jaunty in the saddle, his reins held high and loose in the hand whose fingers turn up gracefully, his whole body free yet firm in the saddle with the seat of the perfect horseman. At the boom of the cannon, when the flag dropped fluttering down to sleep, he would rise in his stirrups and wave his hat to the flag. Then, toward the edge, out into the evening, he would ride on. The dust of his riding would mingle with the dusk of night. We could not see which was the one or the other. We could only hear the hoofbeats passing, boldly and steadily still, but growing fainter, fainter, and more faint.

Zane Grey (1872–1939)

ZANE GREY was born in Zanesville, Ohio, a city founded by one of his maternal ancestors. He wrote his first story, "Jim of the Cave," when he was fifteen. Zane studied dentistry at the University of Pennsylvania on a baseball scholarship, all the while continuing to write. After graduation he played baseball in the minor leagues for several years, then established a dental practice in New York City. After his 1905 marriage to Lina (Dolly) Roth, Grey often spent months away from his wife, fishing, writing, and spending time with his many mistresses, while she remained at home and managed his career and their three children. Dolly edited his writing and had a keen business sense, handling all of Zane's contract negotiations with publishers, movie studios, and agents. His money was split evenly between them, her share covering all of the family expenses. The Greys moved to California in 1918.

From 1918 to 1932, Zane Grey was a regular contributor to *Outdoor Life* magazine. Although he initially had difficulty in getting published, Zane Grey went on to become one of the most prolific and popular Western writers of all time. His best-known book, *Riders of the Purple Sage,* was published in 1912.

"Cowboy Golf" and "A Gentleman of the Range" are from *The Light of Western Stars* (1914).

Cowboy Golf

FROM *The Light of Western Stars*, 1914

In the whirl of the succeeding days it was a mooted question whether Madeline's guests or her cowboys or herself got the keenest enjoyment out of the flying time. Considering the sameness of the cowboys' ordinary life, she was inclined to think they made the most of the present. Stillwell and Stewart, however, had found the situation trying. The work of the ranch had to go on, and some of it got sadly neglected. Stillwell could not resist the ladies any more than he could resist the fun in the extraordinary goings-on of the cowboys. Stewart alone kept the business of cattle-raising from a serious setback. Early and late he was in the saddle, driving the lazy Mexicans whom he had hired to relieve the cowboys.

One morning in June Madeline was sitting on the porch with her merry friends when Stillwell appeared on the corral path. He had not come to consult Madeline for several days—an omission so unusual as to be remarked.

"Here comes Bill—in trouble," laughed Florence.

Indeed, he bore some faint resemblance to a thundercloud as he approached the porch; but the greetings he got from Madeline's party, especially from Helen and Dorothy, chased away the blackness from his face and brought the wonderful wrinkling smile.

"Miss Majesty, sure I'm a sad demoralized old cattleman," he said, presently. "An' I'm in need of a heap of help."

"What's wrong now?" asked Madeline, with her encouraging smile.

"Wal, it's so amazin' strange what cowboys will do. I jest am about to give up. Why, you might say my cowboys were all on strike for vacations. What do you think of that? We've changed the shifts, shortened hours, let one an' another off duty, hired Greasers, an', in fact, done everythin' that could be thought of. But this vacation idee growed worse. When Stewart set his foot down, then the boys begin to get sick. Never in my born days as a cattleman have I heerd of so many diseases. An' you ought to see how lame an' crippled an' weak many of the boys have got all of a sudden. The idee of a cowboy comin' to me with a sore finger an' askin' to be let off for a day! There's Booly. Now I've knowed a hoss to fall all over him, an' onct he rolled down a cañon. Never bothered him at all. He's got a blister on his heel, a ridin' blister, an' he says it's goin' to blood-poisonin' if he doesn't rest. There's Jim Bell. He's developed what he says is spinal mengalootis, or some such like. There's Frankie Slade. He swore he had scarlet fever because his face burnt so red, I guess, an' when I hollered that scarlet fever was contagious an' he must be put away somewhere, he up an' says he guessed it wasn't that. But he was sure awful sick an' needed to loaf around an' be amused. Why, even Nels doesn't want to work these days. If it wasn't for Stewart, who's had Greasers with the cattle, I don't know what I'd do."

"Why all this sudden illness and idleness?" asked Madeline.

"Wal, you see, the truth is every blamed cowboy on the range except Stewart thinks it's his bounden duty to entertain the ladies."

"I think that is just fine!" exclaimed Dorothy Coombs; and she joined in the general laugh.

"Stewart, then, doesn't care to help entertain us?" inquired Helen, in curious interest.

"Wal, Miss Helen, Stewart is sure different from the other cowboys," replied Stillwell. "Yet he used to be like them. There never was a cowboy fuller of the devil than Gene. But he's changed. He's foreman here, an' that must be it. All the responsibility rests on him. He sure has no time for amusin' the ladies."

"I imagine that is our loss," said Edith Wayne, in her earnest way. "I admire him."

"Stillwell, you need not be so distressed with what is only gallantry in the boys, even if it does make a temporary confusion in the work," said Madeline.

"Miss Majesty, all I said is not the half, nor the quarter, nor nuthin' of what's troublin' me," answered he, sadly.

"Very well; unburden yourself."

"Wal, the cowboys, exceptin' Gene, have gone plumb batty, jest plain crazy over this heah game of gol-lof."

A merry peal of mirth greeted Stillwell's solemn assertion.

"Oh, Stillwell, you are in fun," replied Madeline.

"I hope to die if I'm not in daid earnest," declared the cattleman.

"It's an amazin' strange fact. Ask Flo. She'll tell you. She knows cowboys, an' how if they ever start on somethin' they ride it as they ride a hoss."

Florence being appealed to, and evidently feeling all eyes upon her, modestly replied that Stillwell had scarcely misstated the situation. "Cowboys play like they work or fight," she added. "They give their whole souls to it. They are great big simple boys."

"Indeed they are," said Madeline. "Oh, I'm glad if they like the game of golf. They have so little play."

"Wal, somethin's got to be did if we're to go on raisin' cattle at Her Majesty's Rancho," replied Stillwell. He appeared both deliberate and resigned.

Madeline remembered that despite Stillwell's simplicity he was as deep as any of his cowboys, and there was absolutely no gaging him where possibilities of fun were concerned. Madeline fancied that his exaggerated talk about the cowboys' sudden craze for golf was in line with certain other remarkable tales that had lately emanated from him. Some very strange things had occurred of late, and it was impossible to tell whether or not they were accidents, mere coincidence, or deep-laid, skillfully worked-out designs of the fun-loving cowboys. Certainly there had been great fun, and at the expense of her guests, particularly Castleton. So Madeline was at a loss to know what to think about Stillwell's latest elaboration. From mere force of habit she sympathized with him and found difficulty in doubting his apparent sincerity.

"To go back a ways," went on Stillwell, as Madeline looked up expectantly, "you recollect what pride the boys took in fixin' up that gol-lof course out on the mesa? Wal, they worked on that job, an' though I never seen any other course, I'll gamble yours can't be beat. The boys was sure curious about that game. You recollect also how they all wanted to see you an' your brother play, an' be caddies for you? Wal, whenever you'd quit they'd go to work tryin' to play the game. Monty Price, he was the leadin' spirit. Old as I am, Miss Majesty, an' used as I am to cowboy excentrikities, I nearly dropped daid when I heered that little hobble-footed, burned-up Montana cow-puncher say there wasn't any game too swell for him, an' gol-lof was just his speed. Serious as a preacher, mind you, he was. An' he was always practisin'. When Stewart gave him charge of the course an' the club-house an' all them funny sticks, why, Monty was tickled to death. You see, Monty is sensitive that he ain't much good any more for cowboy work. He was glad to have a job that he didn't feel he was hangin' to by kindness. Wal, he practised the game, an' he read the books in the club-house, an' he got the boys to doin' the same. That wasn't very hard, I reckon. They played early an' late an' in the moonlight. For a while Monty was coach, an' the boys stood it. But pretty soon Frankie Slade got puffed on his game, an' he had to have it out with Monty. Wal, Monty beat him bad. Then one after another the other boys tackled Monty. He beat them all. After that they split up an' begin to play matches, two on a side. For a spell this worked fine. But cowboys can't never be satisfied long onless they win all the time. Monty an' Link Stevens, both cripples, you might say, joined forces an' elected to beat all comers. Wal, they did, an' that's the trouble. Long an' patient the other cowboys tried to beat them two game legs, an' hevn't done it. Mebbe if Monty an' Link was perfectly sound in their legs like the other cowboys there wouldn't hev been such a holler. But no sound cowboys'll ever stand for a disgrace like that. Why, down at the bunks in the evenin's it's some mortifyin' the way Monty an' Link crow over the rest of the outfit. They've taken on superior airs. You couldn't reach up to Monty with a trimmed spruce pole. An' Link—wal, he's just amazin' scornful.

"'It's a swell game, ain't it?' says Link, powerful sarcastic. 'Wal, what's hurtin' you low-down common cowmen? You keep harpin' on Monty's game leg an' on my game leg. If we hed good legs we'd beat you all the wuss. It's brains that wins in gol-lof. Brains an' air-stoocratik blood, which of the same you fellers sure hev little.'

"An' then Monty he blows smoke powerful careless an' superior, an' he says:

"'Sure it's a swell game. You cow-headed gents think beef an' brawn ought to hev the call over skill an' gray matter. You'll all hev to back up an' get down. Go out an' learn the game. You don't know a baffy from a Chinee sandwich. All you can do is waggle with a club an' fozzle the ball.'

"Whenever Monty gets to usin' them queer names the boys go round kind of dotty. Monty an' Link hev got the books an' directions of the game, an' they won't let the other boys see them. They show the rules, but that's all. An', of course, every game ends in a row almost before it's started. The boys are all terrible in earnest about this gol-lof. An' I want to say, for the good of ranchin', not to mention a possible fight, that Monty an' Link hev got to be beat. There'll be no peace round this ranch till that's done."

Madeline's guests were much amused. As for herself, in spite of her scarcely considered doubt, Stillwell's tale of woe occasioned her anxiety. However, she could hardly control her mirth.

"What in the world can I do?"

"Wal, I reckon I couldn't say. I only come to you for advice. It seems that a queer kind of game has locoed my cowboys, an' for the time bein' ranchin' is at a standstill. Sounds ridiculous, I know, but cowboys are as strange as wild cattle. All I'm sure of is that the conceit has got to be taken out of Monty an' Link. Onct, just onct, will square it, an' then we can resoome our work."

"Stillwell, listen," said Madeline, brightly. "We'll arrange a match game, a foursome, between Monty and Link and your best picked team. Castleton, who is an expert golfer, will umpire. My sister, and friends, and I will take turns as caddies for your team. That will be fair, considering yours is the weaker. Caddies may coach, and perhaps expert advice is all that is necessary for your team to defeat Monty's."

"A grand idee," declared Stillwell, with instant decision. "When can we have this match game?"

"Why, to-day—this afternoon. We'll ride out to the links."

"Wal, I reckon I'll be some indebted to you, Miss Majesty, an' all your guests," replied Stillwell, warmly. He rose with sombrero in hand, and a twinkle in his eye that again prompted Madeline to wonder. "An' now I'll be goin' to fix up for the game of cowboy gol-lof. Adios."

The idea was as enthusiastically received by Madeline's guests as it had been by Stillwell. They were highly amused and speculative to the point of taking sides and making wagers on their choice. Moreover, this situation so frankly revealed by Stillwell had completed their deep mystification. They were now absolutely nonplussed by the singular character of American cowboys. Madeline was pleased to note how seriously they had taken the old cattleman's story. She had a little throb of wild expectancy that made her both fear and delight in the afternoon's prospect.

The June days had set in warm; in fact, hot during the noon hours; and this had inculcated in her insatiable visitors a tendency to profit by the experience of those used to the Southwest. They indulged in the restful siesta during the heated term of the day.

Madeline was awakened by Majesty's well-known whistle and pounding on the gravel. Then she heard the other horses. When she went out she found her party assembled in gala golf attire, and with spirits to match their costumes. Castleton, especially, appeared resplendent in a golf coat that beggared description. Madeline had faint misgivings when she reflected on what Monty and Nels and Nick might do under the influence of that blazing garment.

"Oh, Majesty," cried Helen, as Madeline went up to her horse, "don't make him kneel! Try that flying mount. We all want to see it. It's so stunning."

"But that way, too, I must have him kneel," said Madeline, "or I can't reach the stirrup. He's so tremendously high."

Madeline had to yield to the laughing insistence of her friends, and after all of them except Florence were up she made Majesty go down on one knee. Then she stood on his left side, facing back, and took a good firm grip on the bridle and pommel and his mane. After she had slipped the toe of her boot firmly into the stirrup she called to Majesty. He jumped and swung her up into the saddle.

"Now just to see how it ought to be done watch Florence," said Madeline.

The Western girl was at her best in riding-habit and with her horse. It was beautiful to see the ease and grace with which she accomplished the cowboys' flying mount. Then she led the party down the slope and across the flat to climb the mesa.

Madeline never saw a group of her cowboys without looking them over, almost unconsciously, for her foreman, Gene Stewart. This afternoon, as usual, he was not present. However, she now had a sense—of which she was wholly conscious—that she was both disappointed and irritated. He had really not been attentive to her guests, and he, of all her cowboys, was the only one of whom they wanted most to see something. Helen, particularly, had asked to have him attend the match. But Stewart was with the cattle. Madeline thought of his faithfulness, and was ashamed of her momentary lapse into that old imperious habit of desiring things irrespective of reason.

Stewart, however, immediately slipped out of her mind as she surveyed the group of cowboys on the links. By actual count there were sixteen, not including Stillwell. And the same number of splendid horses, all shiny and clean, grazed on the rim in the care of Mexican lads. The cowboys were on dress-parade, looking very different in Madeline's eyes, at least, from the way cowboys usually appeared. But they were real and natural to her guests; and they were so picturesque that they might have been stage cowboys instead of real ones. Sombreros with silver buckles and horsehair bands were in evidence; and bright silk scarves, embroidered vests, fringed and ornamented chaps, huge swinging guns, and clinking silver spurs lent a festive appearance.

Madeline and her party were at once eagerly surrounded by the cowboys, and she found it difficult to repress a smile. If these cowboys were still remarkable to her, what must they be to her guests?

"Wal, you-all raced over, I seen," said Stillwell, taking Madeline's bridle. "Get down—get down. We're sure amazin' glad an' proud. An', Miss Majesty, I'm offerin' to beg pawdin for the way the boys are packin' guns. Mebbe it ain't polite. But it's Stewart's orders."

"Stewart's orders!" echoed Madeline. Her friends were suddenly silent.

"I reckon he won't take no chances on the boys bein' surprised sudden by raiders. An' there's raiders operatin' in from the Guadalupes. That's all. Nothin' to worry over. I was just explainin'."

Madeline, with several of her party, expressed relief, but Helen showed excitement and then disappointment.

"Oh, I want something to happen!" she cried.

Sixteen pairs of keen cowboy eyes fastened intently upon her pretty, petulant face; and Madeline divined, if Helen did not, that the desired consummation was not far off.

"So do I," said Dot Coombs. "It would be perfectly lovely to have a real adventure."

The gaze of the sixteen cowboys shifted and sought the demure face of this other discontented girl. Madeline laughed, and Stillwell wore his strange, moving smile.

"Wal, I reckon you ladies sure won't have to go home unhappy," he said. "Why, as boss of this heah outfit I'd feel myself disgraced forever if you didn't have your wish. Just wait. An' now, ladies, the matter on hand may not be amusin' or excitin' to you; but to this heah cowboy outfit it's powerful important. An' all the help you can give us will sure be thankfully received. Take a look across the links. Do you-all see them two apologies for human bein's prancin' like a couple of hobbled broncs? Wal, you're gazin' at Monty Price an' Link Stevens, who have of a sudden got too swell to associate with their old bunkies. They're practisin' for the toornament. They don't want my boys to see how they handle them crooked clubs."

"Have you picked your team?" inquired Madeline.

Stillwell mopped his red face with an immense bandana, and showed something of confusion and perplexity.

"I've sixteen boys, an' they all want to play," he replied. "Pickin' the team ain't goin' to be an easy job. Mebbe it won't be healthy, either. There's Nels and Nick. They just stated cheerful-like that if they didn't play we won't have any game at all. Nick never tried before, an' Nels, all he wants is to get a crack at Monty with one of them crooked clubs."

"I suggest you let all your boys drive from the tee and choose the two who drive the farthest," said Madeline.

Stillwell's perplexed face lighted up.

"Wal, that's a plumb good idee. The boys 'll stand for that."

Wherewith he broke up the admiring circle of cowboys round the ladies.

"Grap a rope—I mean a club—all you cow-punchers, an' march over hyar an' take a swipe at this little white bean."

The cowboys obeyed with alacrity. There was considerable difficulty over the choice of clubs and who should try first. The latter question had to be adjusted by lot. However, after Frankie Slade made several ineffectual attempts to hit the ball from the teeing-ground, at last to send it only a few yards, the other players were not so eager to follow. Stillwell had to push Booly forward, and Booly executed a most miserable shot and retired to the laughing comments of his comrades. The efforts of several succeeding cowboys attested to the extreme difficulty of making a good drive.

"Wal, Nick, it's your turn," said Stillwell.

"Bill, I ain't so all-fired particular about playin'," replied Nick.

"Why? You was roarin' about it a little while ago. Afraid to show how bad you'll play?"

"Nope, jest plain consideration for my feller cow-punchers," answered Nick, with spirit. "I'm appreciatin' how bad they play, an' I'm not mean enough to show them up."

"Wal, you've got to show me," said Stillwell. "I know you never seen a gol-lof stick in your life. What's more, I'll bet you can't hit that little ball square—not in a dozen cracks at it."

"Bill, I'm also too much of a gent to take your money. But you know I'm from Missouri. Gimme a club."

Nick's angry confidence seemed to evaporate as one after another he took up and handled the clubs. It was plain that he had never before wielded one. But, also, it was plain that he was not the kind of man to give in. Finally he selected a driver, looked doubtfully at the small knob, and then stepped into position on the teeing-ground.

Nick Steele stood six feet four inches in height. He had the rider's wiry slenderness, yet he was broad of shoulder. His arms were long. Manifestly he was an exceedingly powerful man. He swung the driver aloft and whirled it down with a tremendous swing. Crack! The white ball disappeared, and from where it had been rose a tiny cloud of dust.

Madeline's quick sight caught the ball as it lined somewhat to the right. It was shooting low and level with the speed of a bullet. It went up and up in swift, beautiful flight, then lost its speed and began to sail, to curve, to drop; and it fell out of sight beyond the rim of the mesa. Madeline had never seen a drive that approached this one. It was magnificent, beyond belief except for actual evidence of her own eyes.

The yelling of the cowboys probably brought Nick Steele out of the astounding spell with which he beheld his shot. Then Nick, suddenly alive to the situation, recovered from his trance and, resting nonchalantly upon his club, he surveyed Stillwell and the boys. After their first surprised outburst they were dumb.

"You-all seen thet?" Nick grandly waved his hand. "Thought I was joshin', didn't you? Why, I used to go to St. Louis an' Kansas City to play this here game. There was some talk of the golf clubs takin' me down East to play the champions. But I never cared fer the game. Too easy fer me! Them fellers back in Missouri were a lot of cheap dubs, anyhow, always kickin' because whenever I hit a ball hard I *always lost it*. Why, I hed to hit sort of left-handed to let 'em stay in my class. Now you-all can go ahead an' play Monty an' Link. I could beat 'em both, playin' with one hand, if I wanted to. But I ain't interested. I jest hit thet ball off the mesa to show you. I sure wouldn't be seen playin' on your team."

With that Nick sauntered away toward the horses. Stillwell appeared crushed. And not a scornful word was hurled after Nick, which fact proved the nature of his victory. Then Nels strode into the limelight. As far as it was possible for this iron-faced cowboy to be so, he was bland and suave. He remarked to Stillwell and the other cowboys that sometimes it was painful for them to judge of the gifts of superior cowboys such as belonged to Nick and himself. He picked up the club Nick had used and called for a new ball. Stillwell carefully built up a little mound of sand and, placing the ball upon it, squared away to watch. He looked grim and expectant. Nels was not so large a man as Nick, and did not look so formidable as he waved his club at the gaping cowboys. Still he was lithe, tough, strong. Briskly, with a debonair manner, he stepped up and then delivered a mighty swing at the ball. He missed. The power and momentum of his swing flung him off his feet, and he actually turned upside down and spun round on his head. The cowboys howled. Stillwell's stentorian laugh rolled across the mesa. Madeline and her guests found it impossible to restrain their mirth. And when Nels got up he cast a reproachful glance at Madeline. His feelings were hurt.

His second attempt, not by any means so violent, resulted in as clean a miss as the first, and brought jeers from the cowboys. Nels's red face flamed redder. Angrily he swung again. The mound of sand spread over the teeing-ground and the exasperating little ball rolled a few inches. This time he had to build up the sand mound and replace the ball himself. Stillwell stood scornfully by, and the boys addressed remarks to Nels.

"Take off them blinders," said one.

"Nels, your eyes are shore bad," said another.

"You don't hit where you look."

"Nels, your left eye has sprung a limp."

"Why, you dog-goned old fule, you cain't hit thet bawl."

Nels essayed again, only to meet ignominious failure. Then carefully he gathered himself together, gaged distance, balanced the club, swung cautiously. And the head of the club made a beautiful curve round the ball.

"Shore it's jest thet crooked club," he declared.

He changed clubs and made another signal failure. Rage suddenly possessing him, he began to swing wildly. Always, it appeared, the illusive little ball was not where he aimed. Stillwell hunched his huge bulk, leaned hands on knees, and roared his riotous mirth. The cowboys leaped up and down in glee.

"You cain't hit thet bawl," sang out one of the noisiest.

A few more whirling, desperate lunges on the part of Nels, all as futile as if the ball had been thin air, finally brought to the dogged cowboy a realization that golf was beyond him.

Stillwell bawled: "Oh, haw, haw, haw! Nels, you're—too old— eyes no good!"

Nels slammed down the club, and when he straightened up with the red leaving his face, then the real pride and fire of the man showed. Deliberately he stepped off ten paces and turned toward the little mound upon which rested the ball. His arm shot down, elbow crooked, hand like a claw.

"Aw, Nels, this is fun!" yelled Stillwell.

But swift as a gleam of light Nels flashed his gun, and the report came with the action. Chips flew from the golf-ball as it tumbled from the mound. Nels had hit it without raising the dust. Then he dropped the gun back in its sheath and faced the cowboys.

"Mebbe my eyes ain't so orful bad," he said, coolly, and started to walk off.

"But look ah-heah, Nels," yelled Stillwell, "we come out to play gol-lof! We can't let you knock the ball around with your gun. What'd you want to get mad for? It's only fun. Now you an' Nick hang round heah an' be sociable. We ain't depreciatin' your company none, nor your usefulness on occasions. An' if you just hain't got inborn politeness sufficient to do the gallant before the ladies, why, remember Stewart's orders."

"Stewart's orders?" queried Nels, coming to a sudden halt.

"That's what I said," replied Stillwell, with asperity. "His orders. Are you forgettin' orders? Wal, you're a fine cowboy. You an' Nick an' Monty, 'specially, are to obey orders."

Nels took off his sombrero and scratched his head. "Bill, I reckon I'm some forgetful. But I was mad. I'd 'a' remembered pretty soon, an' mebbe my manners."

"Sure you would," replied Stillwell. "Wal, now, we don't seem to be proceedin' much with my gol-lof team. Next ambitious player step up."

In Ambrose, who showed some skill in driving, Stillwell found one of his team. The succeeding players, however, were so poor and so evenly matched that the earnest Stillwell was in despair. He lost his temper just as speedily as Nels had. Finally Ed Linton's wife appeared riding up with Ambrose's wife, and perhaps this helped, for Ed suddenly disclosed ability that made Stillwell single him out.

"Let me coach you a little," said Bill.

"Sure, if you like," replied Ed. "But I know more about this game than you do."

"Wal, then, let's see you hit a ball straight. Seems to me you got good all-fired quick. It's amazin' strange." Here Bill looked around to discover the two young wives modestly casting eyes of admiration upon their husbands. "Haw, haw! It ain't so darned strange. Mebbe that'll help some. Now, Ed, stand up and don't sling your club as if you was ropin' a steer. Come round easy-like an' hit straight."

Ed made several attempts which, although better than those of his predecessors, were rather discouraging to the exacting coach. Presently, after a particularly atrocious shot, Stillwell strode in distress here and there, and finally stopped a dozen paces or more in front of the teeing-ground. Ed, who for a cowboy was somewhat phlegmatic, calmly made ready for another attempt.

"Fore!" he called.

Stillwell stared.

"*Fore!*" yelled Ed.

"Why're you hollerin' that way at me?" demanded Bill.

"I mean for you to lope off the horizon. Get back from in front."

"Oh, that was one of them durned crazy words Monty is always hollerin'. Wal, I reckon I'm safe enough hyar. You couldn't hit me in a million years."

"Bill, ooze away," urged Ed.

"Didn't I say you couldn't hit me? What am I coachin' you for? It's because you hit crooked, ain't it? Wal, go ahaid an' break your back."

Ed Linton was a short, heavy man, and his stocky build gave evidence of considerable strength. His former strokes had not been made at the expense of exertion, but now he got ready for a supreme effort. A sudden silence clamped down upon the exuberant cowboys. It was one of those fateful moments when the air was charged with disaster. As Ed swung the club it fairly whistled.

Crack! Instantly came a thump. But no one saw the ball until it dropped from Stillwell's shrinking body. His big hands went spasmodically to the place that hurt, and a terrible groan rumbled from him.

Then the cowboys broke into a frenzy of mirth that seemed to find adequate expression only in dancing and rolling accompaniment to their howls. Stillwell recovered his dignity as soon as he caught his breath, and he advanced with a rueful face.

"Wal, boys, it's on Bill," he said. "I'm a livin' proof of the pigheadedness of mankind. You're captain of the team. You hit straight, an' if I hadn't been obstructin' the general atmosphere that ball would sure have gone clear to the Chiricahuas."

Then making a megaphone of his huge hands, he yelled a loud blast of defiance at Monty and Link.

"Hey, you swell gol-lofers! We're waitin'. Come on if you ain't scared."

Instantly Monty and Link quit practicing, and like two emperors came stalking across the links.

"Guess my bluff didn't work much," said Stillwell. Then he turned to Madeline and her friends. "Sure I hope, Miss Majesty, that you-all won't weaken an' go over to the enemy. Monty is some eloquent, an', besides, he has a way of gettin' people to agree with him. He'll be plumb wild when he heahs what he an' Link are up against. But it's a square deal, because he wouldn't help us or lend the book that shows how to play. An', besides, it's policy for us to beat him. Now, if you'll elect who's to be caddies an' umpire I'll be powerful obliged."

Madeline's friends were hugely amused over the prospective match; but, except for Dorothy and Castleton, they disclaimed any ambition for active participation. Accordingly, Madeline appointed Castleton to judge the play, Dorothy to act as caddie for Ed Linton, and she herself to be caddie for Ambrose. While Stillwell beamingly announced this momentous news to his team and supporters Monty and Link were striding up.

Both were diminutive in size, bow-legged, lame in one foot, and altogether unprepossessing. Link was young, and Monty's years, more than twice Link's, had left their mark. But it would have been impossible to tell Monty's age. As Stillwell said, Monty was burned to the color and hardness of a cinder. He never minded the heat, and always wore heavy sheepskin chaps with the wool outside. This made him look broader than he was long. Link, partial to leather, had, since he became Madeline's chauffeur, taken to leather altogether. He carried no weapon, but Monty wore a huge gun-sheath and gun. Link smoked a cigarette and looked coolly impudent. Monty was dark-faced, swaggering, for all the world like a barbarian chief.

"That Monty makes my flesh creep," said Helen, low-voiced. "Really, Mr. Stillwell, is he so bad—desperate—as I've heard? Did he ever kill anybody?"

"Sure. 'Most as many as Nels," replied Stillwell, cheerfully.

"Oh! And is that nice Mr. Nels a desperado, too? I wouldn't have thought so. He's so kind and old-fashioned and soft-voiced."

"Nels is sure an example of the dooplicity of men, Miss Helen.

Don't you listen to his soft voice. He's really as bad as a side-winder rattlesnake."

At this juncture Monty and Link reached the teeing-ground, and Stillwell went out to meet them. The other cowboys pressed forward to surround the trio. Madeline heard Stillwell's voice, and evidently he was explaining that his team was to have skilled advice during the play. Suddenly there came from the center of the group a loud, angry roar that broke off as suddenly. Then followed excited voices all mingled together. Presently Monty appeared, breaking away from restraining hands, and he strode toward Madeline.

Monty Price was a type of cowboy who had never been known to speak to a woman unless he was first addressed, and then he answered in blunt, awkward shyness. Upon this great occasion, however, it appeared that he meant to protest or plead with Madeline, for he showed stress of emotion. Madeline had never gotten acquainted with Monty. She was a little in awe, if not in fear, of him, and now she found it imperative for her to keep in mind that more than any other of the wild fellows on her ranch this one should be dealt with as if he were a big boy.

Monty removed his sombrero—something he had never done before—and the single instant when it was off was long enough to show his head entirely bald. This was one of the hall-marks of that terrible Montana prairie fire through which he had fought to save the life of a child. Madeline did not forget it, and all at once she wanted to take Monty's side. Remembering Stillwell's wisdom, however, she forebore yielding to sentiment, and called upon her wits.

"Miss—Miss Hammond," began Monty, stammering, "I'm extendin' admirin' greetin's to you an' your friends. Link an' me are right down proud to play the match game with you watchin'. But Bill says you're goin' to caddie for his team an' coach 'em on the fine points. An' I want to ask, all respectful, if thet's fair an' square?"

"Monty, that is for you to say," replied Madeline. "It was my suggestion. But if you object in the least, of course we shall withdraw. It seems fair to me, because you have learned the game; you are expert, and I understand the other boys have no chance with you. Then you have coached Link. I think it would be sportsmanlike of you to accept the handicap."

"Aw, a handicap! Thet was what Bill was drivin' at. Why didn't he say so? Every time Bill comes to a word thet's pie to us old golfers he jest stumbles. Miss Majesty, you've made it all clear as print. An'

I may say with becomin' modesty thet you wasn't mistaken none about me bein' sportsmanlike. Me an' Link was born thet way. An' we accept the handicap. Lackin' thet handicap, I reckon Link an' me would have no ambish to play our most be-ootiful game. An' thankin' you, Miss Majesty, an' all your friends, I want to add thet if Bill's outfit couldn't beat us before, they've got a swell chanct now, with you ladies a-watchin' me an' Link."

Monty had seemed to expand with pride as he delivered this speech, and at the end he bowed low and turned away. He joined the group round Stillwell. Once more there was animated discussion and argument and expostulation. One of the cowboys came for Castleton and led him away to exploit upon ground rules.

It seemed to Madeline that the game never would begin. She strolled on the rim of the mesa, arm in arm with Edith Wayne, and while Edith talked she looked out over the gray valley leading to the rugged black mountains and the vast red wastes. In the foreground on the gray slope she saw cattle in movement and cowboys riding to and fro. She thought of Stewart. Then Boyd Harvey came for them, saying all details had been arranged. Stillwell met them half-way, and this cool, dry, old cattleman, whose face and manner scarcely changed at the announcement of a cattle-raid, now showed extreme agitation.

"Wal, Miss Majesty, we've gone an' made a foozle right at the start," he said, dejectedly.

"A foozle? But the game has not yet begun," replied Madeline.

"A bad start, I mean. It's amazin' bad, an' we're licked already."

"What in the world is wrong?"

She wanted to laugh, but Stillwell's distress restrained her.

"Wal, it's this way. That darn Monty is as cute an' slick as a fox. After he got done declaimin' about the handicap he an' Link was so happy to take, he got Castleton over hyar an' drove us all dotty with his crazy gol-lof names. Then he borrowed Castleton's gol-lof coat. I reckon borrowed is some kind word. He just about took that blazin' coat off the Englishman. Though I ain't sayin' but that Castleton was agreeable when he tumbled to Monty's meanin'. Which was nothin' more 'n to break Ambrose's heart. That coat dazzles Ambrose. You know how vain Ambrose is. Why, he'd die to get to wear that Englishman's gol-lof coat. An' Monty forestalled him. It's plumb pitiful to see the look in Ambrose's eyes. He won't be able to play much. Then what do you think? Monty fixed Ed Linton, all right. Usually Ed is easy-goin' an' cool. But now he's on

the rampage. Wal, mebbe it's news to you to learn that Ed's wife is
powerful, turrible jealous of him. Ed was somethin' of a devil with
the wimmen. Monty goes over an' tells Beulah—that's Ed's wife—
that Ed is goin' to have for caddie the lovely Miss Dorothy with the
goo-goo eyes. I reckon this was some disrespectful, but with all doo
respect to Miss Dorothy she has got a pair of unbridled eyes. Mebbe
it's just natural for her to look at a feller like that. Oh, it's all right;
I'm not sayin' any-thin'! I know it's all proper an' regular for girls
back East to use their eyes. But out hyar it's bound to result disas-
trous. All the boys talk about among themselves is Miss Dot's eyes,
an' all they brag about is which feller is the luckiest. Anyway, sure
Ed's wife knows it. An' Monty up an' told her that it was fine for her
to come out an' see how swell Ed was prancin' round under the light
of Miss Dot's brown eyes. Beulah calls over Ed, figgertively speakin',
ropes him for a minnit. Ed comes back huggin' a grouch as big as a
hill. Oh, it was funny! He was goin' to punch Monty's haid off. An'
Monty stands there an' laughs. Says Monty, sarcastic as alkali water:
'Ed, we-all knowed you was a heap married man, but you're some
locoed to give yourself away.' That settled Ed. He's some touchy
about the way Beulah henpecks him. He lost his spirit. An' now he
couldn't play marbles, let alone gol-lof. Nope, Monty was too smart.
An' I reckon he was right about brains bein' what wins."

The game began. At first Madeline and Dorothy essayed to direct
the endeavors of their respective players. But all they said and did
only made their team play the worse. At the third hole they were far
behind and hopelessly bewildered. What with Monty's borrowed
coat, with its dazzling effect upon Ambrose, and Link's oft-repeated
allusion to Ed's matrimonial state, and Stillwell's vociferated disgust,
and the clamoring good intention and pursuit of the cowboy supporters, and the embarrassing presence of the ladies, Ambrose and Ed
wore through all manner of strange play until it became ridiculous.

"Hey, Link," came Monty's voice booming over the links, "our
esteemed rivals are playin' shinny."

Madeline and Dorothy gave up, presently, when the game became
a rout, and they sat down with their followers to watch the fun.
Whether by hook or crook, Ed and Ambrose forged ahead to come
close upon Monty and Link. Castleton disappeared in a mass of ges-
ticulating, shouting cowboys. When that compact mass disintegrated
Castleton came forth rather hurriedly, it appeared, to stalk back
toward his hostess and friends.

"Look!" exclaimed Helen, in delight. "Castleton is actually excited. Whatever did they do to him? Oh, this is immense!" Castleton was excited, indeed, and also somewhat disheveled. "By Jove! that was a rum go," he said, as he came up. "Never saw such blooming golf! I resigned my office as umpire."

Only upon considerable pressure did he reveal the reason. "It was like this, don't you know. They were all together over there, watching each other. Monty Price's ball dropped into a hazard, and he moved it to improve the lie. By Jove! They've all been doing that. But over there the game was waxing hot. Stillwell and his cowboys saw Monty move the ball, and there was a row. They appealed to me. I corrected the play, showed the rules. Monty agreed he was in the wrong. However, when it came to moving his ball back to its former lie in the hazard there was more blooming trouble. Monty placed the ball to suit him, and then he transfixed me with an evil eye.

"'Dook,' he said. I wish the bloody cowboy would not call me that. 'Dook, mebbe this game ain't as important as international politics or some other things relatin', but there's some health an' peace dependin' on it. Savvy? For some space our opponents have been dead to honor an' sportsmanlike conduct. I calculate the game depends on my next drive. I'm placin' my ball as near to where it was as human eyesight could. You seen where it was same as I seen it. You're the umpire, an', Dook, I take you as a honorable man. Moreover, never in my born days has my word been doubted without sorrow. So I'm askin' you, wasn't my ball layin' just about here?'

"The bloody little desperado smiled cheerfully, and he dropped his right hand down to the butt of his gun. By Jove, he did! Then I had to tell a blooming lie!"

Castleton even caught the tone of Monty's voice, but it was plain that he had not the least conception that Monty had been fooling. Madeline and her friends divined it, however; and, there being no need of reserve, they let loose the fountains of mirth.

A Gentleman of the Range

FROM *The Light of Western Stars*, 1914

When Madeline Hammond stepped from the train at El Cajon, New Mexico, it was nearly midnight, and her first impression was of a huge dark space of cool, windy emptiness, strange and silent, stretching away under great blinking white stars.

"Miss, there's no one to meet you," said the conductor, rather anxiously.

"I wired my brother," she replied. "The train being so late—perhaps he grew tired of waiting. He will be here presently. But, if he should not come—surely I can find a hotel?"

"There's lodgings to be had. Get the station agent to show you. If you'll excuse me—this is no place for a lady like you to be alone at night. It's a rough little town—mostly Mexicans, miners, cowboys. And they carouse a lot. Besides, the revolution across the border has stirred up some excitement along the line. Miss, I guess it's safe enough, if you—"

"Thank you. I am not in the least afraid."

As the train started to glide away Miss Hammond walked toward the dimly lighted station. As she was about to enter she encountered a Mexican with sombrero hiding his features and a blanket mantling his shoulders.

"Is there any one here to meet Miss Hammond?" she asked.

"*No sabe*, Señora," he replied from under the muffling blanket, and he shuffled away into the shadow.

She entered the empty waiting-room. An oil-lamp gave out a thick yellow light. The ticket window was open, and through it she saw there was neither agent nor operator in the little compartment. A telegraph instrument clicked faintly.

Madeline Hammond stood tapping a shapely foot on the floor, and with some amusement contrasted her reception in El Cajon with what it was when she left a train at the Grand Central. The only time she could remember ever having been alone like this was once when she had missed her maid and her train at a place outside of Versailles—an adventure that had been a novel and delightful break in the prescribed routine of her much-chaperoned life. She crossed the waiting-room to a window and, holding aside her veil, looked out. At first she could descry only a few dim lights, and these blurred in her sight. As her eyes grew accustomed to the darkness she saw a superbly built horse standing near the window. Beyond was a bare square. Or, if it was a street, it was the widest one Madeline had ever seen. The dim lights shone from low, flat buildings. She made out the dark shapes of many horses, all standing motionless with drooping heads. Through a hole in the window-glass came a cool breeze, and on it breathed a sound that struck coarsely upon her ear—a discordant mingling of laughter and shout, and the tramp of boots to the hard music of a phonograph.

"Western revelry," mused Miss Hammond, as she left the window. "Now, what to do? I'll wait here. Perhaps the station agent will return soon, or Alfred will come for me."

As she sat down to wait she reviewed the causes which accounted for the remarkable situation in which she found herself. That Madeline Hammond should be alone, at a late hour, in a dingy little Western railroad station, was indeed extraordinary.

The close of her debutante year had been marred by the only unhappy experience of her life—the disgrace of her brother and his leaving home. She dated the beginning of a certain thoughtful habit of mind from that time, and a dissatisfaction with the brilliant life society offered her. The change had been so gradual that it was permanent before she realized it. For a while an active outdoor life— golf, tennis, yachting—kept this realization from becoming morbid introspection. There came a time when even these lost charm for her, and then she believed she was indeed ill in mind. Travel did not help her.

There had been months of unrest, of curiously painful wonderment that her position, her wealth, her popularity no longer sufficed. She believed she had lived through the dreams and fancies of a girl to become a woman of the world. And she had gone on as before, a part of the glittering show, but no longer blind to the truth—that there was nothing in her luxurious life to make it significant.

Sometimes from the depths of her there flashed up at odd moments intimations of a future revolt. She remembered one evening at the opera when the curtain had risen upon a particularly well-done piece of stage scenery—a broad space of deep desolateness, reaching away under an infinitude of night sky, illumined by stars. The suggestion it brought of vast wastes of lonely, rugged earth, of a great, blue-arched vault of starry sky, pervaded her soul with a strange, sweet peace.

When the scene was changed she lost this vague new sense of peace, and she turned away from the stage in irritation. She looked at the long, curved tier of glittering boxes that represented her world. It was a distinguished and splendid world—the wealth, fashion, culture, beauty, and blood of a nation. She, Madeline Hammond, was a part of it. She smiled, she listened, she talked to the men who from time to time strolled into the Hammond box, and she felt that there was not a moment when she was natural, true to herself. She wondered why these people could not somehow, some way be different; but she could not tell what she wanted them to be. If they had been different they would not have fitted the place; indeed, they would not have been there at all. Yet she thought wistfully that they lacked something for her.

And suddenly realizing she would marry one of these men if she did not revolt, she had been assailed by a great weariness, an icy-sickening sense that life had palled upon her. She was tired of fashionable society. She was tired of polished, imperturbable men who sought only to please her. She was tired of being fêted, admired, loved, followed, and importuned; tired of people; tired of houses, noise, ostentation, luxury. She was so tired of herself!

In the lonely distances and the passionless stars of boldly painted stage scenery she had caught a glimpse of something that stirred her soul. The feeling did not last. She could not call it back. She imagined that the very boldness of the scene had appealed to her; she divined that the man who painted it had found inspiration, joy, strength, serenity in rugged nature. And at last she knew what she needed—to be alone, to brood for long hours, to gaze out on lonely, silent, darkening stretches, to watch the stars, to face her soul, to find her real self.

Then it was she had first thought of visiting the brother who had gone West to cast his fortune with the cattlemen. As it happened, she had friends who were on the eve of starting for California, and she made a quick decision to travel with them. When she calmly announced her intention of going out West her mother had exclaimed in consternation; and her father, surprised into pathetic memory of the black sheep of the family, had stared at her with glistening eyes. "Why, Madeline! You want to see that wild boy!" Then he had reverted to the anger he still felt for his wayward son, and he had forbidden Madeline to go. Her mother forgot her haughty poise and dignity. Madeline, however, had exhibited a will she had never before been known to possess. She stood her ground even to reminding them that she was twenty-four and her own mistress. In the end she had prevailed, and that without betraying the real state of her mind.

Her decision to visit her brother had been too hurriedly made and acted upon for her to write him about it, and so she had telegraphed him from New York, and also, a day later, from Chicago, where her traveling friends had been delayed by illness. Nothing could have turned her back then. Madeline had planned to arrive in El Cajon on October 3d, her brother's birthday, and she had succeeded, though her arrival occurred at the twenty-fourth hour. Her train had been several hours late. Whether or not the message had reached Alfred's hands she had no means of telling, and the thing which concerned her now was the fact that she had arrived and he was not there to meet her.

It did not take long for thought of the past to give way wholly to the reality of the present.

"I hope nothing has happened to Alfred," she said to herself. "He was well, doing splendidly, the last time he wrote. To be sure, that was a good while ago; but, then, he never wrote often. He's all right. Pretty soon he'll come, and how glad I'll be! I wonder if he has changed."

As Madeline sat waiting in the yellow gloom she heard the faint, intermittent click of the telegraph instrument, the low hum of wires, the occasional stamp of an iron-shod hoof, and a distant vacant laugh rising above the sounds of the dance. These commonplace things were new to her. She became conscious of a slight quickening of her pulse. Madeline had only a limited knowledge of the West. Like all of her class, she had traveled Europe and had neglected America. A few letters from her brother had confused her already vague ideas of plains and mountains, as well as of cowboys and cattle. She had been astounded at the interminable distance she had traveled, and if there had been anything attractive to look at in all that journey she had passed it in the night. And here she sat in a dingy little station, with telegraph wires moaning a lonely song in the wind. A faint sound like the rattling of thin chains diverted Madeline's attention. At first she imagined it was made by the telegraph wires. Then she heard a step. The door swung wide; a tall man entered, and with him came the clinking rattle. She realized then that the sound came from his spurs. The man was a cowboy, and his entrance recalled vividly to her that of Dustin Farnum in the first act of "The Virginian."

"Will you please direct me to a hotel?" asked Madeline, rising.

The cowboy removed his sombrero, and the sweep he made with it and the accompanying bow, despite their exaggeration, had a kind of rude grace. He took two long strides toward her.

"Lady, are you married?"

In the past Miss Hammond's sense of humor had often helped her to overlook critical exactions natural to her breeding. She kept silence, and she imagined it was just as well that her veil hid her face at the moment. She had been prepared to find cowboys rather striking, and she had been warned not to laugh at them.

This gentleman of the range deliberately reached down and took up her left hand. Before she recovered from her start of amaze he had stripped off her glove.

"Fine spark, but no wedding ring," he drawled. "Lady, I'm glad to see you're not married."

He released her hand and returned the glove.

"You see, the only ho-tel in this here town is against boarding married women."

"Indeed?" said Madeline, trying to adjust her wits to the situation.

"It sure is," he went on. "Bad business for ho-tels to have married women. Keeps the boys away. You see, this isn't Reno."

Then he laughed rather boyishly, and from that, and the way he slouched on his sombrero, Madeline realized he was half drunk. As she instinctively recoiled she not only gave him a keener glance, but stepped into a position where a better light shone on his face. It was like red bronze, bold, raw, sharp. He laughed again, as if good-naturedly amused with himself, and the laugh scarcely changed the hard set of his features. Like that of all women whose beauty and charm had brought them much before the world, Miss Hammond's intuition had been developed until she had a delicate and exquisitely sensitive perception of the nature of men and of her effect upon them. This crude cowboy, under the influence of drink, had affronted her; nevertheless, whatever was in his mind, he meant no insult. "I shall be greatly obliged if you will show me to the hotel," she said.

"Lady, you wait here," he replied, slowly, as if his thought did not come swiftly. "I'll go fetch the porter."

She thanked him, and as he went out, closing the door, she sat down in considerable relief. It occurred to her that she should have mentioned her brother's name. Then she fell to wondering what living with such uncouth cowboys had done to Alfred. He had been wild enough in college, and she doubted that any cowboy could have taught him much. She alone of her family had ever believed in any latent good in Alfred Hammond, and her faith had scarcely survived the two years of silence.

Waiting there, she again found herself listening to the moan of the wind through the wires. The horse outside began to pound with heavy hoofs, and once he whinnied. Then Madeline heard a rapid pattering, low at first and growing louder, which presently she recognized as the galloping of horses. She went to the window, thinking, hoping her brother had arrived. But as the clatter increased to a roar, shadows sped by—lean horses, flying manes and tails, sombreroed riders, all strange and wild in her sight. Recalling what the conductor had said, she was at some pains to quell her uneasiness. Dust-clouds shrouded the dim lights in the windows. Then out of the gloom two figures appeared, one tall, the other slight. The cowboy was returning with a porter.

Heavy footsteps sounded without, and lighter ones dragging along, and then suddenly the door rasped open, jarring the whole room. The cowboy entered, pulling a disheveled figure—that of a priest, a padre, whose mantle had manifestly been disarranged by the rude grasp of his captor. Plain it was that the padre was extremely terrified.

Madeline Hammond gazed in bewilderment at the little man, so pale and shaken, and a protest trembled upon her lips; but it was never uttered, for this half-drunken cowboy now appeared to be a cool, grim-smiling devil; and stretching out a long arm, he grasped her and swung her back to the bench.

"You stay there!" he ordered.

His voice, though neither brutal nor harsh nor cruel, had the unaccountable effect of making her feel powerless to move. No man had ever before addressed her in such a tone. It was the woman in her that obeyed—not the personality of proud Madeline Hammond. The padre lifted his clasped hands as if supplicating for his life, and began to speak hurriedly in Spanish. Madeline did not understand the language. The cowboy pulled out a huge gun and brandished it in the priest's face. Then he lowered it, apparently to point it at the priest's feet. There was a red flash, and then a thundering report that stunned Madeline. The room filled with smoke and the smell of powder. Madeline did not faint or even shut her eyes, but she felt as if she were fast in a cold vise. When she could see distinctly through the smoke she experienced a sensation of immeasurable relief that the cowboy had not shot the padre. But he was still waving the gun, and now appeared to be dragging his victim toward her. What possibly could be the drunken fool's intention? This must be, this surely was a cowboy trick. She had a vague, swiftly flashing recollection of Alfred's first letters descriptive of the extravagant fun of cowboys. Then she vividly remembered a moving picture she had seen— cowboys playing a monstrous joke on a lone school-teacher. Madeline no sooner thought of it than she made certain her brother was introducing her to a little wild West amusement. She could scarcely believe it, yet it must be true. Alfred's old love of teasing her might have extended even to this outrage. Probably he stood just outside the door or window laughing at her embarrassment.

Anger checked her panic. She straightened up with what composure this surprise had left her and started for the door. But the cowboy barred her passage—grasped her arms. Then Madeline divined that her brother could not have any knowledge of this indignity. It was no trick. It was something that was happening, that was real, that threatened she knew not what. She tried to wrench free, feeling hot all over at being handled by this drunken brute. Poise, dignity, culture—all the acquired habits of character—fled before the instinct to fight. She was athletic. She fought. She struggled desperately. But he forced her back with hands of iron. She had never known a man could be so strong. And then it was the man's coolly smiling face, the paralyzing strangeness of his manner, more than his strength, that weakened Madeline until she sank trembling against the bench.

"What—do you—mean?" she panted.

"Dearie, ease up a little on the bridle," he replied, gaily.

Madeline thought she must be dreaming. She could not think

clearly. It had all been too swift, too terrible for her to grasp. Yet she not only saw this man, but also felt his powerful presence. And the shaking priest, the haze of blue smoke, the smell of powder—these were not unreal.

Then close before her eyes burst another blinding red flash, and close at her ears bellowed another report. Unable to stand, Madeline slipped down onto the bench. Her drifting faculties refused clearly to record what transpired during the next few moments; presently, however, as her mind steadied somewhat, she heard, though as in a dream, the voice of the padre hurrying over strange words. It ceased, and then the cowboy's voice stirred her.

"Lady, say *Si—Si*. Say it—quick! Say it—*Si!*"

From sheer suggestion, a force irresistible at this moment when her will was clamped by panic, she spoke the word.

"And now, lady—so we can finish this properly—what's your name?"

Still obeying mechanically, she told him.

He stared for a while, as if the name had awakened associations in a mind somewhat befogged. He leaned back unsteadily. Madeline heard the expulsion of his breath, a kind of hard puff, not unusual in drunken men.

"What name?" he demanded.

"Madeline Hammond. I am Alfred Hammond's sister."

He put his hand up and brushed at an imaginary something before his eyes. Then he loomed over her, and that hand, now shaking a little, reached out for her veil. Before he could touch it, however, she swept it back, revealing her face.

"You're—not—*Majesty* Hammond?"

How strange—stranger than anything that had ever happened to her before—was it to hear that name on the lips of this cowboy! It was a name by which she was familiarly known, though only those nearest and dearest to her had the privilege of using it. And now it revived her dulled faculties, and by an effort she regained control of herself.

"You are *Majesty* Hammond," he replied; and this time he affirmed wonderingly rather than questioned.

Madeline rose and faced him.

"Yes, I am."

He slammed his gun back into its holster.

"Well, I reckon we won't go on with it, then."

"With what, sir? And why did you force me to say *Si* to this priest?"

"I reckon that was a way I took to show him you'd be willing to get married."

"Oh! . . . You—you! . . ." Words failed her. This appeared to galvanize the cowboy into action. He grasped the padre and led him toward the door, cursing and threatening, no doubt enjoining secrecy. Then he pushed him across the threshold and stood there breathing hard and wrestling with himself.

"Here—wait—wait a minute, Miss—Miss Hammond," he said, huskily. "You could fall into worse company than mine—though I reckon you sure think not. I'm pretty drunk, but I'm—all right otherwise. Just wait—a minute."

She stood quivering and blazing with wrath, and watched this savage fight his drunkenness. He acted like a man who had been suddenly shocked into a rational state of mind, and he was now battling with himself to hold on to it. Madeline saw the dark, damp hair lift from his brows as he held it up to the cool wind. Above him she saw the white stars in the deep-blue sky, and they seemed as unreal to her as any other thing in this strange night. They were cold, brilliant, aloof, distant; and looking at them, she felt her wrath lessen and die and leave her calm.

The cowboy turned and began to talk.

"You see—I was pretty drunk," he labored. "There was a *fiesta*—and a wedding. I do fool things when I'm drunk. I made a fool bet I'd marry the first girl who came to town. . . . If you hadn't worn that veil—the fellows were joshing me—and Ed Linton was getting married—and everybody always wants to gamble. . . . I must have been pretty drunk."

After the one look at her when she had first put aside her veil he had not raised his eyes to her face. The cool audacity had vanished in what was either excessive emotion or the maudlin condition peculiar to some men when drunk. He could not stand still; perspiration collected in beads upon his forehead; he kept wiping his face with his scarf, and he breathed like a man after violent exertions.

"You see—I was pretty—" he began.

"Explanations are not necessary," she interrupted. "I am very tired—distressed. The hour is late. Have you the slightest idea what it means to be a gentleman?"

His bronzed face burned to a flaming crimson.

"Is my brother here—in town to-night?" Madeline went on.
"No. He's at his ranch."
"But I wired him."
"Like as not the message is over in his box at the P.O. He'll be in town to-morrow. He's shipping cattle for Stillwell."
"Meanwhile I must go to a hotel. Will you please—"
If he heard her last words he showed no evidence of it. A noise outside had attracted his attention. Madeline listened. Low voices of men, the softer liquid tones of a woman, drifted in through the open door. They spoke in Spanish, and the voices grew louder. Evidently the speakers were approaching the station. Footsteps crunching on gravel attested to this, and quicker steps, coming with deep tones of men in anger, told of a quarrel. Then the woman's voice, hurried and broken, rising higher, was eloquent of vain appeal.

The cowboy's demeanor startled Madeline into anticipation of something dreadful. She was not deceived. From outside came the sound of a scuffle—a muffled shot, a groan, the thud of a falling body, a woman's low cry, and footsteps padding away in rapid retreat.

Madeline Hammond leaned weakly back in her seat, cold and sick, and for a moment her ears throbbed to the tramp of the dancers across the way and the rhythm of the cheap music. Then into the open door-place flashed a girl's tragic face, lighted by dark eyes and framed by dusky hair. The girl reached a slim brown hand round the side of the door and held on as if to support herself. A long black scarf accentuated her gaudy attire.

"Señor—Gene!" she exclaimed; and breathless glad recognition made a sudden break in her terror.

"Bonita!" The cowboy leaped to her. "Girl! Are you hurt?"
"No, Señor."
He took hold of her. "I heard—somebody got shot. Was it Danny?"
"No, Señor."
"Did Danny do the shooting? Tell me, girl."
"No, Señor."
"I'm sure glad. I thought Danny was mixed up in that. He had Stillwell's money for the boys—I was afraid. . . . Say, Bonita, but *you'll* get in trouble. Who was with you? What did you do?"
"Señor Gene—they Don Carlos *vaqueros*—they quarrel over me. I only dance a leetle, smile a leetle, and they quarrel. I beg they be good—watch out for Sheriff Hawe . . . and now Sheriff Hawe put

me in jail. I so frighten; he try make leetle love to Bonita once, and now he hate me like he hate Señor Gene."

"Pat Hawe won't put you in jail. Take my horse and hit the Peloncillo trail. Bonita, promise to stay away from El Cajon."

"*Si,* Señor."

He led her outside. Madeline heard the horse snort and champ his bit. The cowboy spoke low; only a few words were intelligible— "stirrups . . . wait . . . out of town . . . mountain . . . trail . . . now ride!"

A moment's silence ensued, and was broken by a pounding of hoofs, a pattering of gravel. Then Madeline saw a big, dark horse run into the wide space. She caught a glimpse of wind-swept scarf and hair, a little form low down in the saddle. The horse was outlined in black against the line of dim lights. There was something wild and splendid in his flight.

Directly the cowboy appeared again in the doorway.

"Miss Hammond, I reckon we want to rustle out of here. Been bad goings-on. And there's a train due."

She hurried into the open air, not daring to look back or to either side. Her guide strode swiftly. She had almost to run to keep up with him. Many conflicting emotions confused her. She had a strange sense of this stalking giant beside her, silent except for his jangling spurs. She had a strange feeling of the cool, sweet wind and the white stars. Was it only her disordered fancy, or did these wonderful stars open and shut? She had a queer, disembodied thought that somewhere in ages back, in another life, she had seen these stars. The night seemed dark, yet there was a pale, luminous light—a light from the stars—and she fancied it would always haunt her.

Suddenly aware that she had been led beyond the line of houses, she spoke:

"Where are you taking me?"

"To Florence Kingsley," he replied.

"Who is she?"

"I reckon she's your brother's best friend out here."

Madeline kept pace with the cowboy for a few moments longer, and then she stopped. It was as much from necessity to catch her breath as it was from recurring fear. All at once she realized what little use her training had been for such an experience as this. The cowboy, missing her, came back the few intervening steps. Then he waited, still silent, looming beside her.

"It's so dark, so lonely," she faltered. "How do I know . . . what warrant can you give me that you—that no harm will befall me if I go farther?"

"None, Miss Hammond, except that I've seen your face."

Frederic Remington (1861–1909)

FREDERIC REMINGTON was born in Canton, New York, in 1861. His father was a colonel in the Civil War, a newspaper editor, and active in local politics. In his youth, Frederic drew sketches of cowboys and soldiers. As he grew up, he enjoyed hunting and became an avid horseman, following his family's tradition. Remington went to art school at Yale but had to leave when his father died of tuberculosis. At nineteen, he made his first trip West, going to Montana, at first to buy a cattle operation then a mining interest, but realized he did not have sufficient capital for either. On that first trip, Remington sent home quick sketches on wrapping paper, which *Harper's Weekly* later published as his first commercial effort.

In 1883, Remington went to Peabody, Kansas, to become a sheep rancher. He used his entire inheritance for the venture, but sold his ranch and returned East less than a year later. Fortified with funds from his mother, his next Western venture was to become a partner in a saloon in Kansas City. It was there that his paintings began selling. He soon returned to New York once again.

In 1886, Remington was sent to Arizona by *Harper's Weekly* magazine to cover the government's war against Geronimo as an artist-correspondent. Other magazines sent him to remote locations to write articles and to draw depictions of major events.

Remington is most often remembered as a critically acclaimed sculptor/painter of the Old West, but he was a prolific author as well, writing 111 stories and articles for the best magazines of the day, including *Century, Outing, Cosmopolitan,* and *Collier's.*

"Life in the Cattle Country" was published in *Collier's* magazine in 1899.

Life in the Cattle Country

FROM *Collier's* magazine, 1899

The "cattle country" of the West comprises the semi-arid belt lying between the Rocky Mountains and the arable lands of the Missouri and Mississippi Rivers, and extending from Mexico to British America. The name has been given it not because there are more cattle there than elsewhere, but because the land in its present condition is fit for little or nothing but stock raising. One who for the first time traverses the territory known abroad for its cattle, naturally expects to find the broad plains dotted with browsing herds standing knee-deep in lush pasturage; but, in fact, if he travels in the summer season, he sees the brown earth showing through a sparse covering of herbage equally brown, while he may go many miles before he comes upon a straggling bunch of gaunt, long-horned steers picking gingerly at the dry vegetation. In the humid farming regions, where corn and tame grasses can be grown for feeding, the amount of land necessary for the support of a cow is small; but upon the great plains, which lie desolate and practically dead for half the year, the conservative stockman finds it necessary to allow twenty or thirty acres for each head of his herd. No grain is raised there, and none is fed save in great emergency; the only food for the cattle is the wild grass native to the plains. This grass makes its growth in the spring; and when the rains of spring cease it is cured where it stands by the glowing sunlight. This natural hay is scant at the best, and gives little promise to the unpracticed eye; but it is in fact very nutritious, and range cattle will thrive and fatten upon it. Every aspect of the plains suggests the necessity for avoiding the danger of overstocking; the allowance of twenty-five acres for each animal is not extravagant.

For a long time the cattle country of the Northwest was a mere stretch of wild land, wholly unbroken by fences; then the herds ranged freely under semi-occasional oversight from their owners. In that time the "cow-boy" of song and story was in his element. A gradual change has come over that old-time freedom; for where once the land was the property of the Federal government, and open to all who chose to make legitimate use of it, of late years the owners of the herds—the "cattle kings"—have acquired title to their lands, and the individual ranch has taken the place of Nature's range. Railway lines have multiplied; and with individual ownership of land has come the wire fence to mark the bounds of each man's possessions. To the wire fence more than to any other cause is due the passing of the traditional "cow-boy." Of course the fencing of the ranges is not yet universal; but every year sees a nearer approach to that end.

In former time the "round-up" was of much more importance than it is to-day; for with nothing to hinder, the cattle belonging to many owners would mix and mingle intimately, and the process of rounding up was the only method of separating them and establishing ownership. It is altogether likely the people of the next generation will see nothing of this picturesque and interesting activity.

In the cattle lands of the North, the work of rounding up begins so soon as spring is well established. During the winter the herds have been suffered to range freely, and in hard winters will often be found to have drifted far from home. The spring round-up in Nebraska and Dakota begins late in April or in May, and has for its purpose the assembling of the herds which belong to the several ranches of a neighborhood, the separation of each man's cattle from the mass, the branding of calves, etc., and the return of each herd to its own range, where the beef animals are to be put in condition for market, pending the summer and fall round-up. Cattle growers' associations have been formed in the Western States, and when the season opens each association designates the times when the several ranges within its jurisdiction shall round up their cattle, and these times are sought to be arranged that when the first round-up is completed, say in District No. 1, District No. 2, which lies adjoining, will take up the work where No. 1 left off, and No. 3 will follow No. 2 in like manner; and in this way the round-up in the entire State consists not so much of a broken series of drives as of one long drive, with the result that practically every head of stock is discovered, identified and claimed by its owner.

Once the date is fixed for the round-up in a given district, the semi-quiescence of the winter gives instant place to hurry, bustle and strenuous activity. The "cow-ponies" which are to be ridden by the men have been upon the range through the winter, and these must be gathered up and put in condition for riding—often a task of no small difficulty, for after their winter's freedom they are not infrequently so wild as to require to be broken anew to the saddle. But, as Kipling is so fond of saying, that is another story.

The "riders" of the round-up—the men upon whom devolves the actual labor of handling the cattle—rely very greatly upon their saddle ponies. These must necessarily be trained to the work which they are to perform, and know not only the ways of men, but also the more erratic ways of the light-headed steers and cows. Ponies untrained to their duties would make endless trouble, to say nothing of greatly endangering the lives of the men. Each rider takes with him upon the round-up his own "string," consisting of ten or a dozen ponies, which are to be used in turn, so as to insure having a fresh, strong animal in instant readiness for the emergencies which are always arising, but which can never be foretold. Cow-ponies are seldom entirely trustworthy in the matter of habits and temper; but they are stout-hearted, sure-footed little beasts, who know how to keep faith in the crises of driving and "cutting out."

Besides the personal equipment of each man, the ranch sends with the party a general outfit, the principal item of which is a strong and heavy four-horse wagon, carrying bedding, food, cooking utensils, etc., and with this wagon is the man in the hollow of whose skilful hand lies the comfort and welfare of every man on the round-up—that is to say, the camp cook. Nowhere is a good cook more appreciated than in those waste places of the West. The bill of fare for the party on round-up duty is not of very great variety; the inevitable beans, salt pork, canned goods, bread and coffee make the sum total of what the men may expect to eat.

It is of great importance that this food should be well and palatably cooked; and quite independent of his abstract skill, it is always possible for the genius presiding over frying-pan and coffee-pot to make life endurable for men situated as these are. Each ranch which takes part in the round-up sends such an outfit with the men who are delegated to represent it and look after its interests, so that when the camp is pitched upon the plains it presents a very bustling and business-like appearance.

The round-up is under the direct charge of one man, known as the captain, who is sometimes selected by the association at the time of appointing the meeting, and is sometimes chosen by the ranchmen themselves when the party assembles for its work. For the time being the authority of the captain is as nearly absolute as one man's authority can be over American citizens. Violations of his orders are punishable in most cases by the assessment of arbitrary fines; but recourse is not often had to this penalty; for as a rule the men know what is expected of them, and take keen pride in doing their work well. The captain has a lieutenant chosen from the representatives of each ranch taking part in the round-up. Thus officered the force of men is ready for its work.

At the appointed time the delegates from the several ranches come straggling to the place of meeting. There is usually some delay in beginning the work, and while the captain and his aids are planning the details, the riders are wont to engage in a variety of activities, some serious, some designed for amusement—breaking unruly ponies, racing, trading, card-playing, and whatever occurs by way of passing the time. This is all put aside, however, when work actually begins; for the round-up is earnest.

With the opening of spring, when the snows have disappeared from the plains, the cattle will naturally have sought the grazing lands in the neighborhood of the water-courses; therefore, as a rule, the line travelled by the round-up lies along the valley of a small stream, extending back so far as may be necessary upon either hand.

The men are awakened in the morning long before daylight. They have probably slept on the ground, rolled in blankets and with saddles or boots for pillows. Toilets are hurriedly made, for tardiness is not tolerated. The camp breakfast is gulped down in the dark, and every man must be instantly ready to mount when the summons comes. A force of twenty or thirty men is chosen for the day's riding, and this force is divided into two parties, one of which is to cover the territory to the right and the other to the left of the line of the riders' march. For the most part, the land which borders the streams of the far Northwest is broken, rocky and ragged, and to ride a horse over it is certainly not a pleasure trip, to say nothing of the necessity for looking out sharply for straggling bunches of cattle, gathering them up and driving them forward; for range cattle are wild as deer and perverse as swine.

So soon as possible the night's camp is struck and the wagons move forward for five miles or so, where the riders are to assemble after the morning's work. The two parties of riders then strike off in opposite directions, those in each party gradually drawing further and further apart, until the dozen men form a line ten or fifteen miles in length, extending from the site of the night's camp back to the foothills bordering the stream; and then this line, with its members a mile or so apart, moves forward in the direction of the new camp, searching every nook and cranny among the rocks and hills for wandering bunches of grazing cattle. These must be assembled and driven to camp. The man on the inner end of the line keeps close to the stream, riding straight forward, while he at the other end will have to ride for perhaps thirty or forty miles, making a long circling sweep to the hills and then back to the stream. This ride is hard and often perilous, for the land is much broken and cut up by ravines and precipitous "buttes." The half-wild cattle will climb everywhere, and wherever they go the ponies must follow. It may be that in the course of the morning's drive the riders will gather many hundreds or perhaps thousands of cattle; or it is possible that no more than a score or two will be found. At any rate, the drive is carried forward with the intention of reaching camp about midday. Dinner is eaten with a ravenous appetite, but with scant ceremony, and there is no allowance of time for an after-dinner nap, for the herd gathered in the morning must be sorted over and the animals given to their several owners. This is the most trying work of the round-up. It requires clean, strong courage to ride a pony of uncertain temper into the heart of a herd of several hundred or thousand wild cattle which are wrought up, as these are, to a pitch of high nervous excitement; but there is no other recourse.

Each ranch has its individual mark or brand, which is put upon its animals—sometimes a letter or combination of letters, and sometimes a geometrical figure.

The brands are protected by State law, somewhat after the fashion of a copyright, and each is the absolute property of the ranch which uses it. The ranches are commonly known among the cattlemen of the neighborhood by the name of the brand which they use—as "Circle-Bar Ranch," "Lazy L Ranch," etc. A lazy L is an L lying upon its side. In the work of "cutting out," a delegate from a ranch rides into the herd gathered in the morning, singles out one at a time those cattle bearing his ranch's brand, and slowly urges them to the edge of the mass, where they are taken in charge by other riders and kept together in a bunch. Great vigilance is necessary in holding out these separated bunches, for they are constantly striving to return to the main herd. The ponies used in cutting out must be the best, thoroughly broken to the work, and wise as serpents; for in case of some maddened cow or steer forming a sudden disposition to charge, the life of the rider often depends upon the willingness and cool adroitness of his pony in getting out of the way. Once the herd is apportioned to its owners, there remains the labor of branding. Calves with their mothers are easily identified; but there will always be found some mature animals which have escaped the branding-iron in former round-ups, and which are known as mavericks. It may be imagined that the burning of a brand upon the shoulder, flank or side of a lusty two-year-old bull is fraught with considerable excitement. To do this, it is first necessary that the animal be "roped," or lariated, and thrown down. The skill of men trained to handle the rope is really admirable, and it may be remarked in passing that an expert roper is always in demand. The wildly excited steer or bull will be in full flight over the prairie, diving, dodging, plunging this way and that to escape from the inevitable noose swinging over the head of the shrill-yelling rider in pursuit. The greatest skill lies in throwing the noose so that it will settle upon the ground in such wise as to catch the fore or hind legs of the galloping beast; this is the pride of the adept roper. To throw the noose over the head or horns is a trick held in slight esteem. When the noose has settled to its place, the rider gives to his pony a well-understood signal, and the willing beast settles himself for the shock to come when the captive brings up at the end of the taut rope. The pony goes back upon his haunches, the man takes a few turns with the rope around the high horn of his saddle; then with a jerk and a jar the helpless victim throws a furious summersault, and after that there is nothing for it but to submit to fate. A second rider throws his lariat over the other pair of struggling legs, and with the brute thus pinioned the hot branding-iron is set against his side. Where the iron has touched, the hair may grow no more; or if it grows, it will be so discolored as to leave the brand easily recognizable. When the ropes are loosed the fun is fast; for the infuriated animal seeks vengeance, and will charge blindly at any moving thing with sight. The branding of calves is not child's play, but it is tame as compared with the work upon grown animals.

The work of branding concludes the most serious business of the day, save that the herd requires constant watching throughout the twenty-four hours. When night has fallen and the herd has lain down, riders are detailed to circle continually about to guard against the ever-present danger of a stampede. In the night, cattle will take fright upon very slight alarm, and often quite causelessly. One or two will rise bellowing, and in an instant the entire herd is upon its feet, crazed with fright and desiring nothing but flight. To break a stampede, it is necessary to head off the leaders and turn them back into the herd. If the onward rush can be checked and the herd induced to move around in a circle, the present danger is past; but it is impossible to foretell when another break will occur. The rider who deliberately goes in front of a stampeding herd in the pitchy darkness of a prairie night, thoughtless of everything save his duty, must be a man of fine fibre. And indeed I must say at the last that the "cowpunchers" as a class, maligned and traduced as they have been, possess a quality of sturdy, sterling manhood which would be to the credit of men in any walk of life. The honor of the average "puncher" abides with him continually. He will not lie; he will not steal. He keeps faith with his friends; toward his enemies he bears himself like a man. He has his vices—as who has not?—but I like to speak softly of them when set against his unassailable virtues. I wish that the manhood of the cow-boy might come more into fashion further East.

Andy Adams (1859–1935)

ANDY ADAMS was born on a farm in Indiana, the son of pioneers. As a boy he helped with the cattle and horses. In the 1880s he moved to Texas for ten years, where he spent considerable time driving cattle along the Western Trail. He eventually went to Colorado and Nevada for gold mining and settled in Colorado Springs in 1894. He began writing at the age of forty-three and published his most successful book, *The Log of a Cowboy: A Narrative of the Old Trail Days,* in 1903. Although a work of fiction, *The Log of a Cowboy* is based upon Adams' own experiences along the Western Trail, and is considered to be one of the most authentic records of the Wild West days in cattle country. Encouraged by this book's success, he published six more books—four of them in under four years. Andy Adams became one of the pioneers of cowboy writing and the Western genre.

The following story is called "Justice in the Saddle" and is taken from chapters 1–3 of *The Outlet* (1905).

Justice in the Saddle

FROM *The Outlet*, 1905

It was an hour after the usual time when we bedded down the cattle. The wagon had overtaken us about sunset, and the cook's fire piloted us into a camp fully two miles to the right of the trail. A change of horses was awaiting us, and after a hasty supper Tupps detailed two young fellows to visit Ogalalla. It required no urging; I outlined clearly what was expected of their mission, requesting them to return by the way of Flood's wagon, and to receive any orders which my employer might see fit to send. The horse-wrangler was pressed in to stand the guard of one of the absent lads on the second watch, and I agreed to take the other, which fell in the third. The boys had not yet returned when our guard was called, but did so shortly afterward, one of them hunting me up on night-herd.

"Well," said he, turning his horse and circling with me, "we caught onto everything that was adrift. The Rebel and Sponsilier were both in town, in charge of two deputies. Flood and your brother went in with us, and with the lads from the other outfits, including those across the river, there must have been twenty-five of Lovell's men in town. I noticed that Dave and The Rebel were still wearing their six-shooters, while among the boys the arrests were looked upon as quite a joke. The two deputies had all kinds of money, and wouldn't allow no one but themselves to spend a cent. The biggest one of the two—the one who gave you the cigar— would say to my boss: 'Sponsilier, you're a trail foreman from Texas—one of Don Lovell's boss men—but you're under arrest; your cattle are in my possession this very minute. You understand that, don't you? Very well, then; everybody come up and have a drink on the sheriff's office.' That was about the talk in every saloon and dancehall visited. But when we proposed starting back to camp, about midnight, the big deputy said to Flood: 'I want you to tell Colonel Lovell that I hold a warrant for his arrest; urge him not to put me to the trouble of coming out after him. If he had identified himself to me this afternoon, he could have slept on a goose-hair bed to-night instead of out there on the mesa, on the cold ground. His reputation in this town would entitle him to three meals a day, even if he was under arrest. Now, we'll have one more, and tell the damned old rascal that I'll expect him in the morning.'"

We rode out the watch together. On returning to Flood's camp, they had found Don Lovell awake. The old man was pleased with the report, but sent me no special word except to exercise my own judgment. The cattle were tired after their long tramp of the day before, the outfit were saddle weary, and the first rays of the rising sun flooded the mesa before men or animals offered to arise. But the duties of another day commanded us anew, and with the cook calling us, we rose to meet them. I was favorably impressed with Tupps as a segundo, and after breakfast suggested that he graze the cattle over to the North Platte, cross it, and make a permanent camp. This was agreed to, half the men were excused for the day, and after designating, beyond the river, a clump of cottonwoods where the wagon would be found, seven of us turned and rode back for Ogalalla. With picked mounts under us, we avoided the other cattle which could be seen grazing northward, and when fully halfway to town, there before us on the brink of the mesa loomed up the lead of a herd. I soon recognized Jack Splann on the point, and taking a wide circle, dropped in behind him, the column stretching back a mile and coming up the bluffs, forty abreast like an army in loose marching order. I was proud of those "Open A's"; they were my first herd, and though in a hurry to reach town, I turned and rode back with them for fully a mile.

Splann was acting under orders from Flood, who had met him at the ford that morning. If the cattle were in the possession of any deputy sheriff, they had failed to notify Jack, and the latter had already started for the North Platte of his own accord. The "Drooping T" cattle were in the immediate rear under Forrest's segundo, and Splann urged me to accompany him that forenoon, saying: "From what the boys said this morning, Dave and Paul will not be given a hearing until two o'clock this afternoon. I can graze beyond the North Fork by that time, and then we'll all go back together. Flood's right behind here with the 'Drooping T's,' and I think it's his intention to go all the way to the river. Drop back and see him."

The boys who were with me never halted, but had ridden on

towards town. When the second herd began the ascent of the mesa, I left Splann and turned back, waiting on the brink for its arrival. As it would take the lead cattle some time to reach me, I dismounted, resting in the shade of my horse. But my rest was brief, for the clattering hoofs of a cavalcade of horsemen were approaching, and as I arose, Quince Forrest and Bob Quirk with a dozen or more men dashed up and halted. As their herds were intended for the Crow and Fort Washakie agencies, they would naturally follow up the south side of the North Platte, and an hour or two of grazing would put them in camp. The Buford cattle, as well as Flood's herd, were due to cross this North Fork of the mother Platte within ten miles of Ogalalla, their respective routes thenceforth being north and northeast. Forrest, like myself, was somewhat leary of entering the town, and my brother and the boys passed on shortly, leaving Quince behind. We discussed every possible phase of what might happen in case we were recognized, which was almost certain if Tolleston or the Dodge buyers were encountered. But an overweening hunger to get into Ogalalla was dominant in us, and under the excuse of settling for our supplies, after the herd passed, we remounted our horses, Flood joining us, and rode for the hamlet.

There was little external and no moral change in the town. Several new saloons had opened, and in anticipation of the large drive that year, the Dew-Drop-In dance-hall had been enlarged, and employed three shifts of bartenders. A stage had been added with the new addition, and a special importation of ladies had been brought out from Omaha for the season. I use the term *ladies* advisedly, for in my presence one of the proprietors, with marked courtesy, said to an Eastern stranger, "Oh, no, you need no introduction. My wife is the only woman in town; all the balance are ladies." Beyond a shave and a hair-cut, Forrest and I fought shy of public places. But after the supplies were settled for, and some new clothing was secured, we chambered a few drinks and swaggered about with considerable ado. My bill of supplies amounted to one hundred and twenty-six dollars, and when, without a word, I drew a draft for the amount, the proprietor of the outfitting store, as a pelon, made me a present of two fine silk handkerchiefs. Forrest was treated likewise, and having invested ourselves in white shirts, with flaming red ties, we used the new handkerchiefs to otherwise decorate our persons. We had both chosen the brightest colors, and with these knotted about our necks, dangling from pistol-pockets, or protruding from ruffled shirt fronts, our own mothers would scarcely have known us. Jim Flood, whom we met casually on a back street, stopped, and after circling us once, said, "Now if you fellows just keep perfectly sober, your disguise will be complete."

Meanwhile Don Lovell had reported at an early hour to the sheriff's office. The legal profession was represented in Ogalalla by several firms, criminal practice being their specialty; but fortunately Mike Sutton, an attorney of Dodge, had arrived in town the day before on a legal errand for another trail drover. Sutton was a frontier advocate, alike popular with the Texas element and the gambling fraternity, having achieved laurels in his home town as a criminal lawyer. Mike was born on the little green isle beyond the sea, and, gifted with the Celtic wit, was also in logic clear as the tones of a bell, while his insight into human motives was almost superhuman. Lovell had had occasion in other years to rely on Sutton's counsel, and now would listen to no refusal of his services. As it turned out, the lawyer's mission in Ogalalla was so closely in sympathy with Lovell's trouble that they naturally strengthened each other. The highest tribunal of justice in Ogalalla was the county court, the judge of which also ran the stock-yards during the shipping season, and was banker for two monte games at the Lone Star saloon. He enjoyed the reputation of being an honest, fearless jurist, and supported by a growing civic pride, his decisions gave satisfaction. A sense of crude equity governed his rulings, and as one of the citizens remarked, "Whatever the judge said, *went*." It should be remembered that this was in '84, but had a similar trouble occurred five years earlier, it is likely that Judge Colt would have figured in the preliminaries, and the coroner might have been called on to impanel a jury. But the rudiments of civilization were sweeping westward, and Ogalalla was nerved to the importance of the occasion; for that very afternoon a hearing was to be given for the possession of two herds of cattle, valued at over a quarter-million dollars.

The representatives of The Western Supply Company were quartered in the largest hotel in town, but seldom appeared on the streets. They had employed a firm of local attorneys, consisting of an old and a young man, both of whom evidently believed in the justice of their client's cause. All the cattle-hands in Lovell's employ were anxious to get a glimpse of Tolleston, many of them patronizing the bar and table of the same hostelry, but their efforts were futile until the hour arrived for the hearing. They probably have a new court-house in

Ogalalla now, but at the date of this chronicle the building which served as a temple of justice was poorly proportioned, its height being entirely out of relation to its width. It was a two-story affair, the lower floor being used for county offices, the upper one as the court-room. A long stairway ran up the outside of the building, landing on a gallery in front, from which the sheriff announced the sitting of the honorable court of Keith County. At home in Texas, lawsuits were so rare that though I was a grown man, the novelty of this one absorbed me. Quite a large crowd had gathered in advance of the hour, and while awaiting the arrival of Judge Mulqueen, a contingent of fifteen men from the two herds in question rode up and halted in front of the court-house. Forrest and I were lying low, not caring to be seen, when the three plaintiffs, the two local attorneys, and Tolleston put in an appearance. The cavalcade had not yet dismounted, and when Dorg Seay caught sight of Tolleston, he stood up in his stirrups and sang out, "Hello there, Archibald! my old college chum, how goes it?"

Judge Mulqueen had evidently dressed for the occasion, for with the exception of the plaintiffs, he was the only man in the court-room who wore a coat. The afternoon was a sultry one; in that first bottom of the Platte there was scarcely a breath of air, and collars wilted limp as rags. Neither map nor chart graced the unplastered walls, the unpainted furniture of the room was sadly in need of repair, while a musty odor permeated the room. Outside the railing the seating capacity of the court-room was rather small, rough, bare planks serving for seats, but the spectators gladly stood along the sides and rear, eager to catch every word, as they silently mopped the sweat which oozed alike from citizen and cattleman. Forrest and I were concealed in the rear, which was packed with Lovell's boys, when the judge walked in and court opened for the hearing. Judge Mulqueen requested counsel on either side to be as brief and direct as possible, both in their pleadings and testimony, adding: "If they reach the stock-yards in time, I may have to load out a train of feeders this evening. We'll bed the cars, anyhow." Turning to the sheriff, he continued: "Frank, if you happen outside, keep an eye up the river; those Lincoln feeders made a deal yesterday for five hundred three-year-olds.—Read your complaint."

The legal document was read with great fervor and energy by the younger of the two local lawyers. In the main it reviewed the situation correctly, every point, however, being made subservient to their object,—the possession of the cattle. The plaintiffs contended that they were the innocent holders of the original contract between the government and The Western Supply Company, properly assigned; that they had purchased these two herds in question, had paid earnest-money to the amount of sixty-five thousand dollars on the same, and concluded by petitioning the court for possession. Sutton arose, counseled a moment with Lovell, and borrowing a chew of tobacco from Sponsilier, leisurely addressed the court.

"I shall not trouble your honor by reading our reply in full, but briefly state its contents," said he, in substance. "We admit that the herds in question, which have been correctly described by road brands and ages, are the property of my client. We further admit that the two trail foremen here under arrest as accessories were acting under the orders of their employer, who assumes all responsibility for their acts, and in our pleadings we ask this honorable court to discharge them from further detention. The earnest-money, said to have been paid on these herds, is correct to a cent, and we admit having the amount in our possession. But," and the little advocate's voice rose, rich in its Irish brogue, "we deny any assignment of the original contract. The Western Supply Company is a corporation name, a shield and fence of thieves. The plaintiffs here can claim no assignment, because they themselves constitute the company. It has been decided that a man cannot steal his own money, neither can he assign from himself to himself. We shall prove by a credible witness that The Western Supply Company is but another name for John C. Fields, Oliver Radcliff, and the portly gentleman who was known a year ago as 'Honest' John Griscom, one of his many aliases. If to these names you add a few moneyed confederates, you have The Western Supply Company, one and the same. We shall also prove that for years past these same gentlemen have belonged to a ring, all brokers in government contracts, and frequently finding it necessary to use assumed names, generally that of a corporation."

Scanning the document in his hand, Sutton continued: "Our motive in selling and accepting money on these herds in Dodge demands a word of explanation. The original contract calls for five million pounds of beef on foot to be delivered at Fort Buford. My client is a sub-contractor under that award. There are times, your honor, when it becomes necessary to resort to questionable means to attain an end. This is one of them. Within a week after my client had given bonds for the fulfillment of his contract, he made the discovery that he was dealing with a double-faced set of scoundrels. From that day until the present moment, secret-service men have shadowed every action of the plaintiffs. My client has anticipated their every move. When beeves broke in price from five to seven dollars a head, Honest John, here, made his boasts in Washington City over a champagne supper that he and his associates would clear one hundred thousand dollars on their Buford contract. Let us reason together how this could be done. The Western Supply Company refused, even when offered a bonus, to assign their contract to my client. But they were perfectly willing to transfer it, from themselves as a corporation, to themselves as individuals, even though they had previously given Don Lovell a subcontract for the delivery of the beeves. The original award was made seven months ago, and the depreciation in cattle since is the secret of why the frog eat the cabbage. My client is under the necessity of tendering his cattle on the day of delivery, and proposes to hold this earnest-money to indemnify himself in case of an adverse decision at Fort Buford. It is the only thing he can do, as The Western Supply Company is execution proof, its assets consisting of some stud-horse office furniture and a corporate seal. On the other hand, Don Lovell is rated at half a million, mostly in pasture lands; is a citizen of Medina County, Texas, and if these gentlemen have any grievance, let them go there and sue him. A judgment against my client is good. Now, your honor, you have our side of the question. To be brief, shall these old Wisinsteins come out here from Washington City and dispossess any man of his property? There is but one answer—not in the Republic of Keith."

All three of the plaintiffs took the stand, their testimony supporting the complaint, Lovell's attorney refusing even to cross-examine any one of them. When they rested their case Sutton arose, and scanning the audience for some time, inquired, "Is Jim Reed here?" In response, a tall, one-armed man worked his way from the outer gallery through the crowd and advanced to the rail. I knew Reed by sight only, my middle brother having made several trips with his trail cattle, but he was known to every one by reputation. He had lost an arm in the Confederate service, and was recognized by the gambling fraternity as the gamest man among all the trail drovers, while every cowman from the Rio Grande to the Yellowstone knew him as a poker-player. Reed was asked to take the stand, and when questioned if he knew either of the plaintiffs, said:

"Yes, I know that fat gentleman, and I'm powerful glad to meet up with him again," replied the witness, designating Honest John. "That man is so crooked that he can't sleep in a bed, and it's one of the wonders of this country that he hasn't stretched hemp before this. I made his acquaintance as manager of The Federal Supply Company, and delivered three thousand cows to him at the Washita Indian Agency last fall. In the final settlement, he drew on three different banks, and one draft of twenty-eight thousand dollars came back, indorsed, *drawee unknown*. I had other herds on the trail to look after, and it was a month before I found out that the check was bogus, by which time Honest John had sailed for Europe. There was nothing could be done but put my claim into a judgment and lay for him. But I've got a grapevine twist on him now, for no sooner did he buy a herd here last week than Mr. Sutton transferred the judgment to this jurisdiction, and his cattle will be attached this afternoon. I've been on his trail for nearly a year, but he'll come to me now, and before he can move his beeves out of this county, the last cent must come, with interest, attorney's fees, detective bills, and remuneration for my own time and trouble. That's the reason that I'm so glad to meet him. Judge, I've gone to the trouble and expense to get his record for the last ten years. He's so snaky he sheds his name yearly, shifting for a nickname from Honest John to The Quaker. In '80 he and his associates did business under the name of The Army & Sutler Supply Company, and I know of two judgments that can be bought very reasonable against that corporation. His record would convince any one that he despises to make an honest dollar."

The older of the two attorneys for the plaintiffs asked a few questions, but the replies were so unsatisfactory to their side, that they soon passed the witness. During the cross-questioning, however, the sheriff had approached the judge and whispered something to his honor. As there were no further witnesses to be examined, the local attorneys insisted on arguing the case, but Judge Mulqueen frowned them down, saying:

"This court sees no occasion for any argument in the present case. You might spout until you were black in the face and it wouldn't change my opinion any; besides I've got twenty cars to send and a train of cattle to load out this evening. This court refuses to interfere with the herds in question, at present the property of and in possession of Don Lovell, who, together with his men, are discharged from custody. If you're in town to-night, Mr. Reed, drop into the Lone Star. Couple of nice monte games running there; hundred-dollar limit, and if you feel lucky, there's a nice bank roll behind them. Adjourn court, Mr. Sheriff."

Turning the Tables

"Keep away from me, you common cow-hands," said Sponsilier, as a group of us waited for him at the foot of the court-house stairs. But Dave's gravity soon turned to a smile as he continued: "Did you fellows notice The Rebel and me sitting inside the rail among all the big augers? Paul, was it a dream, or did we sleep in a bed last night and have a sure-enough pillow under our heads? My memory is kind of hazy to-day, but I remember the drinks and the cigars all right, and saying to some one that his luck was too good to last. And here we are turned out in the cold world again, our fun all over, and now must go back to those measly cattle. But it's just what I expected."

The crowd dispersed quietly, though the sheriff took the precaution to accompany the plaintiffs and Tolleston back to their hotel. The absence of the two deputies whom we had met the day before was explained by the testimony of the one-armed cowman. When the two drovers came downstairs, they were talking very confidentially together, and on my employer noticing the large number of his men present, he gave orders for them to meet him at once at the White Elephant saloon. Those who had horses at hand mounted and dashed down the street, while the rest of us took it leisurely around to the appointed rendezvous, some three blocks distant. While on the way, I learned from The Rebel that the cattle on which the attachment was to be made that afternoon were then being held well up the North Fork. Sheriff Phillips joined us shortly after we entered the saloon, and informed my employer that the firm of Field, Radcliff & Co. had declared war. They had even denounced him and the sheriff's office as being in collusion against them, and had dispatched Tolleston with orders to refuse services.

"Let them get on the prod all they want to," said Don Lovell to Reed and the sheriff. "I've got ninety men here, and you fellows are welcome to half of them, even if I have to go out and stand a watch on night-herd myself. Reed, we can't afford to have our business ruined by such a set of scoundrels, and we might as well fight it out here and now. Look at the situation I'm in. A hundred thousand dollars wouldn't indemnify me in having my cattle refused as late as the middle of September at Fort Buford. And believing that I will be turned down, under my contract, so Sutton says, I must tender my beeves on the appointed day of delivery, which will absolve my bondsmen and me from all liability. A man can't trifle with the government—the cattle must be there. Now in my case, Jim, what would you do?"

"That's a hard question, Don. You see we're strangers up in this Northwest country. Now, if it was home in Texas, there would be only one thing to do. Of course I'm no longer handy with a shotgun, but you've got two good arms."

"Well, gentlemen," said the sheriff, "you must excuse me for interrupting, but if my deputies are to take possession of that herd this afternoon, I must saddle up and go to the front. If Honest John and associates try to stand up any bluffs on my office, they'll only run on the rope once. I'm much obliged to you, Mr. Lovell, for the assurance of any help I may need, for it's quite likely that I may have to call upon you. If a ring of government speculators can come out here and refuse service, or dictate to my office, then old Keith County is certainly on the verge of decadence. Now, I'll be all ready to start for the North Fork in fifteen minutes, and I'd admire to have you all go along."

Lovell and Reed both expressed a willingness to accompany the sheriff. Phillips thanked them and nodded to the force behind the mahogany, who dexterously slid the glasses up and down the bar, and politely inquired of the double now confronting them as to their tastes. As this was the third round since entering the place, I was anxious to get away, and summoning Forrest, we started for our horses. We had left them at a barn on a back street, but before reaching the livery, Quince concluded that he needed a few more cartridges. I had ordered a hundred the day before for my own personal use, but they had been sent out with the supplies and were then in camp. My own belt was filled with ammunition, but on Forrest buying fifty, I took an equal number, and after starting out of the store, both turned back and doubled our purchases. On arriving at the stable, whom should I meet but the Wyoming cowman who had left us at Grinnell. During the few minutes in which I was compelled to listen to his troubles, he informed me that on his arrival at Ogalalla, all the surplus cow-hands had been engaged by a man named Tolleston for the Yellowstone country. He had sent to his ranch, however, for an outfit who would arrive that evening, and he expected to start his herd the next morning. But without wasting any words, Forrest and I swung into our saddles, waved a farewell to the wayfaring acquaintance, and rode around to the White Elephant. The sheriff and quite a cavalcade of our boys had already started, and on reaching the street which terminated in the only road leading to the North Fork, we were halted by Flood to await the arrival of the others. Jim Reed and my employer were still behind, and some little time was lost before they came up, sufficient to give the sheriff a full half-mile start. But under the leadership of the two drovers, we shook out our horses, and the advance cavalcade were soon overtaken.

"Well, Mr. Sheriff," said old man Don, as he reined in beside Phillips, "how do you like the looks of this for a posse? I'll vouch that they're all good cow-hands, and if you want to deputize the whole works, why, just work your rabbit's foot. You might leave Reed and me out, but I think there's some forty odd without us. Jim and I are getting a little too old, but we'll hang around and run errands and do the clerking. I'm perfectly willing to waste a week, and remember that we've got the chuck and nearly a thousand saddle horses right over here on the North Fork. You can move your office out to one of my wagons if you wish, and whatever's mine is yours, just so long as Honest John and his friends pay the fiddler. If he and his associates are going to make one hundred thousand dollars on the Buford contract, one thing is certain—I'll lose plenty of money on this year's drive. If he refuses service and you take possession, your office will be perfectly justified in putting a good force of men with the herd. And at ten dollars a day for a man and horse, they'll soon get sick and Reed will get his pay. If I have to hold the sack in the end, I don't want any company."

The location of the beeves was about twelve miles from town and but a short distance above the herds of The Rebel and Bob Quirk. It was nearly four o'clock when we left the hamlet, and by striking a free gait, we covered the intervening distance in less than an hour and a half. The mesa between the two rivers was covered with through cattle, and as we neared the herd in question, we were met by the larger one of the two chief deputies. The under-sheriff was on his way to town, but on sighting his superior among us, he halted and a conference ensued. Sponsilier and Priest made a great ado over the big deputy on meeting, and after a few inquiries were exchanged, the latter turned to Sheriff Phillips and said:

"Well, we served the papers and I left the other two boys in temporary possession of the cattle. It's a badly mixed-up affair. The Texas foreman is still in charge, and he seems like a reasonable fellow. The terms of the sale were to be half cash here and the balance at the point of delivery. But the buyers only paid forty thousand down, and the trail boss refuses to start until they make good their agreement. From what I could gather from the foreman, the buyers simply buffaloed the young fellow out of his beeves, and are now hanging back for more favorable terms. He accepted service all right and assured me that our men would be welcome at his wagon until further notice, so I left matters just as I found them. But as I was on the point of leaving, that segundo of the buyers arrived and tried to stir up a little trouble. We all sat down on him rather hard, and as I left he and the Texas foreman were holding quite a big pow-wow."

"That's Tolleston all right," said old man Don, "and you can depend on him stirring up a muss if there's any show. It's a mystery to me how I tolerated that fellow as long as I did. If some of you boys will corner and hold him for me, I'd enjoy reading his title to him in a few plain words. It's due him, and I want to pay everything I owe. What's the programme, Mr. Sheriff?"

"The only safe thing to do is to get full possession of the cattle," replied Phillips. "My deputies are all right, but they don't thoroughly understand the situation. Mr. Lovell, if you can lend me ten men, I'll take charge of the herd at once and move them back down the river about seven miles. They're entirely too near the west line of the county to suit me, and once they're in our custody the money will be forthcoming, or the expenses will mount up rapidly. Let's ride."

The under-sheriff turned back with us. A swell of the mesa cut off a view of the herd, but under the leadership of the deputy we rode to its summit, and there before and under us were both camp and cattle. Arriving at the wagon, Phillips very politely informed the Texas foreman that he would have to take full possession of his beeves for a few days, or until the present difficulties were adjusted. The trail boss was a young fellow of possibly thirty, and met the sheriff's demand with several questions, but, on being assured that his employer's equity in the herd would be fully protected without expense, he offered no serious objection. It developed that Reed had some slight acquaintance with the seller of the cattle, and lost no time in informing the trail boss of the record of the parties with whom his employer was dealing. The one-armed drover's language was plain, the foreman knew Reed by reputation, and when Lovell assured the young man that he would be welcome at any of his wagons, and would be perfectly at liberty to see that his herd was properly cared for, he yielded without a word. My sympathies were with the foreman, for he seemed an honest fellow, and deliberately to take his herd from him, to my impulsive reasoning looked like an injustice. But the sheriff and those two old cowmen were determined, and the young fellow probably acted for the best in making a graceful surrender.

Meanwhile the two deputies in charge failed to materialize, and on inquiry they were reported as out at the herd with Tolleston. The foreman accompanied us to the cattle, and while on the way he informed the sheriff that he wished to count the beeves over to him and take a receipt for the same. Phillips hesitated, as he was no cowman, but Reed spoke up and insisted that it was fair and just, saying: "Of course, you'll count the cattle and give him a receipt in numbers, ages, and brands. It's not this young man's fault that his herd must undergo all this trouble, and when he turns them over to an officer of the law he ought to have something to show for it. Any of Lovell's foremen here will count them to a hair for you, and Don and I will witness the receipt, which will make it good among cowmen."

Without loss of time the herd was started east. Tolleston kept well out of reach of my employer, and besought every one to know what this movement meant. But when the trail boss and Jim Flood rode out to a swell of ground ahead, and the point-men began filing the column through between the two foremen, Archie was sagacious enough to know that the count meant something serious. In the mean time Bob Quirk had favored Tolleston with his company, and when the count was nearly half over, my brother quietly informed him that the sheriff was taking possession. Once the atmosphere cleared, Archie grew uneasy and restless, and as the last few hundred beeves were passing the counters, he suddenly concluded to return to Ogalalla. But my brother urged him not to think of going until he had met his former employer, assuring Tolleston that the old man had made inquiry about and was anxious to meet him. The latter, however, could not remember anything of urgent importance between them, and pleaded the lateness of the hour and the necessity of his immediate return to town. The more urgent Bob Quirk became, the more fidgety grew Archie. The last of the cattle were passing the count as Tolleston turned away from my brother's entreaty, and giving his horse the rowel, started off on a gallop. But

there was a scattering field of horsemen to pass, and before the parting guest could clear it, a half-dozen ropes circled in the air and deftly
settled over his horse's neck and himself, one of which pinioned his
arms. The boys were expecting something of this nature, and fully
half the men in Lovell's employ galloped up and formed a circle
around the captive, now livid with rage. Archie was cursing by both
note and rhyme, and had managed to unearth a knife and was trying
to cut the lassos which fettered himself and horse, when Dorg Seay
rode in and rapped him over the knuckles with a six-shooter, saying,
"Don't do that, sweetheart; those ropes cost thirty-five cents
apiece."

Fortunately the knife was knocked from Tolleston's hand and his
six-shooter secured, rendering him powerless to inflict injury to any
one. The cattle count had ended, and escorted by a cordon of
mounted men, both horse and captive were led over to where a
contingent had gathered around to hear the result of the count. I was
merely a delighted spectator, and as the other men turned from the
cattle and met us, Lovell languidly threw one leg over his horse's
neck, and, suppressing a smile, greeted his old foreman.

"Hello, Archie," said he; "it's been some little time since last we
met. I've been hearing some bad reports about you, and was anxious
to meet up and talk matters over. Boys, take those ropes off his horse
and give him back his irons; I raised this man and made him the cowhand he is, and there's nothing so serious between us that we should
remain strangers. Now, Archie, I want you to know that you are in
the employ of my enemies, who are as big a set of scoundrels as ever
missed a halter. You and Flood, here, were the only two men in my
employ who knew all the facts in regard to the Buford contract. And
just because I wouldn't favor you over a blind horse, you must hunt
up the very men who are trying to undermine me on this drive. No
wonder they gave you employment, for you're a valuable man to
them; but it's at a serious loss,—the loss of your honor. You can't go
home to Texas and again be respected among men. This outfit you
are with will promise you the earth, but the moment that they're
through with you, you won't cut any more figure than a last year's
bird's nest. They'll throw you aside like an old boot, and you'll fall
so hard that you'll hear the clock tick in China. Now, Archie, it hurts
me to see a young fellow like you go wrong, and I'm willing to for-
give the past and stretch out a hand to save you. If you'll quit those
people, you can have Flood's cattle from here to the Rosebud

Agency, or I'll buy you a ticket home and you can help with the fall work at the ranch. You may have a day or two to think this matter over, and whatever you decide on will be final. You have shown little gratitude for the opportunities that I've given you, but we'll break the old slate and start all over with a new one. Now, that's all I wanted to say to you, except to do your own thinking. If you're going back to town, I'll ride a short distance with you."

The two rode away together, but halted within sight for a short conference, after which Lovell returned. The cattle were being drifted east by the deputies and several of our boys, the trail boss having called off his men on an agreement of the count. The herd had tallied out thirty-six hundred and ten head, but in making out the receipt, the fact was developed that there were some six hundred beeves not in the regular road brand. These had been purchased extra from another source, and had been paid for in full by the buyers, the seller of the main herd agreeing to deliver them along with his own. This was fortunate, as it increased the equity of the buyers in the cattle, and more than established a sufficient interest to satisfy the judgment and all expenses.

Darkness was approaching, which hastened our actions. Two men from each outfit present were detailed to hold the cattle that night, and were sent on ahead to Priest's camp to secure their suppers and a change of mounts. The deposed trail boss accepted an invitation to accompany us and spend the night at one of our wagons, and we rode away to overtake the drifting herd. The different outfits one by one dropped out and rode for their camps; but as mine lay east and across the river, the course of the herd was carrying me home. After passing The Rebel's wagon fully a half mile, we rounded in the herd, which soon lay down to rest on the bed-ground. In the gathering twilight, the camp-fires of nearly a dozen trail wagons were gleaming up and down the river, and while we speculated with Sponsilier's boys which one was ours, the guard arrived and took the bedded herd. The two old cowmen and the trail boss had dropped out opposite my brother's camp, leaving something like ten men with the attached beeves; but on being relieved by the first watch, Flood invited Sheriff Phillips and his deputies across the river to spend the night with him.

"Like to, mighty well, but can't do it," replied Phillips. "The sheriff's office is supposed to be in town, and not over on the North Fork, but I'll leave two of these deputies with you. Some of you had better ride in to-morrow, for there may be overtures made looking towards a settlement; and treat those beeves well, so that there can be no charge of damage to the cattle. Good-night, everybody."

Tolleston Butts In

Morning dawned on a scene of pastoral grandeur. The valley of the North Platte was dotted with cattle from hill and plain. The river, well confined within its low banks, divided an unsurveyed domain of green-swarded meadows like a boundary line between vast pastures. The exodus of cattle from Texas to the new Northwest was nearing flood-tide, and from every swell and knoll the solitary figure of the herdsman greeted the rising sun.

Sponsilier and I had agreed to rejoin our own outfits at the first opportunity. We might have exchanged places the evening before, but I had a horse and some ammunition at Dave's camp and was just contentious enough not to give up a single animal from my own mount. On the other hand, Mr. Dave Sponsilier would have traded whole remudas with me; but my love for a good horse was strong, and Fort Buford was many a weary mile distant. Hence there was no surprise shown as Sponsilier rode up to his own wagon that morning in time for breakfast. We were good friends when personal advantages did not conflict, and where our employer's interests were at stake we stood shoulder to shoulder like comrades. Yet Dave gave me a big jolly about being daffy over my horses, well knowing that there is an indescribable nearness between one of our craft and his own mount. But warding off his raillery, just the same and in due time, I cantered away on my own horse.

As I rode up the North Fork towards my outfit, the attached herd was in plain view across the river. Arriving at my own wagon, I saw a mute appeal in every face for permission to go to town, and consent was readily granted to all who had not been excused on a similar errand the day before. The cook and horse-wrangler were included, and the activities of the outfit in saddling and getting away were suggestive of a prairie fire or a stampede. I accompanied them across the river, and then turned upstream to my brother's camp, promising to join them later and make a full day of it. At Bob's wagon they had stretched a fly, and in its shade lounged half a dozen men, while an air of languid indolence pervaded the camp. Without dismounting, I announced myself as on the way to town, and invited any one who

wished to accompany me. Lovell and Reed both declined; half of
Bob's men had been excused and started an hour before, but my
brother assured me that if I would wait until the deposed foreman
returned, the latter's company could be counted on. I waited, and in
the course of half an hour the trail boss came back from his cattle.
During the interim, the two old cowmen reviewed Grant's siege of
Vicksburg, both having been participants, but on opposite sides.
While the guest was shifting his saddle to a loaned horse, I inquired
if there was anything that I could attend to for any one at Ogalalla.
Lovell could think of nothing; but as we mounted to start, Reed
aroused himself, and coming over, rested the stub of his armless
sleeve on my horse's neck, saying:

"You boys might drop into the sheriff's office as you go in and also
again as you are starting back. Report the cattle as having spent a
quiet night and ask Phillips if he has any word for me."

Turning to the trail boss he continued: "Young man, I would suggest that you hunt up your employer and have him stir things up.
The cattle will be well taken care of, but we're just as anxious to turn
them back to you as you are to receive them. Tell the seller that it
would be well worth his while to see Lovell and myself before going
any farther. We can put him in possession of a few facts that may save
him time and trouble. I reckon that's about all. Oh, yes, I'll be at this
wagon all evening."

My brother rode a short distance with us and introduced the
stranger as Hugh Morris. He proved a sociable fellow, had made
three trips up the trail as foreman, his first two herds having gone to
the Cherokee Strip under contract. By the time we reached Ogalalla,
as strong a fraternal level existed between us as though we had
known each other for years. Halting for a moment at the sheriff's
office, we delivered our messages, after which we left our horses at
the same corral with the understanding that we would ride back
together. A few drinks were indulged in before parting, then each
went to attend to his own errands, but we met frequently during the
day. Once my boys were provided with funds, they fell to gambling
so eagerly that they required no further thought on my part until
evening. Several times during the day I caught glimpses of Tolleston,
always on horseback, and once surrounded by quite a cavalcade of
horsemen. Morris and I took dinner at the hotel where the trio of
government jobbers were stopping. They were in evidence, and
amongst the jolliest of the guests, commanding and receiving the best

that the hostelry afforded. Sutton was likewise present, but quiet and unpretentious, and I thought there was a false, affected note in the hilarity of the ringsters, and for effect. I was known to two of the trio, but managed to overhear any conversation which was adrift. After dinner and over fragrant cigars, they reared their feet high on an outer gallery, and the inference could be easily drawn that a contract, unless it involved millions, was beneath their notice.

Morris informed me that his employer's suspicions were aroused, and that he had that morning demanded a settlement in full or the immediate release of the herd. They had laughed the matter off as a mere incident that would right itself at the proper time, and flashed as references a list of congressmen, senators, and bankers galore. But Morris's employer had stood firm in his contentions, refusing to be overawed by flattery or empty promises. What would be the result remained to be seen, and the foreman and myself wandered aimlessly around town during the afternoon, meeting other trail bosses, nearly all of whom had heard more or less about the existing trouble. That we had the sympathy of the cattle interests on our side goes without saying, and one of them, known as "the kid-gloved foreman," a man in the employ of Shanghai Pierce, invoked the powers above to witness what would happen if he were in Lovell's boots. This was my first meeting with the picturesque trail boss, though I had heard of him often and found him a trifle boastful but not a bad fellow. He distinguished himself from others of his station on the trail by always wearing white shirts, kid gloves, riding-boots, inlaid spurs, while a heavy silver chain was wound several times round a costly sombrero in lieu of a hatband. We spent an hour or more together, drinking sparingly, and at parting he begged that I would assure my employer that he sympathized with him and was at his command.

The afternoon was waning when I hunted up my outfit and started them for camp. With one or two exceptions, the boys were broke and perfectly willing to go. Morris and I joined them at the livery where they had left their horses, and together we started out of town. Ordering them to ride on to camp, and saying that I expected to return by way of Bob Quirk's wagon, Morris and myself stopped at the court-house. Sheriff Phillips was in his office and recognized us both at a glance. "Well, she's working," said he, "and I'll probably have some word for you late this evening. Yes, one of the local attorneys for your friends came in and we figured everything up. He thought that if this office would throw off a certain percent of its expense, and Reed would knock off the interest, his clients would consent to a settlement. I told him to go right back and tell his people that as long as they thought that way, it would only cost them one hundred and forty dollars every twenty-four hours. The lawyer was back within twenty minutes, bringing a draft, covering every item, and urged me to have it accepted by wire. The bank was closed, but I found the cashier in a poker-game and played his hand while he went over to the depot and sent the message. The operator has orders to send a duplicate of the answer to this office, and the moment I get it, if favorable, I'll send a deputy with the news over to the North Fork. Tell Reed that I think the check's all right this time, but we'll stand pat until we know for a certainty. We'll get an answer by morning sure."

The message was hailed with delight at Bob Quirk's wagon. On nearing the river, Morris rode by way of the herd to ask the deputies in charge to turn the cattle up the river towards his camp. Several of the foreman's men were waiting at my brother's wagon, and on Morris's return he ordered his outfit to meet the beeves the next morning and be in readiness to receive them back. Our foremen were lying around temporary headquarters, and as we were starting for our respective camps for the night, Lovell suggested that we hold our outfits all ready to move out with the herds on an hour's notice. Accordingly the next morning, I refused every one leave of absence, and gave special orders to the cook and horse-wrangler to have things in hand to start on an emergency order. Jim Flood had agreed to wait for me, and we would recross the river together and hear the report from the sheriff's office. Forrest and Sponsilier rode up about the same time we arrived at his wagon, and all four of us set out for headquarters across the North Fork. The sun was several hours high when we reached the wagon, and learned that an officer had arrived during the night with a favorable answer, that the cattle had been turned over to Morris without a count, and that the deputies had started for town at daybreak.

"Well, boys," said Lovell, as we came in after picketing our horses, "Reed, here, wins out, but we're just as much at sea as ever. I've looked the situation over from a dozen different viewpoints, and the only thing to do is graze across country and tender our cattle at Fort Buford. It's my nature to look on the bright side of things, and yet I'm old enough to know that justice, in a world so full of injustice, is a rarity. By allowing the earnest-money paid at

Dodge to apply, some kind of a compromise might be effected, whereby I could get rid of two of these herds, with three hundred saddle horses thrown back on my hands at the Yellowstone River. I might dispose of the third herd here and give the remuda away, but at a total loss of at least thirty thousand dollars on the Buford cattle. But then there's my bond to The Western Supply Company, and if this herd of Morris's fails to respond on the day of delivery, I know who will have to make good. An Indian uprising, or the enforcement of quarantine against Texas fever, or any one of a dozen things might tie up the herd, and September the 15th come and go and no beef offered on the contract. I've seen outfits start out and never get through with the chuck-wagon, even. Sutton's advice is good; we'll tender the cattle. There is a chance that we'll get turned down, but if we do, I have enough indemnity money in my possession to temper the wind if the day of delivery should prove a chilly one to us. I think you had all better start in the morning."

The old man's review of the situation was a rational one, in which Jim Reed and the rest of us concurred. Several of the foremen, among them myself, were anxious to start at once, but Lovell urged that we kill a beef before starting and divide it up among the six outfits. He also proposed to Flood that they go into town during the afternoon and freely announce our departure in the morning, hoping to force any issue that might be smouldering in the enemy's camp. The outlook for an early departure was hailed with delight by the older foremen, and we younger and more impulsive ones yielded. The cook had orders to get up something extra for dinner, and we played cards and otherwise lounged around until the midday meal was announced as ready. A horse had been gotten up for Lovell to ride and was on picket, all the relieved men from the attached herd were at Bob's wagon for dinner, and jokes and jollity graced the occasion. But near the middle of the noon repast, some one sighted a mounted man coming at a furious pace for the camp, and shortly the horseman dashed up and inquired for Lovell. We all arose, when the messenger dismounted and handed my employer a letter. Tearing open the missive, the old man read it and turned ashy pale. The message was from Mike Sutton, stating that a fourth member of the ring had arrived during the forenoon, accompanied by a United States marshal from the federal court at Omaha; that the officer was armed with an order of injunctive relief; that he had deputized thirty men whom Tolleston had gathered, and proposed taking possession of the two herds in question that afternoon.

"Like hell they will," said Don Lovell, as he started for his horse. His action was followed by every man present, including the one-armed guest, and within a few minutes thirty men swung into saddles, subject to orders. The camps of the two herds at issue were about four and five miles down and across the river, and no doubt Tolleston knew of their location, as they were only a little more than an hour's ride from Ogalalla. There was no time to be lost, and as we hastily gathered around the old man, he said: "Ride for your outfits, boys, and bring along every man you can spare. We'll meet north of the river about midway between Quince's and Tom's camps. Bring all the cartridges you have, and don't spare your horses going or coming."

Priest's wagon was almost on a line with mine, though south of the river. Fortunately I was mounted on one of the best horses in my string, and having the farthest to go, shook the kinks out of him as old Paul and myself tore down the mesa. After passing The Rebel's camp, I held my course as long as the footing was solid, but on encountering the first sand, crossed the river nearly opposite the appointed rendezvous. The North Platte was fordable at any point, flowing but a midsummer stage of water, with numerous wagon crossings, its shallow channel being about one hundred yards wide. I reined in my horse for the first time near the middle of the stream, as the water reached my saddle-skirt; when I came out on the other side, Priest and his boys were not a mile behind me. As I turned down the river, casting a backward glance, squads of horsemen were galloping in from several quarters and joining a larger one which was throwing up clouds of dust like a column of cavalry. In making a cut-off to reach my camp, I crossed a sand dune from which I sighted the marshal's posse less than two miles distant. My boys were gambling among themselves, not a horse under saddle, and did not notice my approach until I dashed up. Three lads were on herd, but the rest, including the wrangler, ran for their mounts on picket, while Parent and myself ransacked the wagon for ammunition. Fortunately the supply of the latter was abundant, and while saddles were being cinched on horses, the cook and I divided the ammunition and distributed it among the men. The few minutes' rest refreshed my horse, but as we dashed away, the boys yelling like Comanches, the five-mile ride had bested him and he fell slightly behind. As we turned into the open valley, it was a question if we or the marshal would reach the stream first; he had followed an old wood road and would strike the river nearly opposite Forrest's camp. The horses were excited and straining every nerve, and as we neared our crowd the posse halted on the south side and I noticed a conveyance among them in which were seated four men. There was a moment's consultation held, when the posse entered the water and began fording the stream, the vehicle and its occupants remaining on the other side. We had halted in a circle about fifty yards back from the river-bank, and as the first two men came out of the water, Don Lovell rode forward several lengths of his horse, and with his hand motioned to them to halt. The leaders stopped within easy speaking distance, the remainder of the posse halting in groups at their rear, when Lovell demanded the meaning of this demonstration.

An inquiry and answer followed identifying the speakers. "In pursuance of an order from the federal court of this jurisdiction," continued the marshal, "I am vested with authority to take into my custody two herds, numbering nearly seven thousand beeves, now in your possession, and recently sold to Field, Radcliff & Co. for government purposes. I propose to execute my orders peaceably, and any interference on your part will put you and your men in contempt of government authority. If resistance is offered, I can, if necessary, have a company of United States cavalry here from Fort Logan within forty-eight hours to enforce the mandates of the federal court. Now my advice to you would be to turn these cattle over without further controversy."

"And my advice to you," replied Lovell, "is to go back to your federal court and tell that judge that as a citizen of these United States, and one who has borne arms in her defense, I object to having snap judgment rendered against me. If the honorable court which you have the pleasure to represent is willing to dispossess me of my property in favor of a ring of government thieves, and on only hearing one side of the question, then consider me in contempt. I'll gladly go back to Omaha with you, but you can't so much as look at a hoof in my possession. Now call your troops, or take me with you for treating with scorn the orders of your court."

Meanwhile every man on our side had an eye on Archie Tolleston, who had gradually edged forward until his horse stood beside that of the marshal. Before the latter could frame a reply to Lovell's ultimatum, Tolleston said to the federal officer: "Didn't my employers tell you that the old — — — — would defy you without a demonstration of soldiers at your back? Now, the laugh's on you, and—"

"No, it's on you," interrupted a voice at my back, accompanied by a pistol report. My horse jumped forward, followed by a fusillade of shots behind me, when the hireling deputies turned and plunged into the river. Tolleston had wheeled his horse, joining the retreat, and as I brought my six-shooter into action and was in the act of leveling on him, he reeled from the saddle, but clung to the neck of his mount as the animal dashed into the water. I held my fire in the hope that he would right in the saddle and afford me a shot, but he struck a swift current, released his hold, and sunk out of sight. Above the din and excitement of the moment, I heard a voice which I recognized as Reed's, shouting, "Cut loose on that team, boys! Blaze away at those harness horses!" Evidently the team had been burnt by random firing, for they were rearing and plunging, and as I fired my first shot at them, the occupants sprang out of the vehicle and the team ran away. A lull occurred in the shooting to eject shells and refill cylinders, which Lovell took advantage of by ordering back a number of impulsive lads, who were determined to follow up the fleeing deputies.

"Come back here, you rascals, and stop this shooting!" shouted the old man. "Stop it, now, or you'll land me in a federal prison for life! Those horsemen may be deceived. When federal courts can be deluded with sugar-coated blandishments, ordinary men ought to be excusable."

Six-shooters were returned to their holsters. Several horses and two men on our side had received slight flesh wounds, as there had been a random return fire. The deputies halted well out of pistol range, covering the retreat of the occupants of the carriage as best they could, but leaving three dead horses in plain view. As we dropped back towards Forrest's wagon, the team in the mean time having been caught, those on foot were picked up and given seats in the conveyance. Meanwhile a remuda of horses and two chuck-wagons were sighted back on the old wood road, but a horseman met and halted them and they turned back for Ogalalla. On reaching our nearest camp, the posse south of the river had started on their return, leaving behind one of their number in the muddy waters of the North Platte.

Late that evening, as we were preparing to leave for our respective camps, Lovell said to the assembled foremen: "Quince will take Reed and me into Ogalalla about midnight. If Sutton advises it, all three of us will go down to Omaha and try and square things. I can't escape a severe fine, but what do I care as long as I have their money to pay it with? The killing of that fool boy worries me more than a dozen fines. It was uncalled for, too, but he would butt in, and you fellows were all itching for the chance to finger a trigger. Now the understanding is that you all start in the morning."

Stuart N. Lake (1889–1964)

STUART N. LAKE was born in Rome, New York, but little information is available about his life. He became an established writer whose material dealt largely with the West. He is best remembered as the author of *Wyatt Earp: Frontier Marshal,* a highly fictionalized 1931 biography that served as the basis for several movies, including John Ford's *My Darling Clementine,* as well as the 1957 television series, *The Life and Legend of Wyatt Earp.* He wrote several other Western movies including *Wells Fargo* in 1937, *The Westerner* in 1940 (for which he was nominated for an Oscar), *Wells Fargo Days* in 1944, *Winchester 33* in 1950, and *Powder River* in 1953.

"At the O.K. Corral" is from Lake's best-known book, *Wyatt Earp: Frontier Marshal* (1931).

At the O. K. Corral

FROM *Wyatt Earp: Frontier Marshal,* 1931

Whiskey has made more fight-talk than fights, and more brag has been slept off with its liquor than ever has made good in battle. Frontier benders pretty generally followed the alcholic rule, but the red-eye that set Ike Clanton's tongue wagging in the Allen Street saloons during the evening of October 25, 1881, was to precipitate the most celebrated encounter between outlaw and peace officer in the history of untamed Arizona. It was also to furnish Ike with dubious immortality through a gun-fight over which the West has wrangled for half a century, and can still argue as heatedly as when the roar of six-shooters echoed in the streets of Tombstone.

Potency under Ike's belt found vent in loose-mouthed boasts that he would kill Wyatt Earp and Doc Holliday before the setting of the next day's sun. When Farmer Daly and Ed Byrnes suggested that the rustler had laid out quite a job, Ike sneered:

"The Earps are not so much. You'll see, tomorrow. We're in town for a showdown."

About midnight Ike went to the Occidental Saloon where his friends were playing poker. Doc Holliday entered and walked directly to Clanton.

"Ike," Doc said, "I hear you're going to kill me. Get out your gun and commence."

"I haven't any gun," Clanton replied.

"I don't believe you," Doc retorted. "I'll take your word for it this time, but if you intend to open your lying mouth about me again, go heeled."

Morgan Earp, who passed the saloon as Holliday was berating Clanton in picturesque profanity, pulled Doc to the sidewalk. Clanton followed with Tom McLowery, insisting that he was not armed, but promising he soon would be and would shoot Doc, on sight. Wyatt and Virgil Earp came along and took Doc to his room, where Wyatt ordered the dentist to keep away from Clanton.

"A gun-fight now, with you in it," Wyatt warned Holliday, "would ruin my chance to round up this bunch."

"All right," Doc promised regretfully, "I'll keep away from him."

Half an hour later, Ike found Wyatt at the Eagle lunch-counter.

"You tell Doc Holliday no man can talk about me the way he did and live," Ike began. I'm wearing a gun now and you can tell Holliday I aim to get him."

"Doc's gone to bed," Wyatt replied. "You're half-drunk. You'll feel better when you've had some sleep."

"I'm stone-cold sober," Ike retorted. "I'm telling you to tell Holliday I'll gun him the first time I see him."

"Don't you tangle with Doc Holliday," Wyatt advised. "He'll kill you before you've started."

"You've been making a lot of talk about me, too," Ike said.

"You've done the talking," Wyatt corrected.

"Well, it's got to stop," Ike declared. "You had the best of me tonight, but I'll have my friends tomorrow. You be ready for a show-down."

"Go sleep it off, Ike," Wyatt suggested. "You talk too much for a fighting man."

Virgil Earp came in the door, as Ike started out. Ike paused and shouted over his shoulder:

"I said tomorrow. You're to blame for this, Wyatt Earp. What I said for Doc Holliday goes for you and your so-and-so brothers."

Wyatt and Morgan Earp went home about four o'clock. Virgil went to the Occidental to keep an eye on Behan, Clanton, McLowery, and the other cowboys until their game broke up; he reached home after daylight.

The Earps were awakened in the morning on October 26 by word that Ike Clanton was at Fifth and Allen Streets, armed with six-guns and a Winchester, bragging that his friends were on the way to Tombstone to help him clean out the Earps. A second message warned that Billy Clanton, Frank McLowery, and Billy Claiborne had just ridden in to join Ike and Tom McLowery and that the five outlaws were at Fourth and Allen Streets. Ike and Frank had been in several saloons asking if the Earps or Holliday had been around that morning. In Vogan's they had boasted they would shoot the first Earp who showed his face in the street.

"Where's Holliday?" Wyatt asked.

"He hasn't been around."

"Let him sleep," Wyatt ordered.

Ike Clanton had not given the Earps much concern, but Billy Clanton, Claiborne, and the two McLowerys, whatever else they might be, were game men, crack shots and killers. The McLowerys were possibly the two fastest men with six-guns in all the outlaw gang. Frank McLowery was admittedly better on the draw-and-shoot than Curly Bill or John Ringo, and held by some to surpass Buckskin Frank Leslie.

Warren Earp was in California with is parents. Jim Earp was physically unable to take a hand. But, outnumbered as they were, none of the three brothers, as he buckled on his guns, had any idea other than that they would go directly to Fourth and Allen Streets.

"You and Morg go up Fremont Street," Wyatt instructed Virgil. "I'll take Allen Street."

He was giving his brothers the better chance of avoiding the out-laws. They knew it, but obeyed, as was their habit.

"If you see Ike Clanton, arrest him," Wyatt said. "But don't shoot unless Ike does. Take his guns away in front of the whole town, if you can, and show him up."

At Fourth Street, Virgil and Morgan turned south and reached the mid-block alley as Ike Clanton eased out of the narrow passage, rifle in hand, eye on the Allen Street corner.

"Looking for me?" Virgil asked in Ike's ear.

Clanton swung around, lifting the rifle. Virgil seized the Winchester with his left hand, jerked a Colt's with his right, and bent the six-gun over Ike's head. Virgil and Morgan lugged their prisoner through the street to Judge Wallace's courtroom, where Morgan guarded him while Virgil went to find the judge. Several persons who had seen Ike arrested went into the courtroom, among them R. J. Coleman, a mining man who figured in later happenings, and Deputy Sheriff Dave Campbell. Ike was raving with fury.

"I'll get you for this, Wyatt Earp!" he yelled as Wyatt came through the door.

"Clanton," Wyatt answered, "I've had about enough from you and your gang. You've been trying for weeks to get up your nerve to assassinate my brothers and me. The whole town's heard you threaten to kill us. Your fight's against me, not my brothers. You leave them out of this. I'd be justified in shooting you on sight, and if you keep on asking for a fight, I'll give it to you."

"Fight's my racket," Ike blustered. "If I had my guns, I'd fight all you Earps, here and now."

Morgan Earp offered one of Ike's sequestered six-guns, butt foremost, to the owner.

"If you want to fight right bad, Ike," Morgan suggested, "take this. I'll use my fists."

"Quit that, Morg," Wyatt snapped. Deputy Sheriff Campbell pushed Ike into a chair.

"All I want with you," Ike shouted, again identifying Wyatt with a few choice epithets, "is four feet of ground and a gun. You wait until I get out of here."

Wyatt walked from the courtroom. At the door he literally bumped into Tom McLowery, hurrying to Ike's assistance.

"You looking for trouble?" McLowery snarled as he recovered his balance.

"I didn't see you coming," Wyatt answered.

"You're a liar!" McLowery retorted.

Bystanders said Wyatt paled an ominous yellow under his tan.

McLowery's gun was at his hip. Faster than the outlaw could think, Wyatt slapped him full in the face. Tom made no move for his pistol.

"You've got a gun on," Wyatt challenged. "Go after it."

McLowery's right hand dropped downward. Wyatt Earp's Buntline Special flashed and the marshal buffaloed Tom McLowery his full length in the gutter. Wyatt turned his back and walked toward Allen Street.

Judge Wallace fined Ike Clanton twenty-five dollars for breach of the peace. As Ike realized he was to get off thus lightly, more of his bravado returned. The courtroom was filled and before this audience the outlaw took a fling at Virgil Earp.

"If I'd been a split-second faster with my rifle," he boasted, "The coroner'd be working on you now."

"I'm taking your rifle and six-guns to the Grand Hotel," Virgil replied. "Don't pick them up until you start for home."

"You won't be there to see me leave town," Ike retorted.

Wyatt Earp had posted himself outside of Hafford's. Frank and

Tom McLowery, Billy Clanton and Billy Claiborne passed him, all wearing six-guns, and went into Spangenberg's gunshop. Virgil Earp came along, carrying Ike Clanton's weapons to the Grand Hotel, and joined Wyatt at a point across Fourth Street from the gunsmith's. They and several Vigilantes who stood with them could see plainly all that went on in the gun-store.

Ike Clanton now hurried into Spangenberg's. He purchased a six-shooter and the five rustlers loaded their cartridge-belts to capacity. Virgil Earp went on to the hotel. Frank McLowery's horse moved onto the walk in front of the gun-store. Wyatt strode across the road and seized the animal's bit. The two McLowerys and Bill Clanton came running from the store.

"Let go of my horse!" Frank shouted.

"Get him off the walk," Wyatt rejoined.

"Take your hands off my horse!" McLowery insisted.

"When he's where he belongs," Wyatt replied, backed the horse into the road and snubbed him close to the hitching-rail.

The three rustlers had their hands on their gun-butts, spectators later testified.

"That's the last horse of mine you'll ever lay hands on!" Frank McLowery assured Wyatt with a string of oaths.

Wyatt turned on his heel and recrossed the street.

The cowboys left Spangenberg's in a group, going to the Dexter Corral on the south side of Allen Street, between Third and Fourth Streets, owned by Johnny Behan and John Dunbar. Wyatt joined Virgil and Morgan at Hafford's corner, where the brothers stood for possibly half an hour while the rustlers made several trips on foot between the corral and nearby saloons, during which most of Tombstone was apprised of their intention to wipe out the Earps.

Captain Murray and Captain Fronck, with half a dozen Vigilantes, were conferring with Wyatt when R. J. Coleman, heretofore mentioned, reported that he had followed the rustlers to the Dexter Corral and on the way back had met Johnny Behan. Coleman said he had told Behan he should disarm the outlaws, as they were threatening to kill the marshal and his brothers, and that Behan had gone on into the corral. As the Earps and the Vigilantes went into Hafford's to get away from the crowd that gathered, Coleman again went down Allen Street to watch the cowboys.

While Virgil Earp was talking with the Vigilantes, Sheriff Behan entered Hafford's and cut into the conversation.

"Ike Clanton and his crowd are down in my corral making a gun-talk against you fellows," Behan said. "They're laying to kill you. What are you going to do about it?"

"I've been hoping that bunch would leave town without doing anything more than talk," Virgil answered. "I guess they've got to have their lesson. I'm going to throw 'em into the calaboose to cool off. I'll put somebody on to see that they don't walk out, too."

"You try that and they'll kill you," Behan warned Virgil.

"I'll take that chance," Virgil replied. "You're sheriff of Cochise County, Behan, and I'm calling on you to go with me while I arrest them."

Behan laughed. "That's your job, not mine," he said, and left the saloon.

Virgil Earp went into the Wells-Fargo office and returned with a sawed-off shotgun, as Coleman came back to Hafford's with word that the rustlers had transferred headquarters from the Dexter to the O. K. Corral and recruited a sixth to their war-party in the person of Wes Fuller, hanger-on and spy for the Curly Bill crowd. Ike Clanton, Tom McLowery, Billy Claiborne, and Fuller had crossed Allen Street to the O. K. Corral without horses, Billy Clanton had ridden his horse and Frank McLowery had led his. All were wearing six-guns, Coleman said, while Billy Clanton and Frank McLowery had rifles slung from their saddles. They had gone past the stalls near the Allen Street entrance to the corral and into the rear lot which opened on Fremont Street. They had posted Wes Fuller on lookout in the alley and Tom McLowery had gone out into Fremont Street, returning within a few minutes.

The reason for Tom's brief absence was established later by Chris Billicke and Dr. B. W. Gardiner who had been standing on the courthouse steps. Tom walked from the corral to Everhardy's butcher-shop, better known as Bauer's. This business had been placed in Everhardy's name after Bauer was indicted as purchaser of cattle which the Curly Bill crowd rustled, but Bauer continued to work at his block. Chris Billicke and Dr. Gardiner saw Tom McLowery talk with Bauer and stuff a roll of bills into his trousers pocket as he left the shop, revealing as he did so the butt of a six-gun at his left, an item to be noted.

After Tom's return, Coleman started to walk through the corral yard and was stopped by the cowboys, who asked if he knew the Earps. When he replied that he did, Frank McLowery and Ike

Clanton gave him two messages, one for the Earps as a whole, the other for Wyatt, in particular.

"Let's have 'em," Wyatt said.

"They told me to tell the Earps that they were waiting in the O. K. Corral, and that if you didn't come down to fight it out, they'd pick you off in the street when you tried to go home."

The strategy which had moved the outlaws from the Dexter to the O. K. Corral now was apparent.

Allen and Fremont Streets ran parallel with the numbered streets crossing them at right angles, and with an alley running east and west through each block. The O. K. Corral had its covered stalls on the north side of Allen Street, and an open yard across the alley on the south side of Fremont. On Fremont Street an adobe assay office stood at the west line of the corral yard, while to the east was C. S. Fly's photograph gallery.

On the north side of Fremont Street, facing the yard, was the original Cochise County Courthouse, a rambling two-story adobe with courtroom on the ground floor, and on the upper the offices of county officials. These offices opened onto an outside gallery, the west end of which was about opposite the west line of Fly's studio. Then came *The Epitaph* office, and an adobe store occupied by Mrs. Addie Bourland, a milliner.

To return to the O. K. Corral, the alley which ran between the stalls and yard gave onto Fourth Street, and in this passageway Wes Fuller was stationed to keep an eye on the Allen Street corner.

The Earps, in going to and from their homes at First and Fremont Streets, customarily followed Fremont Street past the O. K. Corral yard. The only other direct route available took them by the Allen Street entrance. The Clantons and McLowerys could command with their guns, on a moment's notice, either path; thus outlaw strategy forced the Earps to call the turn or quit the play.

"What's the special message for me?" Wyatt Earp asked Coleman.

"They said to tell you that if you'd leave town they wouldn't harm your brothers," Coleman answered, "but that if you stayed, you'd have to come down and make your fight or they'd bring it to you."

Wyatt looked at Virgil and Morgan. Without a word the three Earps started for the door. Captain Murray stopped them.

"Let us take this off your hands, boys," he offered. "Fronck and I have thirty-five Vigilantes waiting for business. We'll surround the corral, make that bunch surrender, and have them outlawed from Tombstone."

"Much obliged," Wyatt answered for his clan, "but this is our job."

"Come on," he said to Virgil and Morgan.

As the Earps swung out of Hafford's door and started, three abreast, along Fourth Street, Doc Holliday came up on the run.

"Where are you going, Wyatt?" Doc demanded.

"Down the street to make a fight."

"About time," Holliday observed. "I'll go along."

"This is our fight," Wyatt said. "There's no call for you to mix in."

"That's a hell of a thing for you to say to me," Doc retorted. "I heard about this while I was eating breakfast, but I didn't figure you'd go without me."

"I know, Doc," Wyatt said, "but this'll be a tough one."

"Tough ones are the kind I like," the gun-fighting dentist answered.

"All right," Wyatt agreed, and Doc Holliday fell into step with the only person on earth for whom he had either respect or regard.

Holliday was wearing a long overcoat and carrying a cane, as he often did when his physical afflictions bore heavily.

"Here, Doc," Virgil Earp suggested, "let me take your cane and stick this shotgun under your coat where it won't attract so much attention."

Holliday handed over the stick and drew his right arm from the overcoat sleeve, so that the garment hung cape-like over that shoulder. Beneath it he held the short Wells-Fargo weapon. As the four men passed the Fourth Street alley, Wes Fuller ran back into the corral where the Clantons and McLowerys were waiting.

"You ought to have cut him down," Doc Holliday observed.

Beyond this laconic suggestion, not one of the quartet of peace offices spoke as they walked rapidly toward Fremont Street.

Johnny Behan and Frank McLowery had been standing together at the corner of Fourth and Fremont Streets as the Earps left Hafford's. The sheriff and the rustlers hurried to the corral yard; Behan talked for a moment with the five cowboys, then hastened back toward the corner some fifty yards away. He had covered less than half the distance when the marshal's posse came into view.

Tombstone's Fremont Street of 1881 was a sixty-foot thoroughfare with the wide roadbed of the hard-packed, rusty desert sand bordered by footpaths at no marked elevation from the road level. The walks, where buildings adjoined, ran beneath the wooden awnings with their lines of hitching-rails. At the O. K. Corral yard, there was necessarily a gap in the awning roofs and rails, which gave unhindered access for the width of the lot. Johnny Behan apparently expected the marshal's force to follow the sidewalk to the corral and hurried along it to meet them.

Along Fourth Street the Earp party had been two abreast, Wyatt and Virgil in the lead, with Virgil on the outside, Morgan behind him, and Doc Holliday back of Wyatt. Each sensed instinctively what could happen if they rounded the corner of Fly's Photograph Gallery abruptly in close order, and at the street intersection they deployed catercorner to walk four abreast, in the middle of the road.

Half a dozen persons who saw the four men on their journey down Fremont Street have described them. The recollections agree strikingly in detail. No more grimly portentous spectacle had been witnessed in Tombstone.

The three stalwart, six-foot Earps—each with the square jaw of his clan set hard beneath his flowing, tawny mustache and his keen blue eyes alert under the wide brim of a high-peaked, black Stetson—bore out their striking resemblance, even in their attire; dark trousers drawn outside the legs of black, high-heeled boots, long-skirted, square-cut, black coats then in frontier fashion, and white, soft-collared shirts with black string-ties to accentuate the purpose of their lean, bronzed faces. Doc Holliday was some two inches shorter than his three companions, but his stature was heightened by cadaverousness, the flapping black overcoat and the black sombrero above his hollow cheeks. Holliday's blond mustache was as long and as sweeping as any, but below it those who saw him have sworn Doc had his lips pursed, whistling softly. As the distance to the O. K. Corral lessened, the four men spread their ranks as they walked. In front of Bauer's butcher-shop, Johnny Behan ran out with upraised hand. The line halted.

"It's all right, boys. It's all right," the sheriff sputtered. "I've disarmed them."

"Did you arrest them?" Virgil Earp asked.

"No," Behan said, "but I will."

"All right," Virgil said. "Come on."

The politician's nerve deserted him.

"Don't go any farther," he cried. "I order you not to. I'm sheriff of this county. I'll arrest them."

"You told me that was my job," Virgil retorted.

The three Earps and Holliday moved on in the road. The sheriff ran along on the walk.

"Don't go down there! Don't go down there!" he cried. "You'll all be killed!"

The four men in the road cleared the line of Fly's studio. Virgil, Wyatt, and Morgan turned sharply left into the corral, Virgil a few feet in the lead, Wyatt and Morgan following in the order named. The wise Doctor Holliday halted with an uninterrupted sweep of Fremont Street. The door of Fly's gallery banged. Johnny Behan had ducked into the building, where a window gave him view of the corral yard and farther along a side-door opened. Across the lot the five rustlers stood, backs to the assay office wall.

The outlaws were vigorous, sinewy fellows—Ike Clanton, burlier than the rest, wearing, as did each McLowery, a thin mustache in Mexican-dandy style—all with a similarity of attire as marked as, but contrasting sharply with, that of the Earps. Huge sand-hued sombreros, gaudy silk neckerchiefs, fancy woolen shirts, tight-fitting doeskin trousers tucked into forty-dollar halfboots—a get-up so generally affected by Curley Bill followers that it was recognized as their uniform—set off the lean, sunbaked hardness of these desert renegades. Ike Clanton and Tom McLowery wore short, rough coats, the other three, fancy sleeveless vests in the best cow-country fashion.

Billy Claiborne was farthest of his group from the walk, perhaps thirty feet from the street line. Next, on his left, was Ike Clanton, then Billy Clanton, Frank, and Tom McLowery. They had avoided bunching and Tom McLowery was about ten feet from the street. Posted to blank possible fire from the assay office corner were two cow-ponies, one Frank McLowery's, the other Billy Clanton's, each carrying a Winchester rifle in a saddle-boot.

One glance at the cowboys revealed that, despite Johnny Behan's declaration, all were armed. Tom McLowery had a six-gun stuck in the waistband of his trousers. Frank McLowery, Billy and Ike Clanton, each had similar weapons slung from their belts. Claiborne had a Colt's at either hip.

The Earps moved in. From the road, Doc Holliday referred to Johnny Behan in one unprintable phrase. Virgil Earp was well into the corral, Wyatt about opposite Billy Clanton and Frank McLowery, Morg facing Tom. Not a gun had been drawn. Wyatt Earp was determined there'd be no gunplay that the outlaws did not begin. "You men are under arrest. Throw up your hands," Virgil Earp commanded. Frank McLowery dropped his hand to his six-gun and snarled defiance in short, ugly words. Tom McLowery, Billy Clanton, and Billy Claiborne followed concerted suit.

"Hold on!" Virgil Earp shouted, instinctively throwing up his right hand, which carried Doc Holliday's cane, in a gesture of restraint. "We don't want that."

For any accurate conception of what followed, one thing must be kept in mind: action which requires minutes to describe was begun, carried through, and concluded faster than human thought may pick up the threads. Two witnesses swore that its whole course was run in fifteen seconds, others fixed the time at twenty seconds, Wyatt Earp testified that it was finished thirty seconds after Frank McLowery went for his gun. Also, careful note of that action furnishes, more than any other episode of his life, the key to the eminence of Wyatt Earp.

Frank McLowery and Billy Clanton jerked and fired their six-guns simultaneously. Both turned loose on Wyatt Earp, the shots with which they opened the famous battle of the O. K. Corral echoing from the adobe walls as one.

Fast as the two rustlers were at getting into action from a start with guns half-drawn, Wyatt Earp was deadlier. Frank McLowery's bullet tore through the skirt of Wyatt's coat on the right, Billy Clanton's ripped the marshal's sleeve, but before either could fire again, Wyatt's Buntline Special roared; the slug struck Frank McLowery squarely in the abdomen, just above his belt buckle. McLowery screamed, clapped his left hand to the wound, bent over and staggered forward. Wyatt knew Frank as the most dangerous of the five outlaws and had set out deliberately to dispose of him.

In this fraction of a second, Tom McLowery jumped behind Frank's horse, drawing his gun and shooting under the animal's neck at Morgan Earp. The bullet cut Morgan's coat. Billy Clanton shot a second and a third time at Wyatt, missing with both as Morgan turned loose on him, aiming for Billy's stomach, but hitting the cowboy's gun hand.

Sensing that Tom McLowery was now the most dangerous adver-

sary, Wyatt ignored Billy Clanton's fire as Tom again shot underneath the pony's neck and hit Morg.

Tom McLowery must be forced into the open. Wyatt shot at the
pony behind which the cowboy crouched, aiming for the withers.
The pony jumped and stampeded for the street, the excitement
taking Billy Clanton's horse with him. As his brother's horse
started, Tom McLowery grabbed for the rifle in the saddle-boot,
but missed it.

At the upper end of the lot, Virgil Earp had been delayed in going
for his gun by the position of his hand and his grasp of Doc Holliday's
cane. Before Virgil could jerk his Colt's free, Billy Claiborne fired at
him twice and missed. Claiborne started across the corral toward the
side-door of Fly's gallery which opened for him, firing point-blank
at Virgil as he passed him and missing again. When Ike Clanton saw
Johnny Behan open the door for Claiborne, his braggart heart
funked. Ike had not drawn his gun; it swung at his hip as in his panic
he headed straight for Wyatt Earp.

Tom McLowery's second slug had hit Morgan Earp in the left
shoulder, glanced on a bone, ripped across the base of his neck, and
torn a gaping hole in the flesh of his right shoulder.

"I've got it!" Morg gasped, as he reeled under the shock.

"Get behind me and keep quiet," Wyatt said.

As Morgan was hit, Virgil Earp fired his first shot in the fight,
breaking Billy Clanton's gun-arm as it covered the cowboy's abdomen. Billy worked the "border shift," throwing his gun from right
to left hand.

Far from obeying Wyatt's command, Morgan, who saw Billy
Clanton's maneuver, shot Billy in the chest as Virgil put a slug into
Clanton's body, just underneath the twelfth rib.

Before Wyatt could throw down on Tom McLowery, as the pony
plunged away, Ike Clanton had covered the few feet across the corral
and seized Wyatt's left arm.

"Don't kill me, Wyatt! Don't kill me!" the pot-valiant Clanton
pleaded. "I'm not shooting!"

"This fight's commenced. Get to fighting or get out," Wyatt
answered, throwing Ike off. The gallery door was held open and Ike
fled after Claiborne.

Tom McLowery was firing his third shot, this at Wyatt as Ike
Clanton hung to the marshal's arm, when Doc Holliday turned loose
both barrels of his shotgun simultaneously from the road. Tom's shot

went wild and McLowery started on a run around the corner of the assay office toward Third Street. Disgusted with a weapon that could miss at such a range, Holliday hurled the sawed-off shotgun after Tom with an oath and jerked his nickel-plated Colt's. Ten feet around the corner, Tom McLowery fell dead with the double charge of buckshot in his belly and a slug from Wyatt Earp's six-gun under his ribs which had hit him as he ran.

Frank McLowery was nearing the road, left hand clutching his abdomen, the right working his gun as he staggered on. Billy Clanton was still on his feet and following. Frank shot at Wyatt. The slug struck short. So did another he sent at Morg.

Wyatt heard the crash of glass from the side-window of Fly's gallery, where Claiborne and Sheriff Behan stood. Two shots from the window followed.

"Look out, boys!" Wyatt called. "You're getting it in the back!"

Morgan Earp wheeled to face this new danger, stumbled and fell, but Doc Holliday sent two bullets through the window. Shooting from the gallery stopped. At this juncture Ike Clanton darted from a rear door across the alley and into the stalls of the O. K. Corral, flinging his fully loaded six-gun into a corner of the yard as he ran. Doc sent two shots after Ike, but was a split-second late. Doc wheeled to face Frank McLowery, who had reached the street, drawn himself upright and, less than ten feet away, was steeling himself for steady aim at Holliday.

"I've got you, you so-and-so such-and-such," McLowery snarled.

"Think so?" Doc found wit to inquire.

When Morgan fell, he rolled to bring his gun-arm free and brought up at full length on his side facing McLowery and Holliday.

"Look out, Doc!" Morg called, shooting as he lay.

McLowery's, Holliday's, and Morgan Earp's pistols roared together. Doc winced and swore. Frank McLowery threw both hands high in the air, spun on his boot-heels, and dropped on his face. Morg got to his feet. Morgan's bullet had drilled clear through Frank McLowery's head, just behind the ears; Doc's had hit the outlaw in the heart. Either would have killed him instantly, while Wyatt's first shot, which had torn through his abdomen, would have brought death in another few seconds. Frank's last bullet had hit Doc Holliday's hip-holster, glanced, and shaved a strip of skin from his back.

Meanwhile, as Wyatt sent a bullet into Tom McLowery when he ran, Virgil Earp and Billy Clanton were shooting it out. Billy was making for the street, firing as he went, when he hit Virgil in the leg. Virgil kept his feet and returned the fire as Wyatt shifted his attention to Billy Clanton. Wyatt's shot hit Billy in the hips, and as the cowboy fell, Virgil's bullet tore through his hat and creased his scalp. With his last ounce of gameness, the rustler raised to a sitting posture and tried to steady his wavering gun on his knee. While Wyatt and Virgil hesitated over shooting at a man who plainly was done, Billy Clanton slumped in the dust. The firing ceased. Billy Claiborne ran from the rear of Fly's on through toward Allen Street. Holliday's trigger clicked futilely.

"What in hell did you let Ike Clanton get away like that for, Wyatt?" Doc complained.

"He wouldn't jerk his gun," Wyatt answered.

The fight was over.

Frank McLowery was dead in the middle of Fremont Street. Tom McLowery's body was around the Third Street corner. Billy Clanton was still breathing but died within a few minutes.

Virgil's leg-wound and Morgan's, in the shoulder, were ugly, but not serious. Doc Holliday's scratch was superficial.

Four of the cowboys had fired seventeen shots; Ike Clanton, whose brag and bluster brought on the battle, none. They had scored just three hits, not one of which put an adversary out of action.

The three Earps and Holliday had fired seventeen shots, four of which Doc Holliday had thrown at random into the gallery window and after Ike Clanton. The remaining thirteen had been hits. Any one of Frank McLowery's wounds would have been fatal. Billy Clanton had been hit six times, three fatally. Either of Tom McLowery's wounds would have killed him, and Wyatt's shot which stampeded the cow-ponies was a bull's-eye; it served Wyatt's exact purpose, stinging the animal to violent action, but not crippling him beyond ability to get out of the way.

As the smoke of battle lifted, Wyatt turned to look up Fremont Street. A yelling mob was headed toward him. The Citizens' Safety Committee had started for the corral in a column of twos, but excitement overcame discipline.

"I distinctly remember," writes John P. Clum, "that the first set of twos was made up of Colonel William Herring, an attorney, and Milton Clapp, cashier of a local bank. Colonel Herring was tall and portly, with an imposing dignity, while Milton Clapp was short and lean and wore large spectacles. The striking contrast in stature and bearing between these two leaders of the 'column' registered an indelible picture which still intrudes as a flash of comedy in an exceedingly grave moment."

Virgil and Morgan Earp were taken to their homes by the Vigilantes and a guard of twenty posted around the Earp property to prevent retaliation by friends of the dead outlaws. Other Vigilante squads patrolled the Tombstone streets.

Ike Clanton was found hiding in a Mexican dancehall, south of Allen Street, and Billy Claiborne near by. They were taken to the calaboose and guarded to prevent either escape or lynching. Ike, at least, had small desire for freedom; he begged to be locked up and protected.

After his brothers had been cared for, Wyatt Earp walked up Fremont Street with Fred Dodge. Across from the sheriff's office, above the O. K. Corral, Johnny Behan stopped them.

"Wyatt," the sheriff said, "I'm arresting you."

"For what?" Wyatt asked in astonishment.

"Murder," Behan answered.

Wyatt's eyes turned cold and his voice hard.

"Behan," he said, "you threw us. You told us you had disarmed those rustlers. You lied to throw us off and get us murdered. *You* arrest *me?* Not today, nor tomorrow either. I'll be where any respectable person can arrest me any time he wants to, but don't you or any of your cheap errand-boys try it."

The sheriff walked away.

That afternoon a coroner's jury refused to hold the Earps and Holliday for death of the cowboys. Johnny Behan, principal witness at the inquiry, was deeply chagrined. At this time Behan thought himself the sole eye-witness to the fight in the corral, other than the participants. He so boasted to C. S. Fly. Fly had seen something of the battle and had noted other witnesses of whom Behan was unaware. Fly was a Vigilante, and close-mouthed. He reported Behan's belief to the Safety Committee, which sagely decided to give the talkative little sheriff all the rope he'd take.

One item which the coroner did uncover was that the three dead outlaws had, among them, more than six thousand dollars in currency, and that Ike Clanton and Billy Claiborne also had carried large sums of cash into the battle. This substantiated subsequent testimony that the rustlers had planned to kill the Earps and Holliday and ride for Old Mexico to stay until public resentment subsided.

The Cochise County grand jury was sitting at Tombstone at the time of the battle in the O. K. Corral and the Vigilantes asked that body to investigate the killings immediately. Behan, still believing there were no non-participating witnesses to contradict him, testified before the grand jury, as did Ike Clanton. Numerous Tombstone citizens were called, but the Earps did not appear. The grand jury announced that it could find no reason to indict four duly appointed peace officers for performance of necessary duty.

Ike Clanton left the calaboose and went with Johnny Behan to the office of *The Nugget*. Wes Fuller and Billy Claiborne were called into conference. With the next issue, *The Nugget* began the prosecution for Outlawry *vs.* Wyatt Earp.

Eugene Manlove Rhodes (1869–1934)

EUGENE MANLOVE RHODES, nicknamed the Cowboy Chronicler, was born in Tekumseh, Nebraska, in January 1869, and moved to New Mexico with his family in 1881, the year that Billy the Kid was killed by Pat Garrett. As a teenager, Rhodes worked as a cowhand. He was an avid reader and was largely self-educated. He attended the University of the Pacific in California, where he began writing anonymously for the college newspaper. After two years he ran out of funds and had to leave college. For the next twenty-five years he worked as a cowboy, ranch hand, horse-breaker, miner, school-teacher, blacksmith, homesteader, carpenter, and rancher. After losing his ranch, he moved East, where he began writing again. Rhodes wrote seven novels during his lifetime (mostly serialized in magazines), but was never financially successful.

"The Trouble Man," like many of his stories, was published in *The Saturday Evening Post* (1909).

The Trouble Man

FROM *The Saturday Evening Post*, 1909

I

Billy Beebe did not understand. There was no disguising the unpalatable fact: Rainbow treated him kindly. It galled him. Ballinger, his junior in Rainbow, was theme for ridicule and biting jest, target for contumely and abuse; while his own best efforts were met with grave, unfailing courtesy.

Yet the boys liked him; Billy was sure of that. And so far as the actual work was concerned, he was at least as good a roper and brand reader as Ballinger, quicker in action, a much better rider.

In irrelevant and extraneous matters—brains, principle, training, acquirements—Billy was conscious of unchallenged advantage. He was from Ohio, eligible to the Presidency, of family, rich, a college man; yet he had abandoned laudable moss-gathering, to become a rolling, bounding, riotous stone. He could not help feeling that it was rather noble of him. And then to be indulgently sheltered as an honored guest, how beloved soever! It hurt.

Not for himself alone was Billy grieved. Men paired on Rainbow. "One stick makes a poor fire"—so their word went. Billy sat at the feet of John Wesley Pringle—wrinkled, wind-brown Gamaliel. Ballinger was the disciple of Jeff Bransford, gay, willful, questionable man. Billy did not like him. His light banter, lapsing unexpectedly from broad Doric to irreproachable New English, carried in solution audacious, glancing disrespect of convention, established institutions, authorities, axioms, "accepted theories of irregular verbs"—too elusive for disproof, too intolerably subversive to be ignored. That Ballinger, his shadow, was accepted man of action, while Billy was still an outsider, was, in some sense, a reflection on Pringle. Vicarious jealousy was added to the pangs of wounded self-love.

Billy was having ample time for reflection now, riding with Pringle up the Long Range to the Block roundup. Through the slow, dreamy days they threaded the mazed ridges and cañons falling eastward to the Pecos from Guadalupe, Sacramento and White Mountain. They drove their string of thirteen horses each; tough circlers, wise cutting-hoses, sedate night horses and patient old Steamboat, who, in the performance of pack duty, dropped his proper designation to be injuriously known as "the Wagon."

Their way lay through the heart of the Lincoln County War country—on winding trails, by glade and pine-clad mesa; by clear streams, bell-tinkling, beginning, with youth's eager haste, their journey to the far-off sea; by Seven Rivers, Bluewater, the Feliz, Penasco and Silver Spring.

Leisurely they rode, with shady halt at midday—leisurely, for an empire was to be worked. It would be months before they crossed the divide at Nogal, "threw in" with Bransford and Ballinger, now representing Rainbow with the Bar W, and drove home together down the west side.

While Billy pondered his problem Pringle sang or whistled tirelessly—old tunes of amazing variety, ranging from Nancy Lee and Auld Robin Gray to La Paloma Azul or the Nogal Waltz. But ever, by ranch house or brook or pass, he paused to tell of deeds there befallen in the years of old war, deeds violent and bloody, yet half redeemed by hardihood and unflinching courage.

Pringle's voice was low and unemphatic; his eyes were ever on the long horizon. Trojan nor Tyrian he favored, but as he told the Homeric tale of Buckshot Roberts, while they splashed through the broken waters of Ruidoso and held their winding way through the cutoff of Cedar Creek, Billy began dimly to understand.

Between him and Rainbow the difference was in kind, not in degree. The shadow of old names lay heavy on the land; these resolute ghosts yet shaped the acts of men. For Rainbow the Roman *virtus* was still the one virtue. Whenever these old names had been spoken, Billy remembered, men had listened. Horseshoers had listened at their shoeing; cardplayers had listened while the game went on; by campfires other speakers had ceased their talk to listen without comment. Not ill-doers, these listeners, but quiet men, kindly, generous; yet the tales to which they gave this tribute were too often of ill deeds. As if they asked not "Was this well done?" but rather "Was this done indeed—so that no man could have done more?" Were the

deed good or evil, so it were done utterly it commanded admiration—therefore, imitation.

Something of all this he got into words. Pringle nodded gravely.
"You've got it sized up, my son," he said. "Rainbow ain't strictly up
to date and still holds to them elder ethics, like Norval on the
Grampian Hills, William Dhu Tell, and the rest of them neck-or-
nothing boys. This Mr. Rolando, that Eusebio sings about, give our
sentiments to a T-Y-ty. He was scrappy and always blowin' his own
horn, but, by jings, he delivered the goods as per invoice and could
take a major league lickin' with no whimperin'. This Rolando he
don't hold forth about gate money or individual percentages. 'Get
results for your team,' he says. 'Don't flinch, don't foul, hit the line
hard, here goes nothin!'

"That's a purty fair code. And it's all the one we got. Pioneerin' is
troublesome—pioneer is all the same word as pawn, and you throw
away a pawn to gain a point. When we drive in a wild bunch, when
we top off the boundin' bronco, it may look easy, but it's always a
close thing. Even when we win we nearly lose; when we lose we
nearly win. And that forms the stay-with-it-Bill-you're doin'-well
habit. See?

"So, we mostly size a fellow up by his abilities as a trouble man.
Any kind of trouble—not necessarily the fightin' kind. If he goes the
route, if he sets no limit, if he's enlisted for the war—why, you
naturally depend on him.

"Now, take you and Jeff. Most ways you've got the edge on him.
But you hold by rules and formulas and laws. There's things you
must do or mustn't do—because somebody told you so. You go into
a project with a mental reservation not to do anything indecorous
or improper; also, to stop when you've taken a decent lickin'. But
Jeff don't aim to stop while he can wiggle; and he makes up new
rules as he goes along, to fit the situation. Naturally, when you get
in a tight place you waste time rememberin' what the authorities
prescribe as the neat thing. Now, Jeff consults only his own self, and
he's mostly unanimous. Mebbe so you both do the same thing,
mebbe not. But Jeff does it first. You're a good boy, Billy, but
there's only one way to find out if you're a square peg or a round
one."

"How's that?" demanded Billy, laughing, but half vexed.

"Get in the hole," said Pringle.

II

"Aw, stay all night! What's the matter with you fellows? I haven't seen a soul for a week. Everybody's gone to the round-up." Wes' shook his head: "Can't do it, Jimmy. Got to go out to good grass. You're all eat out here."

"I'll side you," said Jimmy decisively. "I got a lot of stored-up talk I've got to get out of my system. I know a bully place to make camp. Box cañon to hobble your horses in, good grass, and a little tank of water in the rocks for cookin'. Bring along your little old Wagon, and I'll tie on a hunk of venison to feed your faces with. Get there by dark."

"How come you didn't go to the work your black self?" asked Wes', as Beebe tossed his rope on the Wagon and led him up.

Jimmy's twinkling eyes lit up his beardless face. "They left me here to play shinny-on-your-own-side," he explained.

"Shinny?" echoed Billy.

"With the three Rivers sheep," said Jimmy. "I'm to keep them from crossing the mountain."

"Oh, I see. You've got an agreement that the east side is for cattle and the west side for sheep."

Jimmy's face puckered. "Agreement? H'm yes, leastways, I'm agreed. I didn't ask them, but they've got the general idea. When I ketch 'em over here I drive them back. As I don't ever follow 'em beyond the summit they ought to savvy my the'ries by this time."

Pringle opened the gate. "Let's mosey along—they've got enough water. Which way, kid?"

"Left-hand trail," said Jimmy, falling in behind.

"But why don't you come to an understanding with them and fix on a dividing line?" insisted Beebe.

Jimmy lolled sidewise in his saddle, cocking an impish eye at his inquisitor. "Reckon ye don't have no sheep down Rainbow way? Thought not. Right there's the point exactly. They have a dividing line. They carry it with 'em wherever they go. For the cattle won't graze where sheep have been. Sheep protects their own range, but we've got to look after ours or they'd drive us out. But the understanding's all right, all right. They don't speak no English, and I don't know no *paisano* talk, but I've fixed up a signal code they savvy as well's if they was all college aluminums."

"Oh, yes—sign talk," said Billy. "I've heard of that." Wes' turned his head aside.

"We-ell, not exactly. Sound talk'd be nearer. One shot means 'Git!' two means 'Hurry up!' and three—"

"But you've no right to do that," protested Billy warmly. "They've got just as much right here as your cattle, haven't they?"

"Surest thing they have—if they can make it stick," agreed Jimmy cordially. "And we've got just as much right to keep 'em off if we can. And we can. There ain't really no right to it. It's Uncle Sam's land we both graze on, and Unkie is some busy with conversation on natural resources, and keepin' republics up in South America and down in Asia, and selectin' texts for coins and infernal revenue stamps, and upbuildin' Pittsburgh, and keepin' up the price of wool, and fightin' all the time to keep the laws from bein' better'n the Constitution, like a Bawston puncher trimmin' a growin' colt's foot down to fit last year's shoes. Shucks! He ain't got no time to look after us. We just got to do our own regulatin' or git out."

"How would you like it yourself?" demanded Billy.

Jimmy's eyes flashed. "If my brain was to leak out and I subsequent took to sheep-herdin', I'd like to see any dern puncher drive me out," he declared belligerently.

"Then you can't complain if—"

"He don't," interrupted Pringle. "None of us complain—nary a murmur. If the sheep men want to go they go, an' a little shootin' up the contagious vicinity don't hurt 'em none. It's all over oncet the noise stops. Besides, I think they mostly sorter enjoy it. Sheepherdin' is might dull business, and a little excitement is mighty welcome. It gives 'em something to look forward to. But if they feel hostile they always get the first shot for keeps. That's a mighty big percentage in their favor, and the reports on file with the War Department shows that they generally get the best of it. Don't you worry none, my son. This ain't no new thing. It's been goin' on ever since Abraham's outfit and the L O T boys got to scrappin' on the Jordan range, and then some before that. After Abraham took to the hill country, I remember, somebody jumped one of his wells and two of Isaac's. It's been like that, in the shortgass countries ever since. Human nature's not changed much. By jings! There they be now!"

Through the twilight the winding trail climbed the side of a long ridge. To their left was a deep, impassable cañon; beyond that a parallel ridge; and from beyond that ridge came the throbbing, drumming clamor of a sheep herd.

"The son of a gun!" said Jimmy. "He means to camp in our box cañon. I'll show him!" He spurred by the grazing horses and clattered on in the lead, striking fire from the stony trail.

On the shoulder of the further ridge heaved a gray fog, spreading, rolling slowly down the hillside. The bleating, the sound of myriad trampling feet, the multiplication of bewildering echoes, swelled to a steady, unchanging, ubiquitous tumult. A dog suddenly topped the ridge; another; then a Mexican herder bearing a long rifle. With one glance at Jimmy beyond the blackshadowed gulf he began turning the herd back, shouting to the dogs. They ran in obedient haste to aid, sending the stragglers scurrying after the main bunch.

Jimmy reined up, black and gigantic against the skyline. He drew his gun. Once, twice, thrice, he shot. The fire streamed out against the growing dark. The bullets, striking the rocks, whined spitefully. The echoes took up the sound and sent it crashing to and fro. The sheep rushed huddling together, panic-stricken. Herder and dogs urged them on. The herder threw up a hand and shouted.

"That boy's shootin' mighty close to the *paisano*," muttered Pringle. "He orter quit now. Reckon he's showin' off a leetle." He raised his voice in warning. "Hi! you Jimmy!" he called. "He's a-goin'! Let him be!"

"*Vamos! Hi-i!*" shrilled Jimmy gayly. He fired again. The Mexican clapped his hand to his leg with an angry scream. With the one movement he sank to his knees, his long rifle fell to a level, cuddled to his shoulder, spitting fire. Jimmy's hand flew up; his gun dropped; he clutched at the saddle-horn, missed it, fell heavily to the ground. The Mexican dropped out of sight behind the ridge. It had been but a scant minute since he first appeared. The dogs followed with the remaining sheep. The ridge was bare. The dark fell fast.

Jimmy lay on his face. Pringle turned him over and opened his shirt.

He was quite dead.

III

From Malagra to Willow Spring, the net available water, is the longest jump on the Bar W range. Working the "Long Lane" fenced by

Malpais and White Mountain is easy enough. But after cutting out and branding there was the long wait for the slow day herd, the tedious holding to water from insufficient troughs. It was late when the day's "cut" was thrown in with the herd, sunset when the bobtail had aught their night horses and relieved the weary day herders. The bobtail moves the herd to the bed ground—some distance from camp, to avoid mutual annoyance and alarm—and holds it while night horses are caught and supper eaten. A thankless job, missing the nightly joking and banter over the day's work. Then the first guard comes on and the bobtail goes, famished, to supper. It breakfasts by starlight, relieves the last guard, and holds cattle while breakfast is eaten, beds rolled and horses caught, turning them over to the day herders at sunup.

Bransford and Ballinger were two of the five bobtailers, hungry, tired, dusty and cross. With persuasive, soothing song they trotted around the restless cattle, with hasty, envious glances for the merry groups around the chuck wagon. The horse herd was coming in; four of the boys were butchering a yearling; beds were being dragged out and unrolled. Shouts of laughter arose; they were baiting the victim of some mishap by making public an exaggerated version of his discomfiture.

Turning his back on the camp, Jeff Bransford became aware of a man riding a big white horse down the old military road from Nogal way. The horse was trotting, but wearily; passing the herd he whinnied greeting, again wearily.

The cattle were slow to settle down. Jeff made several circlings before he had time for another campward glance. The horse herd was grazing off, and the boys were saddling and staking their night horses; but the stranger's horse, still saddled, was tied to a soapweed.

Jeff sniffed. "Oh, Solomon was sapient and Solomon was wise!" he crooned, keeping time with old Summersault's steady fox-trot. "And Solomon was marvelously wide between the eyes!" He sniffed again, his nose wrinkled, one eyebrow arched, one corner of his mouth pulled down; he twisted his mustache and looked sharply down his nose for consultation, pursing his lips. "H'm! That's funny!" he said aloud. "That horse is some tired. Why don't he turn him loose? Bransford, you old fool, sit up and take notice! 'Eternal vigilance is the price of liberty.'"

He had been a tired and a hungry man. He put his weariness by as a garment, keyed up the slackened strings, and rode on with every faculty on the alert. It is to be feared that Jeff's conscience was not altogether void of offense toward his fellows.

A yearling pushed tentatively from the herd. Jeff let her go, fell in after her and circled her back to the bunch behind Clay Cooper. Not by chance. Clay was from beyond the divide.

"Know the new man, Clay?" Jeff asked casually, as he fell back to preserve the proper interval.

Clay turned his head. "Sure. Clem Littlefield, Bonita man."

When the first guard came at last Jeff was on the farther side and so the last to go in. A dim horseman overtook him and waved a sweeping arm in dismissal.

"We've got 'em! Light a rag, you hungry man!"

Jeff turned back slowly, so meeting all the relieving guard and noting that Squatty Robinson, of the VV, was not of them, Ollie Jackson taking his place.

He rode thoughtfully into camp. Staking his horse in the starlight he observed a significant fact. Squatty had not staked his regular night horse, but Alizan, his favorite. He made a swift investigation and found that not a man from the east had caught his usual night horse. Clay Cooper's horse was not staked, but tied short to a mesquit, with the bridle still on.

Pete Johnson, the foreman, was just leaving the fire for bed. Beyond the fire the east-side men were gathered, speaking in subdued voices. Ballinger, with loaded plate, sat down near them. The talking ceased. It started again at once. This time their voices rose clear and distinct in customary badinage.

"Why, this is face up," thought Jeff. "Trouble. Trouble from beyond the divide. They're going to hike shortly. They've told Pete that much, anyhow. Serious trouble—for they've kept it from the rest of them. Is it to my address? Likely. Old Wes' and Beebe are over there somewhere. If I had three guesses the first two'd be that them Rainbow chasers was in a tight."

He stumbled into the firelight, carrying his bridle, which he dropped by the wagon wheel. "This day's sure flown by like a week," he grumbled, fumbling around for cup and plate. "My stomach was just askin' was my throat cut."

As he bent over to spear a steak the tail of his eye took in the group beyond and intercepted a warning glance from Squatty to the stranger. There was an almost imperceptible thrusting motion of Squatty's chin and lips; a motion which included Jeff and the unconscious Ballinger. It was enough. Surmise, suspicion flamed to certainty. "My third guess," reflected Jeff sagely, "is just like the other two. Mr. John Wesley Pringle has been doing a running high jump or some such stunt, and has plumb neglected to come down."

He seated himself cross-legged and fell upon his supper vigorously, bandying quips and quirks with the bobtail as they ate. At last he jumped up, dropped his dishes clattering in the dishpan, and drew a long breath.

"I don't feel a bit hungry," he announced plaintively. "Gee! I'm glad I don't have to stand guard. I do hate to work between meals."

He shouldered his roll of bedding. "Good-by, old world—I'm going home!" he said, and melted into the darkness. Leo following, they unrolled their bed. But as Leo began pulling off his boots Jeff stopped him.

"Close that aperture in your face and keep it that way," he admonished guardedly. "You and me has got to do a ghost dance. Project around and help me find them Three Rivers men."

The Three Rivers men, Crosby and Os Hyde, were sound asleep. Awakened, they were disposed to peevish remonstrance.

"Keep quiet!" said Jeff, "Al, you slip on your boots and go tell Pete you and Os is goin' to Carrizo and that you'll be back in time to stand your guard. Tell him out loud. Then you come back here and you and Os crawl into our bed. I'll show him where it is while you're gone. You use our night horses. Me and Leo want to take yours."

"If there's anything else don't stand on ceremony," said Crosby. "Don't you want my toothbrush?"

"You hurry up," responded Jeff. "D'ye think I'm doin' this for fun? We're It. We got to prove an alibi."

"Oh!" said Al.

A few minutes later, the Three Rivers men disappeared under the tarp of the Rainbow bed, while the Rainbow men, on Three Rivers horses, rode silently out of camp, avoiding the firelit circle.

Once over the ridge, well out of sight and hearing from camp, Jeff turned up the draw to the right and circled back toward the Nogal road on a long trot.

"Beautiful night," observed Leo after an interval. "I just love to ride. How far is it to the asylum?"

"Leo," said Jeff, "you're a good boy—a mighty good boy. But I don't believe you'd notice it if the sun didn't go down till after dark."

He explained the situation. "Now, I'm going to leave you to hold the horses just this side of the Nogal road, while I go on afoot and eavesdrop. Them fellows'll be makin' big medicine when they come along here. I'll lay down by the road and get a line on their play. Don't you let them horses nicker."

Leo waited an interminable time before he heard the eastside men coming from camp. They passed by, talking, as Jeff had prophesied. After another small eternity Jeff joined him.

"I didn't get all the details," he reported. "But it seems that the Parsons City people has got it framed up to hang a sheepman some. Wes' is dead set against it—I didn't make out why. So there's a deadlock and we've got the casting vote. Call up your reserves, old man. We're due to ride around Nogal and beat that bunch to the divide."

It was midnight by the clock in the sky when they stood on Nogal divide. The air was chill. Clouds gathered blackly around Capitan, Nogal Peak and White Mountain. There was steady, low muttering of thunder; the far lightnings flashed pale and green and rose.

"Hustle along to Lincoln, Leo," commanded Jeff, "and tell the sheriff they state, positive, that the hangin' takes place prompt after breakfast. Tell him to bring a posse—and a couple of battleships if he's got 'em handy. Meantime, I'll go over and try what the gentle art of persuasion can do. So long! If I don't come back the mule's yours."

He turned up the right-hand road.

IV

"Well?" said Pringle.

"Light up!" said Uncle Pete. "Nobody's goin' to shoot at ye from the dark. We don't do business that way. When we come we'll come in daylight, down the big middle of the road. Light up. I ain't got no gun. I come over for one last try to make you see reason. I knowed thar weren't use talkin' to you when you was fightin' mad. That's why I got the boys to put it off till mawnin'. And I wanted to send to Angus and Salado and the Bar W for Jimmy's friends. He ain't got no kinnery here. They've come. They all see it the same way. Chavez killed Jimmy, and they're goin' to hang him. And, since they've come, there's too many of us for you to fight."

Wes' lit the candle. "Set down. Talk all you want, but talk low and don't wake Billy," he said as the flame flared up.

That he did not want Billy waked up, that there was not even a passing glance to verify Uncle Pete's statement as to being unarmed, was, considering Uncle Pete's errand and his own position, a complete and voluminous commentary on the men and ethics of that time and place.

Pete Burleson carefully arranged his frame on a bench, and glanced around.

On his cot Billy tossed and moaned. His fevered sleep was tortured by a phantasmagoria of broken and hurried dreams, repeating with monstrous exaggeration the crowded hours of the past day. The brain-stunning shock and horror of sudden, bloody death, the rude litter, the night-long journey with their awful burden, the doubtful aisles of pine with star 'galazies' wheeling beyond, the gaunt, bare hill above, the steep zigzag to the sleeping town, the flaming wrath of violent men—in his dream they came and went. Again, hasty messengers flashed across the haggard dawn; again, he shared the pursuit and capture of the sheep-herder. Sudden clash of unyielding wills; black anger; wild voices for swift death, quickly backed by wild, strong hands; Pringle's cool and steady defiance; his own hot, resolute protest; the prisoner's unflinching fatalism; the hard-won respite—all these and more—the lights, the swaying crowd, fierce faces black and bitter with inarticulate wrath—jumbled confusedly in shifting, unsequenced combinations leading ever to some incredible, unguessed catastrophe.

Beside him, peacefully asleep, lay the manslayer, so lately snatched from death, unconscious of the chain that bound him, oblivious of the menace of the coming day.

"He takes it pretty hard," observed Uncle Pete, nodding at Billy.

"Yes. He's never seen any sorrow. But he don't weaken one mite. I tried every way I could think of to get him out of here. Told him to sidle off down to Lincoln after the sheriff. But he was dead on to me."

"Yes? Well, he wouldn't 'a' got far, anyway," said Uncle Pete dryly. "We're watching every move. Still, it's pity he didn't try. We'd 'a' got him without hurtin' him, and he'd 'a' been out o' this."

Wes' made no answer. Uncle Pete stroked his grizzled beard reflectively. He filled his pipe with cut plug and puffed deliberately.

"Now, look here," he said slowly: "Mr. Procopio Chavez killed

Jimmy, and Mr. Procopio Chavez is going to hang. It wa'n't no weakenin' or doubt on my part that made me call the boys off yisterday evenin'. He's got to hang. I just wanted to keep you fellers from gettin' killed. There might 'a' been some sense in your fighting then, but there ain't now. There's too many of us."

"Me and Billy see the whole thing," said Wes', unmoved. "It was too bad Jimmy got killed, but he was certainly mighty brash. The sheep-herder was goin' peaceable, but Jimmy kept shootin', and shootin' close. When that splinter of rock hit the Mexican man he thought he was shot, and he turned loose. Reckon it hurt him like sin. There's a black-and-blue spot on his leg big as the palm of your hand. You'd 'a' done the same as he did.

"I ain't much enthusiastic about sheep-herders. In fact, I jerked my gun at the time; but I was way down the trail and he was out o' sight before I could shoot. Thinkin' it over careful, I don't see where this Mexican's got any hangin' comin'. You know, just as well as I do, no court's goin' to hang him on the testimony me and Billy's got to give in."

"I do," said Uncle Pete. "That's exactly why we're goin' to hang him ourselves. If we let him go it's just encouragin' the *pastores* to kill up some more of the boys. So we'll just stretch his neck. This is the last friendly warnin', my son. If you stick your fingers between the anvil and the hammer you'll get 'em pinched. 'Tain't any of your business, anyway. This ain't Rainbow. This is the White Mountain and we're strictly home rulers. And, moresoever, that war talk you made yesterday made the boys plumb sore."

"That war talk goes as she lays," said Pringle steadily. "No hangin' till after the shootin'. That goes."

"Now, now—what's the use?" remonstrated Uncle Pete. "Ye'll just get yourself hurted and 'twon't do the greaser any good. You might mebbe so stand us off in a good, thick 'dobe house, but not in this old shanty. If you want to swell up and be stubborn about it, it just means a grave apiece for you all and likely for some few of us."

"It don't make no difference to me," said Pringle, "if it means diggin' a grave in a hole in the cellar under the bottomless pit. I'm goin' to make my word good and do what I think's right."

"So am I, by Jupiter! Mr. Also Ran Pringle, it is a privilege to have known you!" Billy, half awake, covered Uncle Pete with a gun held in a steady hand. "Let's keep him here for a hostage and shoot him if they attempt to carry out their lynching," he suggested.

"We can't Billy. Put it down," said Pringle mildly. "He's here under flag of truce."

"I was tryin' to save your derned fool hides," said Uncle Pete benignantly.

"Well—'tain't no use. We're just talkin' round and round in a circle, Uncle Pete. Turn your wolf loose when you get ready. As I said before, I don't noways dote on sheepmen, but I seen this, and I've got to see that this poor devil gets a square deal. I got to!"

Uncle Pete sighed. "It's pity!" he said; "a great pity! Well, we're comin' quiet and peaceful. If there's any shootin' done you all have got to fire the first shot. We'll have the last one."

"Did you ever stop to think that the Rainbow men may not like this?" inquired Pringle. "If they're anyways dissatisfied they're liable to come up here and scratch your eyes out one by one."

"Jesso. That's why you're goin' to fire the first shot," explained Uncle Pete patiently. "Only for that—and likewise because it would be a sorter mean trick to do—we could get up on the hill and smoke you out with rifles at long range, out o' reach of your six-shooters. You all might get away, but the sheepherder's chained fast and we could shoot him to kingdom come, shack and all, in five minutes. But you've had fair warnin' and you'll get an even break. If you want to begin trouble it's your own lookout. That squares us with Rainbow."

"And you expect them to believe you?" demanded Billy.

"Believe us? Sure! Why shouldn't they!" said Uncle Pete simply. "Of course they'll believe us. It'll be so." He stood up and regarded them wistfully. "There don't seem to be any use o' sayin' any more, so I'll go. I hope there ain't no hard feelin's?"

"Not a bit!" said Pringle; but Billy threw his head back and laughed angrily. "Come, I like that! By Jove, if that isn't nerve for you! To wake a man up and announce that you're coming presently to kill him, and then expect to part the best of friends!"

"Ain't I doin' the friendly part?" demanded Uncle Pete stiffly. He was both nettled and hurt. "If I hadn't thought well of you fellers and done all I could for you, you'd 'a' been dead and done forgot about it by now. I give you all credit for doin' what you think is right, and you might do as much for me."

"Great Caesar's ghost! Do you want us to wish you good luck?" said Billy, exasperated almost to tears. "Have it your own way, by all means—you gentle-hearted old assassin! For my part, I'm going to do my level best to shoot you right between the eyes, but there won't be any hard feeling about it. I'll just be doing what I think is right—a duty I owe to the world. Say! I should think a gentleman of your sportsmanlike instincts would send over a gun for our prisoner. Twenty to one is big odds."

"Twenty to one is a purty good reason why you could surrender without no disgrace," rejoined Uncle Pete earnestly. "You can't make nothin' by fightin', cause you lose your point, anyway. And then, a majority of twenty to one—ain't that a good proof that you're wrong?"

"Now, Billy, you can't get around that. That's your own argument," cried Pringle, delighted. "You've stuck to it right along that you Republicans was dead right because you always get seven votes to our six. *Nux vomica,* you know."

Uncle Pete rose with some haste. "Here's where I go. I never could talk politics without gettin' mad," he said.

"Billy, you're certainly making good. You're a square peg. All the same, I wish," said Wes' Pringle plaintively, as Uncle Pete crunched heavily through the gravel, "that I could hear my favorite tune now."

Billy stared at him. "Does your mind hurt your head?" he asked solicitously.

"No, no—I'm not joking. It would do me good if I could only hear him sing it."

"Hear who sing what?"

"Why, hear Jeff Bransford sing The Little Eohippus—right now. Jeff's got the knack of doing the wrong thing at the right time. Hark! What's that?"

It was a firm footstep at the door, a serene voice low chanting:

> "There was once a little animal
> No bigger than a fox,
> And on five toes he scampered—"

"Good Lord!" said Billy. "It's the man himself."

Questionable Bransford stepped through the half-open door, closed it and set his back to it.

"That's my cue! Who was it said eavesdroppers never heard good of themselves?"

V

He was smiling, his step was light, his tones were cheerful, ringing. His eyes had looked on evil and terrible things. In this desperate pass they wrinkled to pleasant, sunny warmth. He was unhurried, collected, confident. Billy found himself wondering how he had found this man loud, arbitrary, distasteful.

Welcome, question, answer; daybreak paled the ineffectual candle. The Mexican still slept.

"I crawled around the opposition camp like a snake in the grass," said Jeff. "There's two things I observed there that's mightily in our favor. The first thing is, there's no whisky goin'. And the reason for that is the second thing—our one best big chance. Mister Burleson won't let 'em. Fact! Pretty much the entire population of the Pecos and tributary streams had arrived. Them that I know are mostly bad actors, and the ones I don't know looked real horrid to me; but your Uncle Pete is the bell mare. 'No booze!' he says, liftin' one finger; and that settled it. I reckon that when Uncle Simon Peter says 'Thumbs up!' those digits'll be elevated accordingly. If I can get him to see the gate the rest will only need a little gentle persuasion."

"I see you persuading them now," said Billy. "This is a plain case of the irresistible force and the immovable body."

"You will," said Jeff confidently. "You don't know what a jollier I am when I get down to it. Watch me! I'll show you a regular triumph of mind over matter."

"They're coming now," announced Wes' placidly. "Two by two, like the animals out o' the ark. I'm glad of it. I never was good at waitin'. Mr. Bransford will now oblige with his monologue entitled 'Givin' a bull the stop signal with a red flag.' Ladies will kindly remove their hats."

It was a grim and silent cavalcade. Uncle Pete rode at the head. As they turned the corner Jeff walked briskly down the path, hopped lightly on the fence, seated himself on the gatepost and waved an amiable hand.

"Stop, look, and listen!" said this cheerful apparition.

The procession stopped. A murmur, originating from the Bar W contingent, ran down the ranks. Uncle Pete reined up and demanded of him with marked disfavor: "Who in merry hell are you?"

Jeff's teeth flashed white under his brown moustache. "I'm Ali

Baba," he said, and paused expectantly. But the allusion was wasted on Uncle Pete. Seeing that no introduction was forthcoming, Jeff went on:

"I've been laboring with my friends inside, and I've got a proposition to make. As I told Pringle just now, I don't see any sense of us gettin' killed, and killin' a lot of you won't bring us alive again. We'd put up a pretty fight—a very pretty fight. But you'd lay us out sooner or later. So what's the use?"

"I'm mighty glad to see some one with a leetle old horse-sense," said Uncle Pete. "Your friends is dead game sports all right, but they got mighty little judgment. If they'd only been a few of us I wouldn't 'a' blamed 'em a mite for not givin' up. But we got too much odds of 'em."

"This conversation is taking an unexpected turn," said Jeff, making his eyes round. "I ain't named giving up that I remember of. What I want to do is to rig up a compromise."

"If there's any halfway place between a hung Mexican and a live one," said Uncle Pete, "mebbe we can. And if not, not. This ain't no time for triflin', young fellow."

"Oh, shucks! I can think of half a dozen compromises," said Jeff blandly. "We might play seven-up and not count any turned-up jacks. But I was thinking of something different. I realize that you outnumber us, so I'll meet you a good deal more than half way. First, I want to show you something about my gun. Don't anybody shoot, 'cause I ain't going to. Hope I may die if I do!"

"You will if you do. Don't worry about that," said Uncle Pete. "And maybe so, anyhow. You're delayin' the game."

Jeff took this for permission. "Everybody please watch and see there is no deception."

Holding the gun, muzzle up, so all could see, he deliberately extracted all the cartridges but one. The audience exchanged puzzled looks.

Jeff twirled the cylinder and returned the gun to its scabbard. "Now!" he said, sparkling with enthusiasm. "You all see that I've only got one cartridge. I'm in no position to fight. If there's any fighting I'm already dead. What happens to me has no bearing on the discussion. I'm out of it.

"I realize that there's no use trying to intimidate you fellows. Any of you would take a big chance with odds against you, and here the odds is for you. So, as far as I'm concerned, I substitute a certainty for chance. I don't want to kill up a lot of rank strangers—or friends, either. There's nothing in it.

"Neither can I go back on old Wes' and Billy. So I take a half-way course. Just to manifest my entire disapproval, if any one makes a move to go through that gate I'll use my one shot—and it won't be on the man goin' through the gate, either. Nor yet on you, Uncle Pete. You're the leader. So, if you want to give the word, go it! I'm not going to shoot you. Nor I ain't going to shoot any of the Bar W push. They're free to start the ball rolling."

Uncle Pete, thus deprived of the initiatory power, looked helplessly around the Bar W push for confirmation. They nodded in concert. "He'll do whatever he says," said Clay Cooper.

"Thanks," said Jeff pleasantly, "for this unsolicited testimonial. Now, boys, there's no dare about this. Just cause and effect. All of you are plumb safe to make a break—but one. To show you that there's nothing personal about it, no dislike or anything like that, I'll tell you how I picked that one. I started at some place near both ends or the middle and counted backward, or forward, sayin' to myself, 'Intra, mintra, cutra, corn, apple seed and brier thorn,' and when I got to 'thorn' that man was stuck. That's all. Them's the rules."

That part of Uncle Pete's face visible between beard and hat was purple through the brown. He glared at Jeff, opened his mouth, shut it tightly, and breathed heavily through his nose. He looked at his horse's ears, he looked at the low sun, he looked at the distant hills; his gaze wondered disconsolately back to the twinkling indomitable eyes of the man on the gatepost. Uncle Pete sighed deeply.

"That's good! I'll just about make the wagon by noon," he remarked gently. He took his quirt from his saddle-horn. "Young man," he said gravely, flicking his horse's flank, "any time you're out of a job come over and see me." He waved his hand, nodded, and was gone.

Clay Cooper spurred up and took his place, his black eyes snapping. "I like a damned fool," he hissed; "but you suit me too well!"

The forty followed; some pausing for quip or jest, some in frowning silence. But each, as he passed that bright, audacious figure, touched his hat in salute to a gallant foe.

Squatty Robinson was the last. He rode close up and whispered confidentially:

"I want you should do me a favor, Jeff. Just throw down on me and take my gun away. I don't want to go back to camp with any such tale as this."

"You see, Billy," explained Jeff, "you mustn't dare the denizens—never! They dare. They're uncultured; their lives ain't noways valuable to society and they know it. If you notice, I took pains not to dare anybody. Quite otherhow. I merely stated annoyin' consequences to some other fellow, attractive as I could, but impersonal. Just like I'd tell you: 'Billy, I wouldn't set the oil can on the fire—it might boil over.'

"Now, if I'd said: 'Uncle Pete, if anybody makes a break I'll shoot your eye out, anyhow,' there'd 'a' been only one dignified course open to him. Him and me would now be dear Alphonsing each other about payin' the ferryman.

"Spose I'd made oration to shoot the first man through the gate. Every man Jack would have come 'a-snuffin'—each one tryin' to be first. The way I put it up to 'em, to be first wasn't no graceful act—playin' safe at some one else's expense—and then they seen that some one else wouldn't be gettin' an equitable vibration. That's all there was to it. If there wasn't any first there couldn't conveniently be any second, so they went home. B-r-r-! I'm sleepy. Let's go by-by. Wake that dern lazy Mexican up and make him keep watch till the sheriff comes!"

Bertha Muzzy Bower (1871–1940)

BERTHA MUZZY BOWER was born in Minnesota in 1871. The Bower family moved West to Montana in 1888. She became a teacher in Montana and married at nineteen. Bower began writing short stories in 1900—her first work was published in serialized form in the magazine *Popular*. Bower's first commercial success was *Chip, of the Flying U Ranch*. Its success spawned several sequels.

Bower wrote tales of romance and adventure. Her books often had surprise endings, and she wasn't afraid to address controversial issues such as divorce and spousal abuse in her work.

Bower lived on a Montana ranch, married three times, and evolved into the best-known female crafter of Westerns, writing more than five dozen novels. The popularity of her work was not lost on Hollywood— twelve movies were made of her novels.

"The Trail Herd" is from *Cow Country* (1921).

The Trail Herd

FROM *Cow Country*, 1921

Day after day the trail herd plodded slowly to the north, following the buffalo trails that would lead to water, and the crude map of one who had taken a herd north and had returned with a tale of vast plains and no rivals. Always through the day the dust cloud hung over the backs of the cattle, settled into the clothes of those who followed, grimed the pink aprons of Buddy and his small sister Dulcie so that they were no longer pink. Whenever a stream was reached, mother searched patiently for clear water and an untrampled bit of bank where she might do the family washing, leaving Ezra to mind the children. But even so the crust and the wear and tear of travel remained to harass her fastidious soul.

Buddy remembered that drive as he could not remember the comfortable ranch house of his earlier babyhood. To him afterward it seemed that life began with the great herd of cattle. He came to know just how low the sun must slide from the top of the sky before the "point" would spread out with noses to the ground, pausing wherever a mouthful of grass was to be found. When these leaders of the herd stopped, the cattle would scatter and begin feeding. If there was water they would crowd the banks of the stream or pool, pushing and prodding one another with their great, sharp horns. Later, when the sun was gone and dusk crept out of nowhere, the cowboys would ride slowly around the herd, pushing it quietly into a smaller compass. Then, if Buddy were not too sleepy, he would watch the cattle lie down to chew their cuds in deep, sighing content until they slept. It reminded Buddy vaguely of when mother popped corn in a wire popper, a long time ago—before they all lived in a wagon and went with the herd. First one and two—then there would be three, four, five, as many as Buddy could count—then the whole herd would be lying down.

Buddy loved the camp-fires. The cowboys would sit around the one where his father and mother sat—mother with Dulcie in her arms—and they would smoke and tell stories, until mother told him it was time little boys were in bed. Buddy always wanted to know what they said after he had climbed into the big wagon where mother had made a bed, but he never found out. He could remember lying there listening sometimes to the niggers singing at their own campfire within call, Ezra always singing the loudest,—just as a bull always could be heard above the bellowing of the herd.

All his life, Ezra's singing and the monotonous bellowing of a herd reminded Buddy of one mysteriously terrible time when there weren't any rivers or any ponds or anything along the trail, and they had to be careful of the water and save it, and he and Dulcie were not asked to wash their faces. I think that miracle helped to fix the incident indelibly in Buddy's mind; that, and the bellowing of the cattle. It seemed a month to Buddy, but as he grew older he learned that it was three days they went without water.

The first day he did not remember especially, except that mother had talked about clean aprons that night, and failed to produce any. The second he recalled quite clearly. Father came to the wagons sometime in the night to see if mother was asleep. Their murmured talk wakened Buddy and he heard father say: "We'll hold 'em, all right, Lassie. And there's water ahead. It's marked on the trail map. Don't you worry—I'll stay up and help the boys. The cattle are uneasy—but we'll hold 'em."

The third day Buddy never forgot. That was the day when mother forgot that q stands for Quagga, and permitted Buddy to call it p, just for fun, because it looked so much like p. And when he said "w is water," mother made a funny sound and said right out loud, "Oh God, please!" and told Buddy to creep back and play with Sister—when Sister was asleep, and there were still x, y and z to say, let alone that mysterious And-so-forth which seemed to mean so much and so little and never was called upon to help spell a word. Never since he began to have lessons had mother omitted a single letter or cut the study hour down the teeniest little bit.

Buddy was afraid of something, but he could not think what it was that frightened him. He began to think seriously about water, and to listen uneasily to the constant lowing of the herd. The increased shouting of the niggers driving the lagging ones held a sudden significance. It occurred to him that the niggers had their hands full, and that they had never driven so big a "drag." It was hotter than ever, too, and they had twice stopped to yoke in fresh oxen. Ezra had boasted all along that ole Bawley would keep his end up till they got clah to Wyoming. But ole Bawley had stopped, and stopped, and at last had to be taken out of the yoke. Buddy began to wish they would hurry up and find a river.

None of the cowboys would take him on the saddle and let him ride, that day. They looked harassed—Buddy called it cross—when they rode up to the wagon to give their horses a few mouthfuls of water from the barrel. Step-and-a-Half couldn't spare any more, they told mother. He had declared at noon that he needed every drop he had for the cooking, and there would be no washing of dishes whatever. Later, mother had studied a map and afterwards had sat for a long while staring out over the backs of the cattle, her face white. Buddy thought perhaps mother was sick.

That day lasted hours and hours longer than any other day that Buddy could remember. His father looked cross, too, when he rode back to them. Once it was to look at the map which mother had studied. They talked together afterwards, and Buddy heard his father say that she must not worry; the cattle had good bottom, and could stand thirst better than a poor herd, and another dry camp would not really hurt anyone.

He had uncovered the water barrel and looked in, and had ridden straight over to the chuck-wagon, his horse walking alongside the high seat where Step-and-a-Half sat perched listlessly with a long-lashed oxwhip in his hand. Father had talked for a few minutes, and had ridden back scowling.

"That old scoundrel has got two ten-gallon kegs that haven't been touched!" he told mother. "Yo' all mustn't water any more horses out of your barrel Send the boys to Step-and-a-Half. Yo' all keep what you've got. The horses have got to have water—to-night it's going to be hell to hold the herd, and if anybody goes thirsty it'll be the men, not the horses. But yo' all send them to the other wagon, Lassie. Mind, now! Not a drop to anyone."

After father rode away, Buddy crept up and put his two short arms around mother. "Don't cry. I don't have to drink any water," he soothed her. He waited a minute and added optimistically, "Dere's a *bi—ig* wiver comin' pitty soon. Oxes smells water a hunerd miles. Ezra says so. An' las' night Crumpy was snuffin' an' snuffin'. I saw 'im do it. He smelt a *big* wiver. *That* bi-ig!" He spread his short arms as wide apart as they would reach, and smiled tremulously.

Mother squeezed Buddy so hard that he grunted.

"Dear little man, of course there is. *We* don't mind, do we? I—was feeling sorry for the poor cattle."

"De're firsty," Buddy stated solemnly, his eyes big. "De're bawlin' fer a drink of water. I guess de're *awful* firsty. Dere's a big wiver comin' now. Crumpy smelt a big wiver."

Buddy's mother stared across the arid plain parched into greater barrenness by the heat that had been unremitting for the past week. Buddy's faith in the big river she could not share. Somehow they had drifted off the trail marked on the map drawn by George Williams.

Williams had warned them to carry as much water as possible in barrels, as a precaution against suffering if they failed to strike water each night. He had told them that water was scarce, but that his cowboy scouts and the deep-worn buffalo trails had been able to bring him through with water at every camp save two or three. The Staked Plains, he said, would be the hardest drive. And this was the Staked Plains—and it was hard driving!

Buddy did not know all that until afterwards, when he heard father talk of the drive north. But he would have remembered that day and the night that followed, even though he had never heard a word about it. The bawling of the herd became a doleful chant of misery. Even the phlegmatic oxen that drew the wagons bawled and slavered while they strained forward, twisting their heads under the heavy yokes. They stopped oftener than usual to rest, and when Buddy was permitted to walk with the perspiring Ezra by the leaders, he wondered why the oxen's eyes were red, like Dulcie's when she had one of her crying spells.

At night the cowboys did not tie their horses and sit down while they ate, but stood by their mounts and bolted food hurriedly, one eye always on the restless cattle, that walked around and around, and would neither eat nor lie down, but lowed incessantly. Once a few animals came close enough to smell the water in a bucket where Frank Davis was watering his sweat-streaked horse, and Step-and-a-Half's wagon was almost upset before the maddened cattle could be driven back to the main herd.

"No use camping," Bob Birnie told the boys gathered around Step-and-a-Half's Dutch ovens. "The cattle won't stand. We'll wear ourselves and them out trying to hold 'em—they may as well be hunting water as running in circles. Step-and-a-Half, keep your cooked grub handy for the boys, and yo' all pack up and pull out.

We'll turn the cattle loose and follow. If there's any water in this damned country they'll find it."

Years afterwards, Buddy learned that his father had sent men out to hunt water, and that they had not found any. He was ten when this was discussed around a spring roundup fire, and he had studied the matter for a few minutes and then had spoken boldly his mind.

"You oughta kept your horses as thirsty as the cattle was, and I bet they'd a' found that water," he criticized, and was sent to bed for his tactlessness. Bob Birnie himself had thought of that afterwards, and had excused the oversight by saying that he had depended on the map, and had not foreseen a three-day dry drive.

However that may be, that night was a night of panicky desperation. Ezra walked beside the oxen and shouted and swung his lash, and the oxen strained forward bellowing so that not even Dulcie could sleep, but whimpered fretfully in her mother's arms. Buddy sat up wide-eyed and watched for the big river, and tried not to be a 'fraid-cat and cry like Dulcie.

It was long past starry midnight when a little wind puffed out of the darkness and the oxen threw up their heads and sniffed, and put a new note into their "M-*baw-aw-aw*-mm!" They swung sharply so that the wind blew straight into the front of the wagon, which lurched forward with a new impetus.

"Glo-ory t' Gawd, Missy! Dey smells watah, sho's yo' bawn!" sobbed Ezra as he broke into a trot beside the wheelers. "'Tain't fur—lookit dat-ah huhd a-goin' it! No 'm, Missy, *dey* ain't woah out—dey smellin' watah an' dey'm gittin' *to* it! 'Tain't fur, Missy."

Buddy clung to the back of the seat and stared round-eyed into the gloom. He never forgot that lumpy shadow which was the herd, traveling fast in dust that obscured the nearest stars. The shadow humped here and there as the cattle crowded forward at a shuffling half trot, the *click*-swash of their shambling feet treading close on one another. The rapping tattoo of wide-spread horns clashing against wide-spread horns filled him with a formless terror, so that he let go the seat to clutch at mother's dress. He was not afraid of cattle—they were as much a part of his world as were Ezra and the wagon and the camp-fires—but he trembled with the dread which no man could name for him.

These were not the normal, everyday sounds of the herd. The herd had somehow changed from plodding animals to one over-whelming purpose that would sweep away anything that came in its path. Two thousand parched throats and dust-dry tongues—and suddenly the smell of water that would go gurgling down two thousand eager gullets, and every intervening second a cursed delay against which the cattle surged blindly. It was the mob spirit, when the mob was fighting for its very existence.

Over the bellowing of the cattle a yelling cowboy now and then made himself heard. The four oxen straining under their yokes broke into a lumbering gallop lest they be outdistanced by the herd, and Dulcie screamed when the wagon lurched across a dry wash and almost upset, while Ezra plied the ox-whip and yelled frantically at first one ox and then another, inventing names for the new ones. Buddy drew in his breath and held it until the wagon rolled on four wheels instead of two,—but he did not scream.

Still the big river did not come. It seemed to Buddy that the cattle would never stop running. Tangled in the terror was Ezra's shouting as he ran alongside the wagon and called to Missy that it was "dat ole Crumpy actin' the fool," and that the wagon wouldn't upset. "No'm, dey's jest in a hurry to git dere fool haids sunk to de eyes in dat watah. Dey ain't aimin' to run away—no'm, dish yer ain't no stampede!"

Perhaps Buddy dozed. The next thing he remembered, day was breaking, with the sun all red, seen through the dust. The herd was still going, but now it was running and somehow the yoked oxen were keeping close behind, lumbering along with heads held low and the sweat reeking from their spent bodies. Buddy heard dimly his mother's sharp command to Ezra:

"Stand back, Ezra! We're not going to be caught in that terrible trap. They're piling over the bank ahead of us. Get away from the leaders. I am going to shoot."

Buddy crawled up a little higher on the blankets behind the seat, and saw mother steady herself and aim the rifle straight at Crumpy. There was the familiar, deafening roar, the acrid smell of black powder smoke, and Crumpy went down loosely, his nose rooting the trampled ground for a space before the gun belched black smoke again and Crumpy's yoke-mate pitched forward. The wagon stopped so abruptly that Buddy sprawled helplessly on his back like an overturned beetle.

He saw mother stand looking down at the wheelers, that backed and twisted their necks under their yokes. Her lips were set firmly together, and her eyes were bright with purple hollows beneath. She held the rifle for a moment, then set the butt of it on the "jockey box" just in front of the dashboard. The wheelers, helpless between the weight of the wagon behind and the dead oxen in front, might twist their necks off but they could do no damage.

"Unyoke the wheelers, Ezra, and let the poor creatures have their chance at the water," she cried sharply, and Ezra, dodging the horns of the frantic brutes, made shift to obey.

Fairly on the bank of the sluggish stream with its flood-worn channel and its treacherous patches of quicksand, the wagon thus halted by the sheer nerve and quick-thinking of mother became a very small island in a troubled sea of weltering backs and tossing horns and staring eyeballs. Riders shouted and lashed unavailingly with their quirts, trying to hold back the full bulk of the herd until the foremost had slaked their thirst and gone on. But the herd was crazy for the water, and the foremost were plunged headlong into the soft mud where they mired, trampled under the hoofs of those who came crowding from behind.

Someone shouted, close to the wagon yet down the bank at the edge of the water. The words were indistinguishable, but a warning was in the voice. On the echo of that cry, a man screamed twice.

"Ezra!" cried mother fiercely. "It's Frank Davis—they've got him down, somehow. Climb over the backs of the cattle—there's no other way—and *get him!*"

"Yas'm, Missy!" Ezra called back, and then Buddy saw him go over the herd, scrambling, jumping from back to back.

Buddy remembered that always, and the funeral they had later in the day, when the herd was again just trail-weary cattle feeding hungrily on the scanty grass. Down at the edge of the creek the carcasses of many dead animals lay half-buried in the mud. Up on a little knoll where a few stunted trees grew, the negroes dug a long, deep hole. Mother's eyes were often filled with tears that day, and the cowboys scarcely talked at all when they gathered at the chuckwagon.

After a while they all went to the hole which the negroes had dug, and there was a long Something wrapped up in canvas. Mother wore her best dress, which was black, and father and all the boys had shaved their faces and looked very sober. The negroes stood back in a group by themselves, and every few minutes Buddy saw them draw their tattered shirtsleeves across their faces. And father—Buddy looked once and saw two tears running down father's cheeks. Buddy was shocked into a stony calm. He had never dreamed that fathers ever cried.

Mother read out of her Bible, and all the boys held their hats in front of them, with their hands clasped, and looked at the ground while she read. Then mother sang. She sang, "We shall meet beyond the river," which Buddy thought was a very queer song, because they were all there but Frank Davis; then she sang "Nearer, My God, to Thee." Buddy sang too, piping the notes accurately, with a vague pronunciation of the words and a feeling that somehow he was helping mother.

After that they put the long, canvas-wrapped Something down in the hole, and mother said "Our Father Who Art in Heaven," with Buddy repeating it uncertainly after her and pausing to say "*treth-patheth*" very carefully. Then mother picked up Dulcie in her arms, took Buddy by the hand and walked slowly back to the wagon, and would not let him turn to see what the boys were doing.

It was from that day that Buddy missed Frank Davis, who had mysteriously gone to Heaven, according to mother. Buddy's interest in Heaven was extremely keen for a time, and he asked questions which not even mother could answer. Then his memory of Frank Davis blurred. But never his memory of that terrible time when the Tomahawk outfit lost five hundred cattle in the dry drive and the stampede for water.

Edgar Beecher Bronson (1856–1917)

EDGAR BEECHER BRONSON was a Nebraska rancher, a West Texas cattleman, an African big-game hunter, a photographer, and later in life, the author of fiction and personal memoirs. He was the nephew of abolitionist Henry Ward Beecher. Born in Bradford County, Pennsylvania, Bronson went to New York as a very young man to write for the *New York Tribune*. In New York, Bronson met Clarence King, the first director of the United States Geological Survey, who was also owner of large mining and cattle operations. In 1877, Bronson went West with King to learn the cattle business. Bronson worked for one season in Wyoming before starting his own ranch in Sioux County, Nebraska.

Bronson came to writing later in life. He first published *Reminiscences of a Ranchman* in 1908, from which "End of the Trail" is taken. He published *The Red-Blooded Heroes of the Frontier* in 1910; "Triggerfingeritis" is from this work.

End of the Trail

FROM *Reminiscences of a Ranchman*, 1908

We were jogging along in the saddle across the divide between the Rawhide and the Niobrara, Concho Curly and I, *en route* from Cheyenne to the ranch to begin the spring calf round-up.

Travelling the lower trail, we had slept out on our saddle-blankets the night before, beside the sodden wreck of a fire in a little cottonwood grove on Rawhide.

While the night there passed was wretched and comfortless to the last degree, for even our slickers were an insufficient protection against the torrents of warm rain that fell upon us hour after hour, the curtain of gray morning mists that hedged us round about was scarce lifted at bidding of the new day's sun, before eyes, ears, and nostrils told us Nature had wrought one of her great miracles while we slept.

All seed life, somnolent so long in whatever earthly cells the winds and rains had assisted to entomb it, had awakened and arisen into a living force; tree vitality, long hibernating invisible, even in sorely wounded, lightning-riven, gray cottonwood torsos, was asserting itself; voices long still, absent God alone knows where, were gladly hailing the return of the spring.

We had lain down in a dull gray dead world, to awaken in a world pulsing with the life and bright with the colour of sprouting seed and revivifying sap.

Our eyes had closed on tree trunks gaunt and pale, a veritable spectral wood; on wide stretches of buffalo grass, withered yellow and prone upon the ground, the funereal aspect of the land heightened by the grim outlines of two Sioux warriors lashed on pole platforms for their last resting-place in the branches above our heads, fragments of a faded red blanket pendent and flapping in the wind beneath one body, a blue blanket beneath the other, grisly neighbours who appeared to approach or recede as our fire alternately

168

blazed and flickered—both plainly warriors, for beneath each lay the whitening bones of his favourite war pony, killed by his tribesmen to provide him a mount in the Spirit Land.

It was a voiceless, soundless night before the storm came, bar the soughing of the wind, the weary creaking of bare branches, the feeble murmur of the brook (drunk almost dry by the thirsty land), and the flap-flap of our neighbours' last raiment.

Our eyes opened upon trees crowned with the pale green glory of bursting buds, upon valley and hill slopes verdant as the richest meadow; our ears were greeted with the sweet voices of birds chanting a welcome to the spring, and the rollicking song of a brimful stream, merry over the largess it now bore for man and beast and bird and plant, while the sweet, humid scents of animate, palpitant nature had driven from our nostrils the dry, horrid odours of the dead.

So comes the spring on the plains—in a single night!

Concho Curly was a raw, unlettered, freckled product of a Texas pioneer's cabin isolated in a nook of the west slope of the hills about the head of the Concho River, near where they pitch down to the waterless, arid reaches of the staked plains.

But the miracle of the spring, appealing to the universal love of the mysterious, had set even Curly's untrained brain questioning and philosophising.

After riding an hour or more silent, his chin buried in the loose folds of his neckerchief, Curly sighed deeply and then observed:

"Ol' man, hit shore 'pears to me Ol' Mahster hain't never strained Hisself none serious tryin' to divide up even the good things o' this yere world o' ourn. Looks like He never tried none, an' ef He did, He's shore made a pow'ful pore job!"

"Why, Curly," I asked, "what makes you think so?"

"Some fellers has so dod-blamed much an' some so dod-burned little," he replied. "Why, back whar you-all comes from, thar's oodles o' grass an' fodder an' water the hull year, ain't they, while out here frequent hit's so fur from grass to water th' critters goes hungry to drink an' dry to graze—don't they?"

"Quite true, Curly," I admitted.

"Wall, back thar, then, 'most every feller must be rich, an' have buggies an' ambulances plenty, an' a big gallery round his *jacal*, an' nothin' to do but set on her all day studdyin' what new bunch o' prittys he'll buy for his woman, an' wettin' his whistle frequent with rot-gut to he'p his thinker select new kinds o' throat-ticklin' grub to feed his face an' new kinds o' humany quilts an' goose-hair pillers to git to lay on, while out here a hull passle o' fellers is so dod-burned pore they don't even own a name, an' hull families lives 'n' dies 'thout ever gittin' to set in a buggy or to eat anythin' but co'n pone an' sow belly, 'thout no fixin's or dulces to chase them, like th' puddin's an' ice cream you gits to town ef you've got th' spondulix an' are willin' to blow yourse'f reckless.

"On th' level, you cain't make me believe Ol' Mahster had anythin' to do with th' makin' o' these yere parts out yere—ef He had, He'd a shore give us fellers a squarer deal; 'pears to me like when His job was nigh done an' He was sorta tired an' restin', the boys musta got loose an' throwed this part o' th' country together, kinda careless-like, outen th' leavin's."

And on and on he monologued, plucking an occasional "yes" or "no" from me, till apparently a new line of reflection diverted him and he fell silent to study where it might lead him.

Presently, when I was lolling comfortably in the saddle, half dozing, he nudged me in the ribs with the butt of his quirt and remarked:

"Say, ol' man! I reckon I musta been sleep-walkin' an' eatin' loco weed, for I been arguin' plumb wrong.

"Come to think o' hit, while we-all that's pore has to work outrageous to make a skimp of a livin', you-all that's rich has to work a scandalous sight harder to git to keep what you got.

"An' then there's ice! Jest think o' ice! Th' rich has her in th' summer, but d—n me ef th' pore don't get her in th' winter, good an' plenty—makin' hit look like th' good things o' this world is whacked up mighty nigh even, after all, an' that we-all hain't got no roar comin' to us."

Thus happily settled his recent worries, Curly himself dropped into a contented doze, and left me to resume mine.

The season opening promised to be an unusually busy one. It was obvious we were nearing the crest of a three-years' boom. Wild range cattle were selling at higher prices than ever before or since. The Chicago beef-market was correspondingly strong. But there were signs of a reaction that made me anxious to gather and ship my fat beeves soon as possible, before the tide turned.

Every winter two thirds of my herd drifted before the bitter blizzards southeast into the sand hills lying between the sink of Snake Creek and the head of the Blue, a splendid winter range where snow never lay long, and out of which cattle came in the spring in unusually good condition.

Thus, at the end of the spring round-up, I was able to cut fifteen hundred beef steers that, after being grazed under close herd a few weeks on the better-cured, stronger feed on the divide between the Niobrara and Snake Creek, were fit for market, and with them we arrived at our shipping point—Ogallala—July 2, 1882.

Leaving the outfit camped, luckily, on a bench twenty feet above the main valley of the Platte, I rode two miles into town to make shipping arrangements.

A wonderful sight was the Platte Valley about Ogallala in those days, for it was the northern terminus of the great Texas trail of the late '70s and early '80s, where trail-drivers brought their herds to sell and northern ranchmen came to bargain.

That day, far as the eye could see up, down, and across the broad, level valley were cattle by the thousand—thirty or forty thousand at least—a dozen or more separate outfits, grazing in loose, open order so near each other that, at a distance, the valley appeared carpeted with a vast Persian rug of intricate design and infinite variety of colours.

Approached nearer, where individual riders and cattle began to take form, it was a topsy-turvy scene I looked down upon.

The day was unusually, tremendously hot—probably 112° in the shade—so hot the shimmering heat-waves developed a mirage that turned town, herds, and riders upside down—all sprung in an instant to gigantic height, the squat frame houses tall as modern skyscrapers, cattle and riders big as elephants, while here and there deep blue lakes lay placidly over broad expanses that a few moments before were a solid field of variegated, brilliant colours.

Arrived at the Spofford House, the one hotel of the town, I found a familiar bunch of famous Texas cattle kings—Seth Mayberry, Shanghai Pierce, Dillon Fant, Jim Ellison, John Lytle, Dave Hunter, Jess Presnall, etc.—each with a string of long horns for sale.

The one store and the score of saloons, dance-halls, and gambling joints that lined up south of the railway track and formed the only street Ogallala could boast, were packed with wild and woolly, long-haired and bearded, rent and dusty, lusting and thirsty, red-sashed brush-splitters in from the trail outfits for a frolic.

And every now and then a chorus of wild, shrill yells and a fusillade of shots rent the air that would make a tenderfoot think a battle-royal was on.

But there was nothing serious doing, then; it was only cowboy frolic.

The afternoon's fierce heat proved a weather breeder, as some had predicted.

Shortly after supper, but long before sundown, a dense black cloud suddenly rose in the north, swept swiftly above and around us till it filled the whole zenith—an ominous, low-hanging pall that brought upon us in a few minutes the utter darkness of a starless night.

Quite as suddenly as the coming of the cloud, the temperature fell 40° or 50°, and drove us into the hotel.

And we were little more than sheltered behind closed doors before torrents of rain descended, borne on gusts of hurricane force that blew open the north door of the dining-room, picked up a great pin-pool board standing across a biscuit-shooting opening in the partition, swept it across the breadth of the office, narrowly missing Mayberry and Fant, and dashed it to splinters against the opposite wall.

Ten minutes later the violence of rain and downpour slackened, almost stopped.

Shanghai went to the door and looked out, shivered, and shut it with the remark:

"By cripes, fellers! 'pears like Ol' Mahster plumb emptied His tanks that clatter; the hull flat's under water."

"Maybe so He's stackin' us up agin' a swimmin' match," was Fant's cheerful comment.

And within another ten minutes it certainly seemed Fant had called the turn.

A tremendous crash of thunder came, with lightning flashes that illumined the room till our oil lamps looked like fireflies, followed by another tornado-driven downpour it seemed hopeless to expect the house could survive.

And while our ears were still stunned by its first roar, suddenly there came flood waters pouring in over door-sills and through floor cracks, rising at a rate that instantly drove us all to refuge on the second floor of the hotel.

We were certainly in the track, if not the centre, of a waterspout!

But barely were we upstairs before the aerial flood-gates closed, till no more than an ordinary heavy soaking rain was falling, and the wind slackened sufficiently to permit us to climb out on the roof of the porch and take stock of the situation.

Our case looked grave enough—grave past hope of escape, or even help.

"Fellers," quietly remarked Shanghai, "here's a game where passin' don't go—leastwise till it's cash in an' pass out o' existence. Here's where I'd sell my chances o' seein' to-morrow's sun at a dollar a head, an' agree not to tally more'n about five head. I've been up agin' Yankee charges, where the air was full of lead and the cold steel 'peared to hide all the rest of the scenery; I've laid in a buffalo wallow two days and nights surrounded by Comanches, and been bushwhacked by Kiowas on the Palo Pinto, but never till now has Shanghai been up agin' a game he couldn't figure out a way to beat."

And so, in truth, it looked.

The whole world was afloat, a raging, tossing flood—our world, at least.

To us a universal flood could mean no more.

Far as the eye could see rolled waters.

And the waters were rising all the time, ever rising, higher and higher; not creeping, but rising, leaping up the pillars of the porch!

It seemed only a matter of moments before the hotel must collapse, or be swept from its foundations.

Already the flood beneath us was dotted thick with drifting flotsam—wrecks of houses, fences, stables, sidewalks.

Men, women, and children were afloat upon the wreckage, drifting they knew not where, safe they knew not how long, shrieking for aid no one could lend.

Dumb beasts and fowls drifted by us, their inarticulate terror cries rising shrill above the piping of the wind—cattle bawling, pigs squealing, dogs howling, horses neighing, chickens clucking madly, and even the ducks and geese quacking notes of alarm.

It seemed the end of the world, no less—at least, of our little corner of it.

However the old Spofford House held to her foundations was a mystery, unless she stood without the line of the strongest current.

But hold she stoutly did until, perhaps fifteen minutes after we were driven upstairs, word was passed out to us by watchers within upon the staircase that the rise had stopped—stopped just about halfway between floor and ceiling of the first story.

And right then, just as we were catching our breath to interchange congratulations, a new terror menaced us—a terror even more appalling than the remorseless flood that still held us in its grip.

An inky-black pall of cloud still shut out the stars and shrouded all the earth, but a pall so riven and torn by constantly recurring flashes of sheet-lightning that our entire field of view was lit almost as bright as by a midday sun.

Suddenly, off in the south, over the divide between the Platte and the Republican, an ominous shape uprose like magic from below the horizon—a balloon-shaped cloud of an ashen-gray that, from reflection of the lightning or other cause, had a sort of phosphorescent glow that outlined its form against the inky background and made plain to our eyes, as the hand held before one's face, that we confronted an approaching cyclone.

Nearing us it certainly was at terrific speed, for it grew and grew as we looked till its broad dome stood half up to the zenith, while its narrow tail was lashing viciously about near and often apparently upon the earth.

On it came, head-on for us, for a space of perhaps four minutes—until, I am sure, any onlooker who had a prayer loose about him was not idle.

And perhaps (who knows?) one or another such appeal prevailed, for just as it seemed no earthly power could save us, off eastward it switched and sped swiftly out of our sight.

It was near midnight before the waters began to fall, and morning before the house was free of them.

And when about eight o'clock horses were brought us, we had to wade and swim them about a quarter of a mile to reach the dry uplands.

From the roof of the hotel we could see that even the trail herds were badly scattered and commingled, and it was the general opinion my herd of un-trail-broke wild beef steers were probably running yet, somewhere.

But when I got out to the benchland where I had left them, there they were, not a single one missing. This to my infinite surprise, for usually an ordinary thunderstorm will drift beef herds more or less, if not actually stampede them.

The reason was quickly explained: the storm had descended upon them so suddenly and with such extraordinary violence that they were stunned into immobility.

Apparently they had been directly beneath the very centre of the waterspout, for the boys told me the rain fell in such solid sheets that they nearly smothered, drowned while mounted and sitting their saddles about the trembling, bellowing herd; came down in such torrents they had to hold their hands in shape of an inverted cup above nose and mouth to get their breath!

Miles of the U.P. track were destroyed that laid us up for three days, awaiting repairs.

The first two days the little village was quiet, trail men out bunching and separating their herds, townsmen taking stock of their losses.

But the third day hell popped good and plenty.

Tempers were so fiery and feelings so tindery that it seemed the recent violence of the very elements themselves had got into men's veins and made them bent to destroy and to kill.

All day long street and saloon swarmed with shouting, quarrelling, shooting punchers, owners and peace officers were alike powerless to control.

About noon the town marshal and several deputies made a bold try to quell the turmoil—and then had to mount and ride for their lives, leaving two of Hunter & Evans's men dead in front of The Cowboys' Rest, and a string of wounded along the street.

This incident stilled the worst of the tumult for two or three hours, for many took up pursuit of the marshal, while the rest were for a time content to quietly talk over the virtues of the departed in the intervals between quadrille-sets—for, of course, the dancing went on uninterrupted.

Toward evening, notwithstanding the orgy had again resumed a fast and furious pace, Fant, Mayberry, and myself were tempted to join the crowd in The Cowboys' Rest, tempted by glimpses of a scene caught from our perch on a corner of the depot platform opposite.

"That *is* blamed funny!" remarked Mayberry. "Come along over and let's see her good. We're no more liable to get leaded there than anywhere else."

So over we went.

"The Rest" belied its name sadly, for rest was about the only thing Jim Tucker was not prepared to furnish his wild and woolly patrons.

Who entered there left coin behind—and was lucky if he left no more.

Stepped within the door, a rude pine "bar" on the right invited the thirsty; on the left, noisy "tin horns," whirring wheels, clicking faro "cases," and rattling chips lured the gamblers; while away to the rear of the room stretched a hundred feet or more of dance-hall, on each of whose rough benches sat enthroned a temptress—hard of eye, deep-lined of face, decked with cheap gauds, sad wrecks of the sea of vice here lurching and tossing for a time.

As we entered, Mayberry's foreman met us and whispered to his boss:

"You-all better stan' back a little, colonel, out o' line o' th' door. Ol' one-eyed John Graham, o' th' Hunter outfit, settin' thar in th' corner's layin' fo' th' sheriff—allows 'twas him sot up th' marshal to shell us up this mo'nin'—an' ol' John's shore pizen when he starts."

So back we moved to the rear end of the bar.

The room was packed: a solid line of men and women before the bar, every table the centre of a crowding group of players, the dance-hall floor and benches jam-full of a roistering, noisy throng.

At the moment all were happy and peace reigned.

But there was one obvious source of discord—there were "not enough gals to go round"; not enough, indeed, if those present had been multiplied by ten, a situation certain to stir jealousies and strife among a lot of wild nomads for whom this was the first chance in four months to gaze into a woman's eyes.

To be sure, one resourceful and unselfish puncher—a foreman of one of the trail outfits—was doing *his* best to relieve the prevailing deficiency in feminine dancers, and it was a distant glimpse of his efforts that had brought us over.

Bearing, if not boasting, the proud old Dutch name of Jake De Puyster, this rollicking six-foot-two blond giant had heard Buck Groner growl:

"Hain't had airy show for a dance yet. Nairy heifer's throwed her eye my way 'fore she's been roped and tied in about a second. Reckon it's shoot for one or pull my freight for camp, and I ain't sleepy none."

"You stake you'self out, son, a few minutes, and I'll git you a she-pardner you'll be glad of a chance to dance with and buy prittys for," reassured Jake, and then disappeared.

Ten minutes later he returned, bringing Buck a partner that stopped drinking, dance, and play—the most remarkably clad figure that ever entered even a frontier dance-hall.

Still wearing his usual costume—wide chaps, spurred heels, and belt—having removed nothing but his tall-crowned Mexican sombrero, Jake had mavericked three certain articles of feminine apparel and contrived to get himself into them.

Cocked jauntily over his right eye he wore a bright red toque crowned with a faded wreath of pale blue flowers, from which a bedraggled green feather drooped wearily over his left ear; about his waist wrinkled a broad pink sash, tied in a great double bow-knot set squarely in front, while fastened also about his waist, pendent no more than midway of his long thighs, hung a garment white of colour, filmy of fabric, bifurcated of form, richly ruffled of extremity—so habited came Jake, and, with a broad grin lurking within the mazes of his great bushy beard and monstrous moustache, sidled mincing to his mate and shyly murmured a hint he might have the privilege of the next quadrille.

At first Buck was furious, growled, and swore to kill Jake for the insult, until, infected by the gales of laughter that swept the room, he awkwardly offered his arm and led his weird partner to an unfilled set.

And a sorry hour was this to the other ladies; for, while there were better dancers and prettier, that first quadrille made "Miss De Puyster" the belle of the ball for the rest of the day and night, and not a few serious affrays over disputes for an early chance of a "round" or "square" with her were narrowly avoided.

Just as we reached the rear end of the bar, the fiddles stopped their cruel liberties with the beautiful measures of "Sobre las Olas" and Buck led his panting partner up to our group and courteously introduced us thus:

Miss De Puyster, here's two mighty slick ol' long-horn mossbacks you wants to be pow'ful shy of, for they'd maverick off their own daddy, an' a little short-horn Yankee orfun I wants to ax you to adopt an' try to make a good mother to. Fellers, this yere's Miss De Puyster; she ain't much for pretty, but she's hell for active on th' floor—so dod-burned active I couldn't tell whether she was waltzin' or tryin' to throw me side-holts."

But before we had time to properly make our acknowledgments, a new figure in the dance was called—a figure which, though familiar enough in Ogallala dance-halls, distracted and held the attention of all present for a few minutes.

Later we learned that, early in the day, a local celebrity—Bill Thompson by name, a tin horn by trade, and a desperado by pretence—had proffered some insult to Big Alice, the leading lady of the house, for which Jim Tucker had "called him down good and plenty," but under such circumstances that to resent it then would have been to court a fairer fight than Bill's kind ever willingly took on.

But, remembering he was brother to Ben Thompson, the then most celebrated man-killer in the State of Texas (who himself was to fall to King Fisher's pistol in Jack Harris's San Antonio variety theatre a few years later), brooding Tucker's abuse of him, figuring what Ben would do in like circumstances, illumining his view of the situation by frequent resorts to red eye, Bill by evening had rowled himself ready for action.

So it happened that at the very moment Buck finished our introduction to "Miss De Puyster," Bill suddenly stepped within the door of the saloon and took a quick snapshot at Tucker, who was directly across the bar from us and in the act of passing Fant a glass of whisky with his left hand.

The ball cut off three of Tucker's fingers and the tip of the fourth, and, the bar being narrow, spattered us with his blood.

Tucker fell, momentarily, from the shock.

Supposing from Tucker's quick drop he had made an instant kill, Bill stuck his pistol in his waistband and started leisurely out of the door and down the street.

But no sooner was he out of the house than Jim sprang up, seized a sawed-off ten-gauge shotgun, ran to the door, leveled the gun across the stump of his maimed left hand, and emptied into Bill's back, at about six paces, a trifle more No. 4 duck-shot than his system could assimilate.

Perhaps altogether ten minutes were wasted on this incident and the time taken to tourniquet and tie up Jim's wound and to pack Bill inside and stow him in a corner behind the faro lookout's chair and then Jim's understudy called, "Pardners fo' th' next dance!" the fiddlers bravely tackled but soon got hopelessly beyond their depth in "The Blue Danube," and dancing and frolic were resumed, with "Miss De Puyster" still the belle of the ball.

Triggerfingeritis*

FROM *The Red-Blooded Heroes of the Frontier*, 1910

On the Plains thirty years ago there were two types of man-killers; and these two types were subdivided into classes. The first type numbered all who took life in contravention of law. This type was divided into three classes: A, Outlaws to whom bloodletting had become a mania; B, Outlaws who killed in defence of their spoils or liberty; C, Otherwise good men who had slain in the heat of private quarrel, and either "gone on the scout" or "jumped the country" rather than submit to arrest. The second type included all who slew in support of law and order. This type included six classes: A, United States marshals; B, Sheriffs and their deputies; C, Stage or railway express guards, called "messengers"; D, Private citizens organized as Vigilance Committees— these often none too discriminating, and not infrequently the blind or willing instruments of individual grudge or greed; E, Unorganized bands of ranchmen who took the trail of marauders on life or property and never quit it; F, "Inspectors" (detectives) for Stock Growers' Associations.

Throughout the seventies and well into the eighties, in Wyoming, Dakota, western Kansas and Nebraska, New Mexico, and west Texas, courts were idle most of the time, and lawyers lived from hand to mouth. The then state of local society was so rudimentary that it had not acquired the habit of appeal to the law for settlement of its differences. And while it may sound an anachronism, it is nevertheless the simple truth that while life was far less secure through that period, average personal honesty then ranked higher and depredations against property were fewer than at any time since.

As soon as society had advanced to a point where the victim could be relied on to carry his wrongs to court, judges began working

---

* *Triggerfingeritis* is an acute irritation of the sensory nerves of the index finger of habitual gun-packers; usually fatal—to some one.

overtime and lawyers fattening. But of the actual pioneers who took their lives in their hands and recklessly staked them in their everyday goings and comings (as, for instance, did all who ventured into the Sioux country north of the Platte between 1875 and 1880) few long stayed—no matter what their occupation—who were slow on the trigger: it was back to Mother Earth or home for them.

Of the supporters of the law in that period Boone May was one of the finest examples any frontier community ever boasted. Early in 1876 he came to Cheyenne with an elder brother and engaged in freighting thence overland to the Black Hills. Quite half the length of the stage road was then infested by hostile Sioux. This meant heavy risks and high pay. The brothers prospered so handsomely that, toward the end of the year, Boone withdrew from freighting, bought a few cattle and horses, and built and occupied a ranch at the stage-road crossing of Lance Creek, midway between the Platte and Deadwood, in the very heart of the Sioux country. Boone was then well under thirty, graceful of figure, dark-haired, wore a slender downy moustache that served only to emphasize his youth, but possessed that reserve and repose of manner most typical of the utterly fearless.

The Sioux made his acquaintance early, to their grief. One night they descended on his ranch and carried off all the stage horses and most of Boone's. Although the "sign" showed there were fifteen or twenty in the party, at daylight Boone took their trail, alone. The third day thereafter he returned to the ranch with all the stolen stock, besides a dozen split-eared Indian ponies, as compensation for his trouble, taken at what cost of strategy or blood Boone never told.

Learning of this exploit from his drivers, Al. Patrick, the superintendent of the stage line, took the next coach to Lance Creek and brought Boone back to Deadwood, enlisted in his corps of "messengers"; he was too good timber to miss.

At that time every coach south-bound from Deadwood to Cheyenne carried thousands in its mail-pouches and express-boxes; and once a week a treasure coach armored with boiler plate, carrying no passengers, and guarded by six or eight "messengers" or "sawed-off shotgun men," conveyed often as high as two hundred thousand dollars of hard-won Black Hills gold bars.

Thus it naturally followed that, throughout 1877 and 1878, it was the exception for a coach to get through from the Chugwater to Jenny's stockade without being held up by bandits at least once.

Any that happened to escape Jack Wadkins in the south were likely to fall prey to Dune Blackburn in the north—the two most desperate bandit-leaders in the country.

In February, 1878, I had occasion to follow some cattle thieves from Fort Laramie to Deadwood. Returning south by coach, one bitter evening we pulled into Lance Creek, eight passengers inside, Boone May and myself on the box with 'Gene Barnett the driver; Stocking, another famous messenger, roosted behind us atop of the coach, fondling his sawed-off shotgun.

From Lance Creek southward lay the greatest danger zone. At that point, therefore, Boone and Stocking shifted from the coach to the saddle, and, as 'Gene popped his whip and the coach crunched away through the snow, both dropped back perhaps thirty yards behind us.

An hour later, just as the coach got well within a broad belt of plum bushes that lined the north bank of Old Woman's Fork, out into the middle of the road sprang a lithe figure that threw a snap shot over 'Gene's head and halted us.

Instantly six others surrounded the coach and ordered us down. I already had a foot on the nigh front wheel, to descend, when a shot out of the brush to the west (Boone's, I later learned) dropped the man ahead of the team.

Then followed a quick interchange of shots for perhaps a minute, certainly no more, and then I heard Boone's cool voice:

"Drive on, 'Gene!"

"Move an' I'll kill you!" came in a hoarse bandit's voice from the thicket east of us.

"Drive on, 'Gene, or *I'll* kill you," came then from Boone, in a tone of such chilling menace that 'Gene threw the bud into the leaders, and away we flew at a pace materially improved by three or four shots the bandits sent singing past our ears and over the team! The next down coach brought to Cheyenne the comforting news that Boone and Stocking had killed four of the bandits and stampeded the other three.

Within six months after Boone was employed, both Dune Blackburn and Jack Wadkins disappeared from the stage road, dropped out of sight as if the earth had opened and swallowed them, as it probably had. Boone had a way of absenting himself for days from his routine duties along the stage road. He slipped off entirely alone after this new quarry precisely as he had followed the Sioux horse-raiders and, while he never admitted it, the belief was general that he had run down and "planted" both. Indeed it is almost a certainty this is true, for beasts of their type never change their stripes, and sure it is that neither were ever seen or heard of after their disappearance from the Deadwood trail.

Late in the Autumn of the same year, 1878, and also at or near the stage-crossing of Old Woman's Fork, Boone and one companion fought eight bandits led by a man named Tolle, on whose head was a large reward. This was earned by Boone at a hold-up of a U. P. express train near Green River.

This band was, in a way, more lucky, for five of the eight escaped; but of the three otherwise engaged one furnished a head which Boone toted in a gunny sack to Cheyenne and exchanged for five thousand dollars, if my memory rightly serves.

This incident was practically the last of the serious hold-ups on the Cheyenne road. A few pikers followed and "stood up" a coach occasionally, but the strong organized bands were extinct.

Throughout 1879 Boone's activities were transferred to the Sidney-Deadwood road, where for several months before Boone's coming, Curly and Lame Johnny had held sway. Lame Johnny was shortly thereafter captured, and hanged on the lone tree that gave the Big Cottonwood Creek its name. A few months later, Curly was captured by Boone and another, but was never jailed or tried: when nearing Deadwood, he tried to escape from Boone, and failed.

With the Sioux pushed back within the lines of their new reservation in southern Dakota and semi-pacified, and with the Sidney road swept clean of road-agents, life in Boone's old haunts became for him too tame. Thus it happened that, while trapping was then no better within than without the Sioux reservation, the Winter of 1879–80 found Boone and four mates camped on the Cheyenne River below the mouth of Elk Creek, well within the reserve, trapping the main stream and its tributaries. For a month they were undisturbed, and a goodly store of fur was fast accumulating. Then one fine morning, while breakfast was cooking, out from the cover of an adjacent hill and down upon them charged a Sioux war party, one hundred and fifty strong.

Boone's four mates barely had time to take cover below the hard-by river bank—under Boone's orders—before fire opened. Down straight upon them the Sioux charged in solid mass, heels kicking and quirts pounding their split-eared ponies, until, having come within a hundred yards, the mass broke into single file and raced past the camp, each warrior lying along the off side of his pony and firing beneath its neck—the usual but utterly stupid and suicidal Sioux tactics, for accurate fire under such conditions is of course impossible. Meantime Boone stood quietly by the camp-fire, entirely in the open, coolly potting the enemy as regularly and surely as a master wing-shot thinning a flight of ducks. Three times they so charged and Boone so received them, pouring into them a steady, deadly fire out of his Winchester and two pistols. And when, after the third charge, the war party drew off for good, forty-odd ponies and twenty-odd warriors lay upon the plain, stark evidence of Boone's wonderful nerve and marksmanship. Shortly after the fight one of his mates told me that while he and three others were doing their best, there was no doubt that nearly all the dead fell before Boone's fire.

A type diametrically opposite to that of the debonair Boone May was Captain Jim Smith, one of the best peace-officers the frontier ever knew. Of Captain Smith's early history nothing was known, except that he had served with great credit as a captain of artillery in the Union Army. He first appeared on the U. P. during construction days in the late sixties. Serving in various capacities as railroad detective, marshal, stock inspector, and the like, for eighteen years Captain Smith wrote more red history with his pistol (barring May's work on the Sioux) than any two men of his time.

The last I knew of him he had enough dead outlaws to his credit—thirty-odd—to start, if not a respectable, at least, a fair-sized grave-yard. Captain Jim's mere look was almost enough to still the heart-beat and paralyze the pistol hand of any but the wildest of them all. His great burning black eyes, glowering deadly menace from cavernous sockets of extraordinary depth, were set in a colossal grim face; his straight, thin-lipped mouth never showed teeth; his heavy, tight-curling black moustache and stiff black imperial always had the appearance of holding the under lip closely glued to the upper. In years of intimacy, I never once saw on his lips the faintest hint of a smile. He had tremendous breadth of shoulders and depth of chest; he was big-boned, lean-loined, quick and furtive of movement as a panther. In short, Captain Jim was altogether the most fearsome-looking man I ever saw, the very incarnation of a relentless, inexorable, indomitable, avenging Nemesis.

Like most men lacking humor, Captain Jim was devoid of vices;

like all men lacking sentiment, he cultivated no intimacies. Throughout those years loved nothing, animate or inanimate, but his guns—the full length "45" that nestled in its breast scabbard next his heart, and the short "45," sawed off two inches in front of the cylinder, that he always carried in a deep side-pocket of his long sack coat. This was often a much patched pocket, for Jim was a notable economist of time, and usually fired from within the pocket. That he loved those guns I know, for often have I seen him fondle them as tenderly as a mother her first-born.

In 1879 Sidney, Neb., was a hell-hole, filled with the most desperate toughs come to prey upon overland travellers to and from the Black Hills. Of these toughs McCarthy, proprietor of the biggest saloon and gambling-house in town, was the leading spirit and boss. Nightly, men who would not gamble were drugged or slugged or leaded. Town marshals came and went—either feet first or on a keen run.

So long as its property remained unmolested the U. P. management did not mind. But one night the depot was robbed of sixty thousand dollars in gold bullion. Of course, this was the work of the local gang. Then the U. P. got busy. Pete Shelby summoned Captain Jim to Omaha and committed the Sidney situation to his charge. Frequenting haunts where he knew the news would be wired to Sidney, Jim casually mentioned that he was going out there to clean out the town, and purposed killing McCarthy on sight. This he rightly judged would stampede, or throw a chill into, many of the pikers—and simplify his task.

Arrived in Sidney, Jim found McCarthy absent, at North Platte, due to return the next day. Coming to the station the next morning, Jim found the express reported three hours late, and returned to his room in the Railway House, fifty yards north of the depot. He doffed his coat, shoulder scabbard, and boots, and lay down, shortly falling into a doze that nearly cost him his life. Most inconsiderately the train made up nearly an hour of its lost time. Jim's awakening was sudden, but not soon enough. Before he had time to rise at the sound of the softly opening door, McCarthy was over him with a pistol at his head.

Jim's left hand nearly touched the gun pocket of his coat, and his right lay in reach of the other gun; but his slightest movement meant instant death.

"Heerd you come to hang my hide up an' skin the town, but

you're under a copper and my open play wins, Black Jim! See?" growled McCarthy.

"Well, Mac," coolly answered Jim, "you're a bigger damn fool than I allowed. Never heard of you before makin' a killin' there was nothin' in. What's the matter with you and your gang? I'm after that bullion, and I've got a straight tip: Lame Johnny's the bird that hooked onto it. If you're standing in with him, you better lead me aplenty, for if you don't I'll sure get him."

"Honest? Is that right, Jim? Ain't lyin' none?" queried McCarthy, relieved of the belief that his gang were suspected.

"Sure, she's right, Mac."

"But I heerd you done said you was comin' to do me," persisted McCarthy.

"Think I'm fool enough to light in diggin' my own grave, by sendin' love messages like that to a gun expert like you, Mac?" asked Captain Jim.

Whether it was the subtle flattery or Jim's argument, Mac lowered his gun, and while backing out of the room, remarked: "Nothin' in mixin' it with you, Jim, if you don't want me."

But Mac was no more than out of the room when Jim slid off the bed quick as a cat; softly as a cat, on his noiseless stockinged feet he followed Mac down the hall; crafty as a cat, he crept down the creaking stairs, tread for tread, a scant arm's length behind his prey—why, God alone knows, unless for a savage joy in longer holding another thug's life in his hands. So he hung, like a leech to the blood it loves, across the corridor and to the middle of the trunk room that lay between the hall and the hotel office. There Jim spoke: "Oh! Mr. McCarthy!"

Mac whirled, drawing his gun, just in time to receive a bullet squarely through the heart.

During the day Jim got two more scalps. The rest of the McCarthy gang got the impression that it was up to them to pull their freight out of Sidney, and acted on it.

In 1882 the smoke of the Lincoln County War still hung in the timber of the Ruidoso and the Bonito, a feud in which nearly three hundred New Mexicans lost their lives. Depredations on the Mescalero Reservation were so frequent that the Indians were near open revolt.

Needing a red-blooded agent, the Indian Bureau sought and got one in Major W. H. H. Llewellyn, since Captain of Rough Riders, Troup H, then a United States marshal with a distinguished record.

The then Chief of the Bureau offered the Major two troops of cavalry to preserve order among the Mescaleros and keep marauders off the reservation, and was astounded when Llewellyn declined and said he would prefer to handle the situation with no other aid than that of one man he had in mind.

Captain Jim Smith was the man. And pleased enough was he when told of the turbulence of the country and the certainty of plenty doing in his line.

But by the time they reached the Mescalero Agency, the feud was ended; the peace of exhaustion after years of open war and ambush had descended upon Lincoln County, and the Mescaleros were glad enough quietly to draw their rations of flour and coffee, and range the Sacramentos and Guadalupes for game. For Jim and the band of Indian police which he quickly organized there was nothing doing.

Inaction soon cloyed Captain Jim. It got on his nerves. Presently he conceived a resentment toward the agent for bringing him down there under false pretences of daring deeds to be done, that never materialized. One day Major Llewellyn imprudently countermanded an order Jim had given his Chief of Police, under conditions which the Captain took as a personal affront. The next thing the Major knew, he was covered by Jim's gun listening to his death sentence.

"Major," began Captain Jim, "right here is where you cash in. Played me for a big fool long enough. Toted me off down here on the guarantee of the best show of fightin' I've heard of since the war—here where there ain't a man in the Territory with nerve enough left to tackle a prairie dog, 's far 's I can see. Lied to me a plenty, didn't you? Anything to say before you quit?"

Since that time Major Llewellyn has become (and is now) a famous pleader at the New Mexican bar, but I know he will agree that the most eloquent plea he has to this day made was that in answer to Captain Jim's arraignment. Luckily it won.

A month later Jim called on me at El Paso. At the time I was President of the West Texas Cattle Growers' Association, organized chiefly to deal with marauding rustlers.

"Howdy, Ed," Jim began, "I've jumped the Mescalero Reservation, headed north. Nothin' doin' down here now. But, say, Ed, I hear they're crowdin' the rustlers a plenty up in the Indian Territory and the Pan Handle, and she's a cinch they'll be down on you thick in a few months. And, say, Ed, don't forget old Jim; when the rustlers come, send for him. You know he's the cheapest proposition ever— never any lawyers' fees or court costs, nothin' to pay but just Jim's wages."

That was the last time we ever met, and lucky it will probably be for me if we never meet again; for if Jim still lives and there is aught in this story he sees occasion to take exception to, I am sure to be due for a mix-up I can very well get on without.

From 1878 to 1880 Billy Lykins was one of the most efficient inspectors of the Wyoming Stock Growers' Association, a short man of heavy muscular physique and a round, cherubic, pink and white face, in which a pair of steel-blue glittering eyes looked strangely out of place. A second glance, however, showed behind the smiling mouth a set of the jaw that did not belie the fighting eyes. So far as I can now recall, Billy never failed to get what he went after while he remained in our employ.

Probably the toughest customer Billy ever tackled was Doc Middleton. As an outlaw, Doc was the victim of an error of judgment. When he first came among us, hailing from Llano County, Texas, Doc was as fine a puncher and jolly, good-tempered range-mate as any in the Territory. Sober and industrious, he never drank or gambled. But he had his bit of temper, had Doc, and his chunk of good old Llano nerve. Thus, when a group of carousing soldiers, in a Sidney saloon, one night lit in to beat Doc up with their six-shooters for refusing to drink with them, the inevitable happened in a very few seconds; Doc killed three of them, jumped his horse, and split the wind for the Platte.

And therein lay his error.

The killing was perfectly justifiable; surrendered and tried, he would surely have been acquitted. But his breed never surrender, at least, never before their last shell is emptied. Flight having made him an outlaw, the Government offered a heavy reward for him, dead or alive. For a time he was harbored among his friends on the different ranches; indeed was a welcome guest of my Deadman Ranch for several days; but in a few weeks the hue and cry got so hot that he had to jump for the Sand Hills south of the Niobrara.

Ever pursued, he found that honest wage-earning was impossible. Presently he was confronted with want, not of much, indeed of very little, but that want was vital—he wanted cartridges. At this time the

Sand Hills were full of deer and antelope; and therefore to him cartridges meant more even than defence of his freedom, they meant food. It was this want that drove him into his first actual crime, the stealing of Sioux ponies, which he ran into the settlements and sold. The downward path of the criminal is like that of the limpid, clean-faced brook, bred of a bubbling spring nestled in some shady nook of the hills, where the air is sweet and pure, and pollution cometh not. But there it may not stay; on and yet on it rushes, as helpless as heedless, till one day it finds itself plunged into some foul current carrying the off-scourings of half a continent. So on and down plunged Doc; from stealing Indian ponies to lifting ranch horses was no long leap in his new code.

Then our Stock Association got busy and Billy Lykins took his trail. Oddly, in a few months the same type of accident in turn saved the life of each. Their first encounter was single-handed. With the better horse, Lykins was pressing Doc so close that Doc raced to the crest of a low conical hill, jumped off his mount, dropped flat on the ground and covered Lykins with a Springfield rifle, meantime yelling to him:

"Duck, you little Dutch fool; I don't want to kill you"; for they knew each other well, and in a way were friends.

But Billy never knew when to stop. Deeper into his pony's flank sank the rowels, and up the hill on Doc he charged, pistol in hand. At thirty yards Doc pulled the trigger, when—wonder of wonders— the faithful old Springfield missed fire. Before Doc could throw in another shell or draw his pistol, Billy was over him and had him covered.

If my memory rightly serves, the Sidney jail held Doc almost a fortnight. A few weeks later Doc had assembled a strong gang about him, rendezvoused on the Piney, a tributary of the lower Niobrara. There he was far east of Lykins's bailiwick, but a good many degrees within Lykins's disposition to quit his trail. Accompanied by Major W. H. H. Llewellyn and an Omaha detective (inappropriately named Hassard), Lykins located Doc's camp, and the three lay near for several days studying their quarry.

One morning Llewellyn and Hassard started up the creek, mounted, on a scout, leaving Lykins and his horse hidden in the brush near the trail. At a sharp bend of the path the two ran plunk into Doc and five of his men. Both being unknown to Doc's gang, and the position and odds forbidding hostilities, they represented themselves as campers hunting lost stock, and turned and rode back down the trail with the outlaws, alert for any play their leader might make.

Recognizing his man, Billy lay with his "45" and "70" Sharps comfortably resting across a log; and when the band were come within twenty yards of him, he drew a careful bead on Doc's head and pulled the trigger. By strange coincidence his Sharps missed fire, precisely as had Doc's Springfield a few weeks before.

Hearing the snap of the rifle hammer, with a curse Doc jerked his gun and whirled his horse toward the brush just as Billy sprang out into the open and threw a pistol shot into Doc that broke his thigh. Swaying in saddle, Doc cursed Hassard for leading him into a trap, and shot him twice before himself pitching to the ground. Hassard stood idly, stunned apparently by a sort of white-hot work he was not used to, and received his death wound without any effort even to draw. Meantime, the firm of Lykins and Llewellyn accounted for two more before Doc's mates got out of range. Thus, like the brook, Doc had drifted down the turbid current of crime till he found himself impounded in the Lincoln penitentiary with the off-scourings of the State.

While it is true that back into such impounding most who once have been there soon return, Doc turned out to be one of the rare exceptions proving the rule; for the last I heard of him, he was the lame but light-hearted and wholly honest proprietor of a respectable Rushville saloon.

When in the early eighties the front camps of the Atchison, Topeka, and Santa Fe and the Texas Pacific met at El Paso, then a village called Franklin, within a few weeks the population jumped from a few hundred to nearly three thousand. Speculators, prospectors for business opportunities, mechanics, miners, and tourists poured in—a chance-taking, high-living, free-spending lot that offered such rich pickings for the predatory that it was not long before nearly every fat pigeon had a hungry, merciless vulture hovering near, watching for a chance to fasten its claws and gorge itself.

The low one-story adobes, fronted by broad, arched portals, that then lined the west side of El Paso Street for several blocks, was a long solid row of variety theatres, dance halls, saloons, and gambling-houses, never closed by day or by night. They were packed with a roistering mob that drifted from one joint to another, dancing, gambling, carousing, fighting. Naturally, at first the predatory confined their attentions to the roisterers.

Of course every lay-out was a brace game, from which no player arose with any notable winning except occasionally when the "house" felt it a good bit of advertising to graduate a handsome winner—and then it was usually a "capper," whose gains were in a few minutes passed back into the till.

The faro boxes were full of springs as a watch; faro decks were carefully cut "strippers." An average good dealer would shuffle and arrange as he liked the favorite cards of known high-rollers. These had been neatly split on either edge and a minute bit of bristle pasted in, which no ordinary touch would feel, but which the sand-papered finger tips of an expert dealer would catch and slip through on the shuffle and place where they would do (the house) the most good. The "tin horns" gave out few but false notes; the roulette balls were kicked silly out of the boxes representing heavily played numbers. Not content with the "kitty's" rake-off, every stud poker table had one or more "cappers" sitting in, to whom the dealers could occasionally throw a stiff pot. The backs of poker decks were so cunningly marked that while the wise ones could read their size and suit across the table, no untaught eye could detect their guile. And wherever a notable roll was once flashed, greedy eyes never left it until it was safe in the till of some game, or its owner "rolled" and relieved of it by force.

For months orgy ran riot and the predatory band grew bolder and cruder in their methods. Killings were frequent. Few nights passed without more or less street hold-ups—usually more. Respectable citizens took the middle of the street, literally gun in hand, when forced to be out of nights. The Mayor and City Council were powerless. City marshals and deputies they hired in bunches, but all to no purpose. Each fresh lot of appointees were short-lived, literally or officially—mostly literally. Finally, a vigilance committee was formed, made up of good citizens not a few of whom were gun experts with their own bit of red record. But nothing came of it. The predatories openly flouted and defied them.

On one notable night when the committee were assembled in front of the old Grand Central Hotel, a mob of two hundred toughs lined up before the thirty-odd of the committee and dared them to open the ball; and it was a miracle the little Plaza was not then and there turned into a slaughter pen bloody as the Alamo. It really looked as if nothing short of martial law and a strong body of troops could pacify the town.

But one night, into the chamber of the City Council stalked a man, the man of the hour, unheralded and unknown. He gave the name of Bill Stoudenmayer. About all that was ever learned of him was that he hailed from Fort Davis. His type was that of a course, brutal, Germanic gladiator, devoid of strategy; a bluff, stubborn, give-and-take fighter, who drove bull-headed at whatever opposed him. But El Paso soon learned that he could handle his guns with as deadly dexterity as did his forebears their nets and tridents.

Asked his business with the Council, he said he had heard they had failed to find a marshal who could hold the town down, and allowed he'd like to try the job if the Council would make it worth his while. Questioned as to his views, he explained that he was there to make some good money for himself and save the city more; if they would pay him five hundred dollars a month for two months, they could discharge all their deputies and he would go it alone and agree to clear the town of toughs or draw no pay. The Mayor and Council were paralyzed in a double sense: by the wild audacity of this proposal, and by their memory of recent threats of the thug-leaders that they would massacre the Council to a man if any further attempts were made to circumscribe their activities. Some were openly for declining the offer, but in the end a majority gained heart of Stoudenmayer's own hardihood sufficiently to hire him.

The rest of the night Stoudenmayer employed in quietly familiarizing himself with the personnel of the enemy. He lost no time. At daylight the next morning, several notices, manually written in a rude hand and each bearing the signature of the rude hand that wrote it, were found conspicuously posted between Oregon Street and the Plaza. The signature was, "Bill Stoudenmayer, City Marshal."

The notice was brief but pointed:

"Any of the hold-ups named below I find in town after three o'clock to-day, I'm going to kill on sight."

Then followed seventy names. The list was carefully chosen: all "pikers" and "four-flushers" were omitted; none but the *élite* of the gun-twirling, black-jack swinging toughs was included. Hardly a single man was named in the list lacking a more or less gory record.

By the toughs Stoudenmayer was taken as a jest, by respectable citizens as a lunatic. Heavy odds were offered that he would not last till noon, with few takers. And yet throughout the morning

Stoudenmayer quietly walked the streets, unaccompanied save by his two guns and his conspicuously displayed marshal's star.

Nothing happened until about two o'clock, when two men sprang out from ambush behind the big cottonwood tree that then stood on the northeast corner of El Paso and San Antonio Streets, one armed with a shotgun and the other with a pistol, and started to "throw down" on Stoudenmayer, who was approaching from the other side of the street. But before either got his artillery into action, the Marshal jerked his two pistols and killed both, then quietly continued his stroll, over their prostrate bodies, and past them, up the street. It was such an obviously workmanlike job that it threw a chill into the hardiest of the sixty-eight survivors,—so much of a chill that, though Stoudenmayer paraded streets and threaded saloon and dance-hall throngs all the rest of the afternoon, seeking his prey, not a single man of them could he find; all stayed close in their dens.

But that the thug-leaders were not idle Stoudenmayer was not long learning. In the last moments of twilight, just before the pall of night fell upon the town, the Marshal was standing on the east side of El Paso Street, midway between Oregon and San Antonio Streets, no cover within reach of him. Suddenly, without the slightest warning, a heavy fusillade opened on him from the opposite side of the street, a fusillade so heavy it would have decimated a company of infantry. At least a hundred men fired at him at the word, and it was a miracle he did not go down at the first volley. But he was not even scathed. Drawing his pistols, Stoudenmayer marched upon the enemy, slowly but steadily, advancing straight, it seemed, into the jaws of death, but firing with such wonderful rapidity and accuracy that seven of his foes were killed and two wounded in almost as many seconds, although all kept close as possible behind the shelter of the *portal* columns. And every second he was so engaged, at least a hundred guns, aimed by cruel trained eyes, that scarce ever before had missed whatever they sought to draw a bead on, were pouring out upon him a hell of lead that must have sounded to him like a flight of bees.

But stand his iron nerve and fatal snap-shooting the thugs could not. Before he was half way across the street, the hostile fire had ceased, and his would-be assassins were flying for the nearest and best cover they could find. Out of the town they slipped that night, singly and in squads, boarding freight trains north and east, stages west and south, stealing teams and saddle stock, some even hitting the trails afoot, in stark terror of the man. The next morning El Paso found herself evacuated of more than two hundred men who, while they had been for a time her most conspicuous citizens, were such as she was glad enough to spare. In twenty-four hours Bill Stoudenmayer had made his word good and fairly earned his wages; indeed he had accomplished single-handed what the most hopeful El Pasoites had despaired of seeing done with less authority and force than two or three troops of regular cavalry.

Then El Paso settled down to the humdrum but profitable task of laying the foundations for the great metropolis of the Farther Southwest. Since then, an occasional sporadic case of *triggerfingeritis* has developed in El Paso, usually in an acute form; but never once since the night Stoudenmayer turned the El Paso Street *portals* into a shambles has it threatened as an epidemic.

Unluckily, Bill Stoudenmayer did not last long to enjoy the glory of his deed. He was a marked man, merely from motives of revenge harbored by friends of the departed (dead or live), but as a man with a reputation so big as to hang up a rare prize in laurels for any with the strategy and hardihood to down him. It was therefore matter of no general surprise when, a few weeks after his resignation as City Marshal, he fell the victim of a private quarrel.

A few years later, Hal Gosling was the U. S. Marshal for the Western District of Texas. Early in Gosling's regime, Johnny Manning became one of his most efficient and trusted deputies. The pair were wide opposites: Gosling, a big, bluff, kindly, rollicking dare-devil afraid of nothing, but a sort that would rather chaff than fight; Manning a quiet, reserved, slender, handsome little man, not so very much bigger than a full-grown "45," who actually sought no quarrels but would rather fight than eat. Each in his own way, the pair made themselves a holy terror to such of the desperadoes as ventured any liberties with Uncle Sam's belongings.

One of their notable captures was a brace of road-agents who had appropriated the Concho stage road and about everything of value that travelled it. The two were tried in the Federal Court at Austin and sentenced to hard labor at Huntsville. Gosling and Manning started to escort them to their new field of activity. Handcuffed but not otherwise shackled, the two prisoners were given a seat together near the middle of a day coach. By permission of the Marshal, the wife of one and the sister of the other sat immediately behind them—

dear old Hal Gosling never could resist any appeal to his sympathies. The seat directly across the aisle from the two prisoners was occupied by Gosling and Manning. With the car well filled with passengers and their men ironed, the Marshal and his Deputy were off their guard. When out of Austin barely an hour, the train at full speed, the two women slipped pistols into the hands of the two convicted bandits, unseen by the officers. But others saw the act, and a stir of alarm among those near by caused Gosling to whirl in his seat next the aisle, reaching for the pistol in his breast scabbard. But he was too late. Before he was half risen to his feet or his gun out, the prisoners fired and killed him.

Then ensued a terrible duel, begun at little more than arm's length, between Manning and the two prisoners, who presently began backing toward the rear door. Quickly the car filled with smoke, and in it pandemonium reigned, women screaming, men cursing, all who had not dropped in a faint ducking beneath the car seats and trying their best to burrow in the floor. When at length the two prisoners reached the platform and sprang from the moving train, Johnny Manning, shot full of holes as a sieve, lay unconscious across Hal Gosling's body; and the sister of one of the bandits hung limp across the back of the seat the prisoners had occupied, dead of a wild shot.

But Johnny had well avenged Hal's death and his own injuries; one of the prisoners was found dead within a few yards of the track, and the other was captured, mortally wounded, a half-mile away.

After many uncertain weeks, when Manning's system had successfully recovered from the overdose of lead administered by the departed, he quietly resumed his star and belt, and no one ever discovered that the incident had made him in the least gun-shy.

Whenever the history of the Territory of New Mexico comes to be written, the name of Colonel Albert J. Fountain deserves and should have first place in it. Throughout the formative epoch of her evolution from semi-savagery to civilization, an epoch spanning the years from 1866 to 1896, Colonel Fountain was far and away her most distinguished and most useful citizen. As soldier, scholar, dramatist, lawyer, prosecutor, Indian fighter, and desperado-hunter, his was the most picturesque personality I have ever known. Gentle and kind-hearted as a woman, a lover of his books and his ease, he nevertheless was always as quick to take up arms and undergo any hazard and hardship in pursuit of murderous rustlers as he was in 1861 to join the California Column (First California Volunteers) on its march across the burning deserts of Arizona to meet and defeat Sibley at Val Verde. A face fuller of the humanities and charities of life than his would be hard to find; but, roused, the laughing eyes shone cold as a wintry sky. He despised wrong, and hated the criminal, and spent his whole life trying to right the one and suppress or exterminate the other. In this work, and of it, ultimately, he lost his life.

In the early eighties, while the New Mexican courts were well-nigh idle, crime was rampant, especially in Lincoln, Dona Ana, and Grant Counties. To the east of the Rio Grande the Lincoln County War was at its height, while to the west the Jack Kinney gang took whatever they wanted at the muzzle of their guns; and they wanted about everything in sight. County peace officers were powerless.

At this stage Fountain was appointed by the Governor "Colonel of State Militia," and given a free hand to pacify the country. As an organized military body, the militia existed only in name. And so Fountain left it. Serious and effective as was his work, no man loved a grand-stand play more than he. He liked to go it alone, to be the only thing in the spot light. Thus most of his work as a desperado-hunter was done single-handed.

On only one occasion that I can recall did he ever have with him on his raids more than one or two men, always Mexicans, temporarily deputized. That was when he met and cleaned out the Kinney gang over on the Miembres, and did it with half the number of the men he was after. Among those who escaped was Kinney's lieutenant. A few weeks later Colonel Fountain learned that this man was in hiding at Concordia, a *placita* two miles below El Paso. He was one of the most desperate Mexican outlaws the border has ever known, a man who had boasted he would never be taken alive, and that he would kill Fountain before he was himself taken dead, a human tiger, whom the bravest peace officer might be pardoned for wanting a great deal of help to take. Yet Fountain merely took his armory's best and undertook it alone: and by mid-afternoon of the very next day after the information reached him he had his man safely manacled at the El Paso depot of the Santa Fe Railway.

While waiting for the train, Colonel George Baylor, the famous Captain of Texas Rangers, chided Fountain for not wearing a cord to fasten his pistol to his belt, as then did all the Rangers, to prevent its loss from the scabbard in a running fight; and he finished by detaching his own cord, and looping one end to Fountain's belt and the other to his pistol. Then Fountain bade his old friend good-bye and boarded the train with his prisoner, taking a seat near the centre of the rear car.

When well north of Canutillo and near the site of old Fort Fillmore, Fountain rose and passed forward to speak to a friend who was sitting a few seats in front of him, a safe enough proceeding, apparently, with his prisoner handcuffed and the train doing thirty-five miles an hour. But scarcely had he reached his friend's side, when a noise behind him caused him to turn—just in time to see his Mexican running for rear door. Instantly Fountain sprang after him, before he got to the door the man had leaped from the platform. Without the slightest hesitation, Fountain jumped after him, hitting the ground only a few seconds behind him but thirty or forty yards away, rolling like a tumbleweed along the ground. By the time Fountain had regained his feet, his prisoner was running at top speed for the mesquite thickets lining the river, in whose shadows he must soon disappear, for it was already dusk. Reaching for his pistol and finding it gone—lost evidently in the tumble—and fearing to lose his prisoner entirely if he stopped to hunt for it, Fountain hit the best pace he could in pursuit. But almost at the first jump something gave him a thump on the shin that nearly broke it, and, looking down, there, dangling on Colonel Baylor's pistol-cord, he saw his gun.

Always a cunning strategist, Fountain dropped to the ground, sky-lined his man on the crest of a little hillock he had to cross, and took a careful two-handed aim, which enabled Rio Grande ranchers thereafter to sleep easier of nights.

And now, just as I am finishing this story, the wires bring the sad news that dear old Pat Garrett, the dean and almost the last survivor of the famous man-hunters of west Texas and New Mexico, has gone the way of his kind—"died with his boots on." I cannot help believing that he was the victim of a foul shot, for in his personal relations I never knew him to court a quarrel or fail to get an adversary. Many a night we have camped, eaten, and slept together. Barring Colonel Fountain, Pat Garrett had stronger intellectuality and broader sympathies than any of his kind I ever met. He could no more do enough for a friend than he could do enough to an outlaw. In his private affairs so easy-going that he began and ended a ne'er-do-well, in his official duties as a peace officer he was so exacting and painstaking that he ne'er did ill. His many intrepid deeds are too well known to need recounting here.

All his life an atheist, he was as stubbornly contentious for his unbelief as any Scotch Covenanter for his best-loved tenets.

Now, laid for his last rest in the little burying-ground of Las Cruces, a tiny, white-paled square of sandy, hummocky bench land where the pink of fragile nopal petals brightens the graves in Spring and the mesquite showers them with its golden pods in Summer; where the sweet scent of the *juajilla* loads the air, and the sun ever shines down out of a bright and cloudless sky; where a diminutive forest of crosses of wood and stone symbolize the faith he in life refused to accept—now, perhaps, Pat Garrett has learned how widely he was wrong.

Peace to his ashes, and repose to his dauntless spirit!

Mark Twain (1835–1910)

SAMUEL LANGHORNE CLEMENS (Mark Twain) was born in Florida, Missouri. The family soon moved to Hannibal, Missouri, where Twain was raised. In 1847, when Twain was eleven, his father died. He left school, having completed the fifth grade, to work as a printer's apprentice for a local newspaper. At eighteen, Twain went to New York City and Philadelphia, where he worked on several different newspapers and also found some success at writing articles. By 1857, Twain returned home to work as a riverboat pilot on the Mississippi River, but the outbreak of the Civil War in 1861 virtually halted river traffic.

Twain's first major success as an author came in 1865 with the publication of the short story, "Jim Smiley and His Jumping Frog." His writing became so popular that he launched yet another career as a lecturer and stage performer. In 1867, hired by a newspaper as a travel writer, Twain took a steamship tour of Europe and the Holy Land. His travel letters were later reworked into his first book, *The Innocents Abroad* (1869).

Between 1874 and 1891, Twain completed the work he is best known for today—novels such as *The Adventures of Tom Sawyer* (1876), *The Prince and the Pauper* (1881), *Life on the Mississippi* (1883), *Adventures of Huckleberry Finn* (1884), and *A Connecticut Yankee in King Arthur's Court* (1889).

Less well-known are Twain's recollections from his Western experiences, when in the mid-1860s he traveled West with his brother, who had been appointed secretary of the Dakota Territory. Twain, lured by the prospect of striking it rich in Nevada's silver rush, ended up spending a treacherous winter in an isolated mountain shack. He subsequently wrote a book titled *Roughing It* (1872) based upon his experiences of near destitution and the struggle for survival. Chapter 24 follows.

Roughing It (1872)

FROM Chapter 24 (excerpt)

I resolved to have a horse to ride. I had never seen such wild, free, magnificent horsemanship outside of a circus as these picturesquely-clad Mexicans, Californians, and Mexicanized Americans displayed in Carson streets every day. How they rode! Leaning just gently forward out of the perpendicular, easy and nonchalant, with broad slouch-hat brim blown square up in front, and long *riata* swinging above the head, they swept through the town like the wind! The next minute they were only a sailing puff of dust on the far desert. If they trotted, they sat up gallantly and gracefully, and seemed part of the horse; did not go jiggering up and down after the silly Miss-Nancy fashion of the riding-schools. I had quickly learned to tell a horse from a cow, and was full of anxiety to learn more. I was resolved to buy a horse.

While the thought was rankling in my mind, the auctioneer came scurrying through the plaza on a black beast that had as many humps and corners on him as a dromedary, and was necessarily uncomely; but he was "going, going, at twenty-two!—horse, saddle and bridle at twenty-two dollars, gentlemen!" and I could hardly resist.

A man whom I did not know (he turned out to be the auctioneer's brother) noticed the wistful look in my eye, and observed that that was a very remarkable horse to be going at such a price; and added that the saddle alone was worth the money. It was a Spanish saddle, with ponderous *tapidaros,* and furnished with the ungainly sole-leather covering with the unspellable name. I said I had half a notion to bid. Then this keen-eyed person appeared to me to be "taking my measure"; but I dismissed the suspicion when he spoke, for his manner was full of guileless candor and truthfulness. Said he: "I know that horse—know him well. You are a stranger, I take it, and so you might think he was an American horse, maybe, but I assure you he is not. He is nothing of the kind; but—excuse my speaking in a low voice, other people being near—he is, without the shadow of a doubt, a Genuine Mexican Plug!"

I did not know what a Genuine Mexican Plug was, but there was something about this man's way of saying it, that made me swear inwardly that I would own a Genuine Mexican Plug, or die.

"Has he any other—er—advantages?" I inquired, suppressing what eagerness I could.

He hooked his forefinger in the pocket of my army shirt, led me to one side, and breathed in my ear impressively these words:

"He can out-buck anything in America!"

"Going, going, going—at *twent-ty*-four dollars and a half, gen—"

"Twenty-seven!" I shouted, in a frenzy.

"And sold!" said the auctioneer, and passed over the Genuine Mexican Plug to me.

I could scarcely contain my exultation. I paid the money, and put the animal in a neighboring livery-stable to dine and rest himself.

In the afternoon I brought the creature into the plaza, and certain citizens held him by the head, and others by the tail, while I mounted him. As soon as they let go, he placed all his feet in a bunch together, lowered his back, and then suddenly arched it upward, and shot me straight into the air a matter of three or four feet! I came as straight down again, lit in the saddle, went instantly up again, came down almost on the high pommel, shot up again, and came down on the horse's neck—all in the space of three or four seconds. Then he rose and stood almost straight up on his hind feet, and I, clasping his lean neck desperately, slid back into the saddle and held on. He came down, and immediately hoisted his heels into the air, delivering a vicious kick at the sky, and stood on his fore feet. And then down he came once more, and began the original exercise of shooting me straight up again.

The third time I went up I heard a stranger say: "Oh, *don't* he buck, though!"

While I was up, somebody struck the horse a sounding thwack with a leathern strap, and when I arrived again the Genuine Mexican Plug was not there. A California youth chased him up and caught him, and asked if he might have a ride. I granted him that luxury. He mounted the Genuine, got lifted into the air once, but sent his spurs home as he descended, and the horse darted away like a telegram. He soared over three fences like a bird, and disappeared down the road toward the Washoe Valley.

I sat down on a stone with a sigh, and by a natural impulse one of my hands sought my forehead, and the other the base of my stomach.

I believe I never appreciated, till then, the poverty of the human machinery—for I still needed a hand or two to place elsewhere. Pen cannot describe how I was jolted up. Imagination cannot conceive how disjointed I was—how internally, externally, and universally I was unsettled, mixed up, and ruptured. There was a sympathetic crowd around me, though.

One elderly-looking comforter said:

"Stranger, you've been taken in. Everybody in this camp knows that horse. Any child, any Injun, could have told you that he'd buck; he is the very worst devil to buck on the continent of America. You hear *me*. I'm Curry. *Old* Curry. Old *Abe* Curry. And moreover, he is a simon-pure, out-and-out, genuine d—d Mexican plug, and an uncommon mean one at that, too. Why, you turnip, if you had laid low and kept dark, there's chances to buy an *American* horse for mighty little more than you paid for that bloody old foreign relic."

I gave no sign; but I made up my mind that if the auctioneer's brother's funeral took place while I was in the territory I would postpone all other recreations and attend it.

After a gallop of sixteen miles the Californian youth and the Genuine Mexican Plug came tearing into town again, shedding foam-flakes like the spume-spray that drives before a typhoon, and, with one final skip over a wheelbarrow and a Chinaman, cast anchor in front of the "ranch."

Such panting and blowing! Such spreading and contracting of the red equine nostrils, and glaring of the wild equine eye! But was the imperial beast subjugated? Indeed, he was not. His lordship the Speaker of the House thought he was, and mounted him to go down to the Capitol; but the first dash the creature made was over a pile of telegraph poles half as high as a church; and his time to the Capitol—one mile and three-quarters—remains unbeaten to this day. But then he took an advantage—he left out the mile, and only did the three-quarters. That is to say, he made a straight cut across lots, preferring fences and ditches to a crooked road; and when the Speaker got to the Capitol he said he had been in the air so much he felt as if he had made the trip on a comet.

In the evening the Speaker came home afoot for exercise, and got the Genuine towed back behind a quartz-wagon. The next day I loaned the animal to the Clerk of the House to go down to the Dana silver-mine, six miles, and *he* walked back for exercise, and got the horse towed. Everybody I loaned him to always walked back; they

never could get enough exercise any other way. Still, I continued to
loan him to anybody who was willing to borrow him, my idea being
to get him crippled, and throw him on the borrower's hands, or
killed, and make the borrower pay for him. But somehow nothing
ever happened to him. He took chances that no other horse ever
took and survived, but he always came out safe. It was his daily habit
to try experiments that had always before been considered impossible, but he always got through. Sometimes he miscalculated a little,
and did not get his rider through intact, but *he* always got through
himself. Of course I had tried to sell him; but that was a stretch of
simplicity which met with little sympathy. The auctioneer stormed
up and down the streets on him for four days, dispersing the popu-
lace, interrupting business, and destroying children, and never got a
bid—at least never any but the eighteen-dollar one he hired a noto-
riously substanceless bummer to make. The people only smiled pleasantly, and restrained their desire to buy, if they had any. Then the
auctioneer brought in his bill, and I withdrew the horse from the
market. We tried to trade him off at private vendue next, offering
him at a sacrifice for second-hand tombstones, old iron, temperance
tracts—any kind of property. But holders were stiff, and we retired
from the market again. I never tried to ride the horse any more.
Walking was good enough exercise for a man like me, that had nothing the matter with him except ruptures, internal injuries, and such
things. Finally I tried to give him away. But it was a failure. Parties
said earthquakes were handy enough on the Pacific coast—they did
not wish to own one. As a last resort I offered him to the Governor
for the use of the "Brigade." His face lit up eagerly at first, but toned
down again, and he said the thing would be too palpable.

Just then the livery stable-man brought in his bill for six weeks'
keeping—stall-room for the horse, fifteen dollars; hay for the horse,
two hundred and fifty! The Genuine Mexican Plug had eaten a ton
of the article, and the man said he would have eaten a hundred if he
had let him.

I will remark here, in all seriousness, that the regular price of hay
during that year and a part of the next was really two hundred and
fifty dollars a ton. During a part of the previous year it had sold at
five hundred a ton, in gold, and during the winter before that there
was such scarcity of the article that in several instances small quantities
had brought eight hundred dollars a ton in coin! The consequence
might be guessed without my telling it: peopled turned their stock

loose to starve, and before the spring arrived Carson and Eagle Valleys were almost literally carpeted with their carcasses! Any old settler there will verify these statements.

I managed to pay the livery bill, and that same day I gave the Genuine Mexican Plug to a passing Arkansas emigrant whom fortune delivered into my hand. If this ever meets his eye, he will doubtless remember the donation.

Now whoever has had the luck to ride a real Mexican plug will recognize the animal depicted in this chapter, and hardly consider him exaggerated—but the uninitiated will feel justified in regarding his portrait as a fancy sketch, perhaps.

Max Brand (1892–1944)

MAX BRAND was born Frederick Schiller Faust in Seattle, May 1892. He grew up in California and later worked as a cowhand on a ranch in the San Joaquin Valley. Brand attended the University of California, Berkeley, where he began writing. He wrote his first Western story for *All-Story Weekly* in 1918. Brand later moved to New York where he wrote for weekly pulp magazines. In 1925, he moved his family to Europe. With World War II looming, Faust returned with his family to the United States, settling in Hollywood, and working as a scriptwriter for several film studios. He created the Western character Destry, featured in several film versions of *Destry Rides Again*.

Considered one the most prolific American writers of all time, Brand wrote more than thirty million words and published five hundred novels for magazines as well as an untold number of stories.

The first chapter from the novel *Ronicky Doone* (1921) follows.

A Horse in Need

FROM *Ronicky Doone*, 1921

He came into the town as a solid, swiftly moving dust cloud. The wind from behind had kept the dust moving forward at a pace just equal to the gallop of his horse. Not until he had brought his mount to a halt in front of the hotel and swung down to the ground did either he or his horse become distinctly visible. Then it was seen that the animal was in the last stages of exhaustion, with dull eyes and hanging head and forelegs braced widely apart, while the sweat dripped steadily from his flanks into the white dust on the street. Plainly he had been pushed to the last limit of his strength.

The rider was almost as far spent as his mount, for he went up the steps of the hotel with his shoulders sagging with weariness, a wide-shouldered, gaunt-ribbed man. Thick layers of dust had turned his red kerchief and his blue shirt to a common gray. Dust, too, made a mask of his face, and through that mask the eyes peered out, surrounded by pink skin. Even at its best the long, solemn face could never have been called handsome. But, on this particular day, he seemed a haunted man, or one fleeing from an inescapable danger.

The two loungers at the door of the hotel instinctively stepped aside and made room for him to pass, but apparently he had no desire to enter the building. Suddenly he became doubly imposing, as he stood on the veranda and stared up and down at the idlers. Certainly his throat must be thick and hot with dust, but an overmastering purpose made him oblivious of thirst.

"Gents," he said huskily, while a gust of wind fanned a cloud of dust from his clothes, "is there anybody in this town can gimme a hoss to get to Stillwater, inside three hours' riding?"

He waited a moment, his hungry eyes traveling eagerly from face to face. Naturally the oldest man spoke first, since this was a matter of life and death.

"Any hoss in town can get you there in that time, if you know the short way across the mountain."

"How do you take it? That's the way for me."

But the old fellow shook his head and smiled in pity. "Not if you ain't rode it before. I used to go that way when I was a kid, but nowadays nobody rides that way except Doone. That trail is as tricky as the ways of a coyote; you'd sure get lost without a guide."

The stranger turned and followed the gesture of the speaker. The mountain rose from the very verge of the town, a ragged mass of sand and rock, with miserable sagebrush clinging here and there, as dull and uninteresting as the dust itself. Then he lowered the hand from beneath which he had peered and faced about with a sigh. "I guess it ain't much good trying that way. But I got to get to Stillwater inside of three hours."

"They's one hoss in town can get you there," said the old man. "But you can't get that hoss today."

The stranger groaned. "Then I'll make another hoss stretch out and do."

"Can't be done. Doone's hoss is a marvel. Nothing else about here can touch him, and he's the only one that can make the trip around the mountain, inside of three hours. You'd kill another hoss trying to do it, what with your weight."

The stranger groaned again and struck his knuckles against his forehead. "But why can't I get the hoss? Is Doone out of town with it?"

"The hoss ain't out of town, but Doone is."

The traveler clenched his fists. This delay and waste of priceless time was maddening him. "Gents," he called desperately, "I got to get to Martindale today. It's more than life or death to me. Where's Doone's hoss?"

"Right across the road," said the old man who had spoken first. "Over yonder in the corral—the bay."

The traveler turned and saw, beyond the road, a beautiful mare, not very tall, but a mare whose every inch of her fifteen three proclaimed strength and speed. At that moment she raised her head and looked across to him, and the heart of the rider jumped into his throat. The very sight of her was an omen of victory, and he made a long stride in her direction, but two men came before him. The old fellow jumped from the chair and tapped his arm.

"You ain't going to take the bay without getting leave from Doone?"

"Gents, I got to," said the stranger. "Listen! My name's Gregg, Bill Gregg. Up in my country they know I'm straight; down here you ain't heard of me. I ain't going to keep that hoss, and I'll pay a hundred dollars for the use of her for one day. I'll bring or send her back safe and sound, tomorrow. Here's the money. One of you gents, that's a friend of Doone, take it for him."

Not a hand was stretched out; every head shook in negation.

"I'm too fond of the little life that's left to me," said the old fellow. "I won't rent out that hoss for him. Why, he loves that mare like she was his sister. He'd fight like a flash rather than see another man ride her."

But Bill Gregg had his eyes on the bay, and the sight of her was stealing his reason. He knew, as well as he knew that he was a man, that, once in the saddle on her, he would be sure to win. Nothing could stop him. And straight through the restraining circle he broke with a groan of anxiety.

Only the old man who had been the spokesman called after him: "Gregg, don't be a fool. Maybe you don't recognize the name of Doone, but the whole name is Ronicky Doone. Does that mean anything to you?"

Into the back of Gregg's mind came several faint memories, but they were obscure and uncertain. "Blast your Ronicky Doone!" he replied. "I got to have that hoss, and, if none of you'll take money for her rent, I'll take her free and pay her rent when I come through this way tomorrow, maybe. S'long!"

While he spoke he had been undoing the cinches of his own horse. Now he whipped the saddle and bridle off, shouted to the hotel keeper brief instructions for the care of the weary animal and ran across the road with the saddle on his arm.

In the corral he had no difficulty with the mare. She came straight to him in spite of all the flopping trappings. With prickly ears and eyes lighted with kindly curiosity she looked the dusty fellow over.

He slipped the bridle over her head. When he swung the saddle over her back she merely turned her head and carelessly watched it fall. And when he drew up the cinches hard, she only stamped in mock anger. The moment he was in the saddle she tossed her head eagerly, ready to be off.

He looked across the street to the veranda of the hotel, as he passed through the gate of the corral. The men were standing in a long and awe-stricken line, their eyes wide, their mouths agape. Whoever Ronicky Doone might be, he was certainly a man who had won the respect of this town. The men on the veranda looked at Bill Gregg as though he were already a ghost. He waved his hand defiantly at them and the mare, at a word from him, sprang into a long-striding gallop that whirled them rapidly down the street and out of the village.

The bay mare carried him with amazing speed over the ground. They rounded the base of the big mountain, and, glancing up at the ragged canyons which chopped the face of the peak, he was glad that he had not attempted that short cut. If Ronicky Doone could make that trail he was a skillful horseman.

Bill Gregg swung up over the left shoulder of the mountain and found himself looking down on the wide plain which held Stillwater. The air was crystal-clear and dry; the shoulder of the mountain was high above it; Gregg saw a breathless stretch of the cattle country at one sweep of his eyes.

Stillwater was still a long way off, and far away across the plain he saw a tiny moving dot that grew slowly. It was the train heading for Stillwater, and that train he must beat to the station. For a moment his heart stood still; then he saw that the train was distant indeed, and, by the slightest use of the mare's speed, he would be able to reach the town, two or three minutes ahead of it.

But, just as he was beginning to exult in the victory, after all the hard riding of the past three days, the mare tossed up her head and shortened her stride. The heart of Gregg stopped, and he went cold. It was not only the fear that his journey might be ruined, but the fear that something had happened to this magnificent creature beneath him. He swung to the side in the saddle and watched her gallop. Certain she went laboring, very much as though she were trying to run against a mighty pull on the reins.

He looked at her head. It was thrown high, with pricking ears. Perhaps she was frightened by some foolish thing near the road. He touched her with the spurs, and she increased her pace to the old length and ease of stride; but, just as he had begun to be reassured, her step shortened and fell to laboring again, and this time she threw her head higher than before. It was amazing to Bill Gregg; and then it seemed to him that he heard a faint, far whistling, floating down from high above his head.

Again that thin, long-drawn sound, and this time, glancing over his right shoulder, he saw a horseman plunging down the slope of the mountain. He knew instantly that it was Ronicky Doone. The man had come to recapture his horse and had taken the short cut across the mountain to come up with her. Just by a fraction of a minute Doone would be too late, for, by the time he came down onto the trail, the bay would be well ahead, and certainly no horse lived in those mountains capable of overtaking her when she felt like running. Gregg touched her again with the spurs, but this time she reared straight up and, whirling to the side, faced steadily toward her onrushing master.

Stewart Edward White (1873–1946)

STEWART EDWARD WHITE was born in Grand Rapids, Michigan, the son of a successful lumberman. In 1898, White graduated from the University of Michigan, after which he worked as a lumberjack, a cowboy, and a gold prospector.

White's first collection of stories, *The Claim Jumpers,* appeared in 1901. His first real success came with the publication of *The Blazed Trail* in 1902. In 1904, *The Blazed Trail Stories* were published. For the next twenty years, White would publish many more short stories, novels, and articles about his experiences in the mining and lumber camps of California and his many adventure trips.

"On Cowboys" is from *The Mountains* (1904).

On Cowboys

FROM *The Mountains*, 1904

Your cowboy is a species variously subdivided. If you happen to be traveled as to the wild countries, you will be able to recognize whence your chance acquaintance hails by the kind of saddle he rides, and the rigging of it; by the kind of rope he throws, and the method of the throwing; by the shape of hat he wears; by his twist of speech; even by the very manner of his riding. Your California "vaquero" from the Coast Ranges is as unlike as possible to your Texas cowman, and both differ from the Wyoming or South Dakota article. I should be puzzled to define exactly the habitat of the "typical" cowboy. No matter where you go, you will find your individual acquaintance varying from the type in respect to some of the minor details.

Certain characteristics run through the whole tribe, however. Of these some are so well known or have been so adequately done elsewhere that it hardly seems wise to elaborate on them here. Let us assume that you and I know what sort of human beings cowboys are,—with all their taciturnity, their surface gravity, their keen sense of humor, their courage, their kindness, their freedom, their lawlessness, their foulness of mouth, and their supreme skill in the handling of horses and cattle. I shall try to tell you nothing of all that.

If one thinks down doggedly to the last analysis, he will find that the basic reason for the differences between a cowboy and other men rests finally on an individual liberty, a freedom from restraint either of society or convention, a lawlessness, an accepting of his own standard alone. He is absolutely self-poised and sufficient; and that self-poise and that sufficiency he takes pains to assure first of all. After their assurance he is willing to enter into human relations. His attitude toward everything in life is, not suspicious, but watchful. He is "gathered together," his elbows at his side.

This evidences itself most strikingly in his terseness of speech. A man dependent on himself naturally does not give himself away to the first comer. He is more interested in finding out what the other fellow is than in exploiting his own importance. A man who does much promiscuous talking he is likely to despise, arguing that man incautious, hence weak.

Yet when he does talk, he talks to the point and with a vivid and direct picturesqueness of phrase which is as refreshing as it is unexpected. The delightful remodeling of the English language in Mr. Alfred Lewis's "Wolfville" is exaggerated only in quantity, not in quality. No cowboy talks habitually in quite as original a manner as Mr. Lewis's Old Cattleman; but I have no doubt that in time he would be heard to say all the good things in that volume. I myself have note-books full of just such gorgeous language, some of the best of which I have used elsewhere, and so will not repeat here.

This vividness manifests itself quite as often in the selection of the apt word as in the construction of elaborate phrases with a half-humorous intention. A cowboy once told me of the arrival of a tramp by saying, "He *sifted* into camp." Could any verb be more expressive? Does not it convey exactly the lazy, careless, out-at-heels shuffling gait of the hobo? Another in the course of description told of a saloon scene, "They all *bellied up to* the bar." Again, a range cook, objecting to purposeless idling about his fire, shouted: "If you fellows come *moping* around here any more, *I'll sure make you hard to catch!*" "Fish in that pond, son? Why, there's some fish in there big enough to rope," another advised me. "I quit shoveling," one explained the story of his life, "because I couldn't see nothing ahead of shoveling but dirt." The same man described ploughing as, "Looking at a mule's tail all day." And one of the most succinct epitomes of the motifs of fiction was offered by an old fellow who looked over my shoulder as I was reading a novel. "Well, son," said he, "what they doing now, *kissing or killing?*"

Nor are the complete phrases behind in aptness. I have space for only a few examples, but they will illustrate what I mean. Speaking of a companion who was "putting on too much dog," I was informed, "He walks like a man with a new suit of *wooden underwear!*" Or again, in answer to my inquiry as to a mutual acquaintance, "Jim? Oh, poor old Jim! For the last week or so he's been nothing but an insignificant atom of humanity hitched to a boil."

But to observe the riot of imagination turned loose with the bridle off, you must assist at a burst of anger on the part of one of these men. It is mostly unprintable, but you will get an entirely new idea of what profanity means. Also you will come to the conclusion that you, with your trifling *damns,* and the like, have been a very good boy indeed. The remotest, most obscure, and unheard of conceptions are dragged forth from earth, heaven, and hell, and linked together in a sequence so original, so gaudy, and so utterly blasphemous, that you gasp and are stricken with the most devoted admiration. It is genius. Of course I can give you no idea here of what these truly magnificent oaths are like. It is a pity, for it would liberalize your education. Occasionally, like a trickle of clear water into an alkali torrent, a straight English sentence will drop into the flood. It is refreshing by contrast, but weak.

"If your brains were all made of dynamite, you couldn't blow the top of your head off."

"I wouldn't speak to him if I met him in hell carrying a lump of ice in his hand."

"That little horse'll throw you so high the blackbirds will build nests in your hair before you come down."

These are ingenious and amusing, but need the blazing settings from which I have ravished them to give them their due force.

In Arizona a number of us were sitting around the feeble camp-fire the desert scarcity of fuel permits, smoking our pipes. We were all contemplative and comfortably silent with the exception of one very youthful person who had a lot to say. It was mainly about himself. After he had bragged awhile without molestation, one of the older cow-punchers grew very tired of it. He removed his pipe deliberately, and spat in the fire.

"Say, son," he drawled, "if you want to say something big, why don't you say 'elephant'?"

The young fellow subsided. We went on smoking our pipes.

Down near the Chiracahua Range in southeastern Arizona, there is a butte, and halfway up that butte is a cave, and in front of that cave is a ramshackle porch-roof or shed. This latter makes the cave into a dwelling-house. It is inhabited by an old "alkali" and half a dozen bear dogs. I sat with the old fellow one day for nearly an hour. It was a sociable visit, but economical of the English language. He made one remark, outside our initial greeting. It was enough, for in terseness, accuracy, and compression, I have never heard a better or more comprehensive description of the arid countries.

"Son," said he, "in this country thar is more cows and less butter, more rivers and less water, and you kin see farther and see less than in any other country in the world." Now this peculiar directness of phrase means but one thing,— freedom from the influence of convention. The cowboy respects neither the dictionary nor usage. He employs his words in the manner that best suits him, and arranges them in the sequence that best expresses his idea, untrammeled by tradition. It is a phase of the same lawlessness, the same reliance on self, that makes for his taciturnity and watchfulness.

In essence, his dress is an adaptation to the necessities of his calling; as a matter of fact, it is an elaboration on that. The broad heavy felt hat he has found by experience to be more effective in turning heat than a lighter straw; he further runs to variety in the shape of the crown and in the nature of the band. He wears a silk handkerchief about his neck to turn the sun and keep out the dust, but indulges in astonishing gaudiness of color. His gauntlets save his hands from the rope; he adds a fringe and a silver star. The heavy wide "chaps" of leather about his legs are necessary to him when he is riding fast through brush; he indulges in such frivolities as stamped leather, angora hair, and the like. High heels to his boots prevent his foot from slipping through his wide stirrup, and are useful to dig into the ground when he is roping in the corral. Even his six-shooter is more a tool of his trade than a weapon of defense. With it he frightens cattle from the heavy brush; he slaughters old or diseased steers; he "turns the herd" in a stampede or when rounding it in; and especially is it handy and loose to his hip in case his horse should fall and commence to drag him.

So the details of his appearance spring from the practical, but in the wearing of them and the using of them he shows again that fine disregard for the way other people do it or think it.

Now in civilization you and I entertain a double respect for firearms and the law. Firearms are dangerous, and it is against the law to use them promiscuously. If we shoot them off in unexpected places, we first of all alarm unduly our families and neighbors, and in due course attract the notice of the police. By the time we are grown up we look on shooting a revolver as something to be accomplished after an especial trip for the purpose.

But to the cowboy shooting a gun is merely what lighting a match would be to us. We take reasonable care not to scratch that match on the wall nor to throw it where it will do harm. Likewise the cowboy takes reasonable care that his bullets do not land in some one's anatomy nor in too expensive bric-a-brac. Otherwise any time or place will do. The picture comes to me of a bunk-house on an Arizona range. The time was evening. A half-dozen cowboys were sprawled out on the beds smoking, and three more were playing poker with the Chinese cook. A misguided rat darted out from under one of the beds and made for the empty fireplace. He finished his journey in smoke. Then the four who had shot slipped their guns back into their holsters and resumed their cigarettes and drawling low-toned conversation.

On another occasion I stopped for noon at the Circle I ranch. While waiting for dinner, I lay on my back in the bunk-room and counted three hundred and sixty-two bullet-holes in the ceiling. They came to be there because the festive cowboys used to while away the time while lying as I was lying, waiting for supper, in shooting the flies that crawled about the plaster.

This beautiful familiarity with the pistol as a parlor toy accounts in great part for a cowboy's propensity to "shoot up the town" and his indignation when arrested therefor.

The average cowboy is only a fair target-shot with the revolver. But he is chain lightning at getting his gun off in a hurry. There are exceptions to this, however, especially among the older men. Some can handle the Colts 45 and its heavy recoil with almost uncanny accuracy. I have seen individuals who could from their saddles nip lizards darting across the road; and one who was able to perforate twice before it hit the ground a tomato-can tossed into the air. The cowboy is prejudiced against the double-action gun, for some reason or other. He manipulates his single-action weapon fast enough, however.

His sense of humor takes the same unexpected slants, not because his mental processes differ from those of other men, but because he is unshackled by the subtle and unnoticed nothingnesses of precedent which deflect our action toward the common uniformity of our neighbors. It must be confessed that his sense of humor possesses also a certain robustness.

The J. H. outfit had been engaged for ten days in busting broncos. This the Chinese cook, Sang, a newcomer in the territory, found vastly amusing. He liked to throw the ropes off the prostrate broncos, when all was ready; to slap them on the flanks; to yell shrill Chinese yells; and to dance in celestial delight when the terrified animal arose and scattered out of there. But one day the range men drove up a little bunch of full-grown cattle that had been bought from a smaller owner. It was necessary to change the brands. Therefore a little fire was built, the stamp-brand put in to heat, and two of the men on horseback caught a cow by the horns and one hind leg, and promptly upset her. The old brand was obliterated, the new one burnt in. This irritated the cow. Promptly the branding-men, who were of course afoot, climbed to the top of the corral to be out of the way. At this moment, before the horsemen could flip loose their ropes, Sang appeared.

"Hol' on!" he babbled. "I take him off"; and he scrambled over the fence and approached the cow.

Now cattle of any sort rush at the first object they see after getting to their feet. But whereas a steer makes a blind run and so can be avoided, a cow keeps her eyes open. Sang approached that wild-eyed cow, a bland smile on his countenance.

A dead silence fell. Looking about at my companions' faces I could not discern even in the depths of their eyes a single faint flicker of human interest.

Sang loosened the rope from the hind leg, he threw it from the horns, he slapped the cow with his hat, and uttered the shrill Chinese yell. So far all was according to programme.

The cow staggered to her feet, her eyes blazing fire. She took one good look, and then started for Sang.

What followed occurred with all the briskness of a tune from a circus band. Sang darted for the corral fence. Now, three sides of the corral were railed, and so climbable, but the fourth was a solid adobe wall. Of course Sang went for the wall. There, finding his nails would not stick, he fled down the length of it, his queue streaming, his eyes popping, his talons curved toward an ideal of safety, gibbering strange monkey talk, pursued a scant arm's length behind by that infuriated cow. Did any one help him? Not any. Every man of that crew was hanging weak from laughter to the horn of his saddle or the top of the fence. The preternatural solemnity had broken to little bits. Men came running from the bunk-house, only to go into spasms outside, to roll over and over on the ground, clutching handfuls of herbage in the agony of their delight.

At the end of the corral was a narrow chute. Into this Sang escaped as into a burrow. The cow came too. Sang, in desperation, seized a pole, but the cow dashed such a feeble weapon aside. Sang caught sight of a little opening, too small for cows, back into the main corral. He squeezed through. The cow crashed through after him, smashing the boards. At the crucial moment Sang tripped and fell on his face. The cow missed him by so close a margin that for a moment we thought she had hit. But she had not, and before she could turn, Sang had topped the fence and was halfway to the kitchen. Tom Waters always maintained that he spread his Chinese sleeves and flew. Shortly after a tremendous smoke arose from the kitchen chimney. Sang had gone back to cooking.

Now that Mongolian was really in great danger, but no one of the outfit thought for a moment of any but the humorous aspect of the affair. Analogously, in a certain small cow-town I happened to be transient when the postmaster shot a Mexican. Nothing was done about it. The man went right on being postmaster, but he had to set up the drinks because he had hit the Mexican in the stomach. That was considered a poor place to hit a man.

The entire town of Willcox knocked off work for nearly a day to while away the tedium of an enforced wait there on my part. They wanted me to go fishing. One man offered a team, the other a saddle-horse. All expended much eloquence in directing me accurately, so that I should be sure to find exactly the spot where I could hang my feet over a bank beneath which there were "a plumb plenty of fish." Somehow or other they raked out miscellaneous tackle. But they were a little too eager. I excused myself and hunted up a map. Sure enough the lake was there, but it had been dry since a previous geological period. The fish were undoubtedly there too, but they were fossil fish. I borrowed a pickaxe and shovel and announced myself as ready to start.

Outside the principal saloon in one town hung a gong. When a stranger was observed to enter the saloon, that gong was sounded. Then it behooved him to treat those who came in answer to the summons.

But when it comes to a case of real hospitality or helpfulness, your cowboy is there every time. You are welcome to food and shelter without price, whether he is at home or not. Only it is etiquette to leave your name and thanks pinned somewhere about the place. Otherwise your intrusion may be considered in the light of a theft, and you may be pursued accordingly.

Contrary to general opinion, the cowboy is not a dangerous man to those not looking for trouble. There are occasional exceptions, of course, but they belong to the universal genus of bully, and can be found among any class. Attend to your own business, be cool and good-natured, and your skin is safe. Then when it is really "up to you," be a man; you will never lack for friends.

The Sierras, especially towards the south where the meadows are wide and numerous, are full of cattle in small bands. They come up from the desert about the first of June, and are driven back again to the arid countries as soon as the autumn storms begin. In the very high land they are few, and to be left to their own devices; but now we entered a new sort of country.

Below Farewell Gap and the volcanic regions one's surroundings change entirely. The meadows become high flat valleys, often miles in extent; the mountains—while registering big on the aneroid—are so little elevated above the plateaus that a few thousand feet is all of their apparent height; the passes are low, the slopes easy, the trails good, the rock outcrops few, the hills grown with forests to their very tops. Altogether it is a country easy to ride through, rich in grazing, cool and green, with its eight thousand feet of elevation. Consequently during the hot months thousands of desert cattle are pastured here; and with them come many of the desert men.

Our first intimation of these things was in the volcanic region where swim the golden trout. From the advantage of a hill we looked far down to a hair-grass meadow through which twisted tortuously a brook, and by the side of the brook, belittled by distance, was a miniature man. We could see distinctly his every movement, as he approached cautiously the stream's edge, dropped his short line at the end of a stick over the bank, and then yanked bodily the fish from beneath. Behind him stood his pony. We could make out in the clear air the coil of his raw-hide "rope," the glitter of his silver bit, the metal points on his saddle skirts, the polish of his six-shooter, the gleam of his fish, all the details of his costume. Yet he was fully a mile distant. After a time he picked up his string of fish, mounted, and jogged loosely away at the cow-pony's little Spanish trot toward the south. Over a week later, having caught golden trout and climbed Mount Whitney, we followed him and so came to the great central camp at Monache Meadows.

Imagine an island-dotted lake of grass four or five miles long by two or three wide to which slope regular shores of stony soil planted with trees. Imagine on the very edge of that lake an especially fine grove perhaps a quarter of a mile in length, beneath whose trees a dozen different outfits of cowboys are camped for the summer. You must place a herd of ponies in the foreground, a pine mountain at the back, an unbroken ridge across ahead, cattle dotted here and there, thousands of ravens wheeling and croaking and flapping everywhere, a marvelous clear sun and blue sky. The camps were mostly open, though a few possessed tents. They differed from the ordinary in that they had racks for saddles and equipments. Especially well laid out were the cooking arrangements. A dozen accommodating springs supplied fresh water with the conveniently regular spacing of faucets.

Towards evening the men jingled in. This summer camp was almost in the nature of a vacation to them after the hard work of the desert. All they had to do was to ride about the pleasant hills examining that the cattle did not stray nor get into trouble. It was fun for them, and they were in high spirits.

Our immediate neighbors were an old man of seventy-two and his grandson of twenty-five. At least the old man said he was seventy-two. I should have guessed fifty. He was as straight as an arrow, wiry, lean, clear-eyed, and had, without food, ridden twelve hours after some strayed cattle. On arriving he threw off his saddle, turned his horse loose, and set about the construction of supper. This consisted of boiled meat, strong tea, and an incredible number of flapjacks built of water, baking-powder, salt, and flour, warmed through—not cooked—in a frying-pan. He deluged these with molasses and devoured three platefuls. It would have killed an ostrich, but apparently did this decrepit veteran of seventy-two much good.

After supper he talked to us most interestingly in the dry cowboy manner, looking at us keenly from under the floppy brim of his hat. He confided to us that he had had to quit smoking, and it ground him—he'd smoked since he was five years old.

"Tobacco doesn't agree with you any more?" I hazarded.

"Oh, 'taint that," he replied; "only I'd ruther chew."

The dark fell, and all the little camp-fires under the trees twinkled bravely forth. Some of the men sang. One had an accordion. Figures, indistinct and formless, wandered here and there in the shadows, suddenly emerging from mystery into the clarity of firelight, there to disclose themselves as visitors. Out on the plain the cattle lowed, the horses nickered. The red firelight flashed from the metal of suspended equipment, crimsoned the bronze of men's faces, touched with pink the high lights on their gracefully recumbent forms. After a while we rolled up in our blankets and went to sleep, while a band of coyotes wailed like lost spirits from a spot where a steer had died.

William MacLeod Raine (1871–1954)

WILLIAM MACLEOD RAINE was born in London in 1871. He immigrated with his family to the United States when he was ten years old, and the family settled in Arkansas. Raine graduated from Oberlin College in Ohio in 1894 and moved to Seattle, where he worked as a ranch hand. Raine became a newspaper reporter, moved to Denver, and worked for several Denver newspapers to earn a living until his first Western novel, *Wyoming* (1908), was published. Its success enabled him to support himself solely through his writing.

Raine wrote more than fifty books during his career, including *A Texas Ranger* (1910), *Yukon Trail* (1917), and *A Man Four-Square* (1919).

With fast-paced plots and a variety of settings, Raine's fiction and nonfiction works embodied the spirit of the West, often in cowboy vernacular. They also inspired many films.

Raine died in 1954 and was posthumously inducted into the Hall of Great Westerners in the National Cowboy and Western Heritage Museum in Oklahoma City, in 1959.

"A Shot from Ambush" is from *Mavericks* (1912).

A Shot from Ambush

FROM *Mavericks,* 1912

From the valley there drifted up a breeze-swept sound. The rider on the rock-rim trail above, shifting in his saddle to one of the easy, careless attitudes of the habitual horseman, recognized it as a rifle shot.

Presently, from a hidden wash rose little balloon-like puffs of smoke, followed by a faint, far popping, as if somebody had touched off a bunch of firecrackers. Men on horseback, dwarfed by distance to pygmy size, clambered to the bank—now one and then another firing into the mesquite that ran like a broad tongue from the roll of hills into the valley.

"Looks like something's broke loose," the young man drawled aloud. "The band's sure playing a right lively tune this glad mo'ning."

Save for one or two farewell shots, the firing ceased. The riders had disappeared into the chaparral.

The rider did not need to be told that this was a man hunt, destined perhaps to be one of a hundred unwritten desert tragedies. Some subtle instinct in him differentiated between these hurried shots and those born of the casual exuberance of the cow-puncher at play. He had a reason for taking an interest in it—an interest that was more than casual.

Skirting the rim of the saucer-shaped valley, he rode forward warily, came at length to a cañon that ran like a sword cleft into the hills, and descended cautiously by a cattle trail, its scarred slope.

Through the defile ran a mountain stream, splashing over and round boulders in its swift fall.

"I reckon we'll slide down, Keno, and work out close to the fire zone," the rider said to his horse, as they began to slither down the precipitous slope, starting rubble at every motion.

Man and horse were both of the frontier, fit to the minute for any

222

call that might be made on them. The broncho was a roan, with muscles of elastic leather, sure-footed as a mountain goat. Its master—a slim, brown man, of medium height, well knit and muscular—looked on the world, quietly and often humorously, with shrewd gray eyes.

As he reached the bottom of the gulch, his glance fell upon another rider—a woman. She crossed the stream hurriedly, her pony flinging water at every step, and cantered up toward him.

Her glance was once and again over her shoulder, so that it was not until she was almost upon him that she saw the young man among the cottonwoods, and drew her pony to an instant halt. The rifle that had been lying across her saddle leaped halfway to her shoulder, covering him instantly.

"*Buenos dios, senorita.* Are you going for to shoot my head off?" he drawled.

"The rustler!" she cried.

"The alleged rustler, Miss Sanderson," he corrected gently.

"Let me past," she panted.

He observed that her eyes mirrored terror of the scene she had just left.

"It's you that has got the drop on me, isn't it?" he suggested.

The rifle went back to the saddle. Instantly the girl was in motion again, flying up the cañon past the white-stockinged roan, her pony's hindquarters gathered to take the sheep trail like those of a wild cat.

Keller gazed after her. As she disappeared, he took off his hat, bowed elaborately, and remarked to himself, in his low, soft drawl:

"Good mo'ning, ma'am. See you again one of these days, mebbe, when you ain't in such a hurry."

But though he appeared to take the adventure whimsically his mind was busy with its meaning. She was in danger, and he must save her. So much he knew at least.

He had scarcely turned the head of his horse toward the mouth of the cañon when the pursuit drove headlong into sight. Galloping men pounded up the arroyo, and came to halt at his sharp summons. Already Keller and his horse were behind a huge boulder, over the top of which gleamed the short barrel of a wicked-looking gun.

"Mornin', gentlemen. Lost something up this gulch, have you?" he wanted to know amiably.

The last rider, coming to a gingerly halt in order not to jar an arm bandaged roughly in a polka-dot bandanna, swore roundly. He was a large, heavy-set man, still on the sunny side of forty, imperious, a born leader, and, by the look of him, not one lightly to be crossed. "He's our man, boys. We'll take him alive if we can; but, dead or alive, he's ours." He gave crisp orders.

"Oh! It's me you've lost? Any reward?" inquired the man behind the rock.

For answer, a bullet flattened itself against the boulder. The wounded man had whipped up a rifle and fired.

Keller called out a genial warning. "I wouldn't do that. There's too many of you bunched close together, and this old gun spatters like hail. You see, it's loaded with buckshot."

One of the cowboys laughed. He was rather a cool hand himself, but such audacity as this was new to him.

"What's ailing you, Pesky? It don't strike me as being so damned amusing," growled his leader.

"Different here, Buck. I was just grinning because he's such a cheerful guy. Of course, I ain't got one of his pills in my arm, like you have."

"He won't be so gay about it when he's down, with a couple of bullets through him," predicted the other grimly. "But we'll take his advice, just the same. You boys scatter. Cross the creek and sneak up along the other wall, Ned. Curly, you and Irwin climb up this side until you get him in sight. Pesky and I will stay here."

"Hold on a minute! Let's get at the rights of this. What's all the row about?" the cornered man wanted to know.

"You know dashed well what it's about, you blanked bush-whacker. But you didn't shoot straight enough, and you didn't fix it so you could make your getaway. I'm going to hang you high as Haman."

"Thank you. But your intentions aren't directed to the right man. I'm a stranger in this country. Whyfor should I want to shoot you?"

"A stranger. Where from?" demanded Buck Weaver crisply.

"Douglas."

"What doing here?"

"Homesteading."

"Name?"

"Keller."

"Killer, you mean, I reckon. You're a hired assassin, brought in to shoot me. That's what you are."

"No."

"Yes. The man we want came into this gulch, not three minutes ahead of us. If you're not the man, where is he?"

"I haven't got him in my vest pocket."

"I reckon you've got him right there in your coat and pants."

"I ain't so dead sure, Buck," spoke up Pesky. "We didn't see the man so as to know him."

"Riding a roan, wasn't he?" snapped the owner of the Twin Star outfit.

"Looked that way," admitted the cowpuncher.

"Well, then?"

"Keller! Why, that's the name given by the rustler who broke away from us two weeks ago," Curly spoke out.

"No use jawing. I'm going to hang his skin up to dry," Weaver ground out between set teeth.

"By his own way of it, he's only one of them dashed nesters," Irwin added.

Keller was putting two and two together, in amazement. The would-be assassin had, during the past few minutes, been driven into this gulch, riding a roan horse. He could swear that only one person had come in before these pursuers—and that one was a woman on a roan. Her frightened eyes, the fear that showed in every motion, her hurried flight, all contributed to the same inevitable conclusion. It was difficult to believe it, but impossible to deny. This wild, sylvan creature, with the shy, wonderful eyes, had lain in ambush to kill her father's enemy, and was flying from the vengeance on her heels.

His lips were sealed. Even if he were not under heavy obligations to her he could no more save himself at the expense of this brown sylph than he could have testified against his own mother.

"All right. If you feel lucky, come on. You'll get me, of course, but it may prove right expensive," he said quietly.

"That's all right. We're footing our end of the bill," Pesky retorted.

By this time, he and Weaver had dismounted, and were sheltered behind rocks. Already bullets were beginning to spit back and forth, though the flankers had not yet got into action.

"Durn his hide, I hate like sin to puncture it," Pesky told his boss. "I tell you we're making a mistake, Buck. This fellow's a pure—he ain't any hired killer. You can tie to that."

"He's the man that pumped a bullet into my arm from ambush. That's enough for me," the cattleman swore.

"No use being revengeful, especially if it happens he ain't the man. By his say-so, that's a shotgun he's carrying. Loaded with buckshot, he claims. What hit you was a bullet from a Winchester, or some such gun. Mighty easy to prove whether he's lying."

"We'll be able to prove it afterward, all right."

"What's the matter with proving it now? I don't stand for any murder business myself. I'm going to find out what's what."

The cow-puncher tied the red bandanna from his neck round the end of his revolver, and shoved it above the rock in front of him.

"Flag of truce!" he shouted.

"All right. Come right along. Better leave your gun behind," Keller called back.

Pesky waddled forward—a short, thick-set, bow-legged man in chaps, spurs, flannel shirt, and white sombrero. When he took off this last, as he did now, it revealed a head bald as a billiard ball.

"How're they coming?" he inquired genially of the besieged man, as he rounded the rock barricade.

Larrabie's steel eyes relaxed to a hint of a friendly smile. He knew this type of man like a brother.

"Fine and dandy here. Hope you're well yourself, seh."

"Tol'able. Buck's up on his ear, o' course. Can't blame him, can you? Most any man would, with that kind of a pill sent to his address so sudden by special delivery. Wasn't that some inconsiderate of you, Mr. Keller?"

"I thought I explained it was another party did that."

Pesky rolled a cigarette and lit it.

"Right sure of that, are you? Wouldn't mind my taking a look at that gun of yours? You see, if it happens to be what you said it was, that kinder lets you out."

Keller handed over the gun promptly. The cow-puncher broke it, extracted a shell, and with his knife picked out the wad. Into his palm rolled a dozen buckshot.

"Good enough! I told Buck he was barking up the wrong tree. Now, I'll go back and have a powwow with him. I reckon you'll be willing to surrender on guarantee of a square deal?"

"Sure—that's all I ask. I never met your friend—didn't know who he was from Adam. I ain't got any option to shoot all the red-haided men I meet. No, sir! You've followed a cross trail."

"Looks like. Still, it's blamed funny." Pesky scratched his shining poll, and looked shrewdly at the other. "We certainly ran Mr. Bushwhacker into the cañon. I'd swear to that. We was right on his heels, though we couldn't see him very well. But he either come in here or a hole in the ground swallowed him."

He waited tentatively for an answer, but none came other than the white-toothed smile that met him blandly.

"I reckon you know more than you aim to tell, Mr. Keller," continued Pesky. "Don't you figure it's up to you, if we let you out of this thing, to whack up any information you've got? The kind of reptile that kills from ambush don't deserve any consideration."

Half an hour ago, the other would have agreed with him. The man that shot his enemy from cover was a coyote—nothing less. But about that brown slip of a creature, who had for three minutes crossed his orbit, he wanted to reserve judgment.

"I expect I haven't got a thing to tell you that would help any," he drawled, his eye full on that of the cowpuncher.

Pesky threw away his cigarette. "All right. You're the doctor. I'll amble back, and report to the boss."

He did so, with the result that a truce was arranged.

Keller gave up his post of vantage, and came forward to surrender.

Weaver met him with a hard, wintry eye. "Understand, I don't concede your innocence. You're my prisoner, and, by God, if I get any more proof of your guilt, you've got to stand the gaff."

The other nodded quietly, meeting him eye to eye. Nor did his gaze fall, though the big cattleman was the most masterful man on the range. Keller was as easy and unperturbed as when he had been holding half a dozen irate men at bay.

"No kick coming here. But, if it's just the same to you, I'll ask you to get the proof first and hang me afterward."

"If you're homesteading, where's your place?"

"Back in the hills, close to the headwaters of Salt Creek."

"Huh! You'll make that good before I get through with you. And I want to tell you this, too, Mr. Keller. It doesn't make any hit with me that you're one of those thieving nesters. Moreover, there's another charge against you. In the Malpais country we hang rustlers. The boys claim to have you cinched. We'll see."

"Who's that with Curly?" Pesky called out. "By Moses, it's a woman!"

"It is the Sanderson girl," Weaver said in surprise.

Keller swung round as if worked by a spring. The cow-puncher had told the truth. Curly's companion was not only a woman, but *the* woman—the same slim, tanned creature who had flashed past him on a wild race for safety, only a few minutes earlier.

All eyes were focused upon her. Weaver waited for her to speak. Instead, Curly took up the word. He was smiling broadly, quite unaware of the mine he was firing.

"I found this young lady up on the rock rim. Since we were rounding up, I thought I'd bring her down."

"Good enough. Miss Sanderson, you've been where you could see if anyone passed into the cañon. How about it? Anybody go up in the last ten minutes?"

Phyllis moistened her dry lips and looked at the prisoner. "No," she answered reluctantly.

Weaver wheeled on Keller, his eyes hard as jade. "That ties the rope round your neck, my man."

"No," Phyllis cried. "He didn't do it."

The cattleman's stone wall eyes were on her now.

"Didn't? How do you know he didn't?"

"Because I—I passed him here as I rode up a few minutes ago."

"So you rode up a few minutes ago." Buck's lids narrowed. "And he was here, was he? Ever meet Mr. Keller before?"

"Yes."

"When? Speak up. Mind, no lying."

This, struck the first spark of spirit from her. The deep eyes flashed. "I'm not in the habit of lying, sir."

"Then answer my question."

"I've met him at the office when he came for his mail. And the boys arrested him by mistake for a rustler. I saw him when they brought him in."

"By mistake. How do you know it was by mistake?"

"It was I accused him. But I did it because I was angry at him."

"You accused an innocent man of rustling because you were sore at him. You're ce'tainly a pleasant young lady, Miss Sanderson."

Her look flashed defiance at him, but she said nothing. In her slim erectness was a touch of feminine ferocity that gave him another idea.

"So you just rode into the cañon, did you?"

"Yes."

"Meet up with anybody in the valley before you came in?"

"No."

His eyes were like steel drills. They never left her. "Quite sure?"

"Yes."

"What were you doing there?"

She had no answer ready. Her wild look went round in search of a friend in this circle of enemies. They found him in the man who was a prisoner. His steadfast eyes told her to have no fear.

"Did you hear what I said?" demanded Weaver.

"I was—riding."

"Alone?"

The answer came so slowly that it was barely audible. "Yes."

"Riding in Antelope Valley?"

"Yes."

"Let me see that gun." Weaver held out his hand for the rifle.

Phyllis looked at him and tried to fight against his domination; then slowly she handed him the rifle. He broke and examined it. From the chamber he extracted an empty shell.

Grim as a hanging judge, his look chiselled into her.

"I expect the lead that was in here is in my arm. Isn't that right?"

"I—I don't know."

"Who does, then? Either you shot me or you know who did."

Her gaze evaded his, but was forced at last to the meeting.

"I did it."

She was looking at him steadily now. Since the thing must be faced, she had braced herself to it. It was amazing what defiant pluck shone out of her soft eyes. This man of iron saw it, and, seeing, admired hugely the gameness that dwelt in her slim body. But none of his admiration showed in the hard, weather-beaten face.

"So they make bushwhackers out of even the girls among your rustling, sheep-herding outfit!" he taunted.

"My people are not rustlers. They have a right to be on earth, even if you don't want them there."

"I'll show them what rights they have got in this part of the country before I get through with them. But that ain't the point now. What I want to know is how they came to send a girl to do their dirty killing for them."

"They didn't send me. I just saw you, and—and shot on an impulse. Your men have clubbed and poisoned our sheep. They wounded one of our herders, and beat his brother when they caught him unarmed. They have done a hundred mean and brutal things. You are at the bottom of it all; and when I saw you riding there, looking like the lord of all the earth, I just——"

"Well?"

"Couldn't help—what I did."

"You're a nicely brought up young woman—about as savage as the rest of your wolf breed," jeered Weaver.

Yet he exulted in her—in the impulse of ferocity that had made her strike swiftly, regardless of risk to herself, at the man who had hounded and harried her kin to the feud that was now raging. Her shy, untamed beauty would not itself have attracted him; but in combination with her fierce courage it made to him an appeal which he conceded grudgingly.

"What in Heaven's name brought you back after you had once got away?" Weaver asked.

The girl looked at Keller without answering.

"I reckon I can tell you that, seh," explained that young man. "She figured you would jump on me as the guilty party. It got on her conscience that she had left an innocent man to stand for it. I shouldn't wonder but she got to seeing a picture of you-all hanging me or shooting me up. So she came back to own up, if she saw you had caught me."

Weaver nodded. "That's the way I figure it, too. Gamest thing I ever saw a woman do," he said in an undertone to Keller, with whom he was now standing a little apart.

The latter agreed. "Never saw the beat of it. She's scared stiff, too. Makes it all the pluckier. What will you do with her?"

"Take her along with me back to the ranch."

"I wouldn't do that," said the young man quickly.

"Wouldn't you?" Weaver's hard gaze went over him haughtily. "When I want your advice, I'll ask you for it, young man. You're in luck to get off scot-free yourself. That ought to content you for one day."

"But what are you going to do with her? Surely not have her imprisoned for attacking you?"

"I'll do as I dashed please, and don't you forget it, Mr. Keller. Better mind your own business, if you've got any."

With which Buck Weaver turned on his heel, and swung slowly to the saddle. His arm was paining him a great deal, but he gave no sign of it. He expected his men to game it out when they ran into bad luck, and he was stoic enough to set them an example without making any complaints.

The little group of riders turned down the trail, passed through the gateway that led to the valley below, and wound down among the cow-backed hills toward the ranch roofs, which gleamed in the distance. They were the houses of the Twin Star outfit, the big concern owned by Buck Weaver, whose cattle fed literally upon a thousand hills.

It suited Buck's ironic humor to ride beside the girl who had just attempted his life. He bore her no resentment. Had the offender been a man, Buck would have snuffed out his life with as little remorse as he would a guttering candle. But her sex and her youth, and some quality of charm in her, had altered the equation. He meant to show her who was master, but he would choose a different method.

What sport to tame the spirit of this wild desert beauty until she should come like one of her own sheep dogs at his beck and call! He had never yet met the woman he could not dominate. This one, too, would know a good many new emotions before she rejoined her tribe in the hills.

He swung from the saddle at the ranch plaza, and greeted her with a deep bow that mocked her.

"Welcome, Miss Sanderson, to the best the Twin Star outfit has to offer. I hope you will enjoy your visit, which is going to be a long one."

To a Mexican woman, who had come out to the porch in answer to his call, he delivered the girl, charging her duty in two quick sentences of Spanish. The woman nodded her understanding, and led Phyllis inside.

Weaver noticed with delight that his captive's eye met his steadily, with the defiant fierceness of some hunted wild thing. Here was a woman worth taming, even though she was still a girl in years. His exultant eye, returning from the last glimpse of the lissom figure as it disappeared, met the gaze of Keller. That young man was watching him with an odd look of challenge on his usually impassive face.

The cattleman felt the spur of a new antagonism stirring his blood. There was something almost like a sneer on his lips as he spoke:

"Sorry to lose your company, Mr. Keller. But if you're homesteading, of course, we'll have to let you go back to the hills right away. Couldn't think of keeping you from that spring plowing that's waiting to be done."

"You're putting up a different line of talk from what you did. How about that charge of rustling against me, Mr. Weaver? Don't you want to hold me while you investigate it?"

"No, I reckon not. Your lady friend gives you a clean bill of health. She may or may not be lying. I'm not so sure myself. But without her the case against you falls."

Keller knew himself dismissed cavalierly, and, much as he would have liked to stay, he could find no further excuse to urge. He could hardly invite himself to be either the guest or the prisoner of a man who did not want him.

"Just as you say," he nodded, and turned carelessly to his pony.

Yet he was quite sure it would not be as Weaver said if he could help it. He meant to take a hand in the game, no matter what the other might decree. But for the present he acquiesced in the inevitable. Weaver was technically within his rights in holding her until he had communicated with the sheriff. A generous foe might not have stood out for his pound of flesh, but Buck was as hard as nails. As for the reputation of the girl, it was safe at the Twin Star ranch. Buck's sister, a maiden lady of uncertain years, was on hand to play chaperone.

Larrabie swung to the saddle. His horse's hoofs were presently flinging dirt toward the Twin Star as he loped up to the hills.

Nat Love (1854–1921)

NAT LOVE was born a slave on a plantation in Tennessee in 1854. Despite laws that outlawed black literacy, he learned to read and write with the help of his father. As a teenager Love left home and drifted West to find cowboy work chasing herds of cattle north out of Texas. He found work in Dodge City, Kansas, as part of a group of cowboys, and it wasn't long before he displayed talent in roping and herding cattle. Love entered a rodeo on the Fourth of July in 1876 in the town of Deadwood, South Dakota. He won the rope, throw, tie, bridle, saddle, and bronco-riding contests. Love impressed the crowds and earned the nickname "Deadwood Dick." In 1877, he was captured by Pima Indians while rounding up stray cattle near the Gila River in Arizona. Love reported that his life was spared because the Indians respected his fighting ability. Thirty days after being captured, he stole a pony and managed to escape into West Texas.

Nat Love is one of the more celebrated African-American cowboys but by no means is he unique. Cowboys came in all colors and thousands of former slaves made new lives for themselves in the American West.

For fifteen or sixteen years Love lived as a cowboy. He later memorialized his experiences in *The Life and Adventures of Nat Love* (1907). An excerpt from chapter 13 follows.

The Life and Adventures of Nat Love
1907

FROM Chapter 13 (excerpt)

In the spring of 1876 orders were received at the home ranch for three thousand head of three-year-old steers to be delivered near Deadwood, South Dakota. This being one of the largest orders we had ever received at one time, every man around the ranch was placed on his mettle to execute the order in record time. Cow boys mounted on swift horses were dispatched to the farthest limits of the ranch with orders to round up and run in all the three-year-olds on the place, and it was not long before the ranch corrals began to fill up with the long horns as they were driven by the several parties of cow boys; as fast as they came in we would cut out, under the bosses' orders such cattle as were to make up our herd.

In the course of three days we had our herd ready for the trail and we made our preparations to start on our long journey north. Our route lay through New Mexico, Colorado and Wyoming, and as we had heard rumors that the Indians were on the war path and were kicking up something of a rumpus in Wyoming, Indian Territory and Kansas, we expected trouble before we again had the pleasure of sitting around our fire at the home ranch. Quite a large party was selected for this trip owing to the size of the herd and the possibility of trouble on the trail from the Indians. We, as usual, were all well armed and had as mounts the best horses our ranch produced, and in taking the trail we were perfectly confident that we could take care of our herd and ourselves through anything we were liable to meet. We had not been on the trail long before we met other outfits who told us that General Custer was out after the Indians and that a big fight was expected when the Seventh U. S. Cavalry, General Custer's command, met the Crow tribe and other Indians under the leadership of Sitting Bull, Rain-in-the-Face, Old Chief Joseph, and other chiefs of lesser prominence, who had for a long time been terrorizing the settlers of that section and defying the Government.

As we proceeded on our journey it became evident to us that we were only a short distance behind the soldiers. When finally the Indians and soldiers met in the memorable battle or rather massacre in the Little Big Horn Basin on the Little Big Horn River in northern Wyoming, we were only two days behind them, or within 60 miles, but we did not know that at the time or we would have gone to Custer's assistance. We did not know of the fight or the outcome until several days after it was over. It was freely claimed at the time by cattle men who were in a position to know and with whom I talked that if Reno had gone to Custer's aid as he promised to do, Custer would not have lost his entire command and his life.

It was claimed Reno did not obey his orders, however that may be, it was one of the most bloody massacres in the history of this country. We went on our way to Deadwood with our herd, where we arrived on the 3rd of July, 1876, eight days after the Custer massacre took place.

The Custer Battle was June 25, '76, the battle commenced on Sunday afternoon and lasted about two hours. That was the last of General Custer and his Seventh Cavalry. How I know this so well is because we had orders from one of the Government scouts to go in camp, that if we went any farther North we were liable to be captured by the Indians.

We arrived in Deadwood in good condition without having had any trouble with the Indians on the way up. We turned our cattle over to their new owners at once, then proceeded to take in the town. The next morning, July 4th, the gamblers and mining men made up a purse of $200 for a roping contest between the cow boys that were then in town, and as it was a holiday nearly all the cow boys for miles around were assembled there that day. It did not take long to arrange the details for the contest and contestants, six of them being colored cow boys, including myself. Our trail boss was chosen to pick out the mustangs from a herd of wild horses just off the range, and he picked out twelve of the most wild and vicious horses that he could find.

The conditions of the contest were that each of us who were mounted was to rope, throw, tie, bridle and saddle and mount the particular horse picked for us in the shortest time possible. The man accomplishing the feat in the quickest time to be declared the winner.

It seems to me that the horse chosen for me was the most vicious of the lot. Everything being in readiness, the "45" cracked and we all sprang forward together, each of us making for our particular mustang.

I roped, threw, tied, bridled, saddled and mounted my mustang in exactly nine minutes from the crack of the gun. The time of the next nearest competitor was twelve minutes and thirty seconds. This gave me the record and championship of the West, which I held up to the time I quit the business in 1890, and my record has never been beaten. It is worthy of passing remark that I never had a horse pitch with me so much as that mustang, but I never stopped sticking my spurs in him and using my quirt on his flanks until I proved his master. Right there the assembled crowd named me Deadwood Dick and proclaimed me champion roper of the western cattle country.

The roping contest over, a dispute arose over the shooting question with the result that a contest was arranged for the afternoon, as there happened to be some of the best shots with rifle and revolver in the West present that day. Among them were Stormy Jim, who claimed the championship; Powder Horn Bill, who had the reputation of never missing what he shot at; also White Head, a half breed, who generally hit what he shot at, and many other men who knew how to handle a rifle or 45-colt.

The range was measured off 100 and 250 yards for the rifle and 150 for the Colt 45. At this distance a bulls eye about the size of an apple was put up. Each man was to have 14 shots at each range with the rifle and 12 shots with the Colts 45.

I placed every one of my 14 shots with the rifle in the bulls eye with ease, all shots being made from the hip; but with the 45 Colts I missed it twice, only placing 10 shots in the small circle, Stormy Jim being my nearest competitor, only placing 8 bullets in the bulls eye clear, the rest being quite close, while with the 45 he placed 5 bullets in the charmed circle. This gave me the championship of rifle and revolver shooting as well as the roping contest, and for that day I was the hero of Deadwood, and the purse of $200 which I had won on the roping contest went toward keeping things moving, and they did move, as only a large crowd of cattle men can move things. This lasted for several days when most of the cattle men had to return to their respective ranches, as it was the busy season, accordingly our outfit began to make preparations to return to Arizona.

In the meantime news had reached us of the Custer massacre, and the indignation and sorrow was universal, as General Custer was personally known to a large number of the cattle men of the West. But we could do nothing now, as the Indians were out in such strong force. There was nothing to do but let Uncle Sam revenge the loss of the General and his brave command, but it is safe to say not one of us would have hesitated a moment in taking the trail in pursuit of the blood thirsty red skins had the opportunity offered. Everything now being in readiness with us we took the trail homeward bound, and left Deadwood in a blaze of glory. On our way home we visited the Custer battle field in the Little Big Horn Basin. There was ample evidence of the desperate and bloody fight that had taken place a few days before. We arrived home in Arizona in a short time without further incident, except that on the way back we met and talked with many of the famous Government scouts of that region, among them Buffalo Bill (William F. Cody), Yellow Stone Kelley, and many others of that day, some of whom are now living, while others lost their lives in the line of duty, and a finer or braver body of men never lived than these scouts of the West. It was my pleasure to meet Buffalo Bill often in the early 70s, and he was as fine a man as one could wish to meet, kind, generous, true and brave.

Buffalo Bill got his name from the fact that in the early days he was engaged in hunting buffalo for their hides and furnishing U. P. Railroad graders with meat, hence the name Buffalo Bill. Buffalo Bill, Yellowstone Kelley, with many others were at this time serving under Gen. C. C. Miles.

The name of Deadwood Dick was given to me by the people of Deadwood, South Dakota, July 4, 1876, after I had proven myself worthy to carry it, and after I had defeated all comers in riding, roping, and shooting, and I have always carried the name with honor since that time.

We arrived at the home ranch again on our return from the trip to Deadwood about the middle of September, it taking us a little over two months to make the return journey, as we stopped in Cheyenne for several days and at other places, where we always found a hearty welcome, especially so on this trip, as the news had preceded us, and I received enough attention to have given me the big head, but my head had constantly refused to get enlarged again ever since the time I sampled the demijohn in the sweet corn patch at home.

Arriving at home, we received a send off from our boss and our comrades of the home ranch, every man of whom on hearing the

news turned loose his voice and his artillery in a grand demonstration
in my honor.

But they said it was no surprise to them, as they had long known
of my ability with the rope, rifle and 45 Colt, but just the same it was
gratifying to know I had defeated the best men of the West, and
brought the record home to the home ranch in Arizona. After a good
rest we proceeded to ride the range again, getting our herds in good
condition for the winter now at hand.

★   ★   ★

In the spring of 1877, now fully recovered from the effects of the
very serious wounds I had received at the hands of the Indians and
feeling my old self again, I joined the boys in their first trip of the
season, with a herd of cattle for Dodge City. The trip was uneventful
until we reached our destination. This was the first time I had been
in Dodge City since I had won the name of "DEADWOOD DICK," and
many of the boys, who knew me when I first joined the cow boys
there in 1869, were there to greet me now. After our herd had been
delivered to their new owners, we started out to properly celebrate
the event, and for a space of several days we kept the old town on
the jump.

And so when we finally started for home all of us had more or less
of the bad whiskey of Dodge City under our belts and were feeling
rather spirited and ready for anything.

I probably had more of the bad whiskey of Dodge City than any
one and was in consequence feeling very reckless, but we had about
exhausted our resources of amusement in the town, and so were
looking for trouble on the trail home.

On our way back to Texas, our way led past old Fort Dodge.
Seeing the soldiers and the cannon in the fort, a bright idea struck
me, but a fool one just the same. It was no less than a desire to rope
one of the cannons. It seemed to me that it would be a good thing
to rope a cannon and take it back to Texas with us to fight Indians
with.

The bad whiskey which I carried under my belt was responsible
for the fool idea, and gave me the nerve to attempt to execute the
idea. Getting my lariat rope ready I rode to a position just opposite
the gate of the fort, which was standing open. Before the gate paced
a sentry with his gun on his shoulder and his white gloves showing
up clean and white against the dusty grey surroundings. I waited until
the sentry had passed the gate, then putting spurs to my horse I

dashed straight for and through the gate into the yard. The surprised sentry called halt, but I paid no attention to him. Making for the cannon at full speed my rope left my hand and settled square over the cannon, then turning and putting spurs to my horse I tried to drag the cannon after me, but strain as he might my horse was unable to budge it an inch. In the meantime the surprised sentry at the gate had given the alarm and now I heard the bugle sound, boots and saddles, and glancing around I saw the soldiers mounting to come after me, and finding I could not move the cannon, I rode close up to it and got my lariat off then made for the gate again at full speed. The guard jumped in front of me with his gun up, calling halt, but I went by him like a shot, expecting to hear the crack of his musket, but for some reason he failed to fire on me, and I made for the open prairie with the cavalry in hot pursuit.

My horse could run like a wild deer, but he was no match for the big, strong, fresh horses of the soldiers and they soon had me. Relieving me of my arms they placed me in the guard house where the commanding officer came to see me. He asked me who I was and what I was after at the fort. I told him and then he asked me if I knew anyone in the city. I told him I knew Bat Masterson. He ordered two guards to take me to the city to see Masterson. As soon as Masterson saw me he asked me what the trouble was, and before I could answer, the guards told him I rode into the fort and roped one of the cannons and tried to pull it out. Bat asked me what I wanted with a cannon and what I intended doing with it. I told him I wanted to take it back to Texas with me to fight the Indians with; then they all laughed. Then Bat told them that I was all right, the only trouble being that I had too much bad whiskey under my shirt. They said I would have to set the drinks for the house. They came to $15.00, and when I started to pay for them, Bat said for me to keep my money that he would pay for them himself, which he did. Bat said that I was the only cowboy that he liked, and that his brother Jim also thought very much of me. I was then let go and I joined the boys and we continued on our way home, where we arrived safely on the 1st of June, 1877.

We at once began preparing for the coming big round up. As usual this kept us very busy during the months of July and August, and as we received no more orders for cattle this season, we did not have to take the trail again, but after the round up was over, we were kept busy in range riding, and the general all around work of the big cattle ranch. We had at this time on the ranch upwards of 30,000 head of cattle, our own cattle, not to mention the cattle belonging to the many other interests without the Pan Handle country, and as all these immense herds used the range of the country, in common as there was no fences to divide the ranches, consequently the cattle belonging to the different herds often got mixed up and large numbers of them strayed.

At the round ups it was our duty to cut out and brand the young calves, take a census of our stock, and then after the round up was over we would start out to look for possible strays. Over the range we would ride through canyons and gorges, and every place where it was possible for cattle to stray, as it was important to get them with the main herd before winter set in, as if left out in small bunches there was danger of them perishing in the frequent hard storms of the winter. While range riding or hunting for strays, we always carried with us on our saddle the branding irons of our respective ranches, and whenever we ran across a calf that had not been branded we had to rope the calf, tie it, then a fire was made of buffalo chips, the only fuel besides grass to be found on the prairie.

The irons were heated and the calf was branded with the brand of the finder, no matter who it personally belonged to. It now became the property of the finder. The lost cattle were then driven to the main herd. After they were once gotten together it was our duty to keep them together during the winter and early spring. It was while out hunting strays that I got lost, the first and only time I was ever lost in my life, and for four days I had an experience that few men ever went through and lived, as it was a close pull for me.

I had been out for several days looking for lost cattle and becoming separated from the other boys and being in a part of the country unfamiliar to me. It was stormy when I started out from the home ranch and when I had ridden about a hundred miles from home it began to storm in earnest, rain, hail, sleet, and the clouds seemed to touch the earth and gather in their inpenetrable embrace every thing thereon. For a long time I rode on in the direction of home, but as I could not see fifty yards ahead it was a case of going it blind. After riding for many weary hours through the storm I came across a little log cabin on the Palidore river. I rode up to within one hundred yards of it where I was motioned to stop by an old long haired man who stepped out of the cabin door with a long buffalo gun on his arm. It was with this he had motioned me to stop.

I promptly pulled up and raised my hat, which, according to the custom of the cowboy country, gave him to understand I was a cowboy from the western cow ranges. He then motioned me to come on. Riding up to the cabin he asked me to dismount and we shook hands.

He said, when I saw you coming I said to myself that must be a lost cowboy from some of the western cow ranges. I told him I was lost all right, and I told him who I was and where from. Again we shook hands, he saying as we did so, that we were friends until we met again, and he hoped forever. He then told me to picket out my horse and come in and have some supper, which very welcome invitation I accepted.

His cabin was constructed of rough hewn logs, somewhat after the fashion of a Spanish block house. One part of it was constructed under ground, a sort of dug out, while the upper portion of the cabin proper was provided with many loop holes, commanding every direction.

He later told me these loop holes had stood him in handy many a time when he had been attacked by Indians, in their efforts to capture him. On entering his cabin I was amazed to see the walls covered with all kinds of skins, horns, and antlers. Buffalo skins in great numbers covered the floor and bed, while the walls were completely hidden behind the skins of every animal of that region, including large number of rattle snakes skins and many of their rattles.

His bed, which was in one corner of the dug out, was of skins, and to me, weary from my long ride through the storm, seemed to be the most comfortable place on the globe just then. He soon set before me a bountious supper, consisting of buffalo meat and corn dodgers, and seldom before have I enjoyed a meal as I did that one. During supper he told me many of his experiences in the western country. His name was Cater, and he was one of the oldest buffalo hunters in that part of Texas, having hunted and trapped over the wild country ever since the early thirties, and during that time he had many a thrilling adventure with Indians and wild animals.

I stayed with him that night and slept soundly on a comfortable bed he made for me. The next morning he gave me a good breakfast and I prepared to take my departure as the storm had somewhat moderated, and I was anxious to get home, as the boys knowing I was out would be looking for me if I did not show up in a reasonable time.

My kind host told me to go directly northwest and I would strike the Calones flats, a place with which I was perfectly familiar. He said it was about 75 miles from his place. Once there I would have no difficulty in finding my way home. Cater put me up a good lunch to last me on my way, and with many expressions of gratitude to him, I left him with his skins and comfortable, though solitary life. All that day and part of the night I rode in the direction he told me, until about 11 o'clock when I became so tired I decided to go into camp and give my tired horse a rest and a chance to eat. Accordingly I dismounted and removed the saddle and bridle from my horse I hobbled him and turned him loose to graze on the luxuriant grass, while I, tired out, laid down with my head on my saddle fully dressed as I was, not even removing my belt containing my 45 pistol from my waist, laying my Winchester close by. The rain had ceased to fall, but it was still cloudy and threatening. It was my intention to rest a few hours then continue on my way; and as I could not see the stars on account of the clouds and as it was important that I keep my direction northwest in order to strike the Flats, I had carefully taken my direction before sundown, and now on moving my saddle I placed it on the ground pointing in the direction I was going when I stopped so that it would enable me to keep my direction when I again started out. I had been laying there for some time and my horse was quietly grazing about 20 yards off, when I suddenly heard something squeal. It sounded like a woman's voice. It frightened my horse and he ran for me. I jumped to my feet with my Winchester in my hand. This caused my horse to rear and wheel and I heard his hobbles break with a sharp snap. Then I heard the sound of his galloping feet going across the Pan Handle plains until the sound was lost in the distance. Then I slowly began to realize that I was left alone on the plains on foot, how many miles from home I did not know. Remembering I had my guns all right, it was my impulse to go in pursuit of my horse as I thought I could eventually catch him after he had got over his scare, but when I thought of my 40 pound saddle, and I did not want to leave that, so saying to myself that is the second saddle I ever owned, the other having been taken by the Indians when I was captured, and this saddle was part of the outfit presented to me by the boys, and so tired and as hungry as a hawk, I shouldered my saddle and started out in the direction I was going when I went into camp, saying to myself as I did so, if my horse could pack me and my outfit day and night, I can at least pack my outfit. Keeping my direction as well as I could I started out over the prairie through the dark, walking all that night and all the next day without anything to eat or drink until just about sundown and when I had begun to think I would have to spend another night on the prairie without food or drink, when I emerged from a little draw on to a raise on the prairie, then looking over on to a small flat I saw a large herd of buffalo. These were the first I had seen since I became lost and the sight of them put renewed life and hope in me as I was then nearly famished, and when I saw them I knew I had something to eat.

Off to one side about 20 yards from the main herd and about 150 yards from me was a young calf. Placing my Winchester to my shoulder I glanced along the shining barrel, but my hands shook so much I lowered it again, not that I was afraid of missing it as I knew I was a dead shot at that distance, but my weakness caused by my long enforced fast and my great thirst made my eyes dim and my hands shake in a way they had never done before, so waiting a few moments I again placed the gun to my shoulder and this time it spoke and the calf dropped where it had stood. Picking up my outfit I went down to where my supper was laying. I took out my jack knife and commenced on one of his hind quarters. I began to skin and eat to my hearts content, but I was so very thirsty. I had heard of people drinking blood to quench their thirst and that gave me an idea, so cutting the calf's throat with my knife I eagerly drank the fresh warm blood.

It tasted very much like warm sweet milk. It quenched my thirst and made me feel strong, when I had eaten all I could, I cut off two large chunks of the meat and tied them to my saddle, then again shouldering the whole thing I started on my way feeling almost as satisfied as if I had my horse with me. I was lost two days, and two nights, after my horse left me and all that time I kept walking packing my 40 pounds saddle and my Winchester and two cattle pistols.

On the second night about daylight the weather became more threatening and I saw in the distance a long column which looked like smoke. It seemed to be coming towards me at the rate of a mile a minute. It did not take it long to reach me, and when it did I struggled on for a few yards but it was no use, tired as I was from packing my heavy outfit for more than 48 hours and my long tramp, I had not the strength to fight against the storm so I had to come alone. When I again came to myself I was covered up head and foot in the snow, in the camp of some of my comrades from the ranch.

It seemed from what I was told afterwards that the boys knowing I was out in the storm and failing to show up, they had started out to look for me, they had gone in camp during the storm and when the blizzard had passed they noticed an object out on the prairie in the snow, with one hand frozen, clenched around my Winchester and the other around the horn of my saddle, and they had hard work to get my hands loose, they picked me up and placed me on one of the horses and took me to camp where they stripped me of my clothes and wrapped me up in the snow, all the skin came off my nose and mouth and my hands and feet had been so badly frozen that the nails came off. After I had got thawed out in the mess wagon and took me home in 15 days I was again in the saddle ready for business but I will never forget those few days I was lost and the marks of that storm I will carry with me always.

Frank V. Webster

THE NAME FRANK V. WEBSTER was a pseudonym for a list of multiple unknown authors who were work-for-hire flat fee writers. The Webster books were all productions of the Stratemeyer Syndicate, founded by Edward Stratemeyer in 1905. Stratemeyer himself had been a ghost writer for several Horatio Alger Jr. novels. Stratemeyer felt that there was more money in holding the copyright to the cowboy stories, so he hired ghost writers to author his various Western books. It was their job to execute stories according to his outlines. Each novel was about 60,000 words and for this the ghost writer received a flat fee. The Webster books were published in inexpensive editions and were extremely popular.

Though Frank V. Webster is credited with writing nine cowboy Westerns, it is unknown which of the ghost writers actually wrote "After Stray Cattle" (1915).

After Stray Cattle

FROM *Cowboy Dave: or, The Roundup at Rolling River,* 1915

"Hi! Yi! Yip!"

"Woo-o-o-o! Wah! Zut!"

"Here we come!"

What was coming seemed to be a thunderous cloud of dust, from the midst of which came strange, shrill sounds, punctuated with sharp cries, that did not appear to be altogether human.

The dust-cloud grew thicker, the thunder sounded louder, and the yells were shriller.

From one of a group of dull, red buildings a sun-bronzed man stepped forth.

He shaded his eyes with a brown, powerful hand, gazed for an instant toward the approaching cloud of animated and vociferous dust and, turning to a smiling Chinese who stood near, with a pot in his hand, remarked in a slow, musical drawl:

"Well Hop Loy, here they are, rip-roarin' an' snortin' from th' round-up!"

"Alle samee hungly, too," observed the Celestial with unctious blandness.

"You can sure make a point of that Hop Loy," went on the other. "Hungry is their middle name just now, and you'd better begin t' rustle th' grub, or I wouldn't give an empty forty-five for your pig-tail."

"Oi la!" fairly screamed the Chinese, as, with a quick gesture toward his long queue, he scuttled toward the cook house, which stood in the midst of the other low ranch buildings. "Glub leady alle samee light now!" Hop Loy cried over his shoulder.

"It better be!" ominously observed Pocus Pete, foreman of the Bar U ranch, one of the best-outfitted in the Rolling River section. "It better be! Those boys mean business, or I miss my guess," the foreman went on. "Hard work a-plenty, I reckon. Wonder how they made out?" he went on musingly as he started back toward the bunk house, whence he had come with a saddle strap to which he was attaching a new buckle. "If things don't take a turn for th' better soon, there won't any of us make out," and, with a gloomy shake of his head, Pocus Pete, to give him the name he commonly went by, tossed the strap inside the bunk house, and went on toward the main building, where, by virtue of his position as head of the cowboys, he had his own cot.

Meanwhile the crowd of yelling, hard-riding, sand dust-stirring punchers, came on faster than ever.

"Hi! Yi! Yip!"

"Here we come!"

"Keep th' pot a-bilin'! We've got our appetites with us!"

"That's what!"

Some one fired his big revolver in the air, and in another moment there was an echo of many shots, the sharp crack of the forty-fives mingling with the thunder of hoofs, the yells, and the clatter of stirrup leathers.

"The boys coming back, Pete?" asked an elderly man, who came to the door of the main living room of the principal ranch house.

"Yes, Mr. Carson, they're comin' back, an' it don't need a movin' picture operator an' telegraphic despatch t' tell it, either."

"No, Pete. They seem to be in good spirits, too."

"Yes, they generally are when they get back from round-up. I want to hear how they made out, though, an' what th' prospects are."

"So do I, Pete," and there was an anxious note in the voice of Mr. Randolph Carson, owner of the Bar U ranch. Matters had not been going well with him, of late.

With final yells, and an increase in the quantity of dust tossed up as the cowboys pulled their horses back on their haunches, the range-riding outfit of the ranch came to rest, not far away from the stable. The horses, with heaving sides and distended nostrils that showed a deep red, hung their heads from weariness. They had been ridden hard, but not unmercifully, and they would soon recover. The cowboys themselves tipped back their big hats from their foreheads, which showed curiously white in contrast to their bronzed faces, and beat the dust from their trousers. A few of them wore sheepskin chaps.

One after another the punchers slung their legs across the saddle horns, tossed the reins over the heads of their steeds, as an intimation that the horses were not to stray, and then slid to the ground, walking with that peculiarly awkward gait that always marks one who has spent much of his life in the saddle.

"Grub ready, Hop Loy?" demanded one lanky specimen, as he used his blue neck kerchief to remove some of the dust and sweat from his brown face.

"It better be!" added another, significantly; while still another said, quietly:

"My gal has been askin' me for a long, long time to get her a Chinaman's pig-tail, an' I'm shore goin' t'get one now if I don't have my grub right plenty, an' soon!"

"Now you're talkin'!" cried a fourth, with emphasis.

There was no need of saying anything further. The Celestial had stuck his head out of the cook house to hear these ominous words of warning, and now, with a howl of anguish, he drew it inside again, wrapping his queue around his neck. Then followed a frantic rattling of pots and pans.

"You shore did get him goin', Tubby!" exclaimed a tall, lanky cowboy, to a short and squatty member of the tribe.

"Well, I aimed to Skinny," was the calm reply. "I am some hungry."

The last of the cowboys to alight was a manly youth, who might have been in the neighborhood of eighteen or nineteen years of age. He was tall and slight, with a frank and pleasing countenance, and his blue eyes looked at you fearlessly from under dark brows, setting off in contrast his sunburned face. Had any one observed him as he rode up with the other cowboys, it would have been noticed that, though he was the youngest, he was one of the best riders.

He advanced from among the others, pausing to pet his horse which stuck out a wet muzzle for what was evidently an expected caress. Then the young man walked forward, with more of an air of grace than characterized his companions. Evidently, though used to a horse, he was not so saddle-bound as were his mates.

As he walked up to the ranch house he was met by Mr. Carson and Pocus Pete, both of whom looked at him rather eagerly and anxiously.

"Well, son," began the ranch owner, "how did you make out?"

"Pretty fair, Dad," was the answer. "There were more cattle than you led us to expect, and there were more strays than we calculated on. In fact we didn't get near all of them."

"Is that so, Dave?" asked Pocus Pete, quickly. "Whereabouts do you reckon them strays is hidin'?"

"The indications are they're up Forked Branch way. That's where we got some, and we saw more away up the valley, but we didn't have time to go for them, as we had a little trouble; and Tubby and the others thought we'd better come on, and go back for the strays to-morrow."

"Trouble, Dave?" asked Mr. Carson, looking up suddenly.

"Well, not much, though it might have been. We saw some men we took to be rustlers heading for our bunch of cattle, but they rode off when we started for them. Some of the boys wanted to follow but it looked as though it might storm, and Tubby said we'd better move the bunch while we could, and look after the rustlers and strays later."

"Yes, I guess that was best," the ranch owner agreed. "But where were these rustlers from, Dave?"

"Hard to say, Dad. Looked to be Mexicans."

"I reckon that'd be about right," came from Pocus Pete. "We'll have to be on th' watch, Mr. Carson."

"I expect so, Pete. Things aren't going so well that I can afford to lose any cattle. But about these strays, Dave. Do you think we'd better get right after them?"

"I should say so, Dad."

"Think there are many of them?"

"Not more than two of us could drive in. I'll go to-morrow with one of the men. I know just about where to look for them."

"All right, Dave. If you're not too much done out I'd like to have you take a hand."

"Done out, Dad! Don't you think I'm making a pretty good cow-puncher?"

"That's what he is, Mr. Carson, for a fact!" broke in Pete, with admiration. "I'd stake Cowboy Dave ag'in' any man you've got ridin' range to-day. That's what I would!"

"Thanks, Pete," said the youth, with a warm smile.

"Well, that's the truth, Dave. You took to this business like a duck takes to water, though the land knows there ain't any too much water in these parts for ducks."

"Yes, we could use more, especially at this season," Mr. Carson admitted. "Rolling River must be getting pretty dry; isn't it, Dave?"

"I've seen it wetter, Dad. And there's hardly any water in Forked Branch. I don't see how the stray cattle get enough to drink."

"It is queer they'd be off up that way," observed Pete. "But that might account for it," he went on, as though communing with himself.

"Account for what?" asked Dave, as he sat down in a chair on the porch.

"Th' rustlers. If they were up Forked Branch way they'd stand between th' strays and th' cattle comin' down where they could get plenty of water in Rolling River. That's worth lookin' into. I'll ride up that way with you to-morrow, Dave, an' help drive in them cattle."

"Will you, Pete? That will be fine!" the young cowboy exclaimed. Evidently there was a strong feeling of affection between the two. Dave looked to Mr. Carson for confirmation.

"Very well," the ranch owner said, "you and Pete may go, Dave. But don't take any chances with the rustlers if you encounter them."

"We're not likely to," said Pocus Pete, significantly.

From the distant cook house came the appetizing odor of food and Dave sniffed the air eagerly.

"Hungry?" asked Mr. Carson.

"That's what I am, Dad!"

"Well, eat heartily, get a good rest, and tomorrow you can try your hand at driving strays."

Evening settled down over the Bar U ranch; a calm, quiet evening, in spite of the earlier signs of a storm. In the far west a faint intermittent light showed where the elements were raging, but it was so far off that not even the faintest rumble of thunder came over Rolling River, a stream about a mile distant, on the banks of which were now quartered the cattle which the cowboys had recently rounded up for shipment.

The only sounds that came with distinctness were the occasional barking and baying of a dog, as he saw the rising moon, and the dull shuffle of the shifting cattle, which were being guarded by several cowboys who were night-riding.

Very early the next morning Dave Carson and Pocus Pete, astride their favorite horses, and carrying with them a substantial lunch, set off after the strays which had been dimly observed the day before up Forked Branch way.

This was one of the tributaries of Rolling River, the valley of which was at one time one of the most fertile sections of the largest of our Western cattle states. The tributary divided into two parts, or branches, shortly above its junction with Rolling River. Hence its name. Forked Branch came down from amid a series of low foothills, forming the northern boundary of Mr. Randolph Carson's ranch.

"We sure have one fine day for ridin'," observed Pocus Pete, as he urged his pony up alongside Dave's.

"That's right," agreed the youth.

For several miles they rode on, speaking but seldom, for a cowboy soon learns the trick of silence—it is so often forced on him.

As they turned aside to take a trail that led to Forked Branch, Dave, who was riding a little ahead, drew rein. Instinctively Pocus Pete did the same, and then Dave, pointing to the front, asked:

"Is that a man or a cow?"

⋆   ⋆   ⋆

Pocus Pete shaded his eyes with his hand and gazed long and earnestly in the direction indicated by Dave Carson. The two cowponies, evidently glad of the little rest, nosed about the sun-baked earth for some choice morsel of grass.

"It might be either—or both," Pete finally said.

"Either or both?" repeated Dave. "How can that be?"

"Don't you see two specks there, Dave? Look ag'in."

Dave looked. His eyes were younger and perhaps, therefore, sharper than were those of the foreman of Bar U ranch, but Dave lacked the training that long years on the range had given the other.

"Yes, I do see two," the youth finally said, "But I can't tell which is which."

"I'm not altogether sure myself," Pete said, quietly and modestly. "We'll ride a little nearer," he suggested, "an' then we can tell for sure. I guess we're on th' track of some strays all right."

"Some strays, Pete? You mean our strays; don't you?" questioned Dave.

"Well, some of 'em 'll be, probably," was the quiet answer. "But you've got t' remember, Dave, that there's a point of land belongin' t' Centre O ranch that comes up there along the Forked Branch trail. It may be some of Molick's strays."

"That's so. I didn't think of that, Pete. There's more to this business than appears at first sight."

"Yes, Dave; but you're comin' on first-rate. I was a leetle opposed to th' Old Man sendin' you East to study, for fear it would knock out your natural instincts. But when you picked up that man as soon as you did," and he waved his hand toward the distant specks, "when you did that, I know you've not been spoiled, an' that there's hope for you."

"That's good, Pete!" and Dave laughed.

"Yes, I didn't agree with th' Old Man at first," the foreman went on, "but I see he didn't make any mistake."

Mr. Carson was the "Old Man" referred to, but it was not at all a term of disrespect as applied to the ranch owner. It was perfectly natural to Pete to use that term, and Dave did not resent it.

"Yes, I'm glad Dad did send me East," the young man went on, as they continued on their way up the trail. "I was mighty lonesome at first, and I felt—well, cramped, Pete. That's the only way to express it."

"I know how you felt, Dave. There wasn't room to breathe in th' city."

"That's the way I felt. Out here it—it's different."

He straightened up in the saddle, and drew in deep breaths of the pure air of the plains; an air so pure and thin, so free from mists, that the very distances were deceiving, and one would have been positive that the distant foot-hills were but half an hour's ride away, whereas the better part of a day must be spent in reaching them.

"Yes, this is livin'—that's what it is," agreed Pocus Pete." You can make them out a little better now, Dave," and he nodded his head in the direction of the two distant specks. They were much larger now.

"It's a chap on a horse, and he's going in the same direction we are," Dave said, after a moment's observation.

"That's right. And it ain't every cowpuncher on Bar U who could have told that."

"I can see two—three—why, there are half a dozen cattle up there, Pete."

"Yes, an' probably more. I reckon some of th' Centre O outfit has strayed, same as ours. That's probably one of Molick's men after his brand," Pete went on.

The Bar U ranch (so called because the cattle from it were branded with a large U with a straight mark across the middle) adjoined, on the north, the ranch of Jason Molick, whose cattle were marked with a large O in the centre of which was a single dot, and his brand consequently, was known as Centre O.

"Maybe that's Len," suggested Dave, naming the son of the adjoining ranch owner.

"It may be. I'd just as soon it wouldn't be, though. Len doesn't always know how to keep a civil tongue in his head."

"That's right, Pete. I haven't much use for Len myself."

"You an' he had some little fracas; didn't you?"

"Oh, yes, more than once."

"An' you tanned him good and proper, too; didn't you Dave?" asked the foreman with a low chuckle.

"Yes, I did." Dave did not seem at all proud of his achievement." But that was some time ago," he added." I haven't seen Len lately."

"Well, you haven't missed an awful lot," said Pete, dryly.

The two rode on in silence again, gradually coming nearer and nearer to the specks which had so enlarged themselves, by reason of the closing up of the intervening distance, until they could be easily distinguished as a number of cattle and one lone rider. The latter seemed to be making his way toward the animals.

"Is he driving them ahead of him?" asked Dave, after a long and silent observation.

"That's the way it looks," said Pocus Pete. "It's Len Molick all right," he added, after another shading of his eyes with his hand.

"Are you sure?" Dave asked.

"Positive. No one around here rides a horse in that sloppy way but him."

"Then he must have found some of his father's strays, and is taking them to the ranch."

"I'm not so sure of that," Pete said.

"Not so sure of what?"

"That the cattle are all his strays. I wouldn't be a bit surprised but what some of ours had got mixed up with 'em. Things like that have been known to happen you know."

"Do you think—" began Dave.

"I'm not goin' to take any chances thinkin'," Pete said significantly. "I'm going to make sure."

"Look here, Dave," he went on, spurring his pony up alongside of the young cowboy's. "My horse is good an' fresh an' Len's doesn't seem to be in such good condition. Probably he's been abusin' it as he's done before. Now I can take this side trail, slip around through the bottom lands, an' get ahead of him."

"But it's a hard climb up around the mesa, Pete."

"I know it. But I can manage it. Then you come on up behind Len, casual like. If he has any of our cattle—by mistake," said Pete, significantly, "we'll be in a position to correct his error. Nothin' like correctin' errors right off the reel, Dave. Well have him between two fires, so to speak."

"All right, Pete. I'll ride up behind him, as I'm doing now, and you'll head him off; is that it?"

"That's it. You guessed it first crack out of th' box. If nothin's wrong, why we're all right; we're up this way to look after our strays. And if somethin' is wrong, why we'll be in a position to correct it— that's all."

"I see." There was a smile on Dave's face as his cowboy partner, with a wave of his hand, turned his horse into a different trail, speeding the hardy little pony up so as to get ahead of Len Molick.

Dave rode slowly on, busy with many thoughts, some of which had to do with the youth before him. Len Molick was about Dave's own age, that is apparently, for, strange as it may seem, Dave was not certain of the exact number of years that had passed over his head.

It was evident that he was about eighteen or nineteen. He had recently felt a growing need of a razor, and the hair on his face was becoming wiry. But once, when he asked Randolph Carson, about a birthday, the ranch owner had returned an evasive answer.

"I don't know exactly when your birthday does come, Dave," he had said. "Your mother, before she—before she died, kept track of that. In fact I somtimes forget when my own is. I think yours is in May or June, but for the life of me I can't say just which month. It doesn't make a lot of difference, anyhow."

"No, Dad, not especially. But just how old am I?"

"Well, Dave, there you've got me again. I think it's around eighteen. But your mother kept track of that, too. I never had the time.

Put it down at eighteen, going on nineteen, and let it go at that. Now say, about that last bunch of cattle we shipped—"

Thus the ranchman would turn the subject. Not that Dave gave the matter much thought, only now, somehow or other, the question seemed to recur with increased force.

"Funny I don't know just when my birthday is," he mused. "But then lots of the cowboys forget theirs."

The trail was smooth at this point, and Dave soon found himself close to Len, who was driving ahead of him a number of cattle. With a start of surprise Dave saw two which bore the Bar U brand.

"Hello, Len," he called.

Len Molick turned with a start. Either he had not heard Dave approach, or he had pretended ignorance.

"Well, what do you want?" demanded the surly bully.

"Oh, out after strays, as you are," said Dave, coolly. "Guess your cattle and ours have struck up an acquaintance," he added, with assumed cheerfulness.

"What do you mean?"

"I mean they're traveling along together just as if they belonged to the same outfit."

"Huh! I can't help it, can I, if your cows tag along with our strays?" demanded Len with a sneer.

"That's what I'm here for—to help prevent it," Dave went on, and his voice was a trifle sharp. "The Bar U ranch can't afford to lose any strays these days," he resumed. "The Carson outfit needs all it can get, and, as representative of the Carson interests I'll just cut out those strays of ours, Len, and head them the other way."

"Huh! What right have you got to do it?"

"What right? Why my father sent me to gather up our strays. I saw some of them up here yesterday."

"Your father?" The sneer in Len's voice was unmistakable.

"Yes, of course," said Dave, wondering what was the matter with Len. "My father, Randolph Carson."

"He isn't your father!" burst out Len in angry tones. "And you aren't his son! You're a nameless picked-up nobody, that's what you are! A nobody! You haven't even a name!"

And with this taunt on his lips Len spurred his horse away from Dave's.

*　　*　　*

Something seemed to strike Dave Carson a blow in the face. It was as though he had suddenly plunged into cold water, and, for the moment, he could not get his breath. The sneering words of Len Molick rang in his ears:

"You're a nameless, picked-up nobody!"

Having uttered those cruel words, Len was riding on, driving before him some of his father's stray cattle, as well as some belonging to the Bar U ranch. The last act angered Dave, and anger, at that moment, was just what was needed to arouse him from the lethargy in which he found himself. It also served, in a measure, to clear away some of the unpleasant feeling caused by the taunt.

"Hold on there a minute, Len Molick!" called Dave, sharply.

Len never turned his head, and gave no sign of hearing.

A dull red spot glowed in each of Dave's tanned cheeks. With a quick intaking of his breath he lightly touched the spurs to his horse—lightly, for that was all the intelligent beast needed. Dave passed his taunting enemy on the rush, and planting himself directly in front of him on the trail, drew rein so sharply that his steed reared. The cows, scattered by the sudden rush, ambled awkwardly on a little distance, and then stopped to graze.

"What do you mean by getting in my way?" growled Len.

"I mean to have you stop and answer a few questions," was the calm retort.

"If it's about these cattle I tell you I'm not trying to drive off any of yours," said Len, in whining tones. He knew the severe penalty attached to this in a cow country, and Dave was sufficiently formidable, as he sat easily on his horse facing the bully, to make Len a little more respectful.

"I'm not going to ask you about these cattle—at least not right away," Dave went on. "This is about another matter. You said something just now that needs explaining."

"I say a good many things," Len admitted, and again there sounded in his voice a sneer. "I don't have to explain to you everything I say; do I?"

"You do when it concerns me," and Dave put his horse directly across the trail, which, at this point narrowed and ran between two low ranges of hills. "You said something about me just now—you called me a nameless, picked-up nobody!"

Dave could not help wincing as he repeated the slur.

"Well, what if I did?" demanded the bully.

"I want to know what you mean. You insinuated that Mr. Carson was not my father."

"He isn't!"

"Why do you say that, and how do you know?" Dave asked. In spite of his dislike of Len, and the knowledge that the bully was not noted for truth-telling, Dave could not repress a cold chill of fear that seemed to clutch his heart.

"I say that because it's so, and how I know it is none of your affair," retorted Len.

"Oh yes, it is my affair, too!" Dave exclaimed. He was fast regaining control of himself. "It is very much my affair. I demand an explanation. How do you know Mr. Carson isn't my father?"

"Well, I know all right. He picked you up somewhere. He doesn't know what your name is himself. He just let you use his, and he called you Dave. You're a nobody I tell you!"

Dave spurred his horse until it was close beside that of Len's. Then leaning over in the saddle, until his face was very near to that of the bully's, and with blazing eyes looking directly into the shrinking ones of the other rancher's son, Dave said slowly, but with great emphasis:

"Who—told—you?"

There was menace in his tone and attitude, and Len shrank back.

"Oh, don't be afraid!" Dave laughed mirthlessly. "I'm not going to strike you—not now."

"You—you'd better not," Len muttered.

"I want you first to answer my questions," Dave went on. "After that I'll see what happens. It's according to how much truth there is in what you have said."

"Oh, it's true all right," sneered the bully.

"Then I demand to know who told you!"

Dave's hand shot out and grasped the bridle of the other's horse, and Len's plan of flight was frustrated.

"Let me go!" he whiningly demanded.

"Not until you tell me who said I am a nobody—that Mr. Carson is not my father," Dave said, firmly.

"I—I—" began the shrinking Len, when the sound of another horseman approaching caused both lads to turn slightly in their saddles. Dave half expected to see Pocus Pete, but he beheld the not very edifying countenance of Whitey Wasson, a tow-headed cowpuncher belonging to the Centre O outfit. Whitey and Len were reported to be cronies, and companions in more than one not altogether pleasant incident.

"Oh, here you are; eh; Len?" began Whitey. "And I see you've got the strays."

"Yes, I've got 'em," said Len, shortly.

"Any trouble?" went on Whitey, with a quick glance at Dave. The position of the two lads—Dave with his hand grasping Len's bridle—was too significant to be overlooked.

"Trouble?" began Len. "Well, he—he—"

"He made a certain statement concerning me," Dave said, quietly, looking from Len to Whitey, "and I asked him the source of his information. That is all."

"What did he say?"

"He said I was a nameless, picked-up nobody, and that Mr. Carson was not my father. I asked him how he knew, and he said some one told him that."

"So he did!" exclaimed Len.

"Then I demand to know who it was!" cried Dave.

For a moment there was silence, and then Whitey Wasson, with a chuckle said:

"I told Len myself!"

"You did?" cried Dave.

"Yes, he did! Now maybe you won't be so smart!" sneered Len. "Let go my horse!" he cried, roughly, as he swung the animal to one side. But no force was needed; as Dave's nerveless hand fell away from the bridle. He seemed shocked—stunned again.

"You—you—how do you know?" he demanded fiercely, raising his sinking head, and looking straight at Whitey.

"Oh, I know well enough. Lots of the cowboys do. It isn't so much of a secret as you think. If you don't believe me ask your father—no, he ain't your father—but ask the Old Man himself. Just ask him what your name is, and where you came from, and see what he says."

Whitey was sneering now, and he chuckled as he looked at Len. Dave's face paled beneath his tan, and he did not answer.

A nameless, picked-up nobody! How the words stung! And he had considered himself, proudly considered himself, the son of one of the best-liked, best-known and most upright cattle raisers of the Rolling River country. Now who was he?

"Come on, Len," said Whitey. "If you've got the strays we'll drive them back. Been out long enough as 'tis."

He wheeled his horse, Len doing the same, and they started after the straying cattle.

"Hold on there, if you please," came in a drawling voice. "Jest cut out them Bar U steers before you mosey off any farther, Whitey," and riding around a little hillock came Pocus Pete.

"Um!" grunted Whitey.

"Guess you'll be needin' a pair of specks, won't you, Whitey?" went on the Bar U foreman, without a glance at Len or Dave. "A Centre O brand an' a Bar U looks mighty alike to a feller with poor eyes, I reckon," and he smiled meaningly.

"Oh, we can't help it, if some of the Randolph cattle get mixed up with our strays," said Len.

"Who's talkin' to you?" demanded Pocus Pete, with such fierceness that the bully shrank back.

"Now you cut out what strays belong to you, an' let ours alone, Mr. Wasson," went on Pocus Pete with exaggerated politeness. "Dave an' I can take care of our own I reckon. An' move quick, too!" he added menacingly.

Whitey did not answer, but he and Len busied themselves in getting together their own strays. Pocus Pete and Dave, with a little effort, managed to collect their own bunch, and soon the two parties were moving off in opposite directions. Dave sat silent on his horse. Pete glanced at him from time to time, but said nothing. Finally, however, as they dismounted to eat their lunch, Pete could not help asking:

"Have any trouble with them, Dave?"

"Trouble? Oh no."

Dave relapsed into silence, and Pete shook his head in puzzled fashion. Something had happened, but what, he could not guess.

In unwonted silence Dave and Pete rode back to the Bar U ranch, reaching it at dusk with the bunch of strays. They were turned in with the other cattle and then Dave, turning his horse into the corral, walked heavily to the ranch house. All the life seemed to have gone from him.

"Well, son, did you get the bunch?" asked Mr. Carson as he greeted the youth.

"Yes—I did," was the low answer. Mr. Carson glanced keenly at the lad, and something he saw in his face caused the ranch owner to start.

"Was there any trouble?" he asked. It was the same question Pocus Pete had propounded.

"Well, Len Molick and Whitey Wasson had some of our cattle in with theirs."

"They did?"

"Yes, but Pete and I easily cut 'em out. But—Oh, Dad!" The words burst from Dave's lips before he thought. "Am I your son?" he blurted out. "Len and Whitey said I was a picked-up nobody! Am I? Am I not your son?"

He held out his hands appealingly.

A great and sudden change came over Mr. Carson. He seemed to grow older and more sorrowful. A sigh came from him.

Gently he placed one arm over the youth's drooping shoulders.

"Dave," he said gently. "I hoped this secret would never come out—that you would never know. But, since it has, I must tell you the truth. I love you as if you were my own son, but you are not a relative of mine."

The words seemed to cut Dave like a knife.

"Then if I am not your son, who am I?" Dave asked in a husky voice.

The ticking of the clock on the mantle could be plainly, yes, loudly heard, as Mr. Carson slowly answered in a low voice:

"Dave, I don't know!"